The World's Classics

CCCXC
THE LONELY PLOUGH

OXFORD UNIVERSITY PRESS
AMEN HOUSE, E.C. 4
LONDON EDINBURGH GLASGOW
LEIPZIG NEW YORK TORONTO
MELBOURNE CAPETOWN BOMBAY
CALCUTTA MADRAS SHANGHAI
HUMPHREY MILFORD
PUBLISHER TO THE
UNIVERSITY

THE
LONELY PLOUGH

By

CONSTANCE HOLME

'*It is always one man's work—
always and everywhere.*' KIPLING

OXFORD UNIVERSITY PRESS
LONDON : HUMPHREY MILFORD

'*The Lonely Plough*' was first published in 1914. It was first included in '*The World's Classics*' in 1931, reprinted the same year, and again in 1932.

PRINTED IN GREAT BRITAIN

To

THE PEACE-RULERS

PREFACE

WHEN this novel was published in May 1914, the following summary of it appeared on the cover:

'*The Lonely Plough* is the story of a landed estate, and of a big flood on a northern marsh, bringing out the loyalty of the north-country character, not only to the living but to the dead. It endeavours to show the value of the three-cornered relationship between landlord, agent, and tenant, when each is an honest man, living up to his standard, and having confidence in the others. Especially it points out the difficult position of the steward, the responsibility resting upon him, and the many qualifications he is expected to possess.'

This was written at almost the last moment of the old order of things, and it is perhaps of some slight interest to note how far it applies to-day. Times have altered, of course, and it is impossible to foresee how much they may continue to alter. Many estates have been broken up either wholly or in part; electricity and the motor-bus have changed the conditions of the countryside; farmers' sons are restless, turning away from the call of the land to the call of the engineering spirit of the age; the land itself sometimes seems to be disappearing under the wave of building sweeping across it.

Yet much remains. . . . Property, as yet, remains; requiring, in view of the new problems confronting both landlord and tenant, 'stewards' more sound and sensible than ever. Old customs have obstinately re-established themselves, as if war were the mere gesture of a day, and they the things eternal. And at present the land remains; and while it exists it will always make and manage its own children. Man is subdued to what he works in, and no bungalow-dweller tending a garden but is being captured by the soil. The pull of the land, like the pull of the sea, is in our blood, and any townsman may hear it. Our own lads may wander, but somebody else's will come back.

And the need for loyalty remains—for honesty and straight dealing and confidence in our fellows. The land teaches these virtues, for it will be satisfied with nothing less. 'Be honest with the land', say the farmers, 'and it will be honest with you'—and while we have land we shall have the lesson. These necessities are fundamental and do not alter. *The Lonely Plough* is the story of more than one honest man; and honest men, please God, will never be out of date.

Westmorland.

1931.

CONTENTS

mered along a permanent way of mazy speech, and
when you lived close to her you were always breathless and hurried, and the air was never quiet. She
had the aimless velocity of a trundled hoop, and
accomplished about as much.

Various printed notices drifted across the table on
the rippling and bubbling of worries. She had a
passionate habit of joining societies in all capacities,
from President or Secretary to General Bottle-Washer,
of getting herself appointed on innumerable county
committees. As Lancaster's aunt she was considered
'the right person,' and as Lancaster's aunt she took it
for granted that his fingers should straighten the tangle
of her ensuing bewilderment, and make her trundling
path smooth.

He glanced through the circulars quickly, folding
them neatly and adding them to his own collection.
He was very business-like in his movements. The
sheep and the goats of his correspondence were separated right and left; each envelope had its pencilled
name and date; while the more important took cover
in an elastic band and an inner pocket. His brown
hands were methodical and deft; his weighing eyes
implied a steady brain; his glance at the clock showed
a sense of routine always alert. He was haste without
hurry, while she, like the picture-train, rushed wildly
and got nowhere.

A business-man born and made, you would have
said of Lancelot Lancaster, not of stocks and shares
or rustling parchments, but an acute, sound man of
the land, a lean, light, open-air man often in the
saddle, with no aim beyond a clear-sighted judgment
of terms and tenants, nor any desire more whimsical
than a steady prosperity. It was only when you looked
at his mouth, with its hint of patience and repression,
of longing held in leash and idealism shrouded like a
sin, that you wondered if he was not, after all, only
very well-trained.

CHAPTER I

ACROSS THE DUB

HE felt very old.

Older than the old face at the table before him, than the office furniture, which had been there before he was born, than his father's portrait over the desk; older even than the tulip-tree bowing its graceful head to his window. Very old.

They said the tulip-tree blossomed no more than once in a hundred years. It was an ancient tree, biding its time as ancient things may. But Lancaster felt older even than that.

It had been a trying day. Helwise had made it trying, to begin with. She had come down to breakfast in a black print flickering with white spots, and a whirlpool frame of mind, grievance after grievance spinning musically to the surface, only to be submerged again in the twinkling of an eye. In the intervals of digesting a troublesome correspondence, he found himself flinging life-belts of common sense after long-sunk bits of wreckage, gaining nothing but an impulse of helpless annoyance and a growing dislike for the flickering spots. Helwise was his aunt and housekeeper, and though she could add nearly a score of years to his thirty-seven, the weight of time lay infinitely lighter upon her shoulders than on his; perhaps because she twitched them so gracefully from under every descending yoke. Her delicate face and softly greying hair gave the impression of a serene mind and a fading constitution, and if you were not, vulgarly speaking, up to snuff, you ran and did things for Helwise that Helwise ought to have been doing for you, and she always let you. But the serenity was sheer illusion and the constitution was tough. Closer inspection found her racing through life with the objectless hurry of a cinema express. She shim-

Yes, Helwise had been particularly trying at break-fast. Her post had required a lot of explanation, and his own had included a letter from Bluecaster, one of the kindly, idiotic letters at which Lanty smiled and swore in a breath. There was also a second letter (which of course he had read first) totally contradict-ing the other; and at the bottom of all had been one from the London solicitor, telling him (unofficially) to take no notice of either. Bluecaster's agent pencilled patient comments on the three unnecessary epistles.

He had spent the morning with a prospective tenant who had seemed to take a gloating delight in raising difficulties which would never have so much as occurred to anybody else; the type of sportsman who goes house-hunting for the sheer joy of pointing out to the lessor the contemptible disabilities of his property. Getting back for lunch at the usual time, he found that Helwise had had it early and eaten most of it, afterwards cinematographing off to some meeting at least an hour too soon; and the afternoon had seen him harried from pillar to post by an inspector who kept telephoning trysting-places and never turning up. Helwise was having tea at her meeting, so there was none for him unless he chose to order it, and just as his hand was on the bell, tenants of standing had arrived, wanting him. It was really the tenants who had made him feel old.

Facing him at the office-table, Wolf Whinnerah had the light full upon his fierce old face, with its sunk, dark eyes and thatch of silver hair. He was over seventy, but until recently he had carried his years with an almost miraculous lightness. Now, at last, however, the rigorous hand of Time had touched him suddenly, breaking him in a few weeks. Pneumonia, during a trying season, had carried him very near the grave, and though he had fought his way back, he was nevertheless a beaten man. The strong bones of his keen face showed their clean lines under his furrowed skin. His height was dwindled, his step grown uncertain, his grasp weakened, his sight dulled. The end of the things that mattered had come to old Wolf Whinnerah.

His son—his only child—sat between the other two men, with his back to the fireplace. He had the mountain colouring, for all that he had been bred on a marsh farm—the dark hair, and the grey eyes that have the blue of mountain-mist across them, the dale length and breadth, too, and the long, easy, almost lurching swing in his walk. And he had the slow, soft, deep dale voice, and its gentle, distant dignity of manner.

He sat, for the most part, looking at the table, while his father laid his case before the agent. It was a case that put himself hopelessly in the wrong, but he kept his mouth shut, and stayed undefended. He had learned to keep his mouth shut. Argument with Wolf generally led to something perilously near un-harnessed battle. He was over thirty, now, and during all the years he had worked for his father he had never had a penny's wage. He had been kept and clothed, like a child, had tips for treats doled him like a child, and like a child been ruled in all his ways. He did not resent it; there was no question of in-justice, since it was the custom in his class, and only slowly was it drawing towards change. But it kept a man his father's property in a way curiously patri-archal and out of date to an outsider, making paternal authority a mighty weapon, and filial independence a strange, iconoclastic crime.

'Yon's the way of it, sir!' old Whinnerah finished, leaning back in his chair, and spreading the long fingers of his knotted hand along the table, opening and shutting them slowly, as if they levered the operation of his mind. 'I'm done, and the farm must go; and if the lad won't take it on, as he says he won't, why, then, there's nowt for it but I must go an' all!'

He looked down at his hand as he spoke, and clenched it, for it was trembling. The other men looked at it, too, Lancaster with regretful eyes; but the younger glanced away sharply, and set the line of his mouth a trifle closer.

'It's bad hearing!' the agent said at last, seeing that the son did not mean to speak. 'You've been at Ninekyrkes so long, you Whinnerahs. Naturally we like to keep the farms in the family, if it's a family worth having. We'd be more than sorry to part with you—you don't need telling that. Can't you see your way to stopping on a bit longer yourself?'

The old man raised himself painfully to his feet, looking indeed like a grim old wolf, with the last yard of pace run out of him, and the last ounce of fight gone from him. His name he owed to a family tradition tracing a connection with Hugh Lupus of the Conquest, through his sister Lucia. Wolf's son had the name in its Latin dignity, long since distorted to everyday use.

'I said I was done, Mr. Lancaster! You've eyes in your head as'll show you, right enough. Yon time I was down such a terrible while, a year come Martinmas, that finished me, or I'd have likely been good for another nice few years. But I can't carry the whole farm, now. I must give it over to a younger pair o' hands. Not that I'm grudging that; it comes to all of us, in the end; but I'm rare an' sore they'll not be Whinnerah hands, Mr. Lancaster! The lad's set on going abroad, as I've told you. He says he'll not bide. I could have done a bit on the farm along with him, even yet—odd jobs to earn my board and keep my old bones warmed, but wanting him I'll have to quit for good, and see other folk of another breed in the old spot. It's not what I looked for, sir, not what I meant, and I'll take it hard. I'll take it hard!'

He lowered himself shakily back to his chair, and his hand slid out again on the table, opening and shutting, opening and shutting. Lup did not move, nor did his mouth alter. There came a second silence.

'Well, you know your own business best, of course,' Lancaster said presently, wondering what lay behind; 'but surely'—he turned to the young man—'surely you don't really mean leaving us? There has never been any misunderstanding either on your side or ours that I know of. My father thought a lot of you all—that's old news, isn't it?—and I'm of his mind. What's making you quit, Lup, just when you're needed most?'

Lup looked at the table and his father's hand.

'I can't stop, sir,' he said, respectfully but quite definitely. 'I'm sorry if it's putting folk about, but I reckon I'll be better suited on the other side o' the dub.'

'Canada?' The agent smiled and frowned. 'Come, Lup, we can't part with you, and that's the long and the short of it! They're taking too many of our best men, as it is. I don't want to preach, but doesn't it seem to you that it's your duty to stay with your father as long as he wants you?'

'Happen it be,' laconically.

'Then, for every sake, man, stop!'

'Nay, I'll not.'

He shut his mouth again, and Lancaster looked across to the father with a half shrug, then slewed on another tack.

'It's a good farm, and you've done well by it. There's money behind you, and money before you, which is more than a deal of folk can say. You'll find nothing like Ninekyrkes, over there. Hasn't it any memories for you? I don't mind laying you'll find it tug pretty hard on the other side!' He paused, and tried again. It was a very one-sided conversation. 'I understood you were thinking of getting married —that there was to be a wedding on the far marsh.

Do you propose taking the lady with you "across the dub?"'

The blood flamed over the set obstinacy of the dark face, but died instantly.

'I'll not bide!' he said again, and that was all.

A wave of hysterical revolt broke over the dispossessed at his side. Wolf's self-command was never of a lasting quality, and it had been very sorely tried.

'Nay, but I'll not have you gang!' he cried, shaking from head to foot with the terrible effort of finished age forcing its will upon dogged youth and strength. 'You'll stop till I'm in my grave and through an' by with my job for good! You'll be quit of me *then*, right enough, and free to set about any daft-like scheme you choose, but I'm not under the sod yet, and I'll see you do as you're bid. I was a fool ever to hark to you! I should have said nay and nay to it from the start. It's not so long since I could have broken my stick across you, an' I'm not feared of you, now. Am I like to be feared, d'you think'—a sneer edged his quivering voice—'of a fool as can't stick out a bit of a disappointment, as gets sneck-posset from the lass he's after, and bides door slapped in his face without so much as shoving a foot inside? Nay, I'll tell you what it is, my lad! she cares nowt, I tell you—nowt——!'

He stopped, for Lup had risen to his feet and bent towards him, so that over the table the two dark faces almost met, and before the steady anger of his eyes and locked lips even old Wolf was stilled. Lancaster felt the swift current of hatred and bitterness flash between them, sensed the passionate resentment, puzzle, and pain. Then Lup turned on his heel and went out.

'I'll be yoking up, sir,' he threw over his shoulder as he disappeared, and presently they heard his long, unhurrying tread across the cobbled yard.

'What's the trouble, Wolf?' Lancaster asked gently,

as the clatter of hoofs and the jingle of harness came in through the open window. 'What's put the lad wrong?'

'Nowt but what puts every lad wrong, soon or late!' the other answered bitterly, sinking back. 'It's Dockera's lass, her as went to boarding school for a sight o' years, and come back with a look an' a way with her fit to beat a ladyship! Lup was always set on her, ay, an' she on him, if seeing's believing. They've been courtin' this year past and more, going to singin'-practice an' pill-gills an' such-like, and I've never known her give him a wrong word. And then, when it comes to taking on the farm and getting wed and settling down, she'll have none of it! She was at our spot to supper, the night it first come up. Whinnerahs and Dockeras have always been rarely thick, you'll think on, living alongside, just them two selves right away over yon. You could never put a pin between 'em. Well, as I told you, she was having a bit o' supper with us when I first spoke. I'd had it in my mind for long, ever since I was badly, but I'd put it by, time an' again, and let it be. Likely I was no more ready than most to be set on the shelf, but the lad's getting on, an' he'd a right to his chance. I'd had a hard day, too, and it come over me sudden-like as I was done for good, and in a queer sort o' way I was glad to be through with it all and rest, if it didn't mean quitting. I thought of the old chair in the corner, and the view of a summer evening, and the sea washing at the wall, an'—an' all the other things meaning Ninekyrkes and no other spot whatever! I'm not saying any man cares to sit by and see his son master where he's held the reins, but there was a sort of pleasure in feeling I'd done with my job. I reckon the Almighty sends you that as a kind o' sop, just to keep you from fretting over hard. And so I just up an' told them how it was. I said I'd see you, sir, about handing the farm over, and then I says to

Lup, "Now, Lup, my lad," says I, "You've been courtin' long enough an' to spare, and it's time you settled down. We'll change jobs this Martinmas, an' you can get wed, an', please God, there'll be Whinnerahs at Ninekyrkes for many a long year to come. It's a bargain, lad, that's what it is! So now, Miss Francey, don't you keep him waiting. You be getting your gear an' such-like together, and we'll have the wedding as soon as ever you can make shape to be ready!" Yon's what I said, an' I reckon I put it real smart, eh, Mr. Lancaster?"—the agent nodded response to the appeal for commendation—'but happen it was oversmart-like for Dockera's lass! She never so much as coloured up or turned shy, but she round with her head very slow an' looked at me that calm— she's got quality's ways with her, sir, as I said, very soft an' kind, but with something holding her off at the back—an' says she, in her whyet voice, "And what's all that to do with me, Mr. Winnerah?" Eh! but I was rarely bothered just for the minute! When I come to think of it, there'd never been owt in black an' *white*, after a manner of speaking. Lup's not one for tongue-wagging, you'll have found that for yourself. For all I could ha' sworn to there might never have been talk o' weddin' betwixt 'em at all; but they'd been together a deal, an'—an'—why, I'd seen Lup's eyes on her acrost table, an' I'd be like to know, I reckon, when a Whinnerah's set on a lass! So after a bit o' coughing and fidging, thinking she was happen likely just joking us, I got out as we'd always taken it as she and Lup was sweethearts.

"'Happen we be!' says she, only in quality-talk, and she gives Lup the sweetest little look sideways as set him shining like the Angel Gabriel!

"'Why, then! What, there's nowt to find!' says I, trying not to get above myself. "If you're courtin', you're likely thinking to get wed, and now's your time. What's to hinder? The farm's ready, and the lad.""

' "Ay, but not the lass!" says she, spirity-like. "The right time's my own time, and I'll come when I choose!"

' "You'll come when Lup chooses!" I said, fair lossing my temper out an' out. "Tell her that, my lad. Tell her she'll come when she's fetched!"

'But Lup just sat there like a half-rocked 'un, glowering at nowt an' saying less, as he did just now, and then my lady gets on her feet and has her talk out.

' "You mean kindly," she says, "and to be fair and just, but you don't understand how it looks to me. It's the way things are worked, I know. A lad slaves for his father for years after he's a man grown, with never so much as a penny to put between his teeth, and at last, when the old man's tired, he gives his son his chance. Round comes the agent, and it's, 'You're for getting wed, I reckon? Right!' (if it *is* right), and the contract's made. The lass goes into the contract along with the farm, and along at the beck of the three men to the church. Well, that's your way, but it's not mine, and you may as well know it first as last. I'll come when I'm ready, or I'll never come at all!"

'And with that she took herself off, an' after a minute Lup up an' followed her. He didn't come home while morning—I've an idea he spent the night on the sea-wall—and after that it was Canada. Ay, an' Canada it'll be, sir, and no two words about it!'

He stopped, exhausted, and Lancaster laughed.

'Why, man, you're worrying yourself for nothing! It's a lovers' quarrel—no more. I thought, by the look of you, there was murder in the wind! Come, there's no sense in whistling up your own ill-luck. The girl will be round again at the swing of the pendulum by this time to-morrow. She'll pull up to the pole all right, you take my word!'

The old man shook a dogged contradiction.

'You've seen Lup,' he said. 'You know how far there's bending *him*. Have you seen the lass, sir? Nay? What, then——' on a sudden, cheering impulse—'see here, sir, suppose *you* put in a word?'

'What's that?' Lancaster laughed again, amused but embarrassed. 'You want me to tackle her—talk to her nicely, point out what she's throwing away? That's a bit too much to ask, Wolf! I'm not agent for Bluecaster for that.'

'She'd happen take it from you. She'd ha' took it from your father, Mr. Lancaster. There's a many he's talked into a right way o' thinking—ay, an' women-folk among 'em!—as is glad and proud of it to-day.'

'Yes, but I'm——' Lancaster looked rather help-less—'well—not my father, Wolf!'

'You're your father's son. What a Lancaster says, goes—with most of us. You'll try it, sir?'

'I don't see how I can. What has your wife to say about it?'

'Something of the same mak as Lup, sir—lile or nowt, an' nowt most often of the two. She sticks to it there's trouble ahead, anyhow, and it's no odds what road it travels. She's got a queer trick of sitting an' watching the tide, like as if she's waiting to see something happen.'

'But surely she's tried to make Lup hear reason?'

'Ay, I reckon she has, though she's never let wit on it to me. He's the very apple of her eye; she's not like to let him go unspoken. But you'll have a shot, won't you, Mr. Lancaster? Do, sir—do now!' The tone was first wheedling, then wistful. ''Tisn't only the lad. It means the farm—to me.'

He looked across at the agent with a childlike trustfulness that was almost absurdly pathetic, and Lancaster broke suddenly.

'Well, well, I'll see what I can do!' he said, smiling somewhat wryly, and went out to help the old man into his trap, a growing feeling upon him of having

seen the curtain rise upon some slow working of Fate.
The dog-cart jogged through the gate, and for a
moment he saw Lup's head above the wall as he
turned his horse towards the marsh. The rap of the
hoofs came to him for long enough, dying and returning, until the last hill between swallowed them up.

And he felt old.

CHAPTER II

THE GREEN GATES OF VISION: I. DUSK

HE went back into the house when the distance had
snapped the last vibrating link, but he did not stay
there. The office was still under the domination of
the young man's silent anger, the old man's piteous
revolt. He felt troubled for both, seeing the situation
as each saw it, and was conscious of sharp impatience
with the cause of the deadlock, though in his own
mind he was certain that her obstinacy would not
last. But the whole affair was an unnecessary worry
with which he could have dispensed very thankfully,
and added heavily to his sense of weary irritation.

He found both drawing-room and dining-room
totally unbearable in his present mood, for both
were oppressively characteristic of Helwise; curiously
so, since her character seemed always a shifting thing,
sliding through your fingers and resting nowhere. He
had lost his mother early—before his teens—but the
house, under the firm conservatism of his father and
an old servant, had kept her memory and her tenets
for long. Helwise, however, had banished them very
completely. With a long-nursed resentment he marked
the disorder of the dining-room, the drunken regiment
of chairs, the holes in the lace curtains, the cheap
almanacs pinned haphazard between the good prints.
Helwise loved to surround herself with calendars.
They gave her a sense of keeping even with Time.
He could not steal a march on her by a single day,

while some grocer's tribute marked the black footsteps of his pilgrimage. Yet she rarely availed herself of their services, left them hanging for years—horrible traps to the unwary—her own hasty references being invariably directed to the wrong month.

Lanty frowned distastefully at their almost ribald askewness, at the torn places in the paper where the crooked pins had slipped, at the untidy hearth and wild mass of correspondence on the open desk. It should have been a handsome room, by rights, for it was bright and well-proportioned. The severe furniture that his father had bought had mellowed with time, and the few bits of silver on the sideboard had lost their parvenu air of recent presentation. He had chosen the carpet himself, and its soft, dark tints still pleased him, in spite of the tread worn white by the hurrying feet of his aunt. But there was no ease or homeliness in the room, and it certainly was not handsome, save as an elderly *roué* of once better days is handsome, in a last drunken effort after dignity and repose.

The drawing-room was worse. He had had no hand in the drawing-room, so Helwise had let herself loose upon it, with results that made him creep. He hated it, from the collection of smug pot dogs on the mantelpiece to the bad Marcus Stone imitations on the cold blue of the walls. He hated the cheap books lying about, the spindly furniture, the innumerable chair-backs bristling so fiercely with pins that you dared neither lay your head on them in front nor your hand on them from behind. There was only one comfortable chair in the room, and that was sacred to Helwise. Not that she ever actually claimed it as hers, but if you sat down on it by accident, she wandered helplessly over the wild-patterned carpet as if there wasn't another seat within reach, until you became gradually aware of criminal poaching, and arose with shame. There were almanacs here, too, gaudy things

evidently of a higher grade, matching, with a pleasantly
thoughtful touch, the shrieking tiles of the modern
grate. The wide fireplace of his youth had been a
sacred altar, lighting a torch to many dreams, lifting
the smoke of many prayers; but nobody but a Post-
Impressionist could have prayed to this grate, and its
brazen canopy had never housed a single vision.

With a half-sigh he wandered out again and into
the garden, but even here Helwise had successfully
impressed herself. During one of his very rare
absences she had had the fine box borders removed,
and the paths edged with glittering rockery-stones,
intersected by scrubby and unwilling little ferns.
Lanty never quite forgot what he had felt at sight of
them. There was an old song he had been used to
growl softly as he walked between the box, a tender
thing called 'My Lady's Garden,' and sometimes, at
dusk, after a hard day, he had vaguely thought to
find her there in the cool of the evening, even as
himself and Another. He had always missed her, but
she had been there, he was sure of that. But when the
rockery-stones appeared, she came no more; and to
all his big wants and losses there was added the loss
of a little dream.

That was hard to forgive Helwise, just as it was hard
to forgive her the scars on his precious lawn, where
her heavy niblick had taken greedy mouthfuls, and
the insane bumble-puppy pole, rearing its unsightly
length in the middle of the soft, green stretch. She had
a summer-house, too, a Reckitt's Blue wooden thing
on wheels, with texts all over it, like a Church Army
Van. All the texts were about food, strung together
at random: 'I washed my steps with butter.' 'Is
there any taste in the white of an egg?' 'There is
nothing better for a man than that he should eat and
drink. . . . For who can eat, or who else can hasten
hereunto, more than I?' etc., etc. Lanty passed them
with averted eyes, for they reminded him that he

had had no tea and only the scrapings of his aunt's lunch, and stopped for comfort before the one spot in the garden left untroubled, a stone seat in the terrace wall, with straggling letters running along its curve. 'The whole earth is at rest, and is quiet,' said the quiet seat in the wall, a soothing rede for a tired heart, no matter how the truth might rage and storm without. With its balm upon his lips he dropped into the road through a little stile, and came before long, without pause or thought, to a lane winding across country vaguely south. He looked about him before turning into it. If there had been anybody in sight, he would have taken another way, but there was not a soul even far distant, and he stepped in quickly.

Once within its bounds, however, he slackened his pace to an almost hushed saunter. You did not use this lane as a muscular training-ground or a mere short cut; you crept into it on tiptoe, and caught it unawares. It was a capricious lane, racing up and down tiny hills between its high, warm, leaning hedges, spinning round sharp corners out of sight, or running innocently to alluring gateways, only to leave you stranded on arrival. It was full of surprises, full of secrets. As you walked, you heard all sorts of bewitching sounds above and around you, sounds you had known always and sounds you never heard anywhere else. You knew, for instance, the slur of the plough, the whistle of the blackbird, the whirr of the grass-cutter, the slash of the bill-hook on a far fence, the gnawing of turnips, the wind-talk of dead leaves. But there were others you never placed: elf-like twitterings that never came from any bird's throat, weird, hoarse grunts like some guttural gnome-language that couldn't possibly be just a sheep coughing; and if you caught the right time on the right night, you would hear a rustling along the lower fields as the Brush-Harrow Dobbie went by, with never a horse before it nor a man behind. There was also the famous Bluecaster Black-Dog Dobbie, which slunk stealthily at your side, panting and padding ever so softly in the dusk, and disappearing into the wraith of an old Tithe-Barn long since fallen away, that had once marked the boundary of the estate.

Besides these attractions, Lanty had a ghost of his own, and half his joy in the lane lay in wondering if he should find it. It was a very high lane. You had to look up and up before you saw the feathery tops kissing the sky, and you walked between, very warm and safe and quiet, listening with all your ears at once. And then, all of a sudden, there would be a break on the lower side, and over a couple of moss-grown bars, or an ancient gate thrust in at any and every beautiful angle, you would see the lovely land sweeping down and out beneath you, and rising slowly, slowly again to soft curves and blue vapours. They came all along the lane, these flashing little peeps of a world shut out, like cloister vignettes in some silent Abbey. Your heart went before you hungrily to each, yet was loth to leave any for the next. And which was more dear, the tender quiet or the land through its living frame, it would have been hard to say. Lancaster called the peeps his Green Gates of Vision.

He stopped at the first of all, and his Ghost was there to meet him, a long, faint, knife-edged mountain, flung like a cloud against the south-west sky. It was often missing, and at its clearest the mass of it was no more than a blown web, yet the line of it had always the quivering sharpness of steel. He had grown to believe that the sight of it brought him luck, this Ghost-Mountain of his, so christened because it never seemed but the ghost of a hill, edged with the spirit-fire of something safe escaped from clogging matter. Its absence did not depress him, but its presence, sprung suddenly upon his cloistered walk, always made his heart leap, as at an unexpected promise of goodwill. He welcomed it to-day when he was weary and out of tune, and he leaned his arms on the weathered timber with a sense of rest, drawing his gaze slowly back from the far symbol to the country close at hand.

Four or five dropping fields away, Rakestraw stood in its sheath of woods, the new hay thick in the grey Dutch barns. There were rooks' nests in the trees overhanging the house; even at that distance he could see them. That meant luck for Rakestraw, said the wise. He had always told himself that he would live at Rakestraw when the cease-fire sounded for the work he loved, farm it himself, lead his hay and breed his stock, and perhaps the rooks would build for him, too, as they had built for Dart Newby. He knew in his heart he would never do it, just because it seemed so essentially the beautiful and right thing for him to do. Most of us have our dream-houses somewhere, and plot and plan their future and ours together; and whether we ever win to them or not with a signed conveyance, we have something of them always that is never set down in any legal bond.

To the left he could see the road twisting and dipping but yet steadily rising towards Gilmichel, and another road far away on higher land, with Topthorns set on its edge; then Dick Crag, like a soft, grey bear raising itself on hind legs to look abroad, and, behind it, fold on fold of neutral-tinted, blended fells. On the right the land rose again, only more sharply, until the line of the hedges broke once more into the sky, but over the hill he knew was Gilthrotin in the hollow, with its one little, steep street, its old bridge and ancient church, and its empty, eyeless manor-house topping the terrace over the river. He would come to that presently, when, by slow and delicious chapters, he had read his lane from start to finish.

Leaning there, his eyes resting on restful Rakestraw,

he went back in mind to his late interview and the
task he had undertaken. It was only one among many
unconventional duties falling to him, he reflected,
with the same wry smile. As agent for the Bluecaster
estate, free to use his own discretion in almost every
instance, yet often tied hand and foot by old obser-
vance, he frequently found himself in situations for
the right conduct of which there could be no possible
arbiter but his own judgment. Old duties were his
along with the outside management, duties of house-
steward and administrator, and even where his rule
ended, the claims on him went on. If a casual visitor
at the 'Feathers' was lost out fishing, Lancaster was
called to find him, as a matter of course. If the draper
wished to commit suicide, Lancaster was fetched to
command him to desist. If the doctor objected to the
rates, or the parson struck a bad rock in Local
Government, Lancaster was signalled for aid. Difficulties of all sorts came to him for settlement, from
disputes over neighbours' hens and washing and
fondness for the American organ, to the moot point
whether your money ought or ought not to go to your
wife's relations.

At the age of twenty-four, when scarcely through his
training, he had been thrust into his father's place by
a blast of sudden death which carried off master, heir,
and steward in the same month. The new lord was
only just of age, and glad enough to have a Lancaster
to lean on, so that before the young agent had learned
to stand alone, he had the whole estate upon his
shoulders. Thirteen years it was now since he took
hold. Thirteen years since Jeffrey Kennet Cospatrick,
tenth Baron Bluecaster, greeted his inheritance with a
sigh. He was a kindly, shy young man, one of those
puzzling natures that swing from an almost idiotic
simple-mindedness to sudden touches of shrewdness;
that take everybody at face-value most of the time,
and for the rest can see through a stone wall. He had

few near relations, and for the most part spent his
flying visits to Bluecaster alone, but he always came
when he was wanted, ready to face some traditional
ordeal with a shy effort. He was generous, too—to
a fault—but even in his most ultra-altruistic flights
he could be made to listen to reason. Indeed, his faith
in his agent was almost irritatingly sublime; there
were times when the latter longed earnestly for a man
who could see things steadfastly through his own eyes;
Bluecaster leaned so heavily. Yet he knew himself
wonderfully fortunate, and it was only when he was
very wearied or worried, as he had been of late, that
he felt his shoulders ache. It was scarcely strange that
he should feel old; he had had so little time to be really
young. There were drawbacks to being the son of a
fine man, he thought occasionally. People expected
you to start where your father left off, to keep up his
standard of ripe experience where any other beginner
would be busy learning from his own mistakes. The
tenants had turned to him from the first with the
personal confidence and affection that they had given
his predecessor, scarcely realising that he had not yet
grown to the full stature of control. He had gone
through hard years, often troubling himself unnecessarily, but in the end he had won out. Before he was
thirty he had come to father the whole lot of them,
Bluecaster included. The trust was his dearest possession, but, serving it, he had missed his youth.

His work was the breath of his life; its varied
interests kept him keen and stimulated, but they
increased continually, and every year new legislation
made things more difficult for those engaged with
land. The county, too, had claimed him, and he
had yielded, inch by inch, to the fascination making
almost the sole reward of the Great Unpaid. He had
not had a holiday for years; he was too absorbed, too
pressed, too afraid of getting behind. Besides, no other
place called him. The whole of his heart was here.

Things might have run easier if Helwise had been—well, something quite inconceivably different from what she was. Her descent upon his desolate hearth from unrewarding efforts as companion to successive old ladies, had been welcomed by him at the time, not knowing that it was her special mission in life to make it more desolate still. He had been too busy at first to notice the atmosphere with which she surrounded him, attributing his dreariness of spirit to his father's loss and his over-heavy task; and by the time he had made himself and formed his routine, it was too late to send her away. She was happy after her own parasitical fashion, and to uproot her now would mean a gigantic effort to which neither his will nor his heart felt equal. But of late there had grown upon him a longing for a home of his own making, an atmosphere with which Helwise should never have anything to do. He murmured old Samuel Daniel's words as he leaned against the gate:

> 'To have some silly home I do desire,
> Loth still to warm me by another's fire.'

He had a home, certainly, and one silly enough, too, in its mismanagement and lack of all peace; but it was another silliness for which he yearned, the silliness of little, common home-interests and home-jokes, of crossed glances and talk without words, of parting kisses and meeting hands. He had a fire, of course, as well; that is to say, he paid for it, but in every other sense it was 'another's.' He thought of the drawing-room grate and renounced it violently.

Dusk was drawing down, now, though the Mountain still stayed with him, faintly limned as a dried tear. Milking was over at Rakestraw. He watched the cattle coming out from the shippons to a quiet night in the cool fields. Near at hand a sleepy twittering told him where a late-nested bird was hidden close. The clipped sheep and the sturdy lambs still called to each other, as

if the tender time of mother-love was not yet over; and
far down on the road he could hear children pattering
home from their summer treat. There came into his
head a song he had heard at a musical festival:

> 'What can lambkins do
> All the keen night through?
> Nestle by their woolly mother
> The careful ewe.

> 'What can nestlings do
> In the nightly dew?
> Sleep beneath their mother's wing
> Till day breaks anew.

> 'If in field or tree
> There might only be
> Such a warm soft sleeping-place
> Found for me!'

Well, his hour of comfort and sanctity was nearly
over. His soothed nerves gave him courage to laugh
at his own longings. He must get back to Helwise
and other duties, think out some plan of campaign
with regard to Dockeray's recalcitrant daughter. He
raised himself reluctantly, wondering, at the last
moment, what encouragement his Ghost was about
to send him, when he was brought round sharply by
sounds of frivolous song pouring down the lane. The
shuttered quiet passed. The sheep, newly snuggled
under the hedge, scattered in bleating alarm; fresh
twitterings broke from the late nest, and every shy-
peeping fairy-thing became instantly dumb and dead.

With the song came a shuffling as of dancing, and
panting requests to the singer to 'bang a bit more on
the brass!' and as Lancaster, standing in the rutted
road, looked up to the first frolicking bend, two figures
whirled into sight through the thin veil of eve. Behind,
their obedient accompanist let out his fine voice a
little further. With the singer was a girl.

The dancers, closely clasped in each other's arms,

executed a series of intricate steps from hedge to hedge
with the unanimity and gravity of extremely superior
marionettes. They wore dinner-coats and evening
pumps; their heads were bare, and now and then
Lancaster caught the gleam of shirt-fronts as he
watched them swing down through the dusk. He did
not know them, he felt certain of that, and wondered
in widening circles until he remembered that the eyeless house over the hill had been sold recently, and that
these must be some of its new occupants. Watters was
Gilthrotin property, and therefore not in his hands,
and though he had been present at the sale, he
had forgotten the buyer, though he had marked the
Lancashire name as one with plenty of money behind
it. That accounted for the strangers. It did not
account though, he thought, ruffled and jarred, for
their bad taste in thrusting noisily into his lane just
at fairy-time. With the dogged resentment of the
conscientious objector who stands stolidly in front of
a motor-car, he remained in the middle of the road
until the dancers ran into him. They spun in opposite
directions, clutching at nothing, and the singer broke
on a high note. Lancaster went on standing still.
The girl stepped forward, her whitely grey gown
showing moth-like in the shadows. The disgruntled
performers were busy picking themselves out of the
hedge, breathing somewhat offhand apology.

'I hope they didn't hurt you?' she began anxiously.
'It's the Tango. They don't seem able to stop doing
it, and of course, they are only boys and very foolish.
I do hope you're not hurt!'

Lancaster assured her, smiling a little grimly, that
he was perfectly whole. If anybody was hurt, it was
much more likely to be the Tangoists in the hedge.
These now came up, still panting.

'Licks creation! Stuns the stars! Bangs Banagher!
I say, beastly sorry we barged into you like that. Took
you for a turnip, honest injun we did! We're shooting

over to Bluecaster after a smoke-shop, and we thought
it just as easy to tango there. And I say, look here!
You'll know what time they close, I expect. I suppose
we can do it all right?'

'It's six furlongs, and you've just ten minutes,'
Lancaster answered severely. 'You may do it, with
luck. But if you beat Banagher down the hill in that
costume, you'll probably find yourself in jail in less
time still.'

'Right-o, old cock! What's a furlong, anyway?
Anybody seen a furlong? As to the togs, why, it's
the country, the dear, silly old simple-life country!
You can do anything you like in the country, or else
what's the good of it? Come on, you fellows, we've
got to get that smoke!'

They flew together again in a furious embrace, and
spun away out of sight, whistling like flying engines
at a crossing. The girl and the singer stayed behind,
still apologetic.

'You'd have gone quicker by the main road,'
Lancaster said stiffly, still resentful. 'But of course
you probably know that already.'

She nodded.

'Yes. But the boys wanted to come by the lane.
They love the lane. When they don't tango, they
bring the car and squeeze her along as fast as they
can. The hedges are too high, though; you daren't
risk the turns. If they were only clipped so that you
could see over, it would make a fine test for steering!'

The singer in the background began an appeasing
little chant, as if he knew that Lancaster writhed.

'Perhaps some of us prefer it as it is,' he answered
coldly. 'Hadn't you better be looking after your—
your brothers? There's rather a smart police-sergeant
in Bluecaster.'

'They're not my brothers. They're just stopping
with us, that's all. Are we trespassing?' She lifted an
anxious face. 'I didn't know the lane was yours. I'm

ever so sorry! We'd better go on, hadn't we, after the boys? but we'll come back the other way.'

Lanty reddened, ashamed. The singer gave him a friendly smile over the girl's head.

'It isn't my lane—of course not. There's no reason you shouldn't motor down it if you happen to know a collapsible method of passing carts. It's a favourite walk of mine, that's all. And everything was just about asleep.'

She looked a little puzzled and still troubled.

'I expect you *do* feel it's your own lane, really! I've only been here since March—we're at Watters in Gilthrotin—but I've noticed people seem to think that lots of things belong to them just because they've had them somewhere round all their lives—hills and footpaths and favourite views—things like that. The man in the cottage behind us was dreadfully vexed because we cut down a half-dead sycamore by the river. He said he was used to seeing it from his bedroom window—wasn't it funny of him? That's what you feel about the lane, though, isn't it? I wish I'd known! Any other lane would have done for us.'

Lancaster choked his feelings with an effort.

'Please do not bother about me,' he said curtly, raising his cap. 'You have every right to the lane. And I don't think it was funny at all. Goodnight.'

She responded reluctantly, feeling that she had somehow failed to put things right. She wanted to placate this cross, solitary-minded person who had already turned his thin, serious face back to the break in the hedge. Perhaps he was not really cross. He might be suffering from nerves. They ought not to have worried him, poor thing!

A young moon came up over the hill. For a moment they looked together through the green arch.

'It must be fearfully quiet, down there!' she said, nodding towards the buildings hugging the land close as if they loved it and were loved in return. 'I'm not sure I shall like living in the country. Everything seems to be listening for something that never gets itself said. And why don't they put the poor animals under cover? I should hate to spend the night out of doors, myself!'

He had been watching the moon and his wraith of a mountain, and at her words he winced again. She was shattering his magic with both hands. She had no thought for the summer dew or the nestled lambs, the grey robe of the night or the gentle miracle of dawn. It meant nothing to her, this creeping mystery of eve.

'Thought I heard a policeman's whistle a minute ago,' he observed casually. 'I met the constable following up tramps when I came out. Perhaps your folks have run into him.'

With a sense of relief he found himself alone again at last, but the charm had temporarily vanished, the fairy-things remained away. He wished she had not looked through his Green Gate with her alien eyes; he was afraid of seeing things as she saw them. She had thought it nicer for the stock to be indoors, just as she doubtless thought it better for him to be under his own roof instead of mooning about a ridiculous lane. He loathed the thought of his own house at that moment. He disliked the girl who had broken the happy spell. He leaned over the gate in the gloaming, watching the quietened sheep, and trying to call the magic back.

> 'If in field or tree
> There might only be
> Such a warm, soft sleeping-place
> Found for me!'

CHAPTER III

TROUBLE

He rode over to Ladyford the following afternoon.

Helwise came agitating on to the doorstep, just as his foot was in the stirrup, to tell him that his lordship had returned unexpectedly.

'He telephoned from the House in the middle of the morning,' she went on, with the high-pitched, running ease which always seemed to make every difficult situation doubly trying. 'He said he would like to see you at your earliest convenience, but of course I told him you were engaged both this morning and afternoon, and to-night you were going to take me to that lecture on "The Home Beautiful." (It *was* to-night, wasn't it?) I forgot to tell you at lunch. I always think it just as well, Lancelot, to let his lordship know how extremely busy you are, and not always able to run at his beck and call. I am sure it is quite time you applied for a rise, with all these horrid insurances to add up. We could do quite easily with a small brougham.'

Lanty loosed the stirrup.

'I'm quite satisfied with my screw, thank you,' he answered shortly. 'You know Bluecaster's generosity as well as I do. And I do wish, Helwise' (their old Lancaster names formed the one love they had in common), 'that you wouldn't arrange my business for me. I could have gone to Ladyford to-morrow, and this morning I was no further than the show-field, having a look round. You might have sent Armer with a message. He was only helping you to thread that bead-curtain. I'll go in and ring his lordship up at once.'

He turned towards the door, but she stopped him.

'It's no good; he won't be at home. He said he was going out to lunch—I forget where—but he assured me it would be quite all right if you went up in the morning. So you see there's nothing to prevent you riding over to Ladyford, and as you're passing through Sandwath I do wish you would call at Brunskill's for my watch. The man in Bluecaster is no more good than my shoe. And—oh, Lancelot!—I do believe it's the Annual Meeting of the Nursing Association to-day, and it had gone clean out of my mind! I'm something important, I'm sure—let me see, what was it?—oh, yes, of course, Honorary Secretary—and they'll certainly expect me to be there, but it's absolutely out of the question. I've promised to drive to a bazaar in Witham with Harriet Knewstubb—I believe we're judging something—I've forgotten what—but I can't possibly leave her in the lurch. The report is ready—you went through it for me last week, if you remember—but I simply can't be there to present it. Couldn't you do it for me?'

'No, I couldn't!' Lanty returned firmly, 'I do some queer jobs both for you and for Bluecaster, but I haven't yet got as far as presenting reports at a nursing meeting. Throw over Harriet and get along to your post. If you don't want to walk, you can order a trap from the "Feathers." '

'I dare say, but I shan't try. You know what Harriet is if you go back on her—her language, I mean. The whole nursing committee *and* the patients wouldn't be in it. I do think you might help me, Lancelot! It isn't often I turn to you for assistance.'

The last phrase had been part of his life so long that it did not draw even a mental shrug. In a way he had grown almost to welcome it, since it marked the full stop to some tangled rigmarole. As a rule, he awaited it patiently with shut ears, and answered—something.

'I'll help you by leaving the report as I pass, if you like,' he said, at last, 'but you can't expect me to do more. What time is the meeting? Three? Then I shall only just do it. Fetch the papers along, please, and don't invent any fresh messages for his lordship while I'm away.'

'And while you're getting them,' he threw after her, 'just think up some really plausible lie. Even a committee of women won't swallow that bazaar.'

He stood waiting with a hand on the saddle, too trained to patience even to flick his worn cords with a restless whip. Blacker, the horse, had the same air of long-suffering towards feminine caprice. The black spaniel sank her nose between her paws. Black was the Bluecaster colour, from the flag on the roof to the household liveries and the pigs at the Home Farm. There had been a Bluecaster, fleeing from the Plague, who had put all posterity into mourning for his particular sins.

The odd-job man, who did a little of everything, including stable-work and summer-house texts, leaned somnolently against the horse's shoulder. Lanty exchanged a word with him, and then left him in peace. He had had a hard morning. Helwise was entered for a bumble-puppy competition, in aid of a Dogs' Home, and when he had finished the bead-curtain he had been called out to give her practice.

Through a window above she could be heard engaged in a scatter-brained search, and Lanty wondered vaguely why she kept nursing reports in the bath-room, but to follow the workings of Miss Lancaster's mind was to return Ophelia-like, weaving wreaths for one's distracted head. She appeared at last with a bundle of papers through which he looked carefully, having once been basely misled over Boarding-Out Agenda produced by him on her behalf at a golf-meeting: receiving a volley of instructions as he climbed finally into the saddle.

'If you don't like to mention the bazaar, you must think of something for yourself,' she told him, fol-

lowing him down the drive. 'There are plenty of useful
things to say on these occasions, and nobody believes
them. And you can just tell them I think nothing
of the new district nurse—nothing at all! I've met
her at least three times this week, and she never even
dreams of bowing to me. Of course, I wasn't able to
attend the meeting at which she was interviewed, but
that's no excuse, as she must know as well as I do that
I'm the Treas—no, what was it?—Honorary Secretary.
She cycles with her saddle far too low, too—wait a
minute, though; that was the last but one—and she
spends too much of her time making herself pleasant
to people of no importance whatever—the sort who
are never ill and don't subscribe a penny. Don't
forget the watch, will you, and the slippers—did I
mention the slippers? Bedroom-blue-quilted-one-and-
elevenpence-ha'penny—size 6—Wilson's—no, I can't
get them in Bluecaster, you might have known that—
and be sure you say something useful!'

She turned to seize on the factotum, who had
adroitly vanished to finish his nap in the harness-
cupboard, and Lanty succeeded in leaving her
behind. Once safe in the road, however, he checked
his horse a moment for a survey of the house. It was
a square, grey-stone building, comfortable and com-
pact, old enough to have acquired atmosphere, yet
not too old for convenience. The garden, thanks to
Armer, and in spite of Helwise, was looking well.
There were roses everywhere, creepers and climbers
as well as bushes, and here and there the dark velvet
of violas showed black against the pinks. At the back
of Crabtree, Bluecaster stood in its park, with its
shoulder to the hill, and behind and behind again,
as far as he could see, the fells rose in long ranks until
the Whygills towered above them all.

It was a strange day, very sultry and sunless, and
the hills had an edge to their ominous dark blue. The
stillness had a menace in it, too. Only in the garden,

as he looked at it, where the colours showed vividly, as always before thunder, there seemed a protected peace. The house slept and the garden held its breath, and, caught in the spell, he could almost have believed the place a home indeed. Then his aunt's voice came running (it seemed) from all directions at once, her feet scurrying in search of the slumbering one; and with a sigh he touched up the chafing horse, and made west to the marsh.

He met the district nurse almost immediately, a bright little woman of 100 h.p. energy, and found no difficulty in getting himself recognised; and a mile further on he turned up a drive, drawing rein before a porch arched with sweetbriar, where he pulled the bell without dismounting. Mrs. Yare herself came out to him, and to her he handed the papers. Through the near window he had a glimpse of a selection of hats, framing various degrees of interest and annoyance. His regrets were received with gracefully concealed unbelief.

'We were all wondering what had happened!' she told him. 'We always have the meeting here—I'm a Chief Lady Superintendent or something Mikado-ish of that kind, you know—so I hardly thought Miss Lancaster could have forgotten, especially as she calls the meeting herself! I'm very disappointed she wasn't able to come, but no doubt we shall manage all right. She is well, I hope?' she added courteously.

'She is only—mixed,' Lanty answered curtly, gathering up his reins. 'I'm extremely sorry if you have been put out. Please accept my assurance that it shall not happen again. I was told to say something useful,' he finished grimly, 'so perhaps you will be kind enough to convey a message to the committee? My aunt, with much regret, resigns her position on the Association!'

Bluecaster, House and village, lay some three miles from the narrow bay where it ran in to take the rivers

Bytha, Wythe, and Ulva. Lanty could see the winding estuaries as he topped Hullet, with Wythebarrow standing out to the marsh on the north-west, and the grand barrier of Lake hills behind. Both north and east lay the marsh-farms, part of the rich property which ran from the sea (for the foreshore rights were Bluecaster's) to the Yorkshire and Lancashire borders. But there were only two farms on the north, below Wythebarrow and across the strait—Ladyford and Ninekyrkes, standing alone on the lip of the tide. He lost them again as he dropped into Sandwath, where he executed his orders, turning into the marsh-road towards four o'clock.

The same brooding stillness held the bay in thrall; the same line of warning edged the hills. The tide was dead out, and the sands lay desolate under the heavy sky. Now he had the twin farms again, ahead and across where the bay narrowed in and stopped, unnaturally white on the gloom of their background, and flanked by slender stems of larch and fir. The marsh-road was deep-dyked on either hand, and here and there in the watery bottom he caught the sunny gleam of late goldilocks. On his left was the long seawall known as the Let, guarding the eastern marsh; on his right the land rose gently until it hid the village. Here were Moss End and Meadow's Ing, with Lockholme beyond, and others; and, still beyond, close to the brown waste, Pippin Hall, where he left his horse.

He skirted the grassy bank for some ten minutes, and then struck across the sands to his destination. Walking thus, a lonely speck on the dreary flat, the isolation of the dwellings in front came to him sharply, so that their air of prosperous serenity, of tranquil sureness, seemed almost dangerously provocative. Far away and out, where the bay, between two headlands, ran into open water, a slant of light from the sullen sky laid a shining strip from point to point which he knew to be the sea. It was there and it was

coming, quietly, perhaps, and inoffensively, but there
would be many a night when it would come like a
beast of prey, ravening its path between narrow
shores, devouring the waiting desert. And yet the
farms were not afraid.

The sea-wall had been carried in front of them also,
reaching out to the last inch of broken land, and from
thence merging into the huge, defiant bank which had
once been famous throughout the kingdom. It ran
along the coast for a couple of miles, joining the hill
on which the town of Cunswick climbed, and behind
it the reclaimed land lay safe.

Lancaster's father had built both walls, the success
of the lesser firing him, years later, to throw the larger
gauntlet over the sands. They had christened the low
wall 'Lancaster's Let,' which means merely a
hindrance, but the big bank they had named 'Lancaster's Lugg,' from the Scandinavian 'lugg,' a
forelock, and 'lugga,' which means 'to pull by the
hair,' for Lancaster had knotted the manes of the
white sea-horses together, and dragged them out of
their ancient stable.

It was built with a high daring across the one lung
of the limited passage, and at its back the grassy waste
harboured sheep and waited for man's hand; for
though it had long since been mapped out for building, only one house had risen as yet on the stolen
ground. Lanty had often looked at his father's plans,
and locked them away again. Something held him
back from putting them into shape, and, moreover,
decreasing values and increasing Government drains
had left the income tight at times. Yet he meant some
day to materialise his father's dreams, and had good
hopes of them, for Cunswick was a growing seaside
resort, and would eventually take up the land quickly
enough. Meanwhile the big wall held its own, caring
nothing for the onslaughts of the crouching foe behind
that shining line. Whether the full moon brought the

fierce thrust of a heavy swell, or the west wind, riding a wracked sky, hurried the shock of racing billows, the bank held off the one and flung back the other, steadily throwing the trend of the tide to the further and higher side of the bay. To-day, with never a trickle of water at its base, it looked like a mighty serpent on the uncovered sand, winding its slow and writhing length lazily to the sea, purposeless, abnormal, monstrous in the unnatural light and leashed quiet. The sands themselves were dangerous—dangerous to walk and sail, with their deep, shifting banks, unknown quicksands and tidal bore. The whole place had the terrible fascination of lurking ill, and yet on all hands the farms lay peaceful and content, like trustful women sleeping in a tiger's cage.

Lanty looked at the Lugg, that tremendous thwarter of the tides, and thought of his father. The project had roused a storm of controversy at the time, out of which the thing itself had emerged triumphant. Men had pronounced it a risk to the whole coast, and time had proved them wrong. Lancaster had vindicated himself, leaving the bank as his monument, for, in looking out to it each day, the farms saw also the dead who had planned it. They were not afraid of it there. Because a Lancaster had built it they trusted it, resting tranquilly on his word. It was in their simple confidence that his real monument was raised.

The son came at last to the channel of the Wythe, hurrying to sea past the foot of Ladyford, and from there he hailed the farm, shattering the stillness and causing even himself to start. Somebody answered from behind the buildings, and presently a tall boy appeared on the bank, and scrambled down to the boat below. This was Dockeray's youngest son, the only one at home, and Lanty wondered, watching him pull across, what he and his parents thought of the Whinnerah complication. He had come with no definite plan, after all—simply to see how the land

lay, and whether a timely word might in any way be
possible. Certainly he doubted both the opportunity
and his own wisdom. If the girl were as good-looking
as her brother, he thought idly, she might be forgiven
a little petulant coquetting with destiny.

Rowly greeted him with a smile as he grounded the
boat, and made conversation readily enough as they
went over. His parents were well, and the married
brothers away. His sister? Yes, she was at home,
now—had been for some time. Oh, yes, he was glad
to have her. It was a bit lonely at Ladyford of a
winter's night, and Francey was champion at the
piano and singing. He liked a song himself, and so
did the old folks. They were well, too, at Ninekyrkes,
barring old Wolf. He feared he looked like breaking
up fast; but anyhow, it was time he had a rest, and
let Lup take hold. Ever since the pneumonia he'd
been a different man. But that was all; no sign or
hint of how matters stood, or on which side his
sympathies lay. Lanty knew only too well the deeps
covered by the apparent guilelessness of the breed,
and asked no leading questions. It was early work for
that, in any case. Better bide his time until he had
seen the girl herself.

Michael Dockeray was waiting on the bank when
they pulled in, spare and upright, with wise, quiet
eyes and little to say. A totally different type from
old Wolf—this; refined and tactful where the other
was blunt and unafraid; strong enough, too, but with
none of Wolf's added violence. Yet the two had
always been friends, often disagreeing, but turning
to each other for help as naturally as to one of their
own.

He met Lanty's grasp warmly, and they moved on
up to the house, leaving Rowly to get the boat ashore,
for the tide would be on the turn before long. The
agent came but seldom to the far marsh, and he caught
a wave of welcoming excitement as he approached—

figures passing from kitchen to dairy in a cheerful flurry that yet allowed time for a peep through the nearest window at the coming guest. Mrs. Dockeray's voice could be heard running the full gamut of agitated instruction, dropping to a last whisper behind the pantry door concerning the new strawberry jam. Then she appeared, all pleasant smiles and hearty kindness, and Lanty's homelessness was taken up into her motherly arms and smothered out of existence. Through the half-open door he had a glimpse of a smooth, dark head and a trim figure, and a desire for flight came upon him, in spite of the new strawberry jam. His task, vaguely irritating before, became suddenly impossible and grotesque.

He consented to sit in the parlour, making polite conversation with his host while the ordered ceremonies went forward beyond, but he refused to be given tea there, and was glad when the summons came at last from the atmosphere of wool mats and honesty to the artistic rightness of the kitchen. Across the cool picture of yellowed walls, white-stoned flags, shining linen and china, Francey Dockeray's face stood out cooler still, and as he shook her by the hand he felt painfully clumsy and inadequate before her pleasant self-possession. She knew why he had come —he guessed it from the faint satirical twist in her otherwise charming smile, from the swift summing-up of her grey eyes. The business-matter which he had put forward to her father would not pass muster with her, he felt certain of that. He could have dealt with the ordinary farmer's daughter; he knew to a turn the phrase and manner to adopt with success, but they would not apply here. Wolf had been right when he used the word 'quality' of Francey Dockeray. Her ease of manner had the simplicity of true good breeding, and it was to this that he had unwillingly paid tribute. But she was aloof, as he had said. Affectionate towards her parents, thoughtful for the guest, interested and attentive, she was yet, in some inexplicable fashion, outside and away from them all. Lancaster liked his errand less with every minute that passed.

It was inevitable, of course, that the conversation, veering from land-politics to wrestling and singing-practice for the benefit of the young folks, and back again to the farm, should turn at last to their neighbours. As soon as Whinnerah's name was mentioned, Lanty took his first tentative step.

'You'll know, I suppose, that Wolf's talking of leaving?' he asked casually. 'Lup's off to Canada, he tells me, and that means the old folks clearing out of the farm. I'm sorry for both pieces of news. Whinnerahs are old friends. We can always do with the right sort, and Lup's one of the best.'

He sent a straying glance round the group, only to meet the same blank impassiveness that had resisted his efforts crossing the channel. It seemed as if, in the eyes of her family at least, Francey could do no wrong.

'Ay, the pneumonia did for Wolf!' Dockeray admitted sadly. 'I'll be loth to see the Whinnerahs go. We've known each other a sight o' years, now, and when it comes to old company taking its hand off the plough, I'm like to think my own time won't be so long, neither.'

'Nay, now, master!' Mrs. Dockeray put in quickly. 'What, you're a deal younger than Wolf, and as lish as a whip! You've no call to talk of giving up yet awhile. Not but what you'll be missing them all sadly, I doubt, as I will myself. I'm not one for taking up with new stuff, an' I've sort of grown with Whinnerahs. I'm not saying, though, but what it'll do young Lup a deal o' good to see a bit of the world. He sticks away in the old groove till he gets that tied with his tongue you'd think he hadn't two brains to rub one at back o' t'other!'

'Lup's right enough, mother!' young Rowly put in indignantly. 'Lup's head's as full o' meat as most. You've no need to call him out of his name!'

'Nay, why I've nowt against the lad, not I! But he'd do with a shake an' a slake an' a shine with a polisher, after a manner of speaking. Look at Brack Holliday, now! *Yon's* a lad worth running to see of a Saturday night! Canada done that; happen it'll do something for the other an' all. He hadn't much in the way of schoolin', hadn't Lup—he was that stuck on the farm—and it doesn't do not to keep a few manners put by when there's call for 'em. Why, there's whiles I've heard him talking with our Francey there, he so rough and she that nice-spoken—though I say it as shouldn't, she being my own lass—there's times I've felt right-down sorry Lup shouldn't have no more chance of bettering himself than his own hired man.'

Lanty's circular glance caught the faintest flush on Francey's cheek, and passed to meet Mrs. Dockeray's glance seeking his own; and it came to him, in a flash of inspiration, that she was on Lup's side and her menfolk with her; that the wise mother-mind had its own method of pulling the strings, while the others stood apart, committing themselves to nothing. The matter struck him suddenly as a charming, homely comedy of courtship—no more; and he planted a further step with a firmer tread.

'I was doubly surprised to hear of his departure, because it was quite other news I'd looked for. Folk had it he was getting ready to marry and settle down, and I thought the lady in luck, whoever she might be. I was misinformed, I suppose? Strange how these tales get round!'

A certain uneasiness became apparent in both Michael and Rowly at this, but Mrs. Dockeray never turned a hair.

'Ay, well, courtin' he might be, like enough, but it

isn't every lass would look at Lup, as I mentioned a minute ago, for all he's a good enough lad and steady as yon shuppon. He's not everybody's choice in these days o' lettering and figuring. There's a many as'll seek to look higher than just poor Lup Whinnerah!'

She fixed him again, and he nodded assent, seeing that it was expected of him; and then, from her post at the window, where she had moved at the end of the meal, he met Francey's clear gaze. She stood half-turned to the casement and the stretch of sand beyond, her pale cheek to the brilliant geraniums on the wide ledge, and in her eyes, as they rested on his, something of scorn and yet of wounded appeal. He felt the blood rise to his face as he looked, conscious of having outraged both her feelings and his own good taste. The type he understood would have taken him in jest, or retreated from the room in dudgeon; not have remained without retort, gently contemptuous and quietly hurt. He changed the subject abruptly, wishing the Whinnerahs and their affairs at Jericho.

Lup's name dropped like a stone, but the question of matrimony still hung in the air, for Michael himself came back to it after a lengthy discussion upon the late danger of plague from Irish cattle.

'Ay, there's many a knock-down blow lying in wait for the poor farmer!' he observed, shaking his head over a new and harrowing tale. 'But it's a decent enough life for them as is framed for it and knows how to take it standing. It's done well enough by me. I've a fairish farm and a just landlord, and the sort of missis a man'll be put about to part with when the time comes for his last ride to church!' He looked across at his wife with a mild twinkle. 'Not but what she's a rough side to her tongue, and a mighty short stock o' patience for them as doesn't see same ways as herself; but there's only two sorts o' wives, Mr. Lancaster—them as a man's fain to be shot of, an' them as he'd be right fain to be shot *for*—an' yon last's my missis, sir, and a good bit over!'

Francey left the window, and laid her hands on his shoulders for a moment, her face lightly smiling and tender. Then she was gone from the room, while Mrs. Dockeray, with the suspicion of a shake in her voice, defended her character for patience.

'Eh, well, I reckon we're as easy as most!' she admitted at last with her cheerful laugh. 'You'd do no harm to take copy from us, Mr. Lancaster. We've been looking for you to get wed, any time these last ten years!'

Lanty was used to the suggestion, and repudiated it without embarrassment.

'I'm not a marrying man, I doubt!' he answered; and, even as he spoke, felt a surge of envy sweep over him at the picture of mutual need before him. 'Any more than Lup!' he added, with meaning, and there came another pause, during which Rowly slipped out after his sister.

'You know what's to do, sir, I reckon?' the mother asked presently, as Lancaster waited for his challenge to be accepted; and at his brief—'Wolf told me something'—she unburdened herself of the situation, while Michael stared straight before him with his wise eyes, rocking gently from time to time in his cushioned chair.

'Whinnerah he come across rampin' fit to kill himself, saying as how our lass had been playing fast an' loose with his lad, and there was talk o' Canada and quitting the farm an' such-like! He was set on our putting our foot down, Michael an' me, and giving Francey a piece of our minds, but we told him that hadn't never been our way with her, and it wasn't likely we'd begin now; so he took off again in a rare tantrum, an' that's all there is to it. It's true, as he says, as we've always made sure she and Lup was courtin', but we didn't ask questions, taking it that she'd speak when she'd a mind. I'd be glad to see her wed the lad, ay, an' so would Michael here, though I'm not saying she mightn't do better. But if she's not set on having him, she shan't be driven to it, as long as there's folks at Ladyford to her back. I'm real sorry for Wolf and Lup—ay, an' poor Martha!— and I'd give a deal to see the lad stop, but our own barn comes first, and she shall suit herself, Mr. Lancaster.'

And Michael said: 'Ay. Yon's the way of it. Yon's right!' rocking gently from time to time in his cushioned chair.

'Well, it seems a pity,' Lanty said at last, reluctantly making ready to go, 'but I'm still hoping things will right themselves. It's natural a girl should like to be consulted, though I shouldn't have thought it was just a touch of pride with your daughter. She looks too fine a character for anything as small-minded as that.'

' 'Tisn't only pride, Mr. Lancaster! It's something a deal stronger, it's love upside down. We've nobody but ourselves to thank, as I tell Michael. It's the schoolin' as done it. We'd a bit of money saved, and we took a fancy to have her finished like a lady, but I'm not so sure, nowadays, as we did the right thing by her. It's hard, Mr. Lancaster, when you think a deal o' your own, not to want to give them something better than you've had yourself, but I'll not say as I think it's always wise or kind, leastways, for a woman. A man, happen, can go an' fight his own way in the world, but if a woman's got to bide at home, the schoolin's likely learned her nowt but hankering for what's out of her reach. Not but what Francey's been biddable enough, but I've kept my eye on her. I've been biding my time for this, an' now it's come. We've made her different of our own will, and we've no right to expect her to do as we'd have done. It's us that's to blame—an' the learning. It makes a woman look

at a man like a new sort o' lesson-book. It starts her
wondering what she feels instead o' just feeling. It
sets her seeing with her eyes an' not with her heart.
It's not just brains you want for dealing wi' men-folk,
sir. It's something as sees in the dark with blind eyes,
something as sharp to hark as yon collie-pup, as soft
to touch as a mother's hands! Francey's looking an'
not letting herself feel, and till she's learned that
looking doesn't count in love, there's nobody can
help her. Nobody but Lup—and, happen, life—can
set her right.'

'You'll likely be giving them a look-in at Ninekyrkes, sir, as you're here?' she added, following him
to the door. 'They're terrible down, an' it would
cheer them up a bit. Wolf's that set on your family,
you'd happen think it was Royalty, to hark to him!
He saw a deal o' your father, yon time as the Lugg
was so long building—Mr. Lancaster used to stop
many a night along with him—an' he'll crack for a
week about it if happen he gets the chance. He'd
swear with his eyes shut to everything your father
ever did—says there'll never be his like again. Not
but what he thinks a sight o' *you* an' all, sir! You'll
look in?'

'Yes, I'll step over, now I'm here, but of course I'll
say nothing of what you've told me. If they really
mean leaving, we must get things fixed up. Wolf said
his wife had taken to looking ahead for trouble. Is
that so, do you know?'

He saw a half-embarrassed glance pass between the
two.

'She was always a bit of a worrit,' Michael said at
last, rather hurriedly, 'an' this'll have likely got on
her nerves. I'll set you a piece of the way, sir.'

Wondering, Lancaster followed him out into the
heavy evening.

CHAPTER IV
THE TROUBLE SHAPING

It was milking-time when Lanty left Ladyford, with
Dockeray beside him, and they met the cattle coming
in to the shippons. Their slow swing across the yard
added to the drowsy oppression of the day. It was
as if he walked in sleep along the narrow sea-road
linking the two farms. The flat land behind was in
good cultivation. When it was turned by the plough,
the share came out clean of rust and shining like silver.
A big plantation stood away towards Wythebarrow,
hiding the highway between. A wide cut was cloven
betwixt the far meadows. There was no sign of the
tide as yet, and out on the dry sands the Lugg still lay
meaningless and bare.

Ninekyrkes was nearer the open sea than Ladyford,
less sheltered, less homely, less pleasant to the eye.
The rough, sturdy house stood up bravely to the
winds. There were flowers round Dockeray's, and an
orchard behind it. Whinnerah's had neither. It was
built for storm and stress and fierce happenings, and
bore upon its forehead the mark of an abiding-place
of Fate.

Wolf came round as they appeared, and after a
brief greeting Michael turned home. Lancaster saw
him go with strange reluctance. The grim farm and
its grim tenant fostered a sense of tragedy lying in
wait, gathering itself to spring; but he roused his
business-side determinedly, and kept strictly to
technicalities as he started on his tour of inspection.
Yet still the hand of tragedy obtruded through all.
It was pitiful to hear the old man reverting to plans
for the future as if the doom of dismissal had never
been pronounced. He would stop at some field or
fence, pointing out what he meant to do next year or
later, and Lancaster listened patiently, or brought him

back gently to the real state of things. His self-consciousness with regard to Michael's daughter disappeared in face of the full situation, and his anger grew against the girl, who, for some trivial reason, could stubbornly rob a failing man of his earned desire. For Lup he had sympathy, if a good deal of impatience. He was strong enough, surely, to take what he wanted; yet perhaps it needed something finer than mere strength to capture Francey Dockeray. In any case, he should know his own business best.

They got to the house at last, and within it he felt again the marked contrast with Ladyford. Here, in the kitchen so similar in many ways, the cheerful peace was changed for hinted dread, emanating, he concluded at length, from the frail figure in the chair by the window. He had known Mrs. Whinnerah all his life, and he was not afraid of her unsmiling welcome, but to-night he felt that something hidden suffered and watched behind her chill reserve. The sense of it was so strong that it claimed his thoughts even while he carried on the usual conversational exchange.

They were a pathetic pair, he thought, looking from one bent figure to the other. Wolf was a sad enough picture, a fine man gone to wreck in a few devastating months, but the pathos of the woman went deeper. The hard life on the marsh had broken her long since, stolen her youth in the first years of marriage, crippled her with rheumatism, stamped on her thin face that look of passionless endurance which can be seen in many a farmer's wife who has found her burden too heavy and gone on bearing it. She had been pretty, once. In the line of her cheek and the set of her head was still a beauty of refinement absent from Francey's mother over at Ladyford, and the thin fingers of her worn hands were curiously sensitive and suggestive of a rare intuition. But that was all that was left to her. She was finished, as Wolf was finished, and the one thing that life might yet have held for them was to be taken away. Lanty wondered how Lup could look at them, night after night, sitting there hopeless, and steel his heart to the unbreathed prayer, even though sacrifice might mean daily crucifixion, with the love denied so close at hand. But Lup himself was part of the cruel situation. He did not come to it from outside, as Lancaster came, with fresh eyes full of pity.

Remembering both Wolf's words and the Dockerays' embarrassment, he found himself noting the old woman's constant and fixed gaze out to sea. Her faded eyes were still clear, and the large pupils had the effect of dark pebbles seen through deep pools. Time after time he succeeded in drawing them to his own face, but, his question answered, they returned instantly to some invisible point beyond. Wolf had said she was watching for something, and it certainly seemed like it, for the glance was not the wandering one of custom, but a stare of genuine expectation, suggesting held breath and stiffened muscles. Wolf looked at her uneasily at times, and when she became conscious of his gaze she would bring her own with an effort to the guest, but always, always it went back. The sensation of mystery deepened, and Lancaster stirred restlessly under its touch. The sky had darkened and then filled with fire, and beneath the dull thunder-glow the houses on Bytham Knott looked like flakes of snow dropped on a sullen slab of granite. The thin trees stood like dumb sentinels of fear; the green of the fields smote the eye; a sudden clash of milk-pails from without set every nerve leaping, and then the stillness sank again. And the sands and the bank were stiller than the air. The only moving thing was the shining, quivering line far away to the west.

Mrs. Whinnerah made no complaint of the approaching change. She was ready to go, not with the decision of personal choice, but with the apathy of one led by destiny. Lanty asked at last where they thought of moving when the time came for breaking-up. There was a pause after the question, and he saw Wolf's eyes travel to his wife, as if, in this moment, some urgent problem must be solved, but she gave him no assistance.

'You'll think it queer, likely,' he began, filling his pipe with slow fingers, 'but I'm hoping you'll not say no to an old man's wish. There's yon cottage your father built, you'll think on—that on the new land as they call the "Pride." It's been empty a good bit, but it's taken no harm. The key's here, and I've had a look round now and then. Folk say it's over lone-some; they get flate at night, hearkening to the sea, them as hasn't been bred by it an' learned to like it. I'd never rest without the song of it coming and going, but there's folk can't abide it. Well, I've got a fancy for that cottage, Mr. Lancaster. It's nigh on Nine-kyrkes land, and I'd be able to reach an eye over the old spot from the door. With a bit o' practice I'll likely learn not to mind seeing other folk at my job. It'll not be for that long, I doubt.'

'Come, you're good for many a year yet!' Lancaster put in, as cheerfully as he could. 'I can have the cottage put in order for you if you're really set on it, but don't you think you'd be wiser to pitch your tent somewhere else altogether? Living within a stone's-throw will only set you hankering after the farm. You'd be happier away. What has your wife to say to it?'

He turned to the woman, but before she could answer there came a sharp crack right across the empty sands and with a strangled cry she half rose to her feet, gripping the wooden arms of the chair, her face livid and her arms rigid, her glassy eyes fixed on the inscrutable beyond.

'It's through!' she said in a choked voice, so full of

horror that it drew Lancaster to his feet beside her, but Wolf sat still and snarled from his chair.

'Yon's thunder, nowt else! Look ye there!' and as a fierce flicker of lightning danced down the pane, she sank back into her chair, biting her lips to steady them, and knotting her trembling hands together on her knee. She was calm again almost immediately, and Lancaster, at the window, watching the blue daggers stabbing the dead waste, and hearkening to the long rattle of charging clouds, marvelled that she showed no further signs of agitation. Shock after shock broke overhead, leaving her unmoved, and the vivid flashes scarcely shut her eyes. It was not the storm that had frightened her, he told himself. What was it?

The almost running roar made conversation impossible, so he stood silent, watching the tempest sweep along the open space before him. The passion of it seemed grotesque, as wreaked upon a lifeless thing beyond the reach of hurt. It died away at last in tired, angry spasms and slow gleams, and the thick silence came again into the heavy sky.

When it was spent, Lanty turned to say good-bye, hoping to make home before the storm returned, circling on its tracks like a driven hare, but as he reached the door a strange thing happened.

Through the stillness dropped like a muffling shroud came a new sound, smooth, stealthy, swift, a soft sound as of shod wheels, swept wings and subdued speech; and in the same moment Mrs. Whinnerah collapsed in her chair, until he saw the thin, grey hair coiled at the nape of her neck. With an exclamation, half of pity, half wrath, Wolf turned and went back to her, and, looking out, Lanty saw the bore sweeping up over the vanishing sand. It was small to-day, innocent and slim, with a crest of white on its smooth head, but in the deadly certainty of its advance, the unhasting speed with which it met the sand and took

it, there was a sinister promise of mightier power held
back. The insidious reminder of its faint wash was
almost as terrible as the shout of battle with which
the winter tides came in. It slid lightly along the foot
of the Lugg with barely a ripple, and the bank looked
down almost unaware, like a dreaming greybeard at
a child playing round his knees.

Behind him, with a troubled sense of intrusion, he
could hear Wolf's voice, impatient and distressed,
coaxing the crouching figure in the chair.

'It's by, lass—past an' safe, by now—a whyet
enough water with barely a lift to it. Nay, what, you
must be daft to take on like this! It'll stand many a
long year after we're under the sod. You've no call
to fret. It's a Lancaster's job, Martha, as sure as a
gun an' as right as a bobbin!' He looked up apologetically. 'You'll not take it amiss, sir? She's always
like this at the turn of the tide.'

Lanty sympathised as well as he could, but when he
would have held out his hand in farewell, she shrank
away and hid her face once more.

'The Lancaster hand!' she muttered, winding her
fingers in the woollen antimacassar. 'Oh, God! How
long? How long?'

With a pleading look, Wolf drew him out, and he
went gladly enough, bewildered by the whole situation. There was mystery somewhere, and he did not
like to ask the cause.

'Mrs. Whinnerah seems thoroughly upset,' he ventured at last, in a matter-of-fact tone. 'Living so long
by the sea has got on her nerves, and I don't wonder!
It must be pretty drear out here on a rough night.
You should get her away for a change. She has a
sister over at Bortun, hasn't she? It doesn't do to
play with these things. If she keeps like this, you'll
surely never think of taking the cottage?'

Over the old man's shoulder he could see in the
distance the little grey building behind the Lugg, that

some mocker had ticketed 'Lancaster's Pride.' It had had many tenants, but none had stayed very long. Their courage had not been equal to the dark nights on the lonely waste—nights, when behind the wall a full sea surged and swayed, claiming the land that man had robbed. It stood empty, now, waiting stronger spirits, and it was to this place of fear that Wolf's heart turned, for from its windows he could look to Ninekyrkes all day long.

'Nay, the missis'll do well enough,' he said, in answer to Lancaster's speech. 'She started yon worriting job nigh on a year back, a matter of a few week afore Brack Holliday landed home. He made such a stir, it kind o' fixed it in my mind! She'll likely mend after a bit. Anyway, she'll not quit the marsh no more than me, that's sure an' certain!'

'Why, but man, it's bad enough for her at Ninekyrkes!' the other argued. 'It'll be a good few hundred times worse at the Pride. You'll never get her to go.'

'She'll gang where I gang!' Wolf said obstinately. 'Offer her any other spot on the estate, and see for yourself. She'll bide all right.'

'Well, I can't say I think you're wise. Suppose I won't let you the cottage? I've more than half a mind to refuse.'

'Then I'll see his lordship, Mr. Lancaster! It's not for a steward to be looking awry at a good tenant!' He added, 'Begging your pardon, sir!' with instant contrition.

Lancaster nodded assurance.

'That's all right, Wolf. But I wish you'd reconsider your decision. I don't like the idea of your roosting away in that desolate spot.'

'It's desolate, sir, but it's safe enough. *You've* no call to fear the Lugg, surely?'

'Why, no, the bank's all right!' Lanty answered, with a smile. 'There's never anything my father did but holds good to this day. But, all the same, I don't want you at the Pride.'

'Ay, but all the same you'll let it me, sir! It's this way, Mr. Lancaster. Your father, when he'd made sure the Lugg was standing, he'd just time to build yon lile cot afore he died. He'd framed for a many more, but they had to bide. An', near about the last time he was down, he says to me (I'd been a deal with him up an' down the marsh, and he was the best friend I had, but yon's an old story you don't need to hear), he says to me: "Wolf," says he, "yon'll be just the spot for you if ever you come to quit the farm. I'll have been in my grave many a year by then, but my bank'll see to you for me. I'd like to think of you in the little house, for there's never a stone nor a plank but will call me to mind. Not but what I know you'll not forget. I'll never really die while the Lugg stands and Wolf Whinnerah's over sod!" You'll not say no after that, sir?'

'Well, I'll think it over,' Lanty answered reluctantly. 'By the way, I haven't had a word yet with the girl. Perhaps I'll catch her as I go back, though I doubt it's no use. Good-bye, and I wish to goodness you'd change your minds all round!'

He left him at the yard gate, and strode off along the road. On the other side of the Let the tide lapped tenderly. Deep in frowning thought, he was startled by a voice speaking his name, and, looking up, saw Francey Dockeray on the grassy barrier above him.

CHAPTER V
THE TOOL

HE saw her for a moment poised against the brooding sky, and then she dropped down the bank to his side. They stood alone on the desolate strip of road twisting whitely between black peat, green mound, and brown sand. Midway from farm to farm they met—a fitting point, it seemed to him, for the peculiar arbitration he had in hand.

'Rowly's at the boat, sir, if you're wanting him,' she said politely, and he answered with a curt word of thanks. Then—'They're in a bad way at Nine-kyrkes,' he began, without preamble. 'They seem gone to pieces altogether, both Wolf and his wife. It's hard on an old couple, of course, when it comes to losing both their home and their only child.'

She looked away to the crag behind, and made no reply.

'I've just been round the place with the old man,' he went on, 'and it was pitiable to see how he kept forgetting he'd got to go. It was like turning the knife in the wound to keep reminding him how things were. It's hard, as I said. He might have had his last days in peace.'

Still she did not answer; only her gaze, turned inland, grew troubled and hard pressed.

'It seems so unnecessary!' He felt suddenly impatient before her silent resistance of his efforts. 'Lup's place is here; that's plain enough to anybody with half a conscience. He's fond of the old folks, too. It isn't as if they didn't get on. Normally, he'd never have thought of leaving them. Can't something be done? Can't somebody help?'

She gave a sharp sigh, as if forced against her will over old ground already trodden to weariness, and brought her eyes to his as they rested on her full of demand and penetration.

'Hadn't we better be frank with each other, Mr. Lancaster?' she asked gently. 'You've heard the story—I feel sure of that—and you want to try to talk me round. That's so, isn't it?'

'I've heard some sort of an account—yes; and it looks as if the key of the situation lay with you. Of course, you'll say it's no business of mine, and from one point of view it certainly isn't, but when old

friends are in trouble one wants to stretch a hand.
I wish you'd tell me why you did it—why you went
back on Lup Whinnerah just when he needed you
most. You'll not deny you went back on him, I
suppose?'

'No, I don't deny it.'

'Why, then, there's hope!' He smiled with quick
relief. 'You're surely not the sort to play down upon
a good lad like Lup? You'll never break up his home
for the sake of a whim or a foolish twinge of vanity?'

'I don't want to break up his home. I've tried to
dissuade him from going away. He could stop, if he
chose. I can't see that I make any real difference.'

'You make all the difference.' He was speaking
gently enough, now. 'We like to have married men
on the farms, for one thing; and even supposing Lup
did stop on, what sort of a life would it be for him,
with you always within reach? You're all so depen-
dent on each other, out here. He's been over-hasty,
I consider, but I can't find it in my heart to blame
him greatly. Sticking by the man, of course, you'll
say? Well, perhaps; but in this case there's reason.
Come, Miss Francey, think better of it. If you care
for him at all, you'll never let him go.'

'I'll not keep him,' she said, and they fell silent.

Then—'Why?' he asked again. 'But why?'

She smiled faintly.

'I don't know why—not altogether. It's true that
it's partly pride, I suppose—I'm not sure. I do care
for Lup, and I'd promised to marry him, but when
his father put it all into plain words, spoke out and
told me to fix the date, all the glamour went, somehow.
He had it so cut and dried—I felt as if I were being
sold. It meant no more to him than a change of stock
at a May fair. I'd have had to say no if it had killed
me. He meant all right—of course I know that—and
it would have been right for most, but it wasn't for
me. They wouldn't treat one of your class like that,

would they? But that's the way of mine, and I'd no right to resent it, I suppose, only I've been made over and differently in those long years at school. I couldn't accept it as perhaps I ought to have done. It hurt something in me that I didn't know was there, something that wouldn't be touched. That was part of the reason, I think. Not all.'

'And the rest?' he asked, at last.

'The rest is Lup's, sir. I can't tell you that. I don't see it clear myself, as I said. Put it at pride altogether, if you like.'

'What's pride, if you care?' he argued. 'Let that go by the board! You can, if you try. And the other thing, too, whatever it is. For Lup's sake—for the old folks' sake——'

'I can't. I can't.'

'You'll not regret it.'

'I can't—that's all.'

'Well, I'm not here to marry you against your will!' he growled, aggrieved at the deadlock. 'If you won't, you won't, and there's an end of it. I'd not be so hard on you if I thought the change would mean getting Mrs. Whinnerah away altogether, but it seems that Wolf is set on taking the Pride.'

'The Pride?' They had begun to walk slowly towards the boat, but now she half stopped, looking up at him anxiously.

'That's his idea. I can't very well refuse him, if he really means it, but it looks to me a bad move for the wife. Even Ninekyrkes seems too much for her nerves, as it is. You've seen her lately, I suppose? Can you tell me what's at the back of it all?'

She quickened her step, looking down.

'She's getting old, sir, and she imagines things. You mustn't pay any heed, Mr. Lancaster. It only worries Wolf, if you do.'

'Well, I must say you're a happy family over here at present!' he grumbled, as they came down the

shore. 'I might as well have stopped away, for all
the good I've done. You'll be sorry for this, some
day, Miss Francey!'

'I'm sorry now!' she answered, with so much pathos
and helpless appeal in her voice that he was silenced.
Scrambling into the boat, he was rowed away across
the now wide stretch of water. The first shot of the
new battery burst from the sky as he reached the
other side, and through the playing lightning he saw
Francey Dockeray still on the bank, with the blackness
of all doom around and above her.

CHAPTER VI
HAMER'S HUT

DANDY SHAW looked round the Watters drawing-
room with a little twist of the lips. She was perched
on a high oak stool, with her feet on the rungs, and
through the Chippendale mirror opposite she could
see both her own figure and its setting. It was afternoon, and under the looped yellow silk blinds the sun
pattered on dark wood and faint brocades, a carpet
hushed as moss, elusive little water-colours, china
ephemeral as frost-breath, books with the colouring
of rare gems. There were no photographs in the
room, and there was no silver, no flotsam and jetsam
of Christmas and birthday offerings, but there were
flowers everywhere, not massed with heavy ballroom
effects, nor set at conventional intervals like a well-
drilled regiment, but leading the eye on with unexpected thrills of pleasure from one delicate single
shade to another, like tiny semitones in a fairy scale.
From without, where the river crept beneath the dark
splendour of turned beeches edging the terrace, the
long, low, grey-faced house with its plain windows
looked almost asleep, but there was a very active
brain at work within.

Dandy—otherwise Anne—had no need to fear her image in the mirror, but she frowned at it, nevertheless. Even the image seemed joyously alive, with soft, bright hair, and blue eyes full of candid good-will; and nothing about it clashed at first sight with its surroundings, yet she glanced from it to the old walls with amused yet abashed and apologetic resentment. For the first time in her life Dandy Shaw was discovering that there are things which mean more than people.

From the still house and the simple, beautiful room her thoughts went back to Halsted, her late home on the outskirts of a Lancashire town—to the over-whelming magnificence of its *ménage*, the long, rich meals, the endless contrivances for comfort, the stream of guests, the intricate programmes of amusement. She saw the big, red pile, with the shining cars slurring up its drive, the long lines of hothouses, the priceless roses, the precious orchids flung into elaborate schemes of colour. It was all rich and splendid and inviting, luxurious and perfectly organised; but Watters cared for none of these things.

It was pale and grey and plain and cool and utterly aloof. It did not care a toss whether you looked at it or not, so of course you always did, leaning over the humped bridge, and wondering what ghosts moved in the darkened rooms and met by moonlight on the terrace. If you tried to bring a car up its twisting, cross-grained drive, the odds were you would find yourself in the river or a clump of clipped yews as old as Ernuin the Priest. And the roses at Watters would have died of sheer disgust in the cosmopolitan atmosphere of a rose-show marquee. They grew and scrambled and climbed in their own strong-willed fashion, clothing cold stone with hearts of deep orange, flinging arches of tender pink or glowing crimson against opal skies, or lifting single, dewy heads like pale lamps in the hushed garden after sunset. And at any but simple food it looked rigidly askance, loftily permitting the butcher to drop his beef and mutton, and condescending to game, as a country house of standing, but shutting shocked eyelids upon French menus and foreign cheeses. Anything *bisqué* or *braisé* or *soufflé* or *au gratin* scarcely dared trust itself near the stove, and a pot of *foie-gras* had positively to be smuggled.

It was a curious impulse that had driven the Lancashire tradesman from the home of his own creating to one with which he had apparently nothing in common. Less than a year ago, Dandy had found him on the Halsted drive, with his hands in his pockets and his hat on the back of his head, surveying the symbol of wealth with a puzzled frown.

'There's something wrong, Dandy Anne!' he broke out, as she slid a hand through his arm. 'It's strong and it's good, and it's warm and it's cool, and comfortable and convenient and clean, but it isn't anything else. It doesn't make you think of the past and the future. It doesn't make you want to throw up your hat one minute and dry your eyes on your coat-sleeve the next. It'll never have any troubles or joys bigger than an insurance-card or a mayoral invitation. It's smug—that's what it is! It doesn't feel—it *can't*, and so it can't make you feel, either. When a man's getting on in years, he wants the sort of house that can show him how to grow old kindly. This red elephant would be smug and smiling while I was tottering into the grave. Let's go and find a hut, Dandy Anne, where I can grow old gently.'

And Watters, for some reason known only to himself, had seemed to him just that 'hut.' He had had it decorated by an artist, who, recognising the individuality of the place, seemed to have listened in secret to its whispered wants; and when it was

finished, Hamer Shaw strode happily up and down
it, a burly, incongruous figure with its hat on the
back of its head, satisfied to the very marrow, and
growing younger every day. He had opened his eyes
in a Westmorland cottage, and though he had left it
so speedily that it was scarcely worth mention, some
power, biding its time, had called him back, to his
passionate content. Mrs. Shaw was of the type that
belongs nowhere but to the absorbing house-world of
the moment, and she had borne the transplanting
cheerfully enough, if not with her husband's bubbling
ecstasy. But to Dandy it was almost as terrific an
experience as a total change of planet.

Bred in Lancashire, educated in London, finished
abroad, she had no single tie with her new life and
surroundings. She had been perfectly happy at
Halsted, liking the constant excitement, the flow of
money, the crowd of guests. She had understood
everybody, and they had understood her. She had
been an excellent hostess, and a very charming
uncrowned queen, with not only Halsted, but all
her circle at her feet. She had lived quickly and
strongly, a little noisily, perhaps, but very vividly;
and now, at the age of twenty-four, she was flung out
of the rush into still water. Cessation may prove as
distracting as revolution, and after five months she
was even yet eminently perplexed. She had put no
stone in the way of her father's sudden desire, cheerfully resigning the old life for the new, for she was a
happy creature with an interest in the world at large
that would have stood the shock of almost any change.
But this had proved so puzzling and disconcerting,
yielded so many emotions of an unexpected nature!
Not only was she no longer a queen; she was scarcely
an individual. With her somewhat exceptional
powers of clear vision she soon discovered that. She
was 'the new girl from somewhere awful—I forget
where; daughter of the new people at Watters—I

forget who; new-rich dealers in something—I forget what.'

The word 'new' followed her about like a witch's curse. At Halsted it had been the last touch of praise for everything. If you made a purchase, you called everybody in the house to see it, whether it was a diamond necklace or the tiling in the bathroom. But in Gilthrotin nothing new was tolerated but necessaries like bread and butter; diamonds were nothing accounted of unless they had glittered first on a family neck in a family portrait; and when progress and the plumber forced you to a hot-water system or incandescents, you were always glad that your great-grandfather had not lived to see it. Under her cruel consciousness of 'newness' Dandy was oppressed even to the earth. She frowned at the picture in the glass, much as Hamer had frowned at soulless Halsted.

Few people had called, as yet, except the neighbouring clergy, together with countless daughters of the horse-leech, cased in subscription-lists. More daughters had written. Indeed, begging-letters dropped like hail. Hamer contributed to the first twenty-five, and then sat down to think about the rest. The county came slowly, however; in driblets, so to speak. Things would alter in time, of course, for even in the conservative country Hamer Shaw's money would make its way, as well as—later—Hamer Shaw's sterling worth and fine business capacity. And his daughter would be taken up, when it was discovered that she hadn't actually worked in a mill and worn clogs, but was merely a charming and well-educated member of human society. But she would never be a queen again, even then. She would never be even one of the elect. She would always be 'new.' In a ripe old age she would have progressed no further than 'rather new.' She would always be an outsider at Watters in Gilthrotin.

To do her justice, though she sent a sigh after her

lost crown, that was not the cause of her dissatisfaction. For the first time in her smooth career she was arrested, called to halt by something that thrilled almost to pain. For the first time, too, she saw herself no longer the pivot of her world, an outstanding figure on an obliging background of earth, but a mere unnecessary pigmy on its surface. She found the country cruel and very lonely, full of shut secrets, fearful, yet unquestionably alluring. In this new atmosphere, where the true Romance still brushed by on velvet wings, her unfledged soul shrank a little, and as yet was lost. The name of it in books had stirred her to a vague desire; the reality of it, keen as a sword, rich as purple curtains before God, made her afraid.

The house affected her in the same way. Its tranquillity, its dignity, its rapt air of hiding secrets mystic as the Grail, impressed her as the attributes of a living thing, with a mind and being larger than her own. Its susceptibility, too, amazed her. Halsted, for instance, had cared nothing for weather. When the sun burned, you drew the blinds, and, within, the luxury grew cool and fragrant; and when storm held sway without, again the blinds were drawn, shutting you into soft comfort, where electric light, silver, and china, laughter and the click of balls or the slur of dancing feet, struck always the same note of lapped pleasure. But, at Watters, when the sun shone, the old house stirred dreamily and smiled, and half-forgotten pictured faces looked alive from the dim walls, and threads of hot gold ran molten along the dark floors. There was no need to curtain the sun; the place needed it, and turned its old bones gratefully under its touch. And on days of stress the house shared it with the day; you could not shut the storm from Watters. The wind was in the house itself, lifting the rugs, whistling up the stair, crying like a lost soul in the eaves. The hurrying sky was mirrored in the glass of the panelling, and the beating rain filled the stone eyes with streaming tears. Outside, the full river swung above its banks, and the lost wail of sheep on the mist-hung fell rode on the tortured air.

But the silence was worse than anything, she found —the real silence that is full of notes but never a note that jars. When she woke in the morning, it took her by the throat. No jangling of trams, mill-whistles, and trains; only, at times, faint music from the farm across the way, and the slow, sleepy call of church-bells. She could not lie, as she learned to do in later days, staring with quiet eyes at the sky, wrapped in a happy stillness more soothing than sleep. It often woke her in the night—that full silence.

They had had visitors, at first. Before they were fairly settled in the place, a crowd of friends had descended on them, and Hamer Shaw would sooner have shut his door to a Royal honour than on old acquaintance. But the circle, so pleasant and suitable at Halsted, was altogether out of the picture at Watters. The very house itself would have nothing to say to the guests; indeed, it deliberately sulked at them with grudging fires and lukewarm baths. It had other tricks, too—sudden stairs down which they tumbled in the dark; rattling windows, creaking boards and whistling key-holes for the hag-ridden hours of the night; soot in spotless grates, burst pipes and skilfully-situated coal-buckets; while the outside world co-operated subtly, from the early rooster to the midnight owl. These drawbacks had been un-known at Halsted, and the guests asked each other dismally what could have possessed old Hamer to quit his palace for a God-forsaken monument like Watters. Their torpedo-nosed cars had a kind of abnormality in the little village at the river's edge. The Halsted habitués rent the night with gramophones, and across the cool water flung the frenzied wrangles of snooker. They were Halstedites who had tangoed through a dream in the lane. Dandy found herself shrinking from them unintentionally but unmistakably. She was glad when they went; and yet, when they had gone, she was sorry, for she felt her place to be with them. And the friends bemoaned themselves as they motored home, saying sadly—'That's the end of *you*, Hamer, old man! In another year he'll have forgotten he ever knew us. It's the country does it—the benighted, besotted, be-swank-ridden country. Give him six months more, and he'll be as rooted an old tree-stump as any of them!'

It wasn't anybody's fault, Dandy realised that thankfully. The hosts had been kind as usual, the guests hearty as ever, but the new conditions had laughed the old friendships to scorn. It was very sad, and it was also rather terrible, if you were once fully convinced that a house, a senseless mixture of stone and mortar, had done it all on its own!

Thus Dandy held review as she sat with her feet on the rungs of the high stool. Later in the day, on a sudden impulse, she unburdened her mind to her parents.

'It's going to be a bit hard for me,' she said frankly, 'so you must not be disappointed if I'm a failure! I don't match here, and I've lost my old element, so at present I'm neither flesh, fowl, nor good red herring. I'll have to grow to this place, and that sort of thing takes time. I don't mean that I'm unhappy; it's only that I don't fit in. *You're* all right, aren't you, mummy? You touched ground over the Bluecaster butcher with the Halsted smile. And father's been all right all along. It doesn't seem fair that I should still be struggling in deep water.'

Mrs. Shaw said—'6 tr., 3 lacets, 1 sp., 31 tr.—have you seen the new stair-rods?—4 sl. sts. from third horizontal tr., turn!'

And Hamer took his pipe out of his mouth and added—'It's great!' and put it back again.

'Yes, it's great.' Dandy laughed and sighed. 'So great that I'm not sure I'll ever get round to the far side of it! It's small and mean, too—does *every*body keep a pet charity chained like a dog to nobble new-comers? And those that don't beg seem to be tied up in a pride as big as a bath towel—that nice, cross agent-person, for instance, who looks rather like a high-class keeper, and nabobs you off his land like a reigning duke. *He*'ll never want to be kind to us, I'm sure, and we must have *some*body to pass the time of day with. Perhaps the house will decide. It turned a cold enough shoulder on the poor Halstedites; it owes us somebody in return. I hope it will send an interesting selection soon, though it seems queer to have to let a house choose your friends for you! I get on fairly well with the villagers, though they're not exactly flattering. "Very pleased to meet you, miss, I'm sure! You mind me something surprising of her as was last school-teacher but two!" That was the "Jeanne" frock, mother, that Wiggie used to say looked like concrete moonshine, at Halsted. It looks like the fairy queen in a ballet, *here*. Even my sporting clothes are wrong—they sport too much. And I find I don't know any of the things that matter—when the grass begins to grow, and which weather is coming up from the sea, and what to call it when it *has* come. No, I don't fit in. Perhaps I'll learn, after a while.'

Hamer Shaw said—'The land'll teach you,' and leaned back and shut his eyes. He could hear milk-pails on the flags at the Parsonage Farm.

'And love,' Mrs. Shaw added, very unexpectedly, '7 lacets, 7 tr., 9 ch., turn—don't forget to look at the rods!'

'The land—and love.' Dandy said no more, knowing nothing of either. On the fell opposite a floating wreath of mist was lifting delicately upward like a lawn kerchief drawn from a sleeping face. 'The land—and love.' Great Masters. But the land,

as yet, would have none of her, and love might never
look her way. She could win the one if she chose to
woo it; the other and greater must come unasked.

'Mais, cher dieu, de la tendre et divine épouvante,
Amour, que feraient-ils si vous ne veniez pas?'

CHAPTER VII

THE TROUBLE COMING.—THE GREEN GATES
OF VISION: II. MORNING

'AFRAID I've got to worry you a bit!' Bluecaster began
apologetically in his slow, shy voice. He was big and
broad-shouldered, with a manner toiling anxiously to
meet your approval, and never quite sure of getting
there. Yet there was the charm of breeding in his
diffident speech and pleasant smile, and under all his
patient horror of responsibility was a real desire to do
'the decent thing.' He looked at his agent much as a
conscientious hound looks at a kind and skilful but
strict whip. If you were fond of dogs, you reached
out your hand and patted him when nobody was
looking, and he licked your hand in return.

'You'll wonder, I expect, why I never dropped you
a line to say I was coming, but, as a matter of fact, I
hadn't meant turning up again just yet. Had to leave
the mixed doubles at Sledhammer. Ripping tennis we
were having, too—and yet they say we landowners
never do anything for our property! But the fact is,
I've been put out about something, and I wanted to
talk it over. How have things been going? Any
news?'

Lanty thought of the careful letters he had written
at such short intervals, detailed, explicit letters,
suggesting, accounting, and wondered how much,
if any, of the information had been grasped by his
employer. He did not refer to them, however, but
gave him the outstanding points of several situations

as simply and rapidly as possible. Bluecaster was obviously glad when it was over.

The Ninekyrkes problem, though, had a chapter to itself.

'That's curious!' he said thoughtfully. 'It was about the land round there that I wanted to see you. Nothing to do with the matrimonial mix-up, of course! Very awkward for everybody, the girl cutting up rough like that. I wonder they didn't call *you* in, Lancaster! They seem to think you can settle most things.'

'Well, they did,' the agent confessed, 'but I wasn't a success. I think I made matters worse, if anything! There's no other trouble, though, that I know of, on the marsh. What have you heard, my lord?'

Bluecaster, however, still beat about his particular bush, inquiring after Helwise, the factotum, even the Church Army Van. He always remembered Helwise with little, quietly-administered courtesies, though she pestered him to martyrdom when he came within reach.

'I've had a letter,' he broke out at last, with a rush. 'Yesterday—no, the day before. It's from a tenant, of course; though when I say of course, of course I don't mean of course, because they never do write to me, at least, scarcely ever. They don't need to, when they've you.'

Lancaster wondered a little. A sense of coming ill was in the air.

'They've a right to go straight to you, if they choose,' he said, 'though, as you say, they don't seem to find it necessary, as a rule.'

'Or much use, either!' Bluecaster smiled shamefacedly. 'You're not so much older than I am, but they wouldn't give a brass farthing for my opinion against yours. Neither would I, for the matter of that! I don't believe they ever remember that you're really a young man, yet. They come to you with all their worries and woes, don't they?—even the women! You're the real king of this little, ring-fenced pheasant-run. I'm only a sort of Privy Seal that you carry about on your watch-chain. The tenants know that as well as I do. Half the time they forget my existence, but they believe in you like their prayers—all except this blithering nuisance with his letter.'

'Nothing serious, I hope?' Lancaster was longing for the point.

'Well—that's just it. I don't know. But *you'll* know, of course. That's why I say it seems a bit low-down writing me behind your back, so to speak. Still, perhaps he thought it the right thing to do. You see, it's almost personal.'

'Personal?' Lanty smiled. 'You needn't be worrying about my private character, if that's the trouble.'

'Good Lord, no!' Bluecaster almost blushed. 'Afraid I'm getting mixed and making an ass of myself. But I think you'll take this rather worse than libel, if I'm not mistaken. Your father did so much for the place. It's seems such ghastly cheek, calling any of his work in question.'

'Who's the man, my lord? New, I suppose?'

'Yes, of course. At least, a new freak of an old breed. The others would string themselves up before they'd throw mud at a Lancaster. It's Bracken Holliday over at Thweng—little tin god in a Trilby and a Studebaker-Flanders. Claimed me as a sort of long-lost brother at Cunswick Races, and seemed to think I was by way of being blessed of the gods in having him on the estate. What made you let him Thweng?'

'He's old Holliday's nephew—Willie of Pippin Hall. Willie kept him as an orphaned lad until he cleared out to Canada, and made money there, somehow. He wrote to me from abroad about the farm, and I thought he ought to have his chance.

He's not framing over well, but I'm still hoping the old blood will tell when he's settled down, and that he'll find his level after a bit.'

'Not until he's under the turf, I should say! Well, it seems he's got a down on the Lugg.'

Lancaster opened his eyes. The surface of his mind scoffed, but in that instant the waiting trouble sprang into existence. In every terrible memory there is always one moment more poignantly lasting than the rest. It is generally the moment when fear first springs. All his life he remembered the tone in which Bluecaster said—'The Lugg'—the plain, leather-upholstered room and its harassed master. Yet he scoffed. He answered with a smile.

'What's he got against it? Not æsthetic enough for him? Or has he some new patent facing that he wants to palm off on us?'

'Nothing so mild.' Bluecaster lumbered through all his pockets after a letter lying directly in front of him. 'It's the old story, of course. He says—where's the thing got to, anyhow?—that it isn't safe.' He pushed the envelope across, avoiding the agent's eyes. 'He makes out some sort of a case—but you'll see for yourself.'

It was not an attractive letter, since courtesy had been left in the lurch by an assurance very different from the dignified independence of the men of the old type. The writer had a good conceit of himself— you could almost have deduced the Trilby and the motor from the over-tall capitals—but in spite of the insolent tone, it carried a certain conviction that could not be denied respect. He believed what he said when he called the Lugg a public danger.

'Manners just a shade worse than mine, if anything!' Bluecaster went on nervously. 'His penny a week seems to have gone shouting. Still, perhaps we'd better let him down gently, as he's so worried in his mind. He's nothing against the Let, of course, but he's got his knife pretty deep into the poor old Lugg. I wonder what set him raising this view-hullo? It's in repair, I suppose, and all that kind of thing?'

'I had it overhauled at the end of the bad weather. It's as good to-day as when my father built it.'

'That's over fifteen years ago, isn't it? How the county hummed!—remember? The Let was a pretty piece of work, but the Lugg fetched 'em up all standing. And what a rattling time the old lord had, sitting round and watching while your father ran the thing! He was getting a bit over age for Newmarket and all that, and fighting the sea put him on finely for amusement. People howled, and said it was defying Nature, and so on. The papers kept an eye on it for years, didn't they? Remember that rough winter, when a lot of them sent reporters down to be ready on the spot when the bank broke, and the old serpent simply laughed at them? Why, Lancaster's Lugg made the family famous! We've never done anything startling on our own account—nothing publishable, anyhow. And now this outsider has the old tale by the ears once more. Give me the gist of what he writes, will you?'

'He says—it opens well!—that nothing but the most inflated arrogance would ever have built the Lugg at all; that the land behind it is a death-trap, while the Pride is a sheer insult in the face of the Almighty. But that's only the beginning. His main argument is that the forcing of the tide into a narrower channel is a distinct menace to the farms at the head of the bay. (Thweng's one of them, of course.) He contends that each storm places them in imminent danger, and demands that we break the bank, sacrifice the new land, and give the flood room. (Just the original arguments dug up again.) Failing this, he promises us a tide held waiting in God's Hand, which will arrange matters so effectually that not only the whole present world but all succeeding generations shall gnash their teeth at us and brand us with shame!'

'It's a bit rough, isn't it?' Bluecaster put in ruefully. 'Seems pretty intimate Up Above, doesn't he? Of course, one isn't such a Borgia as to want to risk anybody's life or set death-traps, or anything such rotten bad form as that—I'd sooner let the sea suck up the whole blessed income and have done with it—but your father always said the new land would make money for us eventually, and the Lloyd-Georgian era is very expensive. Surely he's rambling a bit, Lancaster?'

'He's certainly quite unnecessarily anxious. I can't understand what has worked him to this pitch. Sounds almost on the verge of brain-fever about it! We had a few words when he took the farm—there may be something of that at the back of it. Sneered at our old-fashioned methods—we've scarcely any agreements in writing, you know—and said *he* was a business man, anyway, and didn't trust anybody. Of course, after that, I had everything down with him in black and white. This may be just his way of trumping up a grudge on that account. He can't really consider the Lugg a danger, in spite of this fervent epistle. It's stood the test—both ways—for so long. I've heard my father say that nothing short of an earthquake wave could take the bank. I've heard him swear that the head farms were as safe as Heaven. He would never have risked a yard of the land he loved. My father's word is good enough for me.'

'And for me!' Bluecaster added bluntly. 'It was a big undertaking, though,' he went on, with the recurring nervousness in his voice. 'I'd never have had the pluck to broach it myself. The bay does look a bit caught by the throat. I suppose it's just possible that a heavy flood with an exceptional gale behind it—well, well, that's all settled, isn't it?

What's to be done with this man? If he's worrying, can't he change farms or something?'

'I hardly think he'll do that.' Lancaster looked again at the letter. 'I can't help feeling that there's something more that we'll get at, presently. Of course, as a marsh-tenant, he's entitled to a hearing. He might have put his views rather more delicately, but that's neither here nor there. Will you write him, or shall I see him? And if the latter, have you any instructions?'

'Oh, see him, certainly!' Bluecaster looked alarmed. 'And of course you'll know streets better than I do what to say. As long as you think the Lugg's all right, it can't be wrong. I'll stop on a few days, now I'm here, in case you want me, but you'll manage as you think best.' He heaved a sigh, looking away. 'I'm glad you're sure about the old bank! I thought it couldn't be anything but a false alarm, but one never knows. *You* do, though! A Lancaster always knows. It's a jolly good thing for me I've a Lancaster to know for me!'

Lanty sighed, too, when he got outside, but it was a little impatiently. Bluecaster was a splendid chap, considerate, generous, reasonable even when he couldn't see the point, but he so often not only did not see the point but made violent haste to escape it. Difficulties that it was his special province to unravel were transferred from his fingers to his agent's with the rapidity of cat's-cradle. He was no support in any problem; generally, indeed, an added factor to the puzzle. In the growing atmosphere of trouble Lancaster longed earnestly for his father.

On the gravel, a thought struck him, and he retraced his steps. Bluecaster was playing billiards by himself, and urged him to have a game. He looked resigned but amiable when Lancaster reverted to the tiresome subject he had thought happily dropped.

'With your permission, my lord, we'll have the

matter out with all the marsh-tenants. There may be something more behind, as I said. Not but what I'm sure they all trust the Lugg to a man, barring Brack. Still, they shall have their chance of speaking, if you're willing.'

'Of course. Get 'em together when you like. Need I be there?'

'I should prefer it. It isn't a question for me to handle alone. It wouldn't be fair to ask me.'

That fetched Bluecaster at once, as he expected.

'Right you are! I'll not shirk. I say—can't you really spare time for a hundred up?'

But Lanty couldn't. He knew that his eye along the cue would see nothing but the wriggling length of the Lugg, and he got away again as soon as possible, calling to the black spaniel that had waited on the drive. He went out through the gardens and across the park, half his mind busy with the new vexation, the other turned, as usual, upon the general condition of the property. Certainly, he had every reason to be satisfied. The gardens were perfect. The old Tudor house showed plainly enough that a keen eye watched its every need. The park, too, had had its special attention. The winding carriage-road was trim and rolled; the fences were in order, the young trees protected against cattle, and the Home Farm adjoining was a model holding. Bluecaster was certainly very well-groomed.

He climbed a hillock crowned by a ring of oaks, from which he could see for miles in all directions, and pride grew in him as he looked. Bluecaster might have done nothing startling, as its owner had said, might have sent no great statesmen or fighters to its country's service; but it was known throughout the North for its prosperity, its careful management, tempering justice with mercy. Bluecaster tenantry were envied, for, if not pampered, they were always considered, could always find an ear for a grievance.

Class-hatred was almost unknown on this particular property, where so much of it ran into isolated dales and along lonely marsh-borders. The balance between landlord and tenant swung sanely and steadily, for both had trust in the hand that held it. Only the agent himself felt the weight of the scales cut deep.

But he had not failed. He had taken hold where his father had loosed, and had kept his father's standard, stumbling at first, but steadying himself as the years passed. He was squarely on his feet now. His back was straight. No. He had not failed.

He allowed himself this fleeting moment of satisfaction and warm pleasure; and then the chill of the new shadow crept over him, a cloud like a man's hand out of the west, where the marsh-farms lay. He must think the matter out, have his words in order before the tenants met. He turned his back on Bluecaster, and sought his Lane of Vision.

The thunder had passed, and there was a bright breeze flickering over the sun-touched fields like the wind of a gaily-flirted fan. Even in the lane little whiffs of it darted at him over the hedges, kissing his cheek and brushing his lashes, and when he reached the second arch, he saw it twinkling like the racing feet of airy children over the new, green corn. But, as under the brooding sky at Ninekyrkes, so here, in the fresh morning, the foreknowledge of evil weighed him down, and in his state of mental weariness, of reaction from years of over-strain, he was too weak to throw it off.

He had known that Bracken Holliday disliked him, and would be glad to wound him if he got the chance. Fresh home from the colonies, with money in his pocket, Brack was a great man in his own estimation, and if not perhaps quite on the same plane as Bluecaster himself, felt at least a perfect equality with the agent. Lanty had shown him plainly that the feeling was all on one side, and Brack hadn't forgotten it. His acute mind had soon grasped that he could hurt Lancaster quickest through his father, and the fact that he had not had to forge his weapon, but had found it sprung to his hand, had given it a strength vastly superior to any carefully-invented grudge. Lanty's confidence stood firm, but his opponent's equal conviction hacked at his faith like a hedger's bill. Of course it would pass. The meeting would laugh Brack to scorn, and that would be the end of the matter. But for the first time a tenant had openly and venomously questioned his father's judgment and his own, and it rankled. There rose in his heart the cold anger waked by cruel criticism of our helpless dead.

He could see nothing but the corn through the Second Gate of Vision, not even the towering Mountain, though it had met him as he first stepped within. The break came under the hill, and over the timber he could touch the land as it rose close, curved above, and then raced away into the pale sky. The grain had reached the moment when it waits the last fiery kiss of the sun; it was still ungilt and tenderly green. The crop was heavy, this year, rich as he had scarcely ever known it. Standing beneath it, he could see how thick it was down at the roots.

Just opposite the gap there was a break in the wheat no more than half a yard wide, a miniature glade that gambolled straight up into the air and vanished. Lanty found himself wishing that he was just six inches high, in a purple pansy coat, red pimpernel boots and a pale primrose cap, so that he might strut along that wonderful bridle-path, and hear what the forest was saying on either hand. He had just decided that the primrose brim should be edged with thistle-down, and carry a noble lamb's-tail bravely dipping down behind, when a lumbering, ebony body, eminently unfairy-like, with lolling tongue and gleaming eyes, crashed through his forest and down

his glade, bringing up heavy and panting at his very
feet. Behind his shoulder, Hamer Shaw and daughter
besought the fat Labrador to return to civilisation as
typified by the road. He raised his hat curtly. This
girl and her roystering belongings seemed destined
to shatter his most precious moments. She would
think that he was always gaping into vacancy like
the village idiot, leaning over a rotten gate. There
seemed so particularly little, too, to see just there,
unless you had the seeing eye. As before, he felt
annoyed and jarred.

The fat dog was too fat to squeeze, and much too
fat to jump, so, stooping wrathfully, he hauled it into
the lane, leaving the field much as if an elephant had
frisked through it. It greeted its owners with the
passionate relief of an explorer escaped from an
African bush. Lanty's silky spaniel stayed decorously
to heel.

Hamer had seen him at the sale, and introduced
himself, apologising for the Labrador's behaviour.

'He isn't used to things yet,' Dandy explained,
with a hand on the smooth head. 'At Halsted—our
old home—he only had town-walks and motor-rides,
and behaved like an urban human being. Here, he
isn't quite sure what he is, and he's trying very hard
to find out. He's not very strong in the upper storey,
and he can't make up his mind whether he's a retriever
or an otter-hound or only a ferret. I don't know what
he thought he was, just now.'

'A reaper and binder, I should imagine!' Lanty
answered crossly, and then smiled in spite of himself,
conquered by the infectious cheerfulness of Hamer's
laugh. 'You'd better see and get him to heel as soon
as possible,' he added, severe again instantly, 'or
you'll be finding him behind a fence with a plug of
lead in him. The Gilthrotin keepers won't stand any
nonsense, and he'd be difficult to miss.'

'You mean he's too fat?' Dandy asked incredu-

lously. 'Of course, he's better fed than yours.'
She looked pityingly at the graceful spaniel, who
slapped a fluffy tail against the road, but did not
stir. 'Grumphy has always had the same meals as
ourselves. We never leave him to cooks. Perhaps
you don't care for dogs. Yours seems almost afraid
to move!' She hugged the Labrador, who leaned his
head against her and snored loudly, while the spaniel
slapped again in welcome to one who, if not quite of
the right figure, was nevertheless of the only correct
shade. 'Grumphy doesn't know what it is to hear an
unkind word!'

Hamer Shaw laughed again, this time at the helpless disgust in Lancaster's face.

'You think he'd be all the better for it, I expect?
Perhaps I agree with you, but he's Dandy's dog, you
see. My little girl knows nothing of country ways
yet, but she'll learn. By the way, sir, they tell me
you've a lot to do with the fishing, here. I've had
some trouble over my private stretch of the river.
Can you spare me a minute or two?'

They fell into talk, and Dandy, excluded, wandered
to the gap and stood looking at the joy-path of her
stout trespasser. Grumphy was a dear, but he was
certainly also a galumphing idiot. The agent-man
would think she was in the habit of taking her walks
with idiots. It was only the other day that her
variety-troupe had danced through his evening
meditation, and now her variety-dog had pranced
through his corn.

'It will straighten up in a day or two, with luck,'
he broke suddenly into her thoughts, looking with
her up the green aisle. 'And if it doesn't, there's not
much harm done. You needn't put too much blame
on your ten stone of dog.'

'I don't mean to blame him!' she flashed, colouring
a little. 'Didn't I tell you he was looking for himself?
I'm doing the same, if it comes to that. *I* shall make

mistakes, too. If I'm hard on him, I shall have to be hard on myself.'

'You'll both learn the quicker.'

'Yes, but we've been spoilt—haven't we, Grumphy boy? We shouldn't take kindly to the whip.'

'Sometimes the whip is the only teacher.'

He checked himself then, feeling that the intimacy of the gap had misled him. He was in no mood to be friendly, and departed presently with a curt good-bye. Round the turn, he dropped his hand with a faint snap of the fingers, and the spaniel, close at his knees, thrust a gentle nose into his palm, looking up at him with worshipping eyes.

'Starved, are you, old lady?' he asked, with a shrug. 'Neglected? Half-cowed? How would you fancy yourself at the Royal, looking like that fat Astrakhan or Saskatchewan or whatever they call it? We'll give him a bucketing some day over Ewrigg after rabbits. Perhaps he'll have settled what he is, by that time, unless the keepers have settled *him*.'

He mentioned the meeting to Helwise, and asked whether she had called yet. It seemed she had not.

'Of course one always *does* call at Watters, but it isn't the thing to rush. Five or six months is quite soon enough for really *old* inhabitants. But I've been meaning to go. I was only waiting until the balance-sheet of the Kindness to Kitchenmaids came in. They'll be sure to give to that, because, if you don't, it looks as though you couldn't afford a kitchenmaid, like people who profess they adore walking when you stop to offer them a lift. It was so difficult to find out what they *were*—the Watters crowd, I mean. One was afraid they might offer one tea in the kitchen—not that one ever *does* get tea at a first call, but they couldn't be expected to know that. Still, I don't mind going, if you think I ought. There's the Onion-Protesters, too, and the Paper Roses.'

'They seem very decent people,' Lanty answered

shortly. 'Not by any means savages, as you suggest. I should be glad if you could find time to call, as I have already met the daughter twice, but I shall be extremely annoyed if you ask them for a penny at a first visit.'

'But it's my duty to get all I can for my societies,' his aunt urged. 'I do so despise people who take up causes, and then forget all about them! Let me see— is it *one* year's subscription or two that I owe to the Church Army? I suppose you could tell me if I brought you my bank-book? And are you thinking of going to the Roselands garden-party, to-day?'

Lanty said no; he had work on hand, and couldn't be taken from it; and Helwise thought how snappy he had grown of late, taciturn at meals, and quick to take all her statements awry. It was tiresome when a man began to grow middle-aged and surly. She congratulated herself upon being neither the one nor the other.

And Lanty thought of the morning's problem, and longed to speak of it, but did not. He would receive more consolation from the shut lips of his father's portrait than from the mindless mouth of his aunt. He could not tell her, but he fancied he could have told Hamer Shaw. Hamer had captured him, even in their brief meeting. He could picture himself laying the case before the big, sane mind, feeling his burden lightened by the big, generous hand. But he knew he would not speak; he had learned to keep silence too long. He would see this through alone, as he had seen many another anxious point. He went into his office, and shut the door. Helwise spent the rest of the day hunting up subscription-lists.

CHAPTER VIII
NEW WINE IN OLD BOTTLES

THE next afternoon he ran into Harriet Knewstubb, wheeling her bicycle into his front hall. She bestowed upon him the kind of cool nod that you keep for the butcher's boy when you find him loitering at your door without obvious excuse. She was a plain, straight girl, with keen, dark eyes and a breeziness of manner that made the air sing in your ears.

'Helwise asked me to call for her,' she announced— 'explained' implies a certain courtesy very aggressively absent. 'We're going over to throw cards at Watters. You've no objection to my shoving this in here, have you? I hate my machine standing about in the sun.'

Lanty said he was only too pleased, and watched dispassionately while she scraped the door-post with her off-pedal, and a valuable oak chest with the front mud-guard. Then he took it from her and put it in a corner, inviting her to come in and wait, but she refused.

'No, thanks. I'll hang about till she's ready. Hope she won't be long. We arranged to go early, so as to skip kitchen tea. Is it true, do you know? By the way, Helwise said something about driving. Hope it isn't a closed shanty, anyway! I can't stick them, myself. I told her she'd much better cycle. Do her a lot more good than stuffing along in an old 'bus.'

'It's too hot for cycling.' Lanty tried not to look annoyed. 'You'll hardly find it stuffy in the dog-cart, I think. I prefer my aunt to drive. She's so energetic, I'm afraid of her knocking up.'

In reality, he had shrunk from the mental image of Helwise in flickering spots pounding through blazing motor-dust to call at Watters. He had no feeling for Dandy except irritation and misunderstanding, but it would have hurt his pride that she should see his only female relative sliding off a bicycle at her front door. He had even gone to the unprecedented length of suggesting costume, and Helwise, with a conscience shrieking subscription-lists, had consented to oblige. Miss Knewstubb, of course, was at liberty to please herself, as far as he was concerned, and her tastes were certainly plain. She could not be much older than Dandy, he reflected, looking back over years of acquaintance, but she gave no impression of appealing youth. She bullied you at bridge, hammered you at golf, while at tennis she picked you up by the scruff of your neck, shook you, and slammed you down again. These, however, were her amusements. Her main business in life was farming Wild Duck Hall, the pretty farm over the hill, and very successfully she did it. He admitted that, even while resenting her aggressive self-satisfaction, her pistol-shot conversation and general hardness of appearance.

He knew vaguely that Dandy's smart tweeds had been too passionately sporting, the fringed tongues of her polished brogues too elaborate, her little cap worn at too rakish an angle, but she had kept a feminine graciousness, nevertheless. Harriet's skirt and shirt were right for the place, if not exactly for a first call; her smoothly-drawn tie was a tie and not a frivolous butterfly of blue silk; her hat held no suggestion of advertisement *à la mode;* but she was hard from her tall silk collar to the nails in her square shoes. Even her glossy hair looked hard. He thought gloomily that no man would ever want to put his lips to it, or draw her well-set head against his shoulder. Dandy's hair was soft as gossamer. Her little head would nestle as lightly as a downy Buff Orpington. He shook off the wandering thought, surprised and annoyed. She believed that he starved Flower!

Helwise bustled down the stairs in the requested lavender, and fell over the bicycle, which instantly swung round by the head and described a graceful

curve on the paint with a ribbed handle. The master
of the house picked it up, and followed the ladies out,
to find them already mounted. Helwise was anxious
to be off, in case he remembered the subscriptions.
Harriet had dispossessed the factotum of the reins,
without asking anybody, and flourished down the
drive, leaving echoes of 'kitchen tea' behind her.
Lanty went back into the house and looked at the
mark on the wall.

.   .   .   .   .   .

They did have tea, after all, though not in the
kitchen. Hamer would have felt the evading of his
hospitality as a child the rejection of its penny bag
of sweets. He saw to it also that Armer had a square
meal. There were no half-measures about Hamer
Shaw.

He had a warm greeting for Lancaster's aunt, and
laboured heartily through her mixed periods, while
Mrs. Shaw murmured crochet patterns as she made
the tea, and Dandy, with an anxious expression,
hearkened to Harriet's slashing opinions. There was
a fair, pale young man, sitting as close to her as
possible, who also seemed fascinated by the caller's
conversational methods. Harriet was enjoying herself.

'Two and a half, at *least!*' she pronounced firmly,
with a critical eye on Dandy's skirt. 'Anything less
would be certain to trip you in turnips. And I don't
recommend leather—no, I can't say that I recommend
leather! It's very nutty when it first comes home,
but give it a day over plough, and slap it has to go
into the bucket! Those brogues of yours are nailed
all wrong, too. They should be done in threes'—she
extended a foot for inspection—'and plain tongues, of
course, the plainer the better. Those Indian-scalp
imitations would soon hang you up in a fence.'

'Does one run *all* day in the country?' the young
man inquired, deeply interested. Harriet nodded
with condescension.

'One gets about. Of course there are crowds of cat-footers who frowst indoors with a book or a needle, but nobody worth mentioning. One's always off somewhere, either on a push-bike or Shanks's pony. The tennis is getting over, but I can put you up for the hockey, if you care about it, Miss Shaw. I'm captain, and Miss Lancaster is secretary and all that kind of thing. By the way, Helwise, have you got your fixtures out yet?'

Miss Lancaster turned a vague eye.

'Fixtures? I believe Lancelot has them somewhere. He generally arranges them for me—I'm so busy! He likes doing little things like that. Of course, *I* do all the *real* work, shaking hands with the teams when they come, and seeing that they have plenty of hairpins and two cups of tea. *He* only writes the letters and keeps the funds straight.'

'That's her nephew,' Harriet kindly explained to Dandy and the pale young man. 'Agent for Blue-caster—perhaps you've met him. Rather a slow old tortoise, but well-meaning. So it's settled you'll play hockey? Where's your place, I wonder? Forward, I should think, in a decent skirt.'

Dandy thanked her politely, having expressed no opinion whatever on the matter. Hamer looked across with a twinkle in his eye. Both Harriet and Helwise pleased him mightily. The buffeting breeziness of the one moved him to tolerant amusement, while the silvery ineffectiveness of the other claimed his chivalry. He promised subscriptions without demur and Helwise almost purred aloud. Lancelot was so ridiculously narrow and proud. Why, these new people *liked* to be asked!

'You'll be going to the Show, of course?' Harriet demanded. 'Bluecaster Agricultural Show, I mean. What do you do? Oh, you—you *prod*. Sheep and cows and things, that is. I'm showing, of course, and if I don't get anything there'll be a row. Perhaps you know I farm? And you scrap with your friends as to which hunter will grab the card—at least, other people do. I've given it up myself, because I'm always right. Occasionally I get a bit lost at the Royal, and have to fall back on Lanty Lancaster, but I'm always O.K. at these local arrangements. You'll join the choral society, I suppose? I'm nothing of a singist personally, but I always put in an appearance. They like it. Keeps the thing together, don't you know? I'm not sure that it's quite good form to have much of a voice—looks a bit like swank—so you'll be all right. Lanty Lancaster used to belong at one time. He's got a few decent notes somewhere round the bottom C.'

'Wiggie—Mr. Wigmore—sings, too,' Dandy put in meekly, glad of a chance to speak. The pale young man was the only friend from the old life that had managed to get into touch with the new. He had stayed on unobtrusively after the others had departed blatantly, and the house had not repudiated him. Harriet gave him a casual stare.

'Oh?' she said, not at all encouragingly. 'Not platforms and things, I hope? We leave that to the tradespeople, here. Evening-dress and a red handkerchief—*you* know! Are you only stopping, or do you belong? You might enter for my bumble-puppy tournament, next Thursday.'

The pale young man looked regretful.

'I'd love to, but I shan't be here, worse luck! I've got to sing for a few people, that very day. I'm so sorry.'

'Platforms and things, I'm afraid!' Dandy added, with a touch of mischief. 'But a white handkerchief. That's something, isn't it?'

Harriet looked puzzled.

'But don't you *do* anything?' she inquired briskly. 'What's your handicap at golf? You look rather like a bank. *Are* you a bank? Surely you do something besides *sing*?'

Dandy opened her lips sharply, but Wiggie's gentle gaze crossed her own, checking her.

'I play draughts quite nicely,' he said thoughtfully; and Harriet snorted and gave him her shoulder. Dandy looked at the carpet.

'Well, I can rake *you* in, can't I, Miss Shaw? Two bob entrance, grub provided. Helwise, I'm bringing Miss Shaw to practise on your pole! Mine's being painted for the tournament. If Lanty or the scrape-up-behind man will play, we can have a foursome.'

'Pleasure—of course—certainly!' Miss Lancaster responded, dragged from a demand for rummage. 'Armer isn't very safe, though. He *will* play a sort of Aunt Sally, and it hurts. And Lancelot is very worried, just now. Some of his silly tenant-people are leaving, and he's quite put out about it. You'd think he actually *cared* when an old man began to fail, or his children turned out badly! I tell him they all look exactly alike to me, so I'm afraid I can't pretend to be very sympathetic.'

'You mean the Ninekyrkes business?' Harriet asked. 'It's all over the place, of course, about young Whinnerah and Michael's daughter. The girl's been over-educated, that's what's wrong. Thinks herself too good for her own class. They sent for Lanty, didn't they, to try and patch things up?'

'Why, does he always lend a hand in the tenants' love-affairs?' Hamer laughed. 'That's a big order, surely!'

'Oh, they use him as a family iron to smooth out the creases!' Helwise sighed. 'I have no doubt he talked to the girl like a Methuselah. He has no *joie de vivre*. People with no *joie de vivre* are very depressing to live with. Oh, *thank* you, dear Mr. Shaw! That will be a guinea each for the Protesters and the Rummage, half a guinea for the Paper Roses—it *was* the Paper Roses, wasn't it?—and, by the way, did I mention the Torn Tea-Cloths? Oh, you must really allow me to interest you in the Torn Tea-Cloths!'

She had the money in her hand when Lanty was suddenly announced, and Hamer, following his accusing eyes, grasped the situation instantly.

'I've just been getting Miss Lancaster's opinion on your local charities,' he remarked, putting his big, kindly person between the two. 'I'm a whale at charities—you just ask our Dandy Anne! They're a sort of hobby of mine, and I'm glad to have a bit of advice from somebody who knows what's worth helping. Mother, give Miss Lancaster another cup of tea!'

'Hamer doesn't count life worth living if he hasn't a hand in somebody's pie,' his wife added, comfortably following on. 'There was one whole year I declare he talked of nothing but overworked tram-horses! I'm glad to see you, Mr. Lancaster! You know Dandy there, I fancy? That's Mr. Wigmore, an old friend of ours from our old home.'

Lanty found himself engineered to a chair beside the daughter of the house, while his aunt hurried clinking coins into her purse behind Hamer's broad back.

'You needn't scowl at old Helwise like that!' Harriet flung at him, brutally undoing the family diplomacy in a breath. 'Why shouldn't she go round catching pennies if she wants? It's no business of yours!'

Lanty looked at her seethingly, the memory of the bicycle handle still rankling, but before he could answer, Wiggie was at his elbow with a teacup. He remembered him now as the singer in the lane, and a further memory, of much older standing, fretted vainly at the back of his brain. A moment later he heard him telling Helwise that he had found half a sovereign in the gutter, and couldn't in conscience spend it on himself. The gentle voice was so convincing, the purring answer so ecstatic, that he smiled unwillingly, meeting deprecating flower-blue eyes at his side.

'It seems so rotten to rook you at a first call!' he broke out. 'I expect you've come up against a fearful lot of that sort of thing already, and it can't impress you very favourably. That's the worst of the country. Everybody has some sort of a show wanting a leg-up, and all the giving falls on the same people. You've got to help, even when you're not interested, or half the things would never run at all. But new-comers should have a certain amount of rope. You must stand out when it gets to rank robbery, and ask for time!'

'We'll consult Watters!' Dandy said promptly. 'This is a very strong-minded house—did you know? We have to give in to it dreadfully. It was simply hateful to our Halsted friends, especially the Tango ones—*you* didn't like them either, did you?—and now it has taken a dislike to the gardener we brought with us—drops slates on him in a dead calm, smokes him out of the potting-shed, and if he tries to put up a ladder, simply humps its back and throws it off again! I'm afraid he'll have to go. It's bearing *us*, so far, but of course we're very careful. Mother wanted to turn the old nursery into a linen-room, but the minute she suggested it a patch of damp appeared on the ceiling, though there hadn't been any rain for weeks; so we had to give up the idea. It likes Wiggie tremendously, though. His bathwater is always hot, and his room's always full of spiders, and stacks of little sunbeams follow him everywhere, patting him on the head.'

Lanty laughed, and she felt quite disproportionately pleased. When he laughed, he looked years younger and a hundred times less worried. Then Harriet plunged into the lightened atmosphere with the pawing of a battle-horse.

'I say—what about this matrimonial agency of yours? We've all been hearing about Francey

Dockeray and young Lup. What did you say to the
girl, and how did she take it?'

The transient boyish look left his face. Dandy had
drawn him into a quaint little world where tenants
and their trouble had no place, but Harriet hauled
him out again.

'Aren't you asking a bit too much?' he answered as
amiably as he could. 'You're a Bluecaster tenant,
too, remember! You'll like *your* sermon kept private,
I fancy, if ever I come arbitrating in *your* love-affairs!'

It was said merely to chill her curiosity, but its
actual effect was quite unaccountable. Harriet
blushed—a slow, surprising blush from the rigid silk
collar to the smooth hair—but she met his eye with
fierce contempt in spite of it.

'Oh, well, be an oyster, if you choose! *I* shan't die
of it! You didn't do much good, from all accounts.
Have you seen Brack Holliday, lately? They say he's
raking up the old fuss about the Lugg.'

The foreboding slid in and tapped him on the
shoulder. He had not meant to come to Watters, but
something had driven him; perhaps the same need of
Hamer Shaw's strength that he had realised yesterday.
He had left the worry at Hamer's door. Things were
no different, he told himself. The Lugg held no
threat. Brack had no case. But after that one bright
moment of clear-eyed proportion, Harriet had
whistled the fear back to his side.

'Brack's teeming with theories—has his pockets full
of them!' he answered abruptly, getting up. He
moved across to his hostess, excusing himself on
business grounds. Helwise gathered herself together
in a flutter and dropped her open purse, standing
helpless in chattering dismay while everybody else
dived and darted after trundling coins. Lanty took
a last look round the room, while Wiggie, grave and
anxious, moved the coalbox and the fender and the
fire-screen and all the fire-irons to rescue a three-

penny-bit. It was a lovely room, and it soothed him; it made his own still more absurdly desolate and drear; but even this was not his ideal. Somewhere, dimly defined in his imagination, was his holy place, with time-worn furniture and the calling atmosphere of home.

'Queer little body!' Hamer observed, when he had seen Helwise and her purse safely off the horizon. 'Talks like a string of telephone-wires touching in a wind. And the young one sounds as though she was pillow-fighting folk all the time! But they're both ladies—queer how it creeps out, in spite of the top dressing! And the lad's a gentleman too, although he's so short and see-you-damned-first! He's worrying, though, more than a bit. Seems to me he's got something on his mind. Didn't he strike you that way, Dandy Anne—as if he'd something on his mind?'

'He isn't happy,' Dandy answered slowly. 'He's always thinking you're going to hurt him, and getting ready for it. People don't do that when they're happy.'

'Likely he's got too much to carry,' Hamer said thoughtfully. 'He's bitten off a big bite in Bluecaster, and they say the young lord don't help much with the chewing. Some writing-chap has it that the strongest man is the one that can walk under the heaviest weight without staggering, but he doesn't say how soon he drops in his tracks. I've a feeling that that Bluecaster agent isn't so far from dropping.'

Mrs. Shaw laid a hand on his arm and drew him towards the door. Wiggie had petitioned her with a glance.

'Now, Father dear, you leave that particular tram alone! The horse may be a bit overwilling, but it doesn't follow it isn't up to weight. Don't start putting things right before you've found the hitch. Come and help me unpack the new vacuum cleaner.'

'I hate to see any creature overpressed,' Hamer

said pitifully. 'I know what it is—it eats the soul out of you if you haven't some big happiness behind to hold you up. And he hasn't that. I can see he doesn't take kindly to that little aunt of his. I should say they don't pull well together. He's lonely, is that young chap; he's not satisfied—right you are, Mother, I'm coming!'

Wiggie had got his wish—Dandy all to himself—but he did not say anything for quite a long time. Instead, he came as if by accident to the piano, and though he played nothing coherent, he drew out funny little bunches and ripples of sound that somehow made the cool room seem cooler. Now and again he glanced at Dandy, sitting on her favourite stool with her head bent. She was changed already, he thought, and she was only too obviously not thinking of him. She had lost a little of her Halsted brilliance; she was a shade thinner, a shade dimmed, as if some new power had breathed a moment on her soul. Wiggie turned his eyes away when he thought that. His own soul was full of delicate little instincts like the dainty grace-notes tripping under his touch.

Dandy was thinking of Lancaster and wondering why she had felt pleased when he laughed. Was it because in that instant he had ceased to be aloof? Yet how alien he really found her! There was the whole network of outlook between them. More than anybody else he had made her feel 'new.'

Wiggie stopped playing bunches and began to whisper a desperate French appeal—

> 'Ma chandelle est morte,
> Je n'ai plus de feu:
> Ouvre-moi la porte,
> Pour l'amour de Dieu!'

Dandy said 'Don't!' quite suddenly without in the least meaning to, and, without in the least meaning to, he got up and came to her.

'Are you hankering to help the tram horse, too?'
he asked, and she lifted her eyes with a laugh.

'Nothing so unselfish, Wiggie dear! But that song
always makes me shiver. The door is so fast and so
hard. It is bolted and barred, with iron knobs as
big as mushrooms, and nothing gets under it but the
draught of one's sighing.'

'*My* door isn't like that!' Wiggie said quickly. 'It's
as fine as thistledown and as thin as air, but it keeps
you out, all the same. You can see through it all the
dearness within, but—it keeps you out! If it were
hard, you could hammer the ache out of your heart,
and lay your cheek against the mushroom knobs for
pity. But you cannot bruise your fists on gossamer,
and the web of it blows weakly-pitiless against your
cheek.'

'But it's not for you to hammer at doors,' he added
presently. 'They fly open all along your road!'

She shook her head doubtfully.

'I've a feeling I may come to it before I'm through!'
she said whimsically. 'I can see myself in the dust
and the dark, hugging a dead candle, and begging,
begging——'

He stopped her with a gesture.

'Don't cheapen yourself! Don't stand at the door
like the milk. The golden drink should be kept for
the golden chalice.'

'Why, Wiggie, what snobbish butlerage! It is the
stone jar that makes the beauty of the miracle.
Watters has taught me that.'

He took her hands.

'But for me even Cherith's brook is dried up, Dandy
dear?'

Her lips quivered.

'Don't quote Elijah into my mouth, Cyril!'

He let her fingers slip, not abruptly, but with a
lingering touch that left no sense of desolation.

'Forgive me! When one is thirsty, even the golden

wine is not too precious and wonderful to drink. It's all right. I didn't mean to worry. Go on thinking about the tram-horse.'

He went back to the piano and played more bunches. Presently he asked to be taken to see the vacuum cleaner.

CHAPTER IX

THE UPPER AND THE NETHER STONES

THE marsh meeting was held at Pippin Hall, the principal farm at the head of the bay, standing boldly on the edge of the sand and looking strictly out to sea. From it the Lugg could be seen in all its length, and the full sweep of the tide running between the narrow shores. Willie Holliday held Pippin with his two sons, and for all that they had harboured him as a child, they hadn't a good word among them for Cousin Brack of Thweng. Brack was always finding mares' nests and raising alarms, and generally trying to teach his grandmother. It was just like Brack's cheek to think he knew better than a couple of Lancasters and the whole of the marshmen put together!

A quiet little tide was washing under the Let as Lanty drew rein at the farmyard gate. In the blurred distance the back of the Lugg rose from the gently-heaving water like some zoological monster wading happily in a tank. It had a drowsy air of good nature and content as the passing wavelets slapped its side. There was no hint anywhere of tragedy or fear. He had taken the matter far too seriously. Probably the farmers thought him a fool for calling the meeting at all.

Certainly, the group in the yard was treating the affair as a huge joke. Men were asking Will Holliday whether he did daily boat-drill with his stock, and there was much laughter when the local wit, Thomas

Dennison of Lockholme, produced a lifebelt, borrowed from the old Ship Inn, and proceeded solemnly to try it on everybody in turn.

Bluecaster was there already. Lanty could see the black liveries in front of the door. Bluecaster himself, in shabby riding-kit and any sort of a hat, was bravely trying to dispense exactly the same amount of attention to each tenant in turn, and chuckling appreciatively at the trenchant wit of the older men. Yet he did not find the lifebelt quite as funny as the rest, Lancaster noticed with surprise. He had had one or two narrow shaves out yachting, and was recounting them with some earnestness when he caught sight of his agent and came to meet him with a touch of confusion. Lanty wondered a little as he handed Blacker to Willie's younger son.

There was about a dozen of them, all told, including Wolf and Michael from over the sand. Only Brack was missing, and even as they realised it they heard his car on the flat road, and, a minute later, sitting low in his seat, with his hat on one side and a cigarette at the corner of his mouth, he swung gracefully round the stoup. It was a very effective entrance—the pretty curve, the easy pull-up at exactly the right point, the nod and the casual eyelids drooped in general greeting, the flicking of ash with a ringed finger over the glossy door—thoroughly well-staged in every detail. It was a pity that the most important person present should have chosen that particular moment for addressing a miserable barn-cat. Bluecaster had his own methods of conveying his opinions, and he was certainly fronting the right way a minute after, when Denny, carrying the belt like a floral offering, deposited it mournfully upon Brack's bonnet. Brack's temper was slightly on edge as he slid out of the car and stamped on the cigarette.

He was a slim, dark young man, of the type glorified in tailors' windows, and his neat suit and grey spats carried a suggestion of being still behind plate glass. He would have been an ordinary person of rather vivid good looks but for his arresting eyes—of a clear, cold grey, with the pupils very black and steady.

He lifted his hat to Bluecaster where his uncle had lifted a finger. Bluecaster acknowledged gravely. To Lanty he nodded. Lancaster—there is a whole code in the action—nodded back. After which they trooped into the house.

Even there, though, settled round the kitchen table, with his lordship at one end and the agent at the other, there was a frivolous tendency to regard the meeting more as a friendly 'crack' than a call to business. It was some time before Bluecaster, at last allowing Brack's deeply-chagrined countenance to swim gently into his ken, hammered on the table for silence. Then he got to his feet diffidently, stammering and sticking a little, his glance travelling nervously from face to face. He had Will Holliday on his right hand and Dockeray on his left, with Bownass of Moss End beyond, Bradley of Wilson Fold and old Simon Farrer of Meadow's Ing. They looked at each other stolidly, and said 'Ay, ay! Yon's reet!' at intervals.

Brack was about the middle, with Wolf on one side and a joyful Holliday cousin ready with gibes on the other. Denny sat directly across, and pretended to be rowing hard whenever he thought Bluecaster wasn't looking. Brack stared over him and through him, and hated the whole lot of them lock, stock and barrel. It was a pity they were too stuck in the mud to recognise real merit when they ran into it head first.

Lanty listened to Bluecaster's speech with the faint discomfort that he always experienced under his employer's efforts. In the landlord's place, and in his own present grim mood, he would have told the lot of them to stay and be drowned or clear out and be damned, but that wasn't Bluecaster's way at all. On the contrary, he was always pathetically anxious to carry a stray leg of anybody's donkey.

A question had been raised about the Lugg, he told them—was it really as safe as was made out? There was an old theory just brought up again that in flood-time the tide hadn't enough room. Well, it always *had* had enough room, they knew that, but of course nobody could answer for the future. The question was—were they justified in continuing to gamble on the point? The late Mr. Lancaster, whom they had all known, and not only known but respected, had given as his definite opinion that there was no gamble in the matter at all. World-famous engineers had, after the first, backed that opinion, and so far the Lugg had proved them all right. Mr. Lancaster had affirmed that it was no sort of danger to the east side, while it meant a great benefit to the north. Speaking as a landowner, he was naturally anxious to see the estate improved and extended, but, speaking as a man, he was not willing to risk, even upon a mere possibility, good tenants who were also, he hoped, his very good friends. If the Lugg was really a danger, it must go, but he felt sure that wouldn't be necessary. He would now call upon Mr. Bracken Holliday, of Thweng, to put before them his views on the matter.

Brack was only too ready to be up, in spite of cousinly adjurations to 'Hod thy gab, an' let yan o' t'aald yans kick off!' Denny was now swimming violently behind Bradley's back, but Brack ignored him, fixing his eyes on Bluecaster. He was nervous at first—the antagonism in the atmosphere had the passivity but also the resistance of the yard wall—but it ceased to embarrass him as he warmed to his subject. His pace quickened, his words came easily. For the moment he forgot any petty personal animosity, and the sincerity of his belief wrung attention even from the most scathing mocker.

He knew he was a stranger, nowadays, he said,

and what had been good enough for them for so long was sure good enough for him. That was one way of looking at it, no doubt. But—now he didn't want to put on frills!—he'd knocked about the world more than a bit, and he'd seen little jokes played by Nature that here on the marsh they'd just laugh down and out if he was fool enough to waste time telling them. But they had set his mind's eye jumping, and it was still jumping when he settled down at Thweng. At first he had been content to take the word of older men than himself, but after a while that mind's eye of his got jumping again, and told him right out that the Lugg had got the cinch on the top marsh farms. No, he didn't believe they were safe! He had a slap-up, cracker-jack reason for refusing to believe it, but he meant to keep it to himself, along with the jokes in meteorology. They had no guarantee, except an almighty run of luck (that was probably pretty well run out, by now), that the Lugg wasn't throttling the bay. They had never had a real storm to test it, not one of those storms that could buck the roof off creation. The Lugg had never seen the real goods. There had been an imitation, fifty or sixty years back —his uncle would remember it—when the marsh roads were under water for a week. There was no Let then, certainly, but he opined the Let wouldn't have made much difference, and anyway the flood had had full room. That wasn't the case now. They had no guarantee—he struck one hand against the other and the cousin copied him, while Denny swam harder than ever—he didn't mind repeating it, because it was the thing he wanted to hammer plum into their minds—*they had no guarantee that the Lugg wasn't throttling the bay!* It wasn't as if the tides were backing off. He guessed it was the other way about. From what he could remember before he went West, the force of the inflow was greater now than it had been then. He wasn't setting out to say it was much, but the mere fact itself meant a lot. He called upon his uncle to say how close on Pippin walls the last winter tides had brought the sea.

Avuncular love failed him, however, for Willie, disgusted at being thus dragged in without notice, was understood to reply that he wasn't 'in t'dock or any sic-like spot,' and Brack had to fall back once more upon his own unsupported eloquence.

It wasn't as if the Lugg protected the north farms. It hadn't even that excuse. Ninekyrkes and Ladyford were safe enough, W.P. and G.W., with the Let to guard them. But all the Lugg protected was land clean robbed from the sea, while it threatened other land that the sea had given them of its own accord. So far, the sea hadn't fired them out, but it would do it some day. He was dead sure the estate was crowding its luck! As tenant of a marsh farm, sharing what he reckoned a very real danger, he asked his lordship right now to give the matter his earnest attention.

He sat down abruptly, and the cousin patted him violently on the back, disarranging the set of his coat. There was a pause, during which everybody looked at the agent, and after a glance at Bluecaster he slowly obeyed the unspoken call.

Brack's virulent letter in mind, he had been surprised by the temperate tone of his speech. Perhaps he was reserving his private knowledge of the Almighty's intentions for a peroration to be appended later. But thus far he was behaving well enough, and deserved a temperate reply.

They all knew that marsh farms had their drawbacks, he said plainly. The land had belonged to the sea once. There was always a remote chance that the sea might claim it again. In this case he was prepared to say that it was very remote indeed. The farms were certainly not death-traps, as had been very largely suggested, and he was quite unable to see why the Lugg, after a trial of over fifteen years, should not be allowed to continue its existence. There was a big stretch of land behind it, which might one day be very valuable. It ought not to be sacrificed in a moment's panic. His father had taken great pride in the sea-walls, particularly in the Lugg, and, as his son, he was naturally averse to hearing its reliability questioned; but if any real evidence could be brought against it he need not say he should be the first to listen. He did not consider, however, that it had been brought as yet. The increase of pressure also he took leave to doubt. In fact, he was ready to maintain that the danger referred to was practically non-existent, but he would be glad to hear what the older men had to say, men who had known his father, and the Lugg when it was first framed.

Holliday was still upset at being treated as a witness for the prosecution, and couldn't be got to speak, and Bownass and Bradley started to rise at the same moment, and fell back, glowering at each other. Finally, Wolf stirred, taking his time about getting to his feet, and leaning heavily on his stick as he looked round the table. There was curious weight in his slow gaze, curious strength in his slow speech.

'There's them as is born to *do* things,' he began deliberately, 'an' them as is born to find fault! I knew Mr. Lancaster's father a sight o' years, and he was always a-doing, and it was always the right things he did. He was a grand man, the grandest man I ever clapped eyes on! His word was his bond. If you'd his word, there was no call for inkhorn-stuff and such-like—nay, nor a postage-stamp ontilt, neither!' (He looked at Brack, and a smile went pleasantly round.) 'He was a just man. He had fair treatment for everybody. There's folks, likely, as think he favoured me, being over at our place a deal, seeing to the Lugg, but they can just put this in their pipes and smoke it. There was a year after I first took hold as Mr. Lancaster give me notice to quit—said I wasn't doing well by the farm, and wouldn't take telling. Ay, and he was right an' all! I was young and a bit above myself, I reckon, but that fetched me up sharp. The missis begged us on again with a deal o' trouble, and I never looked back after. I'd learned my lesson. Ay, he was a just man!

'And he was a good man. If a farmer got behind, he knew he could go to Mr. Lancaster for help; and if he meant fair an' square, he'd *be* helped, right enough. And we all know he was a man wi' *brains*. There's proof on every mile of the estate. He could see twice as far ahead as most folk, and twice an' a half farther round. Bluecaster knows best what it owes him, though there was always a-plenty folks in his road, same as there was with the Lugg. An' now, just look ye here a minute! Would a just man favour one bit of land over another? Would a good man let traps to folk as trusted him? And would a clever man—a man o' *business*'—this went home quickest, and he knew it—'risk good farms for a bit of a show-off? Mr. Lancaster give us his word the Lugg would do us no harm, and his word has a fifteen years' stamp to it as never come out of no government office. There's young Mr. Lancaster saying the same, an' that's all there is about it. I tell you what it is again—there's them as *does* things, an' them as finds fault. It's easy choosing, I reckon, for folk as has eyes in their head and a bit o' good hoss-sense!'

The funny little gruff salvos of applause that had punctuated this speech ended in a regular fusillade of commendation. Lanty said 'Thanks, Wolf!' quite simply, and looked round for the next speaker. There were two or three ready by now, and they said much the same as Wolf, though they did not handle Brack quite so delicately. Brack had a rare lot of names pinned to his jacket before they were through, and had to sit passive while the conservative farmers followed the track like so many sheep. He was aching to be up again, and had difficulty in restraining himself when Denny, having anxiously awaited his turn, plunged into public speaking.

Denny thought it was time somebody cracked a bit about the present Mr. Lancaster. He himself was a younger man who hadn't farmed under the former agent, but at least he could say he wasn't wanting any better sort than he'd got! If the present Mr. Lancaster said the Lugg was all right, that was full stop and a lick for Thomas Cuthbert Dennison. As for the duke who was shaping to farm Thweng in a Trilby, he'd likely hit upon a thing or two he didn't know if he lived long enough and looked hard. Even he, Denny, could happen learn him a bit about sowing corn an' such-like, and there was more than one of them on the spot who could give him a leg-up over pigs. There was a roar at this, for Brack had a patent drill that sowed each seed separately—so separately that, when the grain came up, you could walk between the stems; and there was also a tale that he had given his pigs water used for boiling hams, with horrible results. Even Bluecaster's presence could not restrain the general joy, and there was not much of Brack's moderation left when he rose to his final effort.

'You've only one argument in your whole outfit!' he raged at them bitterly, 'and that's the old, threadbare wheeze that because your fathers did a thing you're bound to follow their trail. It makes me tired to see the lot of you—narrow, ignorant stick-in-the-ditchers—sitting round with your mouths and ears open for any old thing a Lancaster may choose to pour in! You've got that durned Lugg fixed in your minds as a kind of monument to your late agent. Well, I guess you're right in one way. It *is* a monument, sure—a monument to the biggest piece of swank, the rankest self-conceit I ever struck! Look at the Pride! You'll say it's as safe as Bytham Knott, and yet there's nobody will live in it. They try, but they can't stand it out—and why? Because they know the man that built it laughed in the face of God! You say he was a good man, a just man, but *I* say he was a theatrical guy, with an eye on the gallery and swank fit to jump the earth! I tell you I've my own reasons for knowing what's coming—coming on the hop—and there's somebody sure going to get left. Right now's the time to pull out, if you'd only listen! But you won't. You're too deep in your dusty old beliefs for that. But you'll listen, you may bet your life, and *remember*, in the night when the sea comes knocking at your door!'

There had been silence through his speech, the silence of outrage, and there was still silence when he stopped. His strange eyes looked singularly bright and compelling. Lanty stared curiously at him during the pause, and followed his glance, the men round him doing the same. Brack was looking at Bluecaster.

To a very timid, sensitive nature there is, in the forcing of a decision, something of the inhuman terror of being hunted down. The young man was between two fires. If he stood by the Lugg, he carried the lives of men. If he stood by Brack, the Lancasters went to the wall. The first responsibility had been another's; this was his. Brack was thrusting it upon him with keen eyes that held and coerced him and would not let him go.

'His lordship agrees with me!' the latter cried suddenly, so sharply that more than one man jumped. 'His lordship is on my side—sure! Ask him if his conscience isn't hustling him! Ask him what he thinks away down in his heart of Lancaster's Lugg!'

Bluecaster moved in his chair and opened his lips. There was breeding in the way he mastered his inward shrinking and tried to smooth the warring elements into courtesy.

E

'You are making things a little difficult, Mr. Holliday!' he said gently. 'Won't you sit down and allow us to finish the discussion quietly? You will gain nothing by vilifying an honourable gentleman whom all here remember with affection and regret.'

'I'll sit down when I'm through!' Brack said insolently. 'I'm asking your lordship for a straight answer. Are you on my side or are you not?'

Bluecaster looked down the table. There was no staving it off. He must act if he could get no other to act for him. In his extremity he did what he had always done—dropped his burden for Lanty to pick up.

'I am on the Lancasters' side always,' he answered Brack. 'You have produced no conclusive arguments, and naturally I put their word before yours. If Mr. Lancaster thinks the Lugg should stand, I think so, too. That is all I have to say.'

It was cowardice, and it sounded like courtesy—flight and fear, though it seemed like standing shoulder to shoulder; and only two men present guessed it for what it was. Bluecaster was shirking, and for the moment Lancaster filled with passionate revolt; but out of the wrath and clamour at the injustice something nobler rose and conquered. He heard the call to help that no true fighter ever denies; he saw the young man caught in a trap too cruel for his hesitant soul, and he put out his hand to him at once. He looked up the table with a smile and nodded, and as Bluecaster's face lost its strain, and the trusting dog-look came back into his eyes, he yielded to the old rush of keen affection. Of course, you did things for Bluecaster, though you damned yourself to all eternity!

The decision was left to him, the one person in the world who could not possibly see the problem unbiassed. Even if he had not believed, there could scarcely have been but one answer. And he *did* believe. He did trust the Lugg. The fear that dogged him was not of his own heart, but put into him from outside. Brack could talk a clock into stopping. But there was only one answer.

'I stand by my father's work, of course!' he said cheerfully, and with a passionate exclamation Brack sank into his seat. And then old Wolf spoke again.

'And now you'll let me the Pride, Mr. Lancaster!'

He turned to the other question with a start. Wolf and his worries had been out of his mind for the moment. Now they wove a thread in the weft of his father's warp. He hedged, trying to put the point aside.

'Come, Wolf, I'd hopes you'd change your mind! It isn't fair to your wife—I tell you that plainly.'

Wolf set his mouth.

'That's neither here nor there!' he said doggedly. 'It's betwixt her an' me. I'm asking for the Pride. I'd a reason for wanting it afore. I've a double reason now. You an' me an' the old master, we've passed our word for the Lugg. I'll fly that flag for the whole marsh to lift its hat! Let me the Pride!'

He leaned forward, holding out his hand in his desire, and Brack leaned, too.

'You'd better go the whole hog!' he sneered. 'Here's the proof of your trusting. Give him the Pride!'

The agent hesitated, cornered and distressed. Before his troubled vision rose a fearful old woman, terrified to madness when the tide came in.

'His wife——' he began again, and Brack leaped down his throat with a second jeer.

'Oh, put it on the missis! I guess a bad excuse is better than none. Come, man, own out that you're not honest, or else—let him the Pride!'

'He's all in!' he added, turning to Wolf with a laugh. 'Look at him! He's chilled right through. He'll not give it you—not on your life!'

E.2

'Ay, but he will!' Wolf said quietly, his hand outstretched. 'It's to be yes, sir, isn't it? Isn't it, Mr. Lancaster?'

And Lanty said yes.

.   .   .   .   .

Out in the yard, by Bluecaster's wheel, revulsion swept over him. The weight he had lifted pressed hard. He looked up sharply.

'You trust me too much! Will you never see a thing with your own eyes? Suppose I'm wrong, after all?'

Bluecaster, reins in hand, looked down at him with a shamed bitterness in his face.

'It's better to be wrong and a sportsman than a cur that won't face the drain! I wish to God, Lancaster, you were my elder brother!'

Lanty rode after him across the marsh, his foreboding heart in his stirrups. But as he began to climb at last, and the whole panorama of eastern hills came into view, his burden dropped from him. The die was cast. None but a coward would wish it back. What would come, must. He would rest content.

He could see the Whygills curled asleep on the horizon, like giant elephants cuddled trunk to trunk, their soft, velvet, wrinkled backs hunched into the tender sky. Below them the heather glowed pink and rich on the dark ridges of moor. He drew a deep breath as he rode forward, his heart eased. Yet he had taken not only the whole of the marsh, but Bluecaster himself into his hands.

CHAPTER X

TERROR BY NIGHT

Lup was waiting with the boat when Wolf came down to the channel. The tide was gone now, but where the old man stood the still-shining sand sucked heavily at his boots. The son held the boat while his father climbed in, then pushed off again in silence. They had not spoken unless forced since the moment of fierce contact in Lancaster's office.

It is a very strong Northern trait—perhaps the strongest of all—this absolute refusal to dig up any subject that has once gone deep. In ungenerous natures it takes the form of a dogged sullenness which even Time cannot melt or break, but in the Whinnerahs it was something finer yet even more stubborn, a deadly aloofness, an icy withdrawal. In neither face was there any trace of evil feeling; but in both there was stiff-necked pride, iron resolution, unforgiving decision. Where blood runs thickest and ties hold closest this characteristic is most fiercely marked.

They parted at the bank, and Wolf's tired limbs took him slackly back to the homestead. His wife had tea ready for him, but asked no questions, and he vouchsafed no information. It was typical of him that not until close of day did he manage to say what waited to be said.

Lup had gone up to bed. They could hear him walking about the floor of his room. There was scarcely any light in the kitchen, for in farmland they go upstairs early and spare the candle. The room was full of black, shapeless shadows, and in the grey, drear glimmer from the bay the bent figures showed a little greyer, a little more drear. When Lup's step had ceased for the night, Wolf told what had passed at Pippin Hall.

She took it quietly, so quietly that alarm gripped him, and his voice roughened as he stumbled in his own fashion of excuse.

'There was a deal o' talk among the lot o' them, an' lile or nowt to show for it when all was said! I had my own word soon on, but after that I held my whisht till things was fixed, and then—*then* I asked for the Pride. I'd put in for it afore, but he wasn't for giving it me, wasn't Mr. Lancaster. Nay, what, any man with owt in him would ha' done the same, after Brack calling the old master out of his name an hour or more! You mustn't take it amiss, Martha. 'Twas for the old master.'

'And what call had the agent to say you nay at the start?' the thin voice asked in the dusk.

'Why—why I doubt it was seeing you that put about over the water, yon day as he give us a look in, if you'll think on. He would have it you'd be best off marsh ground altogether. It's the Pride for me, now, come happen what may, but if you'd likely be better suited with your own folk over Bortun way—say, for a bit of a spell—ay, or for good——' He slurred and stopped, for speech was bitter, and there was a pause, while out on the featureless night the woman's eyes kept vigil.

'Nay, I reckon I'll bide till we're through,' she said at last, in the same expressionless voice. 'Lup gone, it's not much differ what comes, one way or another. 'Tisn't your doing, nor even Lancaster's. It's something back of us all, that drives us as stock is driven to the butcher. 'Twas the waiting I couldn't abide. I'll not fret no more, now. But all the trusting in the world won't stop what's in front, cold an' slape an' rivin' an' lowpin'——'

'Whisht, now, whisht!' Wolf begged, raising himself painfully, and presently the grey figures went wearily over the stone floor and melted into the blackness of the stair.

About two in the morning, Lup stirred in his still sleep and saw his mother standing at his open casement. The old folk had changed their room of late to one looking over the moss, but Lup's faced fair and square to the bay. It was just on tide-time, too, he remembered drowsily, and was puzzled.

She had an old Paisley shawl thrown over her night-gown, and in the glow of the dip she carried she looked strangely young and singularly unfearful. There was

almost a smile on her face turned and lifted towards
the sea.

He could feel that she was waiting, and her tense
expectation kept him still. A sandbank broke away
just below with a thud and splash weirdly loud in the
quiet. A chill snap of wind broke through the window,
flaring the flame and clattering the unfastened pane
without. An advance battalion of raindrops smote
the glass like a challenge and died. Stillness again,
and the waiting silence; and then out on the dark
came the steady rush of the night wave.

He raised himself on his elbow, ready to go to her,
but she did not flinch as the sound filled the room, and
her face did not change, even though the after-rain,
riding on the wind, spattered through the open
square. There was a hiss in the water to-night, a
muttered hint of hate. The dead hour and the live
wave together caught him into a vague dread, and
he stayed where he was, wondering. The night and
the water and his mother's face; for she was listening,
so he felt, not only to the incoming tide, but to something that had as yet neither voice nor being. He
almost shivered as the pane beat against the wall like
a chained and frightened thing.

So long she stood, in the tossed light dipping and
leaping like a chased elf, so still she stood, her white
face strained to that which was not yet without, she
grew into his drifting dream as he dropped gradually
to his pillow. But when the water was well past,
brimming the banks and pressing fast up the bay, he
heard her draw in her breath and let it out in a great
sigh.

'*One!*' she said, like a prisoner counting towards
release, or a sufferer looking ahead in unbearable
pain; and then, as she had said to Lancaster, down
below: 'How long? Oh, how long?'

Lup moved again, and this time she heard him and
came to his bed, and when she looked at him he was

not afraid any more, for her eyes, when they rested on her son, saw nothing beyond.

'Nay, what, Mother, you'll get your death of cold!' he broke out in his deep voice. 'Get back to your bed. You'll have the old man seeking you.'

She stayed a moment longer, looking at his ruffled head and drowsy eyes, but she did not speak or stoop to kiss him—only at last stretched out one of her strange, worn hands and smoothed the sheet under his throat.

Lying in the dark when the door had closed, he heard her in the passage. '*One!*' she said again, like the numb stroke of a passing-bell; and through the silent house he followed the piteous voice: 'How long? How many? How long?'

CHAPTER XI

THE TROUBLE COMING—THE GREEN GATES OF VISION—II. MOONLIGHT

'LANCELOT is a different creature to-day!' Helwise observed, hitting hard at the empty air, and getting the ball in her left eye for her pains. 'Almost cheery and inclined to gambol—oh, I *am* sorry! Did it hurt? He was a little put out at breakfast, when the Duchess of Saddleback returned him a sixpenny postal order I had meant for a Home Tattle Limerick, instead of the subscription he had told me to send for her Cemetery Bazaar—Armer, please, *over* my head, not *at* it!—but of course, anybody might do a thing like that, anybody, I mean, as busy as I am. It was the Duchess's letter that upset him—I don't know why, because it was charmingly friendly and polite. Said she hoped the sixpence wouldn't be too late to win him the competition—nice of her, wasn't it? What do *you* think? Lancelot says that now he'll have to double his donation, though I can't see any reason for it myself. Still, he didn't really show temper about it, and I didn't in the least mind asking him to check the month's groceries directly afterwards. Of course, I can't say that he showed any *joie de vivre*—I *do* think he's lacking in *joie de vivre*—but he got the groceries to come out all right, and do you mind if we stop?— the ball's caught in my hair-net.'

'Glad to hear he's recovered!' Harriet returned, watching impatiently while Dandy set her hostess at liberty. 'He was just about the limit, that day at Watters. Never saw such a jaundiced old crab-apple in my life! Rotten of him, though, not to turn up to bumble.'

'He's gone to see his lordship off—your service, I think, Miss Shaw—but he should be back presently. He sent me down some flowers this morning—his lordship, I mean—and a message to say he was prevented from calling. He makes a point of coming in to see me, as a rule, and I tell him all the things that want doing to the house, and we get on splendidly! I sent him an invitation to bumble, but something always seems to stop him. Last time it was toothache, and the time before it was a hair-cut or a motor-smash or some other very close shave.'

Dandy caught echoes of this vocal accompaniment as she smote wildly at dancing hanks of string under Harriet's pitying gaze, seething with helpless rage at the flying ball as it spun over and under and apparently through the racquet, leaving her to plant weighty smashes upon space or the inoffensive pole, There was something diabolical in the way it shot down upon you like a bolt from the blue, and caught you on the nose when you weren't looking. When you *did* hit it (which was seldom) you struck with a murderous zest that nearly dislocated your shoulder, not in the least with the friendly dispatch of a drive at golf, or the *esprit de corps* of a clean clearing-shot at hockey. The one ball was a jolly little nipper you hoped to see again very shortly; the other a sportsman and a pal, the twelfth and keenest member of the team; but this was a jeering devil and an aeroplane and a merry-go-round and a slimy sneak, and you hit it as if you were killing wasps.

She was paired against the ladies with what Harriet called 'the-man-who-scraped-up-behind,' and soon grasped that she had cause to be thankful, since he was not only a much better player than either of the enthusiasts, but was also thoroughly up to their little tricks. Occasionally he tipped Dandy a respectful wink to leave the ball to him, or to send it over instead of round, and she obeyed with anxious alacrity. She soon rose to his tactics, and when she discovered that every time Harriet hit Armer, Armer responded by hitting Helwise, she made every effort to play up to him and keep control of the ball. When, by way of a change, Helwise hit her, and she couldn't always manage to hit Harriet, it was even more exciting, though not so comfortable.

Even Bluecaster noticed the change in his agent as they walked the platform together. He was accustomed to seeing him more as a walking encyclopædia of solid business facts than as a man with half the wine of life yet untasted, and youth still to his hand. But to-day he looked younger and freer than he had done for a long time, his laugh was more ready, and his business worries seemed shelved. Even unanalytic Bluecaster could feel that his blood ran more strongly, and his pulse beat quicker.

Bluecaster himself seemed depressed and rather restless, one moment anathematising the delay of his train, the next hinting that he should stay on, in a tone that openly asked for encouragement. As the train came in at last, he thrust an envelope into Lanty's hand, climbing reluctantly to his place.

'From that infernal Brack, I suppose!' he said in a tone of irritation, going across to close a window which he knew he would reopen immediately. 'There's no name to it, and the address might have been written with the poker, but I think it's pretty obvious.'

Lancaster took it with a shrug—the usual, cheap envelope that carries unsigned slander. The post-mark gave no sort of clue, and the fierce venom of the writing disguised it effectually. Within was a page torn from the Book of Ezekiel, scored carefully so that the phrases ran into a connected message. Lanty read it aloud as he stood by the open door.

'Therefore thus saith the Lord God: Because ye have spoken vanity, and seen lies, therefore, behold, I am against you, saith the Lord God. And mine hand shall be upon the prophets that see vanity and that divine lies . . . and ye shall know that I am the Lord God. Because, even because they have seduced my people, saying Peace; and there was no peace; and one built up a wall . . . say unto them . . . that it shall fall . . . there shall be an overflowing shower; and ye, O great hailstones, shall fall, and a stormy wind shall rend it.

'Thus saith the Lord God; I will even rend it with a stormy wind in my fury; and there shall be an overflowing shower in mine anger, and great hail-stones in my fury to consume it. So will I break down the wall . . . and bring it down to the ground, so that the foundation thereof shall be discovered, and it shall fall . . . and ye shall know that I am the Lord. Thus will I accomplish my wrath upon the wall, and will say unto you, The wall is no more . . . there is no peace, saith the Lord God.'

On the margin was scrawled the one word 'MARCH' in the vitriolic hand of the envelope, but that was all. Everything else had been left to Ezekiel.

Lancaster looked up with a laugh.

'Must be Brack!' he agreed, making as if he would tear the page across, and then, since, after all, it was sacred speech, however distorted, folding it and slipping it into his pocket. 'The same trail of omniscience is over it all! I ran into him in Witham on Saturday, and suggested that, if he was really bothered over the matter, we might put him on to some other place. 'Tisn't business, but it might save us trouble in the end, and Thweng won't go wanting. However, he wasn't having any—talked about sticking to the ship and holding by the fort, like Casabianca and Sankey and Moody mixed. That annoyed me a bit, though he was quite quiet and polite—didn't even offer me his confounded Turkish cigarettes! Just as we separated, he asked quite casually whether I believed in clairvoyance. I said no rather shortly, for I was keen to be off. (I'd have said no, in any case, to *him*.) Then he told me he'd come across a lot of it in America, been rather thick with some chap who went in for it professionally, and would have it Brack had the gift, too. This fellow gave him some rather curious information—the name of the farm he would take in England, for instance. That was certainly queer. Thweng isn't the sort of name you'd naturally get your tongue round without a little assistance! He looked as if he could tell me a lot more if he chose, only I didn't stop for it. He rapped out something after me, but I didn't catch any of it except the word "wool." Wonder if he sits up all night with his Trilby and his Turks, summoning spirits! He's been fearfully ragged by the rest of the marshmen, by the way. Denny left a parcel at Thweng, the other day, which turned out to be some old bathing-togs he had dug up somewhere!'

The train moved off, and he walked a few yards with it.

'You won't be up again just yet, I suppose?'

Bluecaster shook his head.

'Not to stop. I'll run up for the Show, and I'll be home for the audits as usual. I'm shooting a good bit, and then going abroad. Christmas in

Cairo. But I'll be back altogether'—he leaned out and called as the train gathered speed, his expression half-laughing, half-earnest—'I'll be back—in *March!*'

Lanty found his guests reinforced by Wiggie when he got home at last. They were seated round a table in the drawing-room, engaged in an impromptu fox-hunt evolved by the singer, by means of dice, a surprising collection of knick-knacks and the pot dogs off the mantelpiece. He had spent the day in Manchester with Hamer, and looked paler than ever and desperately tired, but he hunted with the infectious zest of a Troughton or a Peel. Even the host, standing with his back to the cheerless grate, smiled as he watched the absurd game.

The room was as hideously comfortless as ever, and smelt abominably of stocks. Tea had been taken away, and it had not occurred to Helwise to offer him a fresh brew. A détour upstairs before entering, prompted by some inexplicable shyness, had shown him his dressing-table standing in water. Evidently the window had been open when the factotum wielded his weekly hose. On the hall-floor he found a telegram requiring immediate answer, and an envelope containing money had slipped off the table into Helwise's umbrella. Yet he felt less irritated than usual as he stood on his mockery of a hearth, while Wiggie, with a throw of double sixes, sprang Climber over an imitation brass inkstand, a framed funeral card and a mug from Morecambe. Helwise looked happy, he thought, tossing dice with breathless intensity. He did a great deal more for her, every day, than this foolish young man was doing at the moment, but it never evoked that spirit of flagrant joy. He realised suddenly that, in spite of her rattle-headed irresponsibility, she had something he had not—a youth of soul at once a blessing and a curse. Perhaps he had taken her too seriously, demanded too much of her, not in practice, but in temperament. The Shaws and Wiggie asked nothing of her except to be her aimless and absurd self. Even Harriet bullied but protected and liked her. He alone kept her, made things easy for her, and found her a pricking thorn. He shrugged his shoulders. After all, it was *his* dressing-table.

Harriet had grabbed the only true hound in the pack, a daintily-finished model that Bluecaster had brought Helwise from Grasmere, and was playing in her usual fashion, barking orders and rattling the dice like an enemy's brains. After Lanty came in, she barked rather louder than before, especially at Wiggie, for whom she seemed to have a measureless contempt. Nobody noticed it, though, but Wiggie himself, with all his little thread-ropes of intuition flung out like so many cables.

Dandy was having very bad luck, laboriously boosting a pincushion-backed dachshund over a pink mountain of Lanty's best blotting-paper. She wooed the fates with a variety of chants and curses, but to no purpose. For her the dice would not fall. Her cheeks were as pink as the paper by the time Pincushion's head came over the hill.

'He despises me for being a wretched town-person!' she said dismally. 'Wiggie's getting on all right, but then Wiggie's a magician. All hairy and feathery and furry things love him. We can't keep the birds out of his bedroom.'

'Birds in your room mean bad luck!' Harriet observed brutally, slinging the dicebox at the magician, and adding 'Butter-thumbs!' when he missed it. 'Rotten luck—illness—death! You'd better be making your will.'

A fresh shadow drifted almost imperceptibly across Wiggie's tired face. Dandy looked up quickly, but, as once before, he smiled her into holding her peace, and with a sharp fling of the dice she scrambled

Pincushion down the mountain and over a wall of matches.

He took heart of grace after that, and began to forge rapidly ahead, passing Helwise's pug-nosed St. Bernard and Wiggie's black-and-tan with the Pomeranian tail. Harriet's hound was leading easily. Her fierce throws seemed to frighten the dice into showing their most lucrative faces. The fox—as represented by an ancient penwiper lately chewed by mice—was in imminent danger.

Pincushion gained, however, straining clumsily after Cragsman's delicate grace. The others withdrew, leaving them to fight it out, and then a curious thing happened. The moment Pincushion's head drew level with Cragsman's lean flank, Harriet began to throw blanks. Cragsman stayed stubbornly glued to the same spot, while Dandy's monstrosity, in a succession of twos, finished the course and claimed the quarry. Harriet reached for her gloves and announced that she must be going. Dandy stood up, too, still looking at the game.

'That was queer, wasn't it?' she asked. 'The finish, I mean? Cragsman stopped playing!'

'The luck changed,' Lancaster said briefly. 'All the same, they say in the fells that if a mongrel joins in the chase the pure-bred hound drops the fox instantly. No wonder Cragsman took stock at that overfed Pincushion of yours!'

'I know a song about that,' Wiggie put in. 'Yes, I *shall* say it if I like!' He began to quote softly—

> 'There was a Love went after a Heart,
>   Haughty and fine and fleet,
> Till it chanced a little Cur-Love took part,
>   That hadn't been at the meet.
> And the Proud Love bowed in a cold despite,
>   And out of the running stept;
> And said—"It's very bad form to fight.
>   *J'accepte!*"'

> But the little Cur-Love made shift to pass,
> For it cared too much for pride,
> And, stealing fearfully through the grass,
> Came out on the other side;
> And said, as it took the Heart to keep
> And hold and cherish and cleave,—
> "I'm glad I wasn't too proud to creep.
> *J'arrive!*"'

Harriet glared at him, dragging on her hard gloves in ruthless snatches, but as he finished he lifted his eyes to her with a smile so full of warm goodwill that her own dropped. Wiggie knew what the ugly room meant to her, and the ridiculous game and the taciturn man, where nobody else had even so much as guessed. But then Wiggie was a magician, so Dandy had said, and magicians don't count.

Dusk was dropping as they came out of the house, and along the quiet fields had risen the heart-high, ghostly carriers of the mist. A far-off touch of frost was in the air, and the clean smell of a bonfire soared with its faint, pale smoke beyond a distant wall.

'I'll walk over to Watters with you, if I may,' Lancaster said, groping in the hall for his cap. 'I've papers for Mr. Shaw.'

'But what about Harriet?' Helwise fluttered. 'You must see her home first, Lancelot, and then you might take Mrs. Shaw that crochet pattern she wants for my Deep-Sea Fishermen—or was it the Night-Cap Club? Eight ch., 1 d.c. into sixth ch., back, 2 ch., 1 d.c.—perhaps I'd better write it down. Of course Harriet mustn't go home alone!'

He apologised at once. Harriet generally cycled over, and he associated her instinctively with the steel steed that turned and rent his walls. However, she brushed him aside with scant ceremony.

'Rot! Of course I can. I'm used to paddling about by myself all over the place, and if you think I'll feel any braver for having a land-lunatic mooning along beside me, grunting about turnips, you're jolly well mistaken! It's no use arguing, because I don't mean to be bothered with you, so you can just crochet yourself over to Watters and have done with it.'

She saluted the party with a sideway jerk of her head in her best ploughboy manner, and strode off, watched by her host with annoyance, and something else, altogether different, that held him back from pursuit. Courtesy conquered, however, and he started after her, only to be stopped by Wiggie. 'Let *me!*' he said, gripping his arm. 'I'll catch you up later'—and sped away on Harriet's swinging trail. The misty air caught him by the throat as he ran. It had been stuffy in the stock-scented room, and he had no wrap of any kind. Perhaps that was why he coughed as he came up. Perhaps he knew that she strained hungry ears to his step, and wished to spare her even a momentary disappointment. In any case, he was certainly not well received.

'You go back!' she snapped, turning on him. 'You're an insult—a howling insult! D'you think I want protecting by a thing that *sings?*'

'I play draughts, too, you know,' he reminded her meekly, and she laughed grudgingly and moved on again, her escort with her. And as he went he talked —strange talk that was new to her, talk that set the torch of fancy flaring through the mist. Vaguely through her dogged resistance there stole a sense of protection that was of the soul. Physically, indeed, she had no fear, as she had said, but the manly stride had covered an effort to escape the clinging pain of her own heart. Around her in the dusk Wiggie wove his net of comfort, of beauty, of magic kindliness, and by the time he let her in at her own gate the first bitterness was past. To-morrow she would remember that he sang and coughed, and looked as though he

needed cod-liver-oil and malt. To-night she only knew
that an angel had walked with her.

.   .   .   .   .   .

Through the dewy garden Lanty led his guest past
the ivied seat and the pink fingers of the cherry-tree,
and so out by the little stile under the mighty shadow
of Bluecaster walls. As they passed the great, wrought
gates, already closed for the night, he caught a
glimpse of the house itself, its bare flagstaff proclaim-
ing mutely that the master was from home. Then
they were under the walls again, sunk in an avenue
of lime, and presently in the Lane.

There was the whole of wonder through the Green
Gates to-night. The chestnuts were already turning
to the pure crimson that comes with the first frost.
Already, in the little plantation backing Rakestraw,
the beeches had red at their feet. A late harvest-field,
stooked and waiting, lay wanly yellow under the
white overworld between dark building and close-
laid fence. There was a moon coming, a big moon
slowly topping the hill, and when it came the hill
would go black, and Rakestraw lights would beckon
like swung lanterns of horn. His first look was for his
Mountain, as usual, but it was not there. From the
day of the marsh meeting he never saw his Ghost-
Mountain again, until his life had been broken utterly
and utterly remade.

Dandy was thinking of Harriet as they walked in
the quiet of the Lane. Both her sudden defeat and
her violent independence had held a touch of pathos.
She asked Lanty how long he had known her.

'All her life, or thereabouts. Her people belong
here—good old yeoman stock, the best in the land.
The backbone of England, some of the books call it!
It's true, too. That's why Harriet's so dead sure of
herself—she's on her own ground. She runs her own
farm with the help of a good head man. I got him
for her. It's quite a model place; you ought to see it.

There isn't much about farming she doesn't know. She's a good hand with a plough, too, and can swing a scythe with anybody. Oh yes, Harriet's all right in her own way! It's only her manners that are wrong, and goodness knows *I*'ve no need to talk! She bullies you no end, but she's absolutely straight—couldn't cheat if she tried. We've never been very thick, she and I, but she gets on with my aunt all right, and she's one of our own people, and that means a lot, after all!'

He laughed as he finished, surprised to find himself so urgent in Harriet's praise. He was thinking purely of his offended guest, but his companion felt, as she had felt at Watters, the intangible barrier of outlook rise between them. She had better manners than Harriet—yes—but she knew nothing whatever about a farm. She was better-tempered, but she couldn't tell the signs of the weather. And she was decidedly better-looking, but she couldn't bumble or scythe or pick out a prize hunter. And all that this first autumn night meant to Lanty, Harriet knew as she couldn't possibly know. She was outside.

The smell of the bonfires came again—the fine, pungent smell that is incense in country nostrils. Lancaster lifted his head as he caught it.

'That's real back-end!' he exclaimed. 'Unless you've lived in the country all your life you can't know what it means. You need only shut your eyes, and it paints little pictures for you. I can see things I loved when I was a boy: shadowy autumn evenings, driving home with my father from Witham, the long, white road and the black hedges and the dim land. Children running in to bed, and the cattle close under the fence, and no birds singing—all the field-things resting. The horse's hoofs going clip-clop, a bit tired, and myself snuggled under my father's elbow, half-asleep. The smell of the bonfires all the way—frost coming—leaves dropping—the lights showing one by

one, and then the quiet night. The smell of the
bonfires all the way, and then—home.'

He was quite evidently talking to himself only, and
again isolation turned her chill. Harriet would have
known what he meant. Harriet, who nodded like a
ploughboy, was born to the mysteries of bonfires and
the back-end.

They reached the third Gate in Lancaster's Lane,
and there a big bank of mist laid its ghost-hands over
their eyes, shutting out the scene beyond. Below it,
on the soft, wet, vivid grass, was a fairy-ring. Dandy
asked the meaning of it.

'Fungus,' he explained, 'but who wants to believe
that? Do you know that picture of Butler's—"Pixie-
Led"—the farm lad caught by the fairies in the
gloaming, with the mist-wreaths twining round his
knees, and the lights of the farm and the low, red
sunset behind? He looks such a clumsy, bewildered
giant, whirled round by the mischievous shreds of
elves! I wonder if he remembered or forgot? They
say, if you dance with the fairies, you're never the
same again.'

'It's worth trying!' she put in half-mischievously.
'They might teach me what the bonfires mean.'

He shook his head.

'That's heritage—and association. By the time
you're old you'll understand, if you go on wanting
to. It's the having grown with you, the being part of
you, that fills the country with glamour. Rain in the
night, the rolling of cart-wheels in the early morn,
hounds giving tongue in a soft November—things like
that—they're riches, handfuls of gold, when you
understand!' He dropped suddenly from the heights
to tug at the ancient bars before them. 'Time there
was some new timber in here, by the look of it! This
rotten stuff'll hardly last the winter.'

The golden lamp of the moon was up by now,
shredding the barrier into misty scarves and skeins,

and showing green-shaded fields where turnips and potatoes were grown alongside. Every shadow grew pitilessly sharp, and from the black hill-sides the lights sprang warm.

'I like to watch the windows open their eyes,' Lancaster said. 'They're so quiet, and yet there's all life behind them. Tragedy, often. At Oxenfoot the old man's dying by half-inches. Up at Topthorns they're slipping slowly down the fell into the work-house. It's nobody's fault, and nobody can help. The young folk at Cowgill—bad hats, every one of them!—make the place a hell among them, with the hate and the quarrelling and the mean striving to best the rest. Better things, too—men and women sticking to in the teeth of bad luck and bad health, paying their rent somehow, and keeping a stiff neck whatever comes along. All life—and yet the lights so quiet and steady, just as if peace were the real thing and the trouble behind only an ugly shadow. You don't remember it, outside. You think of folk sitting happy round a fire or at their evening meal, or slipping away quietly to sleep. You think of home.'

Over Dandy, listening, came a sudden longing for Halsted, cheerful, rampant, unmagicked, clean away from this mist-wrapped lane and the man who made the underneath things seem so real. They were not hers and therefore she feared them, and though they were not even looking at her, cared nothing for her existence, she ran away from them in spirit as fast as she could scamper.

'It doesn't mean home to *me!*' she broke out with reckless hurry. 'At *my* home there's a blaze from hundreds of tantalums, and there are motor-horns tooting on the drive and crowds of people coming up the steps, laughing and talking. There's dancing in the drawing-room, and snooker in the billiard-room, and rinking in the hall. In *your* house there's a bowl of milk and a candle and a smoky chimney and a hard bed'—she was half-hysterical, by now—'but in mine there are spring-mattresses and gramophones and thermos flasks and electric hair-curlers——' She stopped, laughing unsteadily. 'You've made me really home-sick for the first time since I came to Watters!'

He turned from the gap, rebuffed and ashamed.

'Afraid I've bored you!' he apologised bluntly. 'Why didn't you stop me yarning? Harriet said I'd get mooning about turnips, you know. I've only one subject. You'll soon learn to steer clear of it! That's Wigmore behind us, I should say.'

Wiggie joined them, trying very hard to put a morning freshness into his dragging step, and because Dandy had fallen silent, exerted himself to bridge the gulf. He was quite willing to make an ass of himself over the rotation of crops if it saved her the burden of conversation.

Arrived at Watters, there was no getting away from Hamer's hospitality, and Lancaster stayed to dinner with a sardonic consciousness of cold sausage and scrambled eggs awaiting him at Crabtree. They were still at table, however, when the lights of his dogcart flashed on the windows, summoning him to a fire at Far Borrans. Hamer and Dandy followed him out to listen to Armer's explanation. It was the hay, it seemed—like enough the late crop had been got in too fast—and the Hall itself was in danger. There was a big crowd of helpers gone up, and the fire-engine was out from Witham as well as the small one from the House. Armer, full of theories and excitement, had thought the master ought to know at once. He had brought the trap in case he was tired; incidentally, that he might himself assist at the pageant.

Lanty climbed in, said good-bye, and clicked to Blacker, but from an overgrown rambler a thick briar reached out and held him fast. Hamer laughed as he loosed him with difficulty.

'My little girl says Watters has the choosing of our

friends. It's made a pretty tight grab at *you*, anyway!
I hope you'll take it as an omen. See here—can't I
run you to this farm in the car? I could have her out
in five minutes.'

'Thanks, but it's up the dale,' Lancaster said.
'No motor-road. Narrow. Bad surface. Dangerous
to-night, with so many traps going up. I suppose
you wouldn't care to come with me?'

Hamer shook his head.

'Not unless I'd be of use! It hurts me to see good
stuff going by the board. I'd be dreaming all night
it was Watters, and waking Mother twisting ropes out
of the sheets! I'll have a Minimax in every corner
after this, won't I, Dandy Anne?'

He linked his arm in hers, and they followed the
trap as it spun out into the main road and turned
quickly into the Lane. Now and again, over and
through the hedges, they caught the gleam of the
lamps; and once Lanty's head and shoulders stood
out black on the golden air. In the drawing-room at
Watters, Wiggie used the perfect artistry of his *demi-
voix* to set Mrs. Hamer nodding over 1 d.c. between
sixth and seventh d.trs.

Hamer sighed in the Lane, and Dandy knew he was
away on his tram-horse hobby once more.

'I could have lent a hand with a bucket!' he said
regretfully, 'though they've likely more than enough
men on the job already. I could have sent the hat
round, too, though perhaps they'd not say thank you
for that sort of thing, up here, and, of course, they're
insured. But I'm a big weight. I'd have made a
difference to the going, and Lancaster was in a hurry.
But I'd have liked to lend a hand!'

Dandy was not listening. Their wandering had
brought them to the Gate of the Fairy-Ring, and she
drew him up to the fence. There she told him something of the walk home and the talk that had roused
her to revolt.

'I'm a Halstedite still!' she said ruefully. 'I've no right to Watters until I can make little pictures out of the smell of burnt wood and the flicker of a farthing dip—until sight and sound and scent are all mixed more or less into one. At present, when I wake to a slow Scotch drizzle, I don't smell violets, or see mushrooms rushing up, or hear cabbages taking long drinks, but I've got to learn. Do you think I might ask the fairies to put me up to a thing or two—what "fog" means, for instance, and "hoggin' taties," and "a good tommy-spot"; and how you "kill" hay, and why the weather is always wrong for turnips? Let me through, Daddy dear, and I'll see if they've anything to say to me!'

Hamer slipped a bar and let her slide past, and with a laugh she stepped on limber feet into the circle, a fairy-thing herself in her white gown, with the yellow light on her uncovered hair. But even as she caught her dress in her fingers and pointed a foot, she checked, her lips parted, her ear bent to listen. Lancaster's trap, long lost in the myriad turns of the Lane, had emerged into the open road, and the horse's hoofs, quickened to a sharp trot, rang from hill to hill. There are things to be read from a hoof-beat in the country quiet. Up in the dales, when a man gallops, the farmers come to their doors, knowing he rides for succour. Lanty's trot spelt urgency, and more than one voice hailed him as he passed. They heard him answer without stopping; saw the far-off lamps flung on the dark borders; heard the hoofs dwindle and quicken and finally die.

Hamer's wise eyes were on Dandy as she stood, her head stooped for the last message. She had forgotten him as well as the fairies, and her face, in its unconscious revelation, was neither that of a spirit nor of the little girl he loved, but the face of a woman come into her kingdom. With a passionate sense of loss, he strode over and lifted her out of the Ring.

CHAPTER XII

THE REAL THINGS

BRACK was thinking hard as he drove along the north marsh road, his hat pulled low over his eyes against the evening sun. He was on his way to Ninekyrkes, to unearth a rumour and prove it true. Talk had it that one other on marsh ground thought as he did of the Lugg, felt for it the same sinister distrust. The agent himself, at the late purgatorial meeting, had hinted that Whinnerah's wife was far from sharing her husband's attitude, and, since then, other tales had reached his ears. He was a constant visitor at Ladyford since his occupation of Thweng, and had gathered by degrees that there was something curiously wrong at the twin-farm. He meant to find out what it was. He had known Mrs. Whinnerah in his childhood, and even if she had been a stranger, Brack was not the man to be deterred by shyness. He remembered her as a delicate, highly-strung woman, with the fated look that many carry from cradle to grave without obvious fulfilment. She must be getting old now, and should therefore be easily handled. If she could be got to back his opinion, on whatever visionary or sentimental grounds, he might yet win his throw with the Lancasters. He had seen the young lord waver, and guessed that to his particular temperament a feeble woman's mania would carry a strong appeal. Once arouse his pity, his fear of hurting something weaker than himself, and no amount of practical advice would keep him from trying to right however imaginary a grievance. Brack began to formulate a letter from Mrs. Whinnerah, to be dictated by himself. He was fond of framing letters. The biting word that goes home was to him much as a neat wrestling-chip to his boors of cousins at Pippin. He could see Bluecaster's face grow

troubled as he read, watch him pen his apologetic
decision to that sneering image at Crabtree. (Brack
had an imagination.) Once his lordship was started
after his red herring of justice, the pride of the Lancasters would soon be kissing the earth! He bit at
his cigarette so savagely that it broke in half and
nearly choked him, which did not tend to soothe a
jarred temper kept on edge by a fretted pride. He
had had a bad time since the meeting, and though
his cult of super-superiority had withheld him from
the vulgarity of open retaliation, repression had increased a passing dislike to a single-eyed hate.

Born of good farming-stock, Brack had craved for
so-called higher things—he had wished to be a gentleman; and the particular brand which had formed his
ideal he now quite adequately represented. But the
red-hot vanity that had brought him home prancing
with effect had met a rude shock. The grey, old-
world atmosphere had foiled this meretricious
gentility as an ancient manor-wall a flaring poster.
Its mellow feudalism, its pure instinct for 'the real
thing,' laughed at him and cast him out. The parent-
stem mocked at the prize-shoot, and, deep down in
him, something, hated and unacknowledged, recognised its justice. Certain colonies, indeed, in Witham
and Cunswick, drawn chiefly from other and larger
towns, hailed him with enthusiasm, but in this one
instance he was true to the soil and would have none
of them. Yet the soil would have none of him, and
gave him no fellow—neither in Bluecaster, shabby
and halting, but unmistakable, nor in Lancaster, at
home in each man's understanding, and certainly
none in Uncle Willie Holliday, that rugged monument of fitness of place. That which was artist in
Brack, the very thing that had betrayed him, now
made hell for him where he had looked for a paradise
of approval. The bitterness of it obscured the real
motive of his late action, turning a passionate crusade

into a petty wreaking of malice, clouding even the fear that waked him, shaking, in the night.

At Ladyford alone had he found balm. Michael Dockeray's hospitality questioned the self-valuation of no guest under his roof. Francey was baffling but polite, and undoubtedly attractive, while the mistress, playing her own mother's-game, laid no bar to his visits. He would call at Ladyford when he had finished at Ninekyrkes, and have supper with them. He lighted another cigarette, and felt vaguely comforted.

Ninekyrkes seemed like a house of the dead as he came to it in the early autumn evening. Wolf and Lup were at a shorthorn sale over at Cunswick—he happened to know that—so Mrs. Whinnerah would be alone. She came to the door when she saw the car, and received his self-introduction hospitably if without enthusiasm. She led the way into the unloved parlour, and Brack, breathing horsehair and mustiness, was inwardly flattered until assailed by a childish memory of the old Lord Bluecaster at Pippin, smoking on the settle with his feet on the hob. The old lord had d——d the parlour, and refused to bear company with the Family Bible. Brack had an uncomfortable feeling that the still woman opposite would have thought more of him if he had preferred the kitchen.

He talked Canada, farming, and life in general, with the peculiar ease that comes of having left home *sans recommandation*, to return in your own Studebaker-Flanders, and passed to the genial intimacy of interrogation which Northern folk tolerate only from their kind. Lancaster would have got his answers all right, but from Brack it smacked of the travelling bagman, and he discovered presently that he was getting nothing. He dropped it, then, and struck boldly for his point.

'I've come asking for sympathy!' he said with a confidential smile. 'You'll have heard about the meeting, I guess, and how they think they've got the laugh on me over the Lugg, your Wolf and the rest. Well, they can go on laughing till the cows come home, but they'll not make me take anything back. The Lugg's got an eye-opener safe and handy for them, and when that comes along, I guess some of them will laugh on the wrong side of their mouths! But I've a notion—though I'm not saying why or how—that there's somebody thinks as I do of the crawling old son of a gun, somebody that reckons with me that it should never have been built—and that's you yourself right here, Mrs. Whinnerah! Tell me if I'm wrong. Don't mind me!'

She didn't mind him. He was certainly wrong, she told him, with her light, expressionless eyes fixed on his ingratiating countenance. Foiled again, he became less flippant.

'You'll say it's no affair of mine what you think, but when a man has a bang-up honest conviction, it's up to him to get it proved if he can. I'm still smarting at the way they petered me out. I didn't expect they'd catch on right away, but I did look for decent consideration. Oh, they'll hold to it that I've had it —I've got *that* fixed! They'll point to the meeting and say the matter was fairly discussed; but they know as well as I do that the whole arrangement was a barn-stormer fake, stage-managed down to the smallest cue. The agent saw to that! It's the old fairy-tale— Lancaster fiddled and the farmers danced, and the man shouting trouble was bucked out. I'm mighty sore about it, I say. I meant well, and I'm sore!'

He was in earnest now. He drew his chair forward, laying his hand on the string-cover of the round table between them.

'I'll just tell you what first set me hustling Blue-caster, and then perhaps you'll chip in with your little lot. Over the pond I ran up against a queer sort of lie-slinger making a living out of telling folks' futures when he wasn't getting nabbed by the police. He was the real goods, too—I'd stake the whole Thweng outfit on it—though I'm not saying he didn't featherstitch the futures a trifle, just to make them look pretty! But that was when there were dollars on the game; he got none out of me. But he digged in my hotel when he had the cash, and the night before I sailed for England he fetched me up on the stairs. He said: "You're clearing—pulling out for England, ain't you?" I told him he'd guessed it in once. "Well," he said, "you just keep those eyes of yours skinned! There's the gosh-dangdest trouble you ever struck coming for you out of the West. There's some sort of mighty curiosity, wriggling like a snake, that's getting ready to jump its contract; and water; and dead, wet, woolly things. I can't see them—it's so plum dark— only feel them when I reach out. There's a crack like a gun over the sea, but you'll not hear it when it comes, though you'll get cold scares many a night, waiting for it! And where there was road there'll be water, water big enough to drown a house, water and wet, woolly things——" I told him to come off it when he started again on the wet woollies—he was giving me the jim-jams!—and I let him know pretty straight that I thought he was in for the blue devils, but he was too slick in earnest to take me up. He said he couldn't fix it plainer, but I'd find it shine up brisk enough when the clock struck. "It'll beat hell!" he said. He told me I could see it for myself, if I'd practise a spell, that I'd the power as good as he had. I got him to show me how'—he laughed rather uncomfortably, looking away—'and I guess I know what the wet woollies are, anyway! He told me what farm I'd fixed on, after a deal of teeth-grinding and eye-rolling—it's a bit of a twister for the psychic tongue, you'll admit! and then he said: "There's somebody else knows the last card in this deal— somebody in England." That's what he told me,

Mrs. Whinnerah, and I want to know! "There's a woman over there powerful scared"—he eyed her searchingly—"a woman scared clean out of creation——"'

The faintly-ironic lips opened at last.

'Ay? An' did he tell you as our bull-calf had slipped shuppon an' was lakin' wi' yon steam-engine o' yourn?'

Brack's superiority broke on a curse as he tore out to the car. The concrete facts that the bull-calf had smashed his off-lamp and horned fancy patterns on his paint did not lessen his chagrin at his mental defeat. He turned irritably on the calm old woman watching from the porch.

'It's the old wheeze—the same old fusty old wheeze! "What a Lancaster says, goes!" It's Lancaster and Lancaster to it. Guess the whole lot of you'll be something struck of a heap when they turn out plaster imitations at the Judgment!' He leaned on the car, looking at her with tense impatience. 'You'll not speak, but there's folks in plenty putting words in your mouth. Now just listen right here! It wouldn't take more than a cent's worth of shove to set his lordship against the Lugg for good and all. I had him wobbling, as it was. *You* can put the cinch on him, if you choose. Lancaster's only a paid servant, when all's said, and he'd have to knuckle under. You'll never go to the Pride, with the fear of the sea on you, just to help the Lancaster tradition make good? I hope to God I may see them fired out of the countryside before I'm a year older, humbled and cursed and damned and broke!'

She looked at him straightly, then, answering him straightly for the first time.

'I've nowt to say to you, Brack Holliday, and them as says I have, lies! Who made the likes o' *you* judge betwixt me an' the Lancasters? But I'll tell you what it is—you're an overthrong, fidging, meddling

jammy-lang-neck, as teptious as a wamp! You're
nowt but a daft rabbit scuttling to ground afore a
storm. It's not *you* that has anything to fear, and
them as has can get through it without your help.
There's bigger things than you in this world, Canada
Brack—ay, and a parlish lot o' bigger folk an' all!—
and happen you'll learn it sooner than late!'

She wiped him out of existence with her old stare
over the sea, and, raging but silenced, he turned the
Flanders to the gate.

By contrast, the atmosphere of Ladyford was all
pure comfort and grace. Here he was an honoured
guest. Here he could flow conversationally without
fear of ironic silence. The string of self twanged joyfully in the breath of Mrs. Dockeray's admiration. It
was pleasant to sup to the sauce of her interest, to see
Rowley's eyes widen at his effects. Still more pleasant
to stand behind Francey at the piano, asking in a
light tenor, from a far-off point not specified, if they
thought of him in the Dear Old Home. But it was
rarest of all to sit opposite to her, watching her pale
cheek bent over her knitting, while her mother, with
discrimination almost too marked for comfort, called
attention to his good points.

'It's just as I've always said! There's nowt like
seeing the world—having a bit of a look round, if it's
only over the near wall into the next bull coppy!
Westmorland folks is that set on their own yard o'
ground, it takes a travelling crane to hawk 'em out.
Why, Brack, it doesn't bear thinking on what-like
you were as a lad, popin' about like a yard o' pump-
water, wi' toes turning in an' chin poking out—a
reg'lar daft-watty! And now you've come back real
quality, talking as like his lordship as two peacocks,
and in a deal better fettle an' more than a deal better-
like! It fair frets me thinking of folk—folk I could
put a name to—slouching and talking broad, clump-
ing about in great boots and smelling of the shuppons,

with never a thought to spare above stock, an' never a word to throw at a dog! You've capt the lot of us, my lad, showing folks what they can frame for if they'll nobbut try!'

Brack glowed, seeing himself winsome and well tailored, elegant, cultured, 'arrived,' but before the women's eyes rose Lup in his still, dumb dignity of the soil. Mrs. Dockeray was playing high. Armoured in commonplace virtue duly admitted, he would have stood little chance beside Brack's glistening veneer; but mockery and contempt could not but give him place even in the most grudging imagination. Something of the pathos and power of Millet's 'Angelus' clung about him under her rough touch, showing him in full and beautiful accord with both earth and heaven. Unfortunately, Lup himself, coming in with Michael just as they sat down to supper, dispelled the illusion more than a little. His 'bettermer' clothes were heavy and ill-cut, foiling the plate-glass impressions to which Brack added grace. His old-fashioned 'bowler,' several sizes too small, gave him the anxious air of an uncertain juggler, while an astonishing red-and-yellow handkerchief of his father's shrieked at Brack's peeping square of white silk. He followed Michael in with a forgotten catalogue, and was for making off again when Mrs. Dockeray netted him with cumbrous but sure sweep.

'You'll stop and have a bite with us now you're here, surely! It's not so many more chances we'll have of a crack with you. Wolf'll likely be set on getting back, so we'll let him be, but I'll not take nay from you, Lup, so you can just set yourself down! There's Brack here with all Canada at his finger-ends, ready to learn you anything you've a mind to, an' a deal more, I reckon! I'm real glad you looked in. The master's never a word for us home-keeping folk after sales an' such-like. He's that weary he gets sluming in his chair afore he's half-through, and it's

vexing when one's aching for a bit o' news. Brack's not
been; leastways, he's never mentioned it.'

'Oh, say! I have, though,' Brack put in hastily,
conscious that his perfunctory interest in the sale of
an historic herd was bound to go against him. 'Guess
I was too taken up to remember. I'd other business
shouting, but I just blew over for a spell—thought it
was up to me to give 'em a look in.' As for the stock, it
had been very much over-rated, he considered. All
the best stuff went over the pond; everybody knew
that, and he happened to be able to confirm it. Lup
would find it so for himself when he got across. Yes,
sir, *he* had been at the sale, right enough! That was
the best of a car; you could whiz about all over the
place, and see a chunk of everything that was going.

'You stopped just on half an hour,' Lup put in,
fixing him steadily across the table. 'I saw when you
come—you were having a bit of a turn-up with the
Duke's shover; and I saw you quit—at the tail of a
cart to the first motor-shop. And the biggest stock
wasn't in the ring till you'd been gone more than a
while. It was a rare good sale. There's no finer
beasts in the world.'

Brack felt his halo dwindling.

'Engine-trouble—fixed in five minutes!' he answered casually. 'No use my stopping, anyway—
prices ran too all-creation big. You feel mighty
thrilled, of course, watching good stock put to the
hammer, even when you've got to grit your teeth on
your tongue to keep it mum, but I'd another trail to
follow. I don't mind laying that half the farmers
there went just for the fun of the circus—they weren't
out to buy. You and your father, I take it, weren't
on to anything, now that Ninekyrkes is changing
hands and you're for out West?'

Lup flushed, and fell into dogged silence. The
afternoon had been bitter as Dead Sea drink. Time
and again the surface of the situation had been

explained to inquiring minds, and in most cases had
met with disapproval. More than one county gentleman had buttonholed him, asked his plans, and
dropped him with a shrug. His father's contemporaries had wagged censuring heads, and, as often as
not, a tongue to match. Already he felt something
of an outcast. Not that he really cared a whit for
condemnation. It would be a poor-blooded Westmorland farmer that even looked aside at criticism; but
where his pride had shaken off concern, his heart had
not gone unscathed. Even on his accustomed gaze
the pathos of old Wolf had smitten hard. He knew
afterwards—months afterwards—that this was the
last happy day the old man ever had. Mixing with
the huge crowd in the beautiful park, greeting and
greeted at every step, tuned to the excitement of a
big sale, he was young and keen again, forgetting the
future. On this happy flickering of dead joy it was
Lup's business to lay the chill, extinguishing hand of
reality. He wondered how often he had reiterated
the same dull speech: 'Nay, father, what, we want no
more wi' stock, you'll think on!' just as he had wondered, each time, how soon he would have to speak
it again. It was like killing something that would not
die, and in spite of his efforts the old man had insisted
on bidding at Rosedale Queen, until Lup had sought
out Lancaster and begged him to bring him to reason.
Somehow Lanty had succeeded, and Wolf had
dropped out, his eager desire followed by a piteous
apathy. The agent stayed near, trying to cheer him,
but with little result. Old Wolf's swan-song, he thought,
had been that frenzied bidding at Rosedale Queen.

Brack had the whip of the conversation again, and
was making the most of it. All Mrs. Dockeray could
elicit from Lup was that Rose Diamond had sold for
two hundred and fifty guineas, or that Denny had
picked up Rosedale Squire for seventeen, and already
saw himself beating the King at the Royal—state-

ments barely stemming the steady flow of Brack's
assurance. The mother fretted and wondered, watching the girl's eyes as they travelled between the two,
weighing them in the balance.

But Francey could not look at them as she, at the
same age, would have looked. In her case, education
of a high class had sharpened the over-critical faculty
of a fine intelligence until it held her emotional
capacity captive. She saw them more as types than
as human flesh and blood. She could neither be
fascinated by the surface charm of the one, nor lose
herself in the primitive strength of the other. Behind
Brack's refinement and overplayed ease she saw that
he was restless, superficial, lacking in stability.
Around Lup's steady sanity and simple faith she felt
the rough shell of his ignorance. Lup saw as his
fathers saw, loved as they loved, glimpsing life sharply
but narrowly, not in the least with her wider if more
dangerous vision. There were depths in her he would
never fathom, finenesses he might respect but never
grasp, shades of feeling making life vivid that he would
always fail to seize. Brack could seize them, after his
own fashion. She could feel him follow her mood
almost as it turned its coat, where Lup would have
been blundering up blind alleys, or sitting dumbly at
corners, waiting her return. Her interest quickened,
so that Brack flattered himself and shone. It was with
real reluctance that he tore himself from his thrilling
attitude of cock-o'-the-midden.

'Guess I feel leaving Ladyford like leaving home!'
he said sentimentally. 'I saw mighty little of hearth
and home for many a long year.' (The string of the
exiled orphan-nephew twanged with fine effect.)
'Lup, I sure envy you, hanging out just over the
way! Why didn't you hit the trail last year, old man?
I'd have had Ninekyrkes, then, instead of Thweng.
You'd have found me real neighbourly, Mrs. Dockeray!'

The words were meant for Francey, with the tail of an eye on Lup, for he knew well enough the talk that was going; but if he expected to score he was disappointed.

'Folk have it you're feared of a marsh-farm,' the other said indifferently. 'Overmuch water about—sets you dreaming-like! It's only a dowly sort of a night. You'd best to see to your lamps. I'll fix yon far gate for you. It's a trick o' swinging.'

He rose and went out, but not before he heard Brack beg the girl for a meeting at the café in Witham, with a ride in the car to follow. As a preliminary canter, he cajoled her into letting him run her to the far gate, just to show he was to be trusted. She came, to his surprise, but when he would have taken her hand in farewell, she had already melted into shadow behind the car, and the gate, under Lup's ruthless propulsion, was closing steadily upon him. To save his wings he cleared quickly, his fetich of gentility forcing him to shout a cheerful gratitude he was very far from feeling. Well, she would drive with him yet; though after a fashion of which he could not dream.

The night was drear. The dark had none of the velvet comfort that goes with the soft blackness before the rising of the moon. Its touch was harsh, its suggestion sinister. The elm over the gate creaked with rheumatic movement, while the brittle autumn leaves whispered restlessly, like sleepers too tired to be still. The couple stayed beneath.

'You'll be meeting him, likely?' Lup asked suddenly, with no hint of jealousy or vexation in his voice. He had taken his dismissal, and had no intention of presuming on old rights.

'Not I!' Francey answered, with a touch of impatience. 'Why, they say he takes a different girl to the café every week! The men in the smoke-room run a sweep as to which it will be! I came down in

the car for fear you got across with him. He was a bit
above himself to-night, our friend Brack.'

'You were getting on with him rarely at supper.'

'Yes.' She fell thoughtful. 'I can talk to him, but
that's all. It's like playing a game with somebody of
your own form for the sheer pleasure of being in
sympathy with that side of them. You may not give
a snap of the fingers for them otherwise, but at the
moment it doesn't count. *You* don't feel like that,
do you?'

'No,' Lup said simply. 'I like folks, or I can't abide
them. I'm keen to clap eyes on them and have a
crack, or else I want no dealings with them whatever.
I'll not drink with them, nor sell with them, nor pass
the time o' day unless I'm put to it. I've no use for
them at all.'

'That's simple, Lup, but it's blind—blind and
narrow! Folk are not all white or black; they've
different sides, different shades. You can pick out
the one you want, and leave the rest. Even Brack
has his points.'

'Like enough,' he answered carelessly. 'He's
welcome to them as long as he keeps out of my
road——' And she laughed a little and was silent.
Brack's 'points' did not interest her overmuch, either.

They had not quarrelled, these two. Even in the
first bitterness of rejection he had recognised that
she was not moved by cruel or petty perversity. She
had simply faded out of his reach when he was surest
of her, retreating behind some barrier which would
fall to neither of them. He had certainly been
passionately hurt and deeply angry, but he had never
been unjust. Unable to see her standpoint, he yet
bowed to it; only he could not bring himself to stay
and suffer.

'When do you go?' she asked suddenly. He told
her, and then: '*Need* you go?' she added somewhat
nervously, Lancaster's embassy in mind. 'There's

your father and mother—you could keep away—*need* you go?'

He answered briefly, turning his head away from her even in the darkness, and she held her tongue; but after a while she began again in stumbling, disjointed phrases like bodiless thoughts not shaped for the clothing of speech.

'It's my fault—but why? What is it? You'd be good to me, but I want so much. I'm several people, and all asking. One of me loves you, but not all—no, not all! One of me is afraid—that's the strongest one. There are so many closed doors. Can anybody be happy in a single room? Or are there new rooms for us to find together that I don't know of, now, so that the closed doors wouldn't matter? If only I knew! If only you could tell me! Suppose the one room was a prison for always? How am I to know?'

He moved uneasily, and she pulled herself up and made an attempt at coherence.

'Marriage isn't just one thing to me; it's all—love, companionship, understanding for always. How can I face closed doors through eternity? You love me, but half I say has no meaning for you, half I feel passes you by even when we're nearest. It isn't your fault; it isn't mine. You're patient with me, but even love and patience are not enough. All the time we're both of us groping, you for light and I for touch. You're gentler than your father, but at the bottom you're alike. You believe in the same things, you feel about them in the same way. You were vexed for my sake when he forced us into each other's arms over the farm, but you didn't feel that he caught up our dream in rough hands, and made it coarse and common. It was right and natural to you, perhaps even beautiful. Perhaps it was I who broke the glamour for *you*—I hadn't thought of that! But I had to do it. I should do it again. What are the real

things—the things that matter?' And for the second
time she said: 'How am I to know?'

He had been standing looking away from her, but
now he turned and took her gently in his arms, with
one hand raising her face as if it had been a child's.
Perhaps it came to him that in her doubt and trouble
she was indeed a child to his certainty of purpose.
All her acquired wisdom could not give her the
unclouded sureness that love had taught him long
since.

'The real things are the old things,' he said.
'They're all I know, but I reckon you'd find them
enough if you'd only believe it. I'd bide if I thought
I could learn you, but I doubt you're a long way off,
and I can't stop on as things are. I'd sooner be shot
than have to stand it out—the never knowing when
I'd be seeing you, the hearing and feeling you all
around me and not mine. D'you think I'd not know,
passing the house, whether it had you inside of it, or
turn a bend and not go sick with longing for you and
fear to meet you? One of us must shift, and it can't
be you. It's not for you to leave your folks and fend
for yourself—it's for me. I wish the old man didn't
take it so hard, but this is *my* job, and I've got to quit.
As for you, I reckon you'll see clear some day, when
you're older. You're only a bit of a lass yet—I forget
it, you're that wise! I don't rightly know what you
mean about closed doors. A man and a woman each
has thoughts the other can't hold with—they're made
different; but when they're man and wife there's a
lot they can share together as they'd likely have never
known, wanting one another. It seems to me that it's
made up that way. I can't talk to you like Brack. I
reckon I'm not sorry, neither, but I'm not that sort,
anyway. I've my mind a deal on my work, as you
don't need telling, but it's my heart as really learns
me the things that matter. They're few enough—
ay, but they're big enough too! Just trust in the

morning and quiet in the evening, our own folk, and work, and food and sleep—seed-time and harvest, cold and heat, summer and winter, day and night—the things the folks behind us knew afore we were born. The real things are the old things.'

They went back to the beckoning porch in silence.

. . .

. . .

And all night long, in his troubled sleep, Wolf was bidding at Rosedale Queen.

CHAPTER XIII

HAMER'S FIRST TRAM

IN the country there are houses far more truly the recipients of formal visits than their occupants, just as, at public functions, your carriage comes up to your place's name instead of your own; for master and tenant pass away, but the house remaineth. You do not call 'on' Bythams, Lyndesays and Wyllens; you call 'at' Gilthrotin, Crump or The Laithes. It is the house that stands on your visiting-list,—that has become a habit; and your dropped pasteboard is for its door rather than for those beneath its roof.

Watters was one of these 'habits,' but the Legend of the Kitchen Tea, mysteriously promulgated and enlarged, held many aloof who had no particular axe to grind. Mrs. Shaw, divided between crochet and creameries, was indifferent to the quality and size of their social circle. Hamer, sweetly taking the grinders at their personal estimate, was unconscious of any difficulty. It was only Dandy on whom the situation, seen more clearly, pressed unkindly.

She began to grow suspicious of callers, to strain her ears when the sound of the grinding was low, waiting for it to start up with the roar of a motor-cycle. She came to know the grades in leeches—the business-leech and the hobby-leech and the charity-leech and the soul-leech. No matter what their

particular goal, it was reached by the same path—
Hamer Shaw's cheque-book. The grinders did not
want money, as a rule. Their needs as well as their
methods were more subtle, based upon the pure
ethics of elections, local, general or 'by,' demure eyes
turned upon next year's voting-register. It was most
of it 'by,' Dandy reflected, watching their tortuous
procedure. On the whole, she preferred the leeches.

She began to wince a little when Harriet, cheerfully
unconscious of having helped the Legend on its way,
took it for granted that their acquaintance was in
common; and though at Dandy's disclaimer she
would grunt 'Cat-footers! Gees out of repair or
something!' her contempt for the ostraciser did little
to soothe the soul of the ostracised.

Visiting Harriet's farm, Dandy had come, with some
surprise, upon Harriet's father. Harriet seemed to
stand so very much alone; you did not credit her
with such weaknesses as near relations. Yet Fawcett
Knewstubb was a distinct weakness, a very delicate
spot indeed. He was very horsy, very check and
utterly selfish, and a really strong connoisseur in
language and whisky. Harriet kept him and his
hunters, called him 'Stubbs!' in the voice of a sergeant,
and wished him dead, in a bitter heart.

Hamer and his daughter motored to Bluecaster
Show along a road swarming with enthusiasts who
had no notion of making room for anybody. Dandy
felt more of an outsider than ever in the crowded field,
with its jumping and cattle rings, its tents, its long
lines of wooden stands. She saw many faces she had
come to know, but few held return signs of recognition.
The usual people were busy greeting each other, very
contented, very much at home. They were there
because they had always been there since the time
they could first sit on a stand without falling through.
After the greetings they buried their heads in their
catalogues and slouched along from pen to pen,

walking blindly into everybody else, and offering information to the empty air. Anxious to do the thing thoroughly, Dandy and Hamer bought catalogues and slouched, too. By this means they were successful in running into Harriet, leaning up against something extremely solid with four legs and a horn or two, gloating over the blue-ribboned card opposite. When Hamer's catalogue knocked her hat sideways, she merely remarked 'How's that for beef?' and continued to gloat. It was a minute or two before they could call her back to earth, but as soon as she realised their existence she left off gloating, and trotted them round the field in a terrific whirl of instruction, leading them at last, somewhat stunned, to a seat on the grand stand.

The day was brilliant, but Harriet, defended against all odds by Donegal, Burberry and K., with a huge carriage-umbrella tucked under her arm, insisted stoutly that you never could tell. It always rained at Bluecaster Show—everybody knew that—and it would rain to-day; this in a tone indicating that it jolly well better had. Dandy, dressed with the delicacy of a Blue Wyandotte, felt abashed until she discovered that Harriet was practically alone in her gloomily-barometric choice of attire.

Ringed in its green cup brimmed by blue hills, the scene had its own untheatrical charm, but its thrills were mild and long in arriving. Business went forward with little regard to spectators, and after a tedious half-hour, during which four horses, eight cows and twelve sheep stared solemnly at the crowd, while the whole Committee got down into the ring and wrangled about them, she found her thoughts straying to the social ethics of the meeting.

There was a rail dividing the stand, cleaving the two-shilling section from the half-crown. This puzzled her, as the planks on either side were equally hard. Harriet's explanation that you got sixpenny-worth

more water-jump scarcely seemed to go deep enough.
The grinders were half-crowners, she noticed, glued
as a rule to the side of some local celebrity, such as
the Member, or the High Sheriff, or the President;
but the leeches only ran to two shillings—with the
exception of Helwise, who was inviting Bluecaster
to come and see how badly they wanted a new bath
at Crabtree, when she wasn't issuing orders to Lanty
in the ring.

Apart from his aunt, Lancaster was having the
usual harried time of an authority on these occasions.
When he wasn't helping or looking for the judge, he
was calling competitors or catching stray sheep,
artfully eluding business-demands from button-holing
tenants, or rescuing the usual veterans of the ring who
stand so trustingly behind the hurdles. He knew
everybody, it seemed, just as Helwise, talking baths,
knew everybody, and Harriet, flourishing her clumsy
gamp. Names passing from mouth to mouth were no
more than empty sound to herself. The fact that
Seaman was jumping did not fill her with anticipation,
nor could the recent death of a well-known horseman
move her to a sense of loss. She began to be rather
bored by the unhurrying succession of events, and
checked herself guiltily in a yawn. The judge of the
moment was having a real day out with a fine hunter-
class, and had to be practically dragged off each horse
in turn. Hamer was drinking in Harriet's observations
like an eager child, but he was as new to it all as his
daughter.

Even the old hands were getting a little weary, and
found time to turn a speculative eye upon the
strangers—the cheery, handsome man and the slim,
well-groomed girl; and the legend went round in
ascending chromatics of incredulity. Some knew
Hamer by accident, so to speak: 'Behaved very
decently over that Abbey Corner smash, don't you
know! Sporting and all that—gave a thumping big

subscription to to-day's business,' etc. etc., and
wondered vaguely whether he might not be worth
cultivation. The women with sons looked at Dandy
and said that anybody married anybody nowadays,
and that even Kitchen Tea might be made positively
chic if the butter were spread thick enough. The
women with daughters only were not interested.

Dandy had ceased to be self-conscious, however.
She was watching Lancaster at work with the same
dreary chill of separation that she had experienced in
the Lane. This was his life, the interchange of business
and friendship to which she was an absolute stranger.
Harriet was perfectly at ease in it, grumbling, grunting, cracking a joke with a passing farmer or summing
up a prize-winner in a pithy sentence—at ease and
happy.

'Dull enough to *you*, I expect,' she observed,
detecting Dandy's secret yawn. 'We're brought up
to it, of course. Besides, it's my trade. Rotten show,
though! Rotten judging! Fool of a crowd. But all
the same I couldn't stop away, any more than Lanty
Lancaster. I've grown to it, you see. When I was a
kid it was my big blow-out of the year, and I've still
got the same feeling for it, like Christmas Day and
all that piffle. It isn't the thing itself—it gets slacker
and rottener every year, as I'm always telling them,
especially Lanty Lancaster—it's what it stands for,
and all the years behind it. If ever I want to purr,
it's when I'm sitting on this shaky old stand, watching
a flat-footed imitation of a horse going slap for the
water. But you must be about fed up on it, I suppose!
It's as slow as Noah's Ark, and, besides, it always
rains.' She slipped the catch of the gamp to see if it
worked, and shot a glance at the sun which should
have sent it slinking over the horizon like a dog
shouted to kennel. 'We're getting through to the
jumping, though. You'll find that a bit more en-
livening. Stubbs is turning out—did I tell you? He's

got a mount that can jump about as much as a hedge-hog, but he thinks he's going to win all right. It's no use *my* jawing; he won't take anything from *me*. I hope he'll behave decently, that's all, and not get slanging the judges. Trust Stubbs to have been where the sun is shining, even though it always rains!'

The band behind the stand broke into a dirge which proved to be 'The Girl in the Taxi,' and to this suitable *motif* the leapers sidled into the ring for their primary reconnaissance. There was something of the dignity of ritual in their solemn progression from fence to fence, in the measuring thrust of the intelligent heads through the furze. Dandy had her first thrill in spite of the accompaniment. She wanted to beat a little drum in the wake of the processional hoofs.

Harriet knew the riders, gentleman, groom or horse-dealer, just as she knew the mounts,—from the hunter, that did a little gentle following of hounds by the aid of gates, to the professional 'leppers' that never see open country, but spend their time winning prizes at a round of shows, and jump more with their brains than with any other section of their queer-shaped carcasses. She dragged out a pencil like a poker, and settled down to work.

'That's Captain Pole-Pole on Griselda, the little grey. Rushes everything that she doesn't take steck at, and a brute to hold, by the look of her. The big roarer waving its wild tail and doing an imitation of a charging squadron belongs to Bluecaster. Lanty has her out for the fun of the thing. They call her something idiotic—oh yes—*Flossie!* She can jump quite a bit—Heavens knows how—though you can feel the stand shake. There's a groom up—plays the triangle in my village orchestra. The thing called Chipmunk, looking as though it was made of knitting-needles, belongs to the Ritson Bros. One's riding, and the other runs in and throws things if Chippie starts frivolling. There's the winner—the little brown like an oak box with head and legs. You'd think he hadn't the reach for a grass-plot rail, but he's there, every time. Watch his eyes and his good-tempered ears! He's as pleased as Punch all along, and as dead in earnest as a city man sprinting for his train. Yes, he'll win right enough! Why? Because he jumps with his head. You can see him stop to think just before he takes off, and he doesn't give the fence an inch more than is wanted. This is his living—he comes from Saddleback way—and little Seaman doesn't mean to waste himself playing round. Stubbs must be cracked to think he can beat him! The rough-looking black with the rope-reins has been taught to behave like a mad circus and an Ulster riot combined. Its owner is a blacksmith in his spare time, and nobody else can stick on its back. It's clever, too, but it's apt to get carried away by its play-acting and make mistakes. Flyer goes to sleep and leaves his heels behind him, and Grace tries to do the tight-rope act on the pole with all four feet at once. That's Stubbs on his beetle-crusher—Lapwing, *he* calls it! He doesn't look any too genial, does he? We had a row before starting about rotifers, if you know what those are—some sort of a measly swimming microbe or rotten reptile of that kind. It's the only thing he cares a rap about except horses and the inside of a glass, and he was ramping mad because some of the beastly things had got thrown away. I hope Lanty is somewhere about.'

Stubbs was immense—very check, very baggy, and very red in the face. His side-whiskers bristled aggressively, and there was a vicious gleam in his eye. He was riding a boring chestnut with weak quarters and the action of a schoolboy in clogs. Harriet dug the person in front of her with the gamp by way of relieving her feelings. Hamer and Dandy tried to think of things to say, but she cut them short.

'Oh, it won't be the first time he's made fools of **us**

both in public! I can't help feeling a bit grubbed, but I suppose I can stick it out. Anyhow, I've got to stop and see him through. Save them hunting me up if he goes and breaks his neck.'

She thrust her hands in her pockets and scowled. Lapwing had already collided with the brown, and Stubbs, ripe for fight, was beginning to explode. The quiet little boy on Seaman stared in astonishment, until Lancaster, coming up, laid a palm on Lapwing's poking nose and drew him out of range. He had some tale ready, peculiarly adapted to Stubbs' appreciation, and Harriet caught her father's guffaw as he rode to his place. She sighed sharply—with relief, Dandy judged—and addressed herself to shouting 'Good lad!' or 'Good lass!' with supreme and delightful unconsciousness of self.

The sleepy Flyer led off, and left everything in ruins behind him, after which there was a lengthy pause, while rails and bricks were replaced and furze-tops refixed. Griselda gave a charming illustration of the so-called feminine temperament, refusing to look at any jump until forced upon it, and then flying it with a complete trust in Providence and an absolute disregard of economy. After these, the performance of the Bluecaster warrior ranked high, in spite of the roaring and waving accompaniment, and a suggestion of clanking chains as she rocked past. Carrying her proud head at the noble angle affected by some ladies much engaged in good works, she yet contrived, by dint of squinting down her nose at the last moment, to view a jump in time to clear it, and thundered on to the next in an atmosphere of escaped earthquakes. In spite of her size and weight, she tackled the trap quite neatly, and roared down the field to the water. Here she was superb! On the wings of sound she came, gathered herself into a mighty bunch, plunged and was over, leaving mingled impressions of trumpets, bazaar bunting and a motor-exhaust.

Chipmunk did quite a good round, thanks to a continuous shower of hats, sticks and ear-splitting yells, but Grace's tight-rope effects were unsuccessful except with the pole, on which she managed to do quite a delicate little bit of work. Lucifera, the black, was greeted warmly by the crowd, to whom she was well known, and responded by putting her back into things, like any other popular clown. Nothing grudging, she gave them all her tricks, from the preliminary, vicious, white-eyed sidle and spin to the last terrific bound with which she caught the bit in her teeth and rushed the obstacle. She missed the water, however, by trying to do a circle on the back outside edge too far up the field, but made up for it by leathering off into the crowd with a splendid impersonation of a mad runaway.

Little Seaman had only one mannerism, a circular trot like the weaving of a spell that seemed to wind him up for the first hurdle. Dandy's heart went out to the sensible, eager, square little horse with the box-legs. He might have been a machine measured to each length and lift, so obviously did he spare unnecessary effort, had it not been for clear evidence of mind behind, of humanly-patient intelligence and endeavour. At the water, his customary check drew a groan of disappointment, changing to applause as it was seen that he was safely across. Certain ladies were so ear-piercingly enraptured that he had to drop on his knees and bow his little box-head before trotting soberly back to his place.

And, at last—Stubbs.

It was perfectly clear that Nature had never intended Lapwing to 'lep'; clearer still that Lapwing was entirely of Nature's opinion. He was born tired; his foolish head had a weary droop; his heavy hoofs were in curious contrast with his weedy frame. What he could not walk through, he sat on behind. When driven to rise, he hit the swing-gate with such force that he nearly looped the loop along with it. He bundled into the trap like a sack of old clothes, utterly abolished the stone wall, and plumped slick into the water, where he stayed determinedly, in spite of the volcanic eruption in the saddle. Lancaster removed the pair once more, this time with difficulty. Harriet flushed a little under the joy of the crowd, but she said nothing, only gave the same sharp little sigh as she watched the retreating figures and the soothing hand on the check knee.

The second round brought its own disasters. Flyer had finally gone to sleep for the afternoon, and was withdrawn. Chipmunk missed the gate, owing to there being no hat handy. Griselda and Grace both foozled the wall, the one from temper and the other from silliness, and Flossie was so busy being noble that she forgot to squint at the trap and was caught. Lucifera, excited by the crowd, began to overact, tried to sit on the shilling stand and broke a stirrup-leather. Only Seaman steadily kept his form—and Stubbs.

Lapwing came out as if he were going to be hanged. At the first hurdle he manifested pained surprise, stopped dead and began to nibble the furze. Blows and curses brought him to the straw-bound pole, where he again paused to munch. The gate being uneatable, however, he cleared it, pecking heavily, broke the trap into matchwood, and jammed his rider's knee against the wall. Then, evincing a sudden passion for the water, tore up to it *con amore*, only to swerve aside at the wing, leaving Stubbs to go on in the main direction; and as splash, roar and oath ascended to heaven, returned to his nibbling.

The Committee appeared on the spot like mushrooms. Stubbs was fished out, set right end up, condoled with, and, being close in front of the grand stand, requested to hush. But Stubbs did not hush, had no intention of hushing. Stamping and shouting, he informed them what he thought of shows in general and this show in particular. Then he was requested to leave, but he wouldn't do that, either, and by way of reply ran a coil of lurid language round every member of the Association. Men climbed down from the stands and joined the happy party, until presently it seemed as if the whole Agricultural Society was helping in the suppression and ejection of Stubbs.

Harriet, white to the lips, observed 'Rotter! Low-down rotter!' between her teeth and got to her feet; but when she would have made her way down, Hamer caught her by the arm.

'This isn't your job, my girl!' he said cheerfully, pressing her back into her seat. 'You stick to Dandy there, and grit your teeth a minute longer. I'll have things straightened out in two twos.'

He dropped into the ring with extraordinary lightness, while his daughter slipped a hand round Harriet's unreceptive elbow by way of conveying sympathy and keeping her quiet at the same time. Helwise fussed down to them, dropping things and repeating the bath-theme *ad lib.* The people near began to discuss hats and servants with feverish politeness, bringing a faint smile even to the victim's rigid lips. The Member stood up and tried to see something at the back of the stand that wasn't there, and of course all the grinders followed his example.

Hamer broke a path through the crush with his own pleasant directness of purpose. Everybody was trying to make Stubbs behave, and nobody was succeeding: neither Bluecaster, tongue-tied and ashamed, nor Lancaster, soothing and propelling, nor the High Sheriff, the Chief Constable, the Judges, the Secretary and Treasurer, the Referee in All Classes, nor the Police. It was a case of carrying Stubbs off bodily, and nobody liked to do it, for, in spite of language and check and abominable conduct, he was yet One of

Us, and moreover his daughter watched from the stand. To them came Hamer the Outsider.

'Sir,' he observed to Stubbs, with the simple grace of touch that gave his every action charm, 'I understand you to be an authority upon *Rotifera*. I should like your advice upon the mounting of certain specimens of *Bdelloidaceæ* that I have just obtained!'

Stubbs broke off half-way in a stream of adjectives beginning with the second and fourth letters of the alphabet, and stared; and everybody round, after a momentary impression that Hamer was drunk, too, wagged their heads and repeated '*Bdelloidaceæ!*' in a loud chorus, as if it were some kind of charm, until Stubbs himself began to say any bits of it that came foremost, without in the least meaning to.

'I have also some fine samples of *Pedalionidæ*,' Hamer continued in his comforting tones, motioning Lancaster to call up his car as he engineered the offender towards the rope. 'A remarkable species— most remarkable!—but perfectly familiar to you, I've no doubt. The *Flosculariaceæ*, too, not to speak of the *Philodinaceæ*—here we are, and mind the step!'

Stubbs made one last attempt to get up steam, but was throttled with a fresh animalcule, hustled into the car and driven off. Lanty came back to the girls.

'I'm to drive you home, if you'll allow me,' he said to Dandy; and 'Can I find your bicycle?' to Harriet. 'The third round will be through in a few minutes, but I'll hand my job over to somebody, and we'll clear off at once, if you like. Your man has the horse, so he's all right. You've done well, to-day, haven't you? How many firsts did you get? You and Wild Duck are bad to beat!'

Harriet grunted, but her face relaxed. It hardened again, however, as she stood up and took a last defiant look round before walking off the field. She cycled home behind the dogcart, counting the times Lancaster's eyes were turned to Dandy's face. She was a trifle cheered when it began to rain heavily, and she was able to hand over the carriage-umbrella with an air of patronage, and splash along bravely in Burberry and K., but in spite of the 'firsts,' in spite of having been proved infallible, her cup of bitterness, that day, was full.

Helwise chattered all the way as blithely as if erring fathers and shamed daughters did not exist. Bluecaster, it seemed, had promised the bath.

'He was quite agreeable about it, Lancelot—porcelain on legs, nickel-plated hot and cold, *you* know! I really hadn't to hint more than *twice!* That led on, of course, to the Perils to Plumbers—my dear boy, how often have I told you that I never *ask?* He's sending the cheque to-night. You don't think, Miss Shaw, that your charming father——? Really, Lancelot, you needn't bite my head off! You're not a bit grateful about the bath, and I don't agree with you that the old one was all right. I knew I should get a present to-day, because I put on my skirt wrong side out. That always means luck! It was rather awkward, because the wrong side of the stuff doesn't go with the coat, and the picoted seams looked rather queer—I saw people staring, on the stand—but I'm glad I stuck to it! If I'd changed, I shouldn't have got the bath.'

Dandy listened vaguely to the chattering voice, thinking of her father, happily mounted on his favourite hobby. He would love looking after Stubbs, and they would spend the evening forming plans for his regeneration. She had a touch of tenderness for the impossible Stubbs; he had unintentionally given her this blissful ride in the rain. When Helwise stopped for a second, she listened to the hoofs and to Lanty's little clicks and calls of encouragement. She had heard him define horse-travelling as 'company and music.' She remembered it now, and had music in her heart to match. And so, in hearing it, forgot to listen to Helwise altogether.

.   .   .   .   .

And for a whole week the County talked of Hamer, and went about prating of *Bdelloidaceæ* as if they bred them, and looked up rotiferous information on the quiet, in order to confound each other's ignorance. The wives called at Watters and filled the card-tray, and the postman staggered under letters of invitation. Hamer became known as 'sound,' 'useful,' 'a man at a pinch,' 'a dashed good sort all round, don't you know!' and every club in the district fought to own him. He was quite pleased about it all, and never guessed that his impulsive piece of 'tramming' had worked the transformation. Somebody in a hole needing pulling out was all that Hamer wanted to make him happy, and he was seldom out of a job. He welcomed the new friends as he had welcomed the grinders and leeches, and opened to them his heart and his pocket.

That was how Hamer became 'county.'

CHAPTER XIV

THE OLD ORDER

SEATED at his table in the window of the 'Duke,' Lancaster could see the farmers come jogging into Sandwath, rounding the dangerous corner with a loose rein, and, as often as not, a head turned in the opposite direction. There were few dreary faces among them, for the late year had been a good one, with heavy crops and the right sort of weather, and no disease to play havoc with stock. He watched them disappear into the stable-yard, and from thence drift across to the Bank, presently to drift back to the 'Duke' for their receipts. It was the last of the three January rent-audits, Bluecaster, Witham and Sandwath; the last, the smallest, and far the most enjoyable. The others, where the numbers ran in each case to over a hundred, were too big, too busy, too long; but to-day there were only the marshmen and some from nearer home, including Wild Duck, counting barely forty, all told. Here, everybody knew his neighbour, and the tenants were mostly of long holding, so that the half-yearly meeting was more like a gathering of a clan than a business convocation. He knew precisely the time-worn joke that would herald most of them, together with the equally hoary grievance; just as he knew the ancient answer that would spring to his lips of its own accord. He was not bored, even if he had ceased to be much amused. The years had not changed the audit into a mere mechanical necessity, nor stolen one whit of its humanity. These people were part of himself by now, with their shrewdness and simpleness, ignorance and intuition, pungent wit, callous exteriors and sentimental hearts. He had the key to every one of them, knew how far each was to be trusted, how far advice would carry, how much sympathy would be wise. The breaking-up of an old man hurt him as did the downfall of a young one; just as octogenarian vigour or steady success was a matter of almost personal pride. Scarcely any life on the land but touched his own somewhere, definitely or unconsciously working its own effect.

The last three months had passed quickly, and more happily than any since his father's death. It seemed as if, with the settling of the marsh problem, the worry of years had come to a head and ceased; as if, in playing the rôle of Fate, he had acquired something of Fate's serenity. The old, grinding anxiety had vanished, leaving in its place a steady, uplifting consciousness of righteous power.

Outwardly, things were not altered. Bluecaster, though rushed home for the last three days, was generally, if not always postally, at least mentally out of reach. Helwise still hampered him with her activities, like a child pettishly dragging unwieldy toys for a walk and expecting the grown-up to carry them. Harriet's bicycle still scraped his walls; the cares of the estate changed only in detail; the county work still clamoured. But he brought to it all fresh ardour and a new sense of peace, from what source he could not have told. Perhaps it was the new interest over at Watters; perhaps the gathering of strength from a big decision over-past. Just possibly it was the long moment of calm wherewith the gods soothe a man before they strike.

He was at Watters a good deal, nowadays, more often, indeed, than he realised, unconsciously seeking the stimulation of Hamer's vitality and courage. He still kept his difficulties to himself, after long habit, yet he often came away finding them solved. Except for his weakness for leeches, Hamer's tram-horse philosophy was founded upon excellent common-sense, and had nothing of Bluecaster's nervous charity. He saw life pitifully, but never morbidly, and his remedies were for time and not for the moment alone. Lancaster left him braced not only to work but to feel, and to be glad of his capacity for both.

On the other hand, he was of use to the older man in many ways, engineering him over social pitfalls, along the precipice of tradition and through the network of county relationship; while to Mrs. Shaw he was an everlasting support and stay. He knew the best methods of reconciling modern grates with ancient hearths; why the newspaper didn't turn up, and what was wrong with the milk; how to retape venetian blinds and bottle fruit, and where to buy the best blankets and hams; what was a tramp and what wasn't; what you might say to your servants, and what you certainly might not; why it was wrong to tip the Force, and right to use steamers in apple-tarts; the neatest way of clearing cockroaches, and

what the Government was going to do. But with
Dandy he seemed to get very little further. He was
often so absorbed that he forgot to speak to her,
though he seldom forgot—unconsciously, perhaps—
to look at her. He knew vaguely that he liked her,
found her presence pleasing, and was grateful for her
kindly acts; and sometimes, in some hour magnetised
by Wiggie's singing, he turned to her as to the woman
of his dreams. But always he came back doggedly to
his first impression of her in the Lane. She was not
of his world—the world of the soul, where it walks
alone until the silver fingers of its eternal mate make
music on the thrilling door. She did not speak his
language, or love his loves; and sometimes he would
leave the beauty of Watters with a queer relief, to talk
shop with Harriet under a shippon wall.

The latter drove in now, in her smart, new milk-
float, affecting the farmer's jog-trot which would soon
ruin the brisk little cob he had bought for her, he
reflected, with a shrug. She had Wiggie with her, and
threw him the reins while she made the pilgrimage
from the Bank to the 'Duke.' Wiggie knew nothing
about horses, but he would have held a megalosaurus
if Harriet had commanded, so hung on and murmured
all the horse-songs he could think of, from 'The Tin Gee-
Gee' to 'The Arab's Farewell to his Favourite Steed.'

She scowled when Lancaster and the clerk got up as
she entered, and the former offered her a chair. She
resented their reception of her as a lady rather than
as a rent-paying tenant, and her ploughboy manner
was particularly evident upon these occasions. Perhaps, in spite of her strenuous pose, the pilgrimage
ending at Lancaster's table hurt something of her
hidden woman's pride. In any case, she needed to
carry a high head for Stubbs, who marked the day
with a white stone. He always insisted upon attending
the dinner with Harriet's ticket, and the result, if
customary, was none the less galling.

She refused the seat, flipping the bank voucher across the table and thrusting the estate-receipt into an important-looking pocket-book; then, remembering her part, sat down sideways and dug her hands into her pockets.

'What about that pig-hull you promised me?' she demanded, in a Judge Jeffreys tone that made the clerk jump.

Lanty temporised solemnly, with the tactful evasiveness of custom. He knew quite well that she had only said it to impress his subordinate, because the pig-hull had been granted at least a week before, but he wouldn't for worlds have denied her the traditional privilege of the punctual tenant, which was in this case no more than just a little bit of side.

'I see you've Wigmore with you,' he added, looking out to where that unhappy gentleman, to the tune of 'Come, pretty bird, and live with me!' was trying to persuade the cob that the bar-parlour of the 'Duke' was not the mouth of his private stable.

'We've been to see the Vicar—Bluecaster, I mean— so I brought him on. The choral has been asked to oblige with 'Elijah', sometime in March, in aid of missions over the seas and kindred objects. (Would you consider Stubbs, half-seas-over, a kindred object?) Wiggie happened to say he knew something about the music, so I told him he could sing. He hung back a bit at first, but I wasn't standing any nonsense. Mind you turn up with plenty of cash. By the way, there's that match with Bortun to-morrow.' (Hockey understood.) 'You'll be pig-and-whistle as usual, of course? I've got some sort of a team scratched together, but I'm still short of a centre-half. I expect I'll have to play there myself, unless *you*'ll take it on?'

'Too old!' Lanty shook his head. 'Is Wigmore training for a circus, by any chance?'

Harriet rose and came to the window, to behold the cob threading a Ladies' Chain with half a dozen vehicles at the 'Duke's' kerb. Poor Wiggie, utterly at its mercy, chirrupped, sang, and apologised in a breath.

'Why not get *him* to play?' Lancaster added.

'Much use!' Harriet laughed contemptuously. '*He* can't do anything but *sing!* By the way, he wants to know if you'll do him the favour to ask him to the dinner? I offered him my ticket, but Stubbs went out and threw bricks at the hens until I withdrew, so I had to come to you. Dandy wants to know what it's like, so of course Wiggie's ready to break his neck over it. He'd do anything for her—crawl into the boiler and come out with the steam!'

She did not look at him—she was too sporting for that—but she felt as if in herself the sudden twinge of jealousy that for a moment held him still. Then he said 'Of course!' and handed her the ticket; and she turned to the door with a rough-and-ready greeting for the next comer. Lanty's voice followed her.

'Two o'clock—and you'd better tell him to pass the punch! It'll just about finish him if he isn't used to that sort of thing, and he doesn't look over-sturdy. The atmosphere will be pretty dangerous, too. You might mention in passing that there's no need to make a martyr of himself. I can tell Miss Shaw anything she wants to know.'

Harriet said 'Right O!' with a queer smile, adding, —'you'll think on about that pig-hull?' for the benefit of her successor, and went out with the ticket burning in her pocket. It was Dandy's ticket all right, no matter who passed the punch or coughed in the smoke.

Lanty came back to business haunted by the smile and an irritating conviction that he had somehow made a fool of himself. They stayed with him all morning, marring his real contentment; for it was pleasant to have no difficult points to tackle after the good year. Not that the tenants were at pains to emphasise the luck. On the contrary, scarcely one

of them would own to any special favouring of
Providence. Hay might have done well, but it had
been slow weather, if fine, and that meant labour at
an exorbitant wage. 'Why, a man could bare lig his
head on t'pillow fur thinkin' he sud be out an' about,
puttin' the wark through!' Harvest might have been
fair to middlin', 'Ay, but look at t'last two crops!
What, we've not pulled up on *that* lot, yet! It's one
year wi' another i' farmin', an' like as not t'bad year's
t'yan as gits t'job! 'Tisn't as if crops was all, neyther.
Stock's gey ticklish stuff to manish, breet as a button
yan minnit, an' deein' off like flees t'next. Why,
t'whole countryside knaas what luck I've had wi' my
calves!' And then would follow the usual wheedling
demand for midden-steads, lime, shippon-repairs in
their degree, or anything else that 'Mr. Lancaster,
sir' looked good for. It was all part of the game, and
there was little goodwill going missing as they came
and went in the wintry sun. What bitter struggle the
past could show, what grinding fear the future might
hold, were alike forgotten as they stood about in
little groups, weather-beaten faces and ageing backs,
ready to enjoy their pillgill now that the pang of
'parting' was over; for though the Westmorland
farmer must have a grievance even at the wonder-
point of prosperity, he must also, on the very verge of
ruin, crack his joke.

Brack's beautiful entry in the S.-F.—an elaborate
S bend round his Uncle Holliday and old Simon
Farrer, violently exchanging views in the middle of
the road—was spoilt by a large mangold at the end
of a rope, attached to his back axle by Denny, somewhere *en route*. The mangold, not being accomplished
in **S** bends, knocked Simon's feet from under him and
caught Uncle Willie on the knee; and while they were
busy asking Brack what he meant by it, Denny himself ramped in with his high-stepper and the expression
of a lily-white hen.

Taken altogether, it was a gay enough morning but for one solitary episode, when Wolf came in for the last time as tenant of Ninekyrkes. The little interview was one of those that Fate stamps with a fiery thumb.

He drove in alone, acknowledging no greeting, and, when some one came forward to take his horse, climbing down without a word. It seemed a long time before he came out of the Bank, and when at last he crossed the road it was with bitter reluctance, his head bent, ignoring salutation and outstretched hand.

Lanty met him as cheerfully as he could with his usual—'Well, Wolf, how's yourself?' but the time-hallowed reply—'A long way on to ploughin' over Jordan!' drew but a ghost of the old smile from both; and when business was through with, the shaky old figure still sat in the chair, saying nothing and staring at the floor. Lancaster made a movement with his hand, and the clerk got up and went out. The agent waited, sorry and patient.

'How's your missis?' he asked at last, when the silence grew unbearable, trying to keep the same brisk, commonplace tone. Wolf raised his eyes.

'She's a deal better, thank you kindly, sir. She's not like the same woman since things was fixed. She never fashes herself over the water, nowadays. I can't rightly make her out, though—but it's no matter. It'll not be for long.'

'You'll be getting into the Pride soon, I suppose?'

'Ay. In a few weeks.'

'You'll not think better of it?'

'Yon's over an' by with, sir. I reckon we can let it bide.'

Lancaster nodded, and there was a second silence. Wolf sat still, as if unable to make the move which would mean the end of all the former things. Un-spoken, between them was the memory of many other days when he had sat thus, first with the father, and later with the son. Reminiscences surged upward of kindnesses on either side, of mutual sympathy and encouragement. There had been bad years when the farmer had needed help, but on the other hand the agent had had in return many a piece of rough advice, worth its weight in gold. Looking back to his early struggle, Lancaster knew that both to Michael's tolerant handling of a problem and Wolf's fierce cutting at the root, he had owed much. And Wolf was a link between himself and his father. The younger men, even loyal partisans like Denny, did not count the same. Again, as months before in his own office, he felt old, seeing the strong man of his father's time tottering on the last steep slope. This was the end of Wolf's real life, whether he went to his grave a year later or ten. The situation wrung his heart, fretting him with his own helplessness. He could do nothing except attempt, by some recurring instinct, to turn him from the one last boon he craved.

They sat on while the clerk, kicking his heels on the mat, wondered at the silence. This was their real good-bye, without thanks or spoken sorrow, the last speechless God-be-with-you! of two troubled men of the North.

The clerk's attention was distracted by a dog in the bar-parlour—a dog that had a fluffy-haired damsel as background—and into the death-chamber of a passing relationship Brack stepped unchecked. Looking up, Lanty saw him at the door, running his curious eyes over the pair at the table. In spite of what came after, he never in all his life quite forgave Brack for his intrusion at that moment.

Wolf pulled himself up, and was for leaving with the usual unemotional jerk, but Lanty stood up, too, and held out his hand. Still, neither said anything, until the old man, going, spoke up suddenly, playing the game to the last, even as Harriet had tried to play it, posing to hide a wounded heart.

'Yon fodder-gang, sir, as I mentioned? The old
one's as near done as may be. You'll happen think
it over——?' He broke off then, reality gripping
him, and Lanty, biting his lip, said 'I'll see to it,
Wolf!' and turned to the window. Brack laughed
callously as the door closed.

'What's the old boy so almighty stuck about? He's
through with Ninekyrkes to-day, isn't he? Mighty
sick, I should say, and feeling kind of "'Way down
upon the Swanee River"! A bit lost, too, from his
talk. He'll want precious little with fodder-gangs out
at the Pride!'

Lancaster said—'Grand weather for the time of
year,' and handed him his receipt. The eyes of the
two men met, Brack's in a smiling half-sneer; and
then he said 'Champ!' turning, still smiling, to leave.

'I'm not going to hustle you with "wants,"' he
said kindly, 'though I guess that doesn't mean there's
nothing to ask! I reckon the only thing that would
mend Thweng is a keg of gunpowder. But I'd just
like to warn you to keep your boots well strutted.
There'll be powerful cold feet for somebody in March!'

He swung out with his insolent smile, the last word
successfully arresting an impulse that would have sent
him spinning into the road. 'March!' So Brack had
evidently been behind Ezekiel, as conjectured. But
why March? What was at the back of it all? And
what did he think was coming?

Denny burst in just afterwards and dispelled his
wonderings, full of joy about the mangold, and
anxious to know if Mr. Lancaster had seen it. His
rollicking vitality swept the air clean both of regret
and apprehension, so that, by the time Lanty took
his seat at dinner, the surprising touch of jealousy
evoked by Wiggie's request was his only aftermath of
the morning.

The singer was on his left, with a very well-brushed
Stubbs beside him, and Michael Dockeray opposite.

At the head, Bluecaster, not quite certain that he wasn't still in Cairo, had Willie Holliday, as chief tenant, on one hand, and Wolf on the other. The last was Dockeray's place by right, but Bluecaster had contrived to remember the special circumstances and to whisper a word in Michael's ear. The right waived, he called to Wolf, and the little attention brightened the old man considerably. It was by acts like these that Bluecaster kept his hold on his people in spite of his long absences. His larger generosity came to them, tempered by reason, through his agent, but his little touches of consideration had the charm of personal courtesy, and were thereby kept in mind. Lancaster was the strong arm upon which they leaned, but his lordship had his own place in their hearts.

Wiggie had a bad time with the enormous meal, but while he tried to disguise his primary plate of beef as turkey and various other dishes, his mind was busy with his surroundings. He knew that he had before him an ancient system working at its best under the most ideal conditions, a triangular relationship which needed the right men in each department to keep the bearings smooth. Just such a state of things might never come his way again. Men said the system was getting played out, becoming extinct as the dodo; but here at least it seemed as if change, however well-intentioned, could mean little but disintegration. The fascination of that most claiming of problems, the interdependence of human beings, not only for things of the body, but of the spirit, took him as he looked round the ring of faces, after staving off a too-attentive plum-pudding. The townsman knew many employers of labour, men of large hearts and high standards, who had their thousands at a nod in the morning, and could play 'smack-at-back-o'-t'lug' with them of an evening without the faintest troubling of authority. But here was something altogether different, reaching back into far years that

had, even then, given each man present his place.
Here were ease and understanding, but no forcing of
either. The invisible silken strings between the three
elements yielded this way and that to the need of the
moment, but readjusted themselves immediately. You
could shake hands across them, hail flesh and blood
on the other side and hear the beating of good human
hearts, but you could not climb them. They were
always there, stretched by long custom and spun on
many graves.

Brack alone was out of place, with his over-smart
good looks and jarring mannerisms. If he could not
scale the strings he could snip them, and you heard
the click of the scissors. Even Stubbs, already well
on the way to becoming a 'kindred object,' and talking as broad Westmorland as anybody present, was
to be preferred to Brack. Later, however, he began
to get really warmed-up and quarrelsome, and it took
pounds of rotifer magic to keep him quiet. Wiggie had
spent the whole of the previous evening with a weary
eye glued to the microscope, so that he was in a
position to be fluent, and if he made bad breaks at
times, the kindred object was not in a condition to
point them out. Wiggie had a knack of acquiring
information that was of no earthly use to himself, but
smoothed the way for other people; and if the opportunity did not always turn up immediately, that did
not prevent him getting ready for it. Sitting on stiles
waiting for lame dogs was constitutional with
Wiggie.

He had early found his way into Lancaster's good
graces, so that he was rather troubled by his touch of
stiffness at the beginning of the meal. He thawed him,
however, with one of his quaint questions, and Lancaster soon found himself pointing out characters and
fixing labels, supplying histories and opening his
treasury of tales. He forgot that 'Dandy wants to
know' was the driving-power behind Wigmore's

interest, remembering only that he was being given a clear run for the hobby of his heart.

'You know my neighbour here, I suppose—Mr. Dockeray of Ladyford? Oh, well, he's a pillar of the county—Justice of the Peace, R.D.C., Guardian, etc., so we have to behave ourselves at this end of the room! Mr. Wigmore's stopping at Watters, Michael —you've met Mr. Shaw, of course. Brought him over one day, didn't I? Michael's going to give us a song, after a bit. By the way, I hope you'll be kind enough to do something in that line, too. We fancy our singing here, but I don't exactly imagine we've anything to beat you! Brack Holliday?—yes—that's the man you gave a lesson in carburettors in the middle of Leighton Mosses. He offered you a cigarette —one of his Turks—and you took it just to oblige him and coughed for ten minutes after he'd cleared out. How do I know? Because I was on the far side of the hedge, working out valuations, and I was pressed for time, or I'd have come over and held your hand or patted you on the back. The shy, thin man between the big cattle-dealer and Belt-End Gibson is Bowness of Moss End. He's one of your musical people. Been in Sandwath Church choir for years and years, and can't read a part to save his life. Best ploughman in the district, too—barring, perhaps, Lup Whinnerah, but Lup doesn't count now, worse luck! You must come to a ploughing-match, one of these days. They're a bit tedious, though, if you're a stranger. The masters curse them like anything, beforehand, because the men are so keen practising that they plough like snails, stopping all the time to look behind and admire. It's a slow job anyway, of course. Still, Miss Shaw might like to know.'

He couldn't resist the sentence, and saw the blood rise in Wiggie's face. Rather ashamed, he went on hurriedly—

'That's Thomas Cuthbert Dennison with the

twinkle. He's asking Brack if he means to start classes for respiration. Brack thinks they're all going to be drowned on the marsh, you know, and Denny wants to be in practice. He's a great chap! Bit too fond of a joke, that's all. Did you see the mangold? No? Well, that cob *does* take a bit of holding!' He met Wigmore's eye in polite sympathy, and they both laughed.

'There's a tale against Denny that never quite goes out of fashion. When he was a lad he was out with a pretty cousin from Lancaster. After a long while of saying nothing at all, he gives a great sigh. "Why, whatever's the matter?" says the cousin, alarmed. "Nay, I was nobbut thinking," says Denny, very dismal. Well, then, the cousin offers him a penny for his thoughts, but Denny was terribly shy-like, and wouldn't out with them. "Eh, well," he says at last, "I was just thinking as I'd never furgit this here walk with thee!" Cousin fluttered, of course. "Why, I'm sure you're very kind, but you sound terribly serious about it!" "Ay," says Denny, "I reckon I is. I'se gitten on a paar o' Brother Steve's boots, an' they've scratted aw t' skin off my heels!" I say—can't you smother Knewstubb with another microbe or two?'

(The boot story made him think of Brack's parting speech. He wondered what had brought the tale to mind.)

'Yes, Denny's a laddie! He's framed a bit differently with the lasses, since then! But he's a right good sort, taken all round. His lordship's making ready for the Loyal Toast, so you'd better be getting something into that glass of yours. You don't happen to be a parson, do you? That's all right—we can skip the Bishop and Clergy and get ahead. There'll be a deuce of a smoke before long—do you think you ought to sing in it? If you find you can't stick it, there's a door here, just behind my chair.'

And Wiggie nodded his head gratefully, and began

to repeat a mental list as long as the Shorter Catechism, beginning with beef and mutton and silken threads and mangolds and ploughing-matches, and ending with Brother Steve's boots.

After that, the business of the evening began. The cloths cleared, and dessert on the table, together with the long, white churchwardens, Bluecaster rose to propose 'The King!' This having been honoured with fervour, the hands went out to the pipes, and Uncle Willie got to his feet to have his say about the landlord. You could see Bluecaster wriggle until his health was safely through the wine, and the cheers and musical honours safely off the feudal chest. His speech in reply was a mixture of Cairo and crops, recognition, New Year wishes and shy little jokes, haltingly delivered, but it was well intended and very well received; and always the hint of breeding crept out in some graceful thought, however poorly spoken, —regret for a sick man's absence, sympathy in bereavement, congratulation upon some particular success. Towards the end, he stumbled and stuck with half a sentence on his lips, and Lancaster knew that he wanted to say something about the Whinnerahs, but he was barely through the introductory words before the old man reached out a hand, begging: 'Don't, my lord! Don't, now!' and the master huddled up his speech in a last blanket of acknowledgment and sat down.

Michael had the agent's health in trust, and when Lancaster stood up to answer, the faces grew interested, for his was the only serious speech of the evening. He looked at Wiggie first, though, firmly taking from him the pipe with which he was meekly struggling. He jerked his head towards the door.

'This is going to be dull, so clear off for a breath of fresh air, and stop putting chimneys down that precious throat of yours. It's going to be dull, I tell you, and I ought to know! You're not missing any-

thing. As for Miss Shaw, she can read it in the papers,
if she wants!'

That sent the faithful Wiggie flying, as he expected,
to cool his aching head in the drawing-in afternoon;
and with the tail of his eye on Stubbs and his behaviour, Lancaster got to work.

His speech was technical, concentrated, rigidly
pinned down to the main interest, but dull it was not,
so clearly did the plain words round and emphasise
each situation, salting hard facts with the short, dry
wit that stimulates the Northerner like his own first
frosts. Drifting outside to an uncurtained window,
Wiggie was fascinated by the picture within. Through
the mist of smoke he saw the faces at the table turned
with the stillness of complete attention to the forceful
figure at the end. Lancaster was at his best when
speaking. The whole man braced and strengthened,
and the almost dour look, so often seen in those who
come early into big responsibilities, relaxed as some
apt finish sent a slow ripple round the ring, setting its
final seal on his own mouth. There came to Wigmore,
of the town, a sense of the wide qualifications that go
to the making of the ideal steward. A well-known
member of this 'easy' profession has said that the land
agent must be 'a keen judge of character, of a genial
and sympathetic disposition and energetic nature,
must know when to be firm, when yielding, the many
times when he must lead, the few when he must drive,
whom to trust and whom to suspect, what to notice
and what to ignore, where to command and where
merely to suggest, whom to praise and whom censure.
Forethought, vigilance, courtesy, reticence are quali-
ties which will carry him far. . . . He has duties to
perform on behalf of tenants as well as landlord. He
is a human buffer between his employer and the
farmers, and must shield the former from annoyance,
and uphold the just claims of the latter, even to the
sacrifice of his own popularity. He must be as reticent

as the lawyer, as upright as the parson, as firm as the
policeman. He must be well informed on every subject, whether it be Bradshaw or the debenture stocks
of a company—the pedigree of a cow or that of a peer;
the price of a Scotch moor, or the vintage of a claret.'

The 'easy' profession carries with it the immense
penalty of an influence reaching forward into the
future long after death, in a fashion characteristic of
scarcely any other. There are some of us whose chief
honour and glory is to find men of humble station
still appraising right and wrong by the standards
taught them of our fathers.

Wiggie's eye ran along the dark heads etched on the
yellow light, from Stubbs, somnolently fixing Lanty
to the punctuation of a spasmodic 'Hear, hear!' to
Dockeray, thoughtful and quiet, Brack, supercilious
but attentive, Wolf, quiveringly interested and yet
outside, and finally to Bluecaster in his big chair at
the head. He wondered afterwards why, of all the
tragedies at the table—and there was more than one
plain to the eye—Bluecaster's had seemed to him the
most helpless and complete. There is something
terrible in the relentlessness with which inheritance
may force a man into a position he is not framed to
fill, thrusting power into his hands and judgment into
his mouth whether he desire their fiery splendours or
no. He may, of course, pluck the joys of heritage and
leave its duties to look after themselves; but if he has
good blood behind him and a strong hand beside
him, he will come to them, soon or late. Left to himself, with no great name to support, Bluecaster would
have been a tennis champion or somebody's private
skipper, chauffeur or huntsman—anything but the
head of a large estate, with his generous but harassed
brain besieged by the growing problems of the day.
Yet he had hurried home from Egypt to take his
place, to speak the right word as far as he knew, and
was sitting with his patient dog's eyes raised in

courteous attention, keeping his end up not too
unsuccessfully, thanks to the spur of race and the
steady influence of a good servant.

Lancaster finished the survey of the half-year,
covering general events, agricultural conditions and
the new legislation; and then, on an impulse that he
never ceased to regret, referred, in his final sentences,
to a subject already closed.

'I should just like to add that I hope all the marshmen are sleeping well!' he ended, dropping into a
lighter tone. 'Mr. Bracken Holliday was a little
anxious, as we all know, about the beginning of last
autumn, but I trust that by now he has come round
to the general conclusion of safety.' He lifted his
glass. 'I wish all on the marsh a succession of prosperous seasons and no dreams!'

Denny seized this excellent opportunity for sending
round a cardboard nautical imitation labelled 'The
Thweng Life-Boat,' and quite a number of pence was
jangled down in front of Brack. He nodded careless
thanks, but he whitened angrily, and he sent one long
glance up the table which set Lancaster biting his
lip. The farmer said nothing, however, and his lordship, grateful that the difficult subject was not to be
reopened, muttered, 'Bounder got some decent
feeling, after all!' and handed him his own cigarette-
case. Brack coloured, this time, and fell into frowning
thought. The courtesy got home, even through his
armour of conceit, but vaguely he groped for subtler
sympathy behind. Who knew what Bluecaster *really*
thought about the Lugg?

Denny was asked to respond for 'The Bonny Lasses
of Westmorland,' and did so with enthusiasm, quite
unabashed by pointed interrogations, such as: 'Wha
was fust-footer ower to Braithet's?' (Braithwaite had
a crowd of pretty daughters) and, 'Wha's buits hed
ta gitten fur t'job?' etc. etc. Michael opened the
singing in the gentle, light tenor that he raised every

Sunday in the Ladyford family pew where his fathers had worshipped. The song was the inevitable 'Kind Mary,' and Lanty wondered whether he was thinking of his own cheerful, masterful partner as he sang with his mild eyes fixed on the ceiling, marking the rhythm with slow nods. Denny gave them the famous 'Eh, poor Lassie, she was Dumb!' and called upon Brack to oblige with 'Pull for the Shore, Sailor!' or 'Throw out the Life-Line!' but his victim, placated by the cigarette-case, was not to be drawn. Old Simon contributed 'The Mardale Hunt,' hammering out the time with the punch-ladle, and quaveringly commanding the chorus to 'give it weft!' Lanty always sang the same song, his father's song: 'In the Downhill of Life.' Wigmore, drawn gradually back by the music, stood presently in the doorway, listening to the simple faith of an older generation—

'In the Downhill of Life when I find I'm declining,
    May my fate no less fortunate be,
Than a snug Elbow Chair can afford for reclining,
    And a Cot that o'erlooks the wide sea.
With an ambling pad Poney to pace o'er the Lawn,
    While I carol away Idle sorrow,
And blythe as the Lark, that each day hails the dawn,
    Look forward with hope for To-morrow.
Chorus. To-morrow, To-morrow, Look forward with hope
    for To-morrow.

'With a Porch at my door both for shelter and shade too,
    As the sunshine or rain may prevail,
And a small spot of ground, for the use of the spade too,
    With a Barn for the use of the flail;
A Cow for my dairy, a Dog for my game,
    And a Purse when a friend wants to borrow,
I'll envy no Nabob his riches or fame,
    Nor what honours may wait him To-morrow.

'From the bleak northern blast may my Cot be completely
    Secur'd by a neighbouring hill,
And at night may repose steal upon me more sweetly,
    By the sound of a murmuring rill:

And while peace and plenty I find at my board,
    With a heart free from sickness and sorrow,
With my Friends I will share what to-day may afford,
    And let them spread the Table To-morrow.

And when I at last must throw off this frail cov'ring,
    Which I've worn for Threescore Years and Ten,
On the brink of the grave I'll not seek to keep hov'ring,
    Nor my thread wish to spin o'er again;
But my face in the glass I'll serenely survey,
    And with smiles count each wrinkle and furrow;
And this old worn-out stuff which is threadbare to-day,
    May become everlasting To-morrow!'

Stubbs wished to supplement this with 'Riding
down to Bangor,' but was firmly suppressed; and
Wiggie was called in to keep him in order and supply
his share of the entertainment.

'It's fearful cheek to ask you!' Lancaster apologised,
'but they don't know what a big favour it is, and
they'll like it no end. You might just give us something to send us home happy, if you're not afraid of
your voice.'

'I'll sing with pleasure!' Wiggie said contentedly,
standing up beside Lancaster's chair with the same
childlike detachment that he showed on a public
platform. He did not begin at once, though, because
he found the last song very difficult to follow, but
after a moment or two he gave them 'The Song
of Good Heart' in a half-whisper sweet as mountain
church-bells, more as if he were thinking it than
singing it—

> 'Give, dear O Lord,
>   Fine weather in its day,
> Plenty on the board,
>   And a Good Heart all the way.
>
> Kind soil for the share,
>   Kind sun for the ley,
> Fair crop and to spare,
>   And a Good Heart all the way.

Good Hand with the stock,
  Good Help and Hope aye,
Christ-blessing on the flock,
  And a Good Heart all the way.

Gold-yellow on the corn,
  Green-yellow on the hay,
A whistle in the morn,
  And a Good Heart all the way.

Good Heart in the field,
  And the Home-Heart gay,
Ay! Heaven yield
  A Good Heart all the way!

A last prayer in the night
  That God 'ild the day.
Bide still and die light,
  With a Good Heart all the way.'

And after that he sang a grand old German
'Alleluja!' letting out his magnificent power until
the room echoed, and his audience thrilled and
rocked, intoxicated with enthusiasm, mightily growl-
ing out the Royal Salute in various keys of their own,
as Wiggie swept them away to the Table of the Great
Rent-Auditor of all. The voice beat at Lancaster's
brain, dragging at a lost memory. Wigmore was a
bit of a puzzle all round. He had no relations that
one ever heard of, and no home. He was a professional
singer, yet one never seemed to come across his name,
in spite of his undeniable gift. Perhaps he was one of
the unlucky, to whom no roads open. Certainly there
was little of the blatantly successful artist about his
slight, tired figure and unassuming manner. Yet it
was surely genius that was swinging them all out of
their narrow anchorages on that flood of sound. And
only Brack, suddenly fearful and cold, felt the irony
of that 'Alleluja!' on the marshmen's lips, singing
their Easter anthem before ever the agony and the
grave were passed.

They fell upon Wiggie in a body after that, and

clumped him heavily on the back until he gasped, and
told him it was 'champion' and 'reet as a bobbin,'
and 'fit to beat Holliday's Royal bull!' until Bluecaster had to rescue him by giving the final toast, 'To
our next merry meeting!' drunk by Brack with shaking
lips. Old Simon presented an unsolicited testimony.

'There's them as *can* sing an' *waint* sing!' he pronounced emphatically, with a scathing eye on Brack,
'an' the de'il tak' 'em fur a lock o' snirpin' dew-
nowts! An' theer's them as *can't* sing an' *dew* sing—
an' neea thanks tull them, neyther—but niver did I
hear the likes o' yon!'

Lanty shook the singer by the hand, and said,
'Miss Shaw will be pleased to hear of this, anyhow!'
with nothing in his voice but the heartiest liking, and
Wiggie met it instantly. There was never again
between them a shadow of any kind.

At the door, Harriet waited in the float. It was
already dark. The short January day was over, and
as Wiggie shoved Stubbs up the step, he was glad
that he could not see her face. A moment later,
gathering that the kindred object was already fast
asleep, he asked for a lift home, but Harriet suspected
him and snapped refusal. 'It's a long way to walk!'
he remonstrated sadly, and so convincingly that she
yielded, thinking he meant to try. Holding on to
Stubbs as they trotted steadily through the dark, he
asked suddenly why she had come herself instead of
sending the man.

'Because this is *my* job, in spite of Hamer!' she
answered abruptly. 'I've got to see Stubbs through,
whatever he does. He's only a poor exhibit as a
father, but he's all I'm likely to have, and if he
chooses to drink himself to death it's up to me to
stand the racket.' She pulled into the hedge. 'Isn't
that the Watters car?'

'It's so difficult to tell, at night,' the subtle Wiggie
made innocent reply, all the time knowing the note

of it as well as the sound of his own voice. But what he did not know was that inside it was Dandy, come to fetch him in an idle moment. That disappointment had yet to be revealed. Thus is the spilt wine of our good deeds made bitter as waters of Marah.

.   .   .   .   .

Lup walked over to drive the old man home. Lancaster had a word with him on the kerb.

'You might have given us a look-in, for the last time! When next January comes round, you'll be feeling sorry you didn't. When do you leave?'

'In another few weeks, sir. I'll be stopping awhile with an uncle in Liverpool before sailing. I'd meant to go, if I'd had to work my passage, but the old man's seen to the brass. There'll be plenty to start me on the other side an' all. When he'd once given it, he wasn't for stinting me. He's hard, but he's not unjust, and he knows I've earned it all right.'

'It's *you* that's hard, Lup—ay, and unjust, too! You haven't earned the right to spoil your father's last days.'

'He's had his life, sir. This is mine.'

'And much good may it do you! You're a fool!' Lanty swung on his heel to find the Watters chauffeur at his elbow, wearing such a shocked expression that both the other men smiled. Lup said, 'Like enough! Good-night to you, sir!' and rattled off, and Lancaster drifted to the car. Dandy put out a hand to him through the window.

'Whom were you slanging on the pavement? And do you know what has happened to Wiggie? They have it inside that he's gone home already.'

It was explained that he had driven off with Mr. and Miss Knewstubb, and she lifted her eyebrows a little. She was so used to Wiggie's devotion that the wind blew cold at the slightest sign of defection.

'It's quite all right, of course, but we'd promised to send over. I had nothing particular to do, so I just came for the run. I hope he won't get cold after the hot room—I brought the closed car on purpose—especially as he came to please me.'

'He pleased a good many other people, too,' Lanty said warmly. 'He was immense! I can't think why he isn't in the front rank of English singers. Surely somebody ought to have found him out!'

'Oh, he's getting on all right,' she answered, rather hurriedly. 'I'm sure he enjoyed singing for you.'

'Well, yes, I think he did. He was great, anyhow! I'm glad you thought of sending him as your representative.'

'I was interested.' She looked down, so that her head with its halo of yellow light was thrown into relief by the night and her dark furs. There were yellow chrysanthemums opposite.

He laughed with a shade of incredulity.

'We're dull enough at close quarters—just a lot of rough working-men digging up God's gold out of the land. I'd an idea you didn't approve of us; thought we starved our dogs or something!' There came to him a recollection of the last meeting in the Lane. 'You told me once you were home-sick for a collection of oddments of some sort—tantalums, thermos flasks and hair-curlers!'

It was she who laughed now, and so infectiously that Bluecaster, making for his carriage, stopped and asked to be introduced.

'I didn't include *him* in my estimate,' Lanty added, when he had passed on, leaving a word for Hamer and a message of sympathy for Helwise, struggling with a cold. 'He's different from the rest of us—you'd know it on the top of Skiddaw. *He's* never done any digging, and I don't want him to.'

'Digging might be good for him,' Dandy ventured, and was growled at for her pains.

'No, it wouldn't! It might alter him, that's all, but he'd lose all the other things. He's the best chap in

Britain! We're here to do the digging for him, as we've always been. You don't understand. They mean a lot to us—the little thoughtfulnesses and the bottles of cough-medicine and the words in season. If Bluecaster was digging, he'd be too busy to bother. That's what *he*'s here for. But of course it can't mean anything to you.'

'You're rather rude, I think!' she replied gently, with a kind of humorous resignation at which he smiled in spite of himself. Up the street, on the green, a group of caravans was stationed, the lights of a merry-go-round filling the winter evening with colour. A rollicking tune came down to them, mixed with the shouts and laughter of the crowd.

'Come out and have a look!' he suggested, opening the door and offering a hand, and presently they were standing in the ring of light, caught in the deafening blare of the full orchestrion overhead. Some of the farmers had stayed for a final flourish to the day's festivity. Denny was mounted on a tiger, with his brother's little girl in front of him, and one of Braithwaite's pleasing daughters behind. The big cattle-dealer was perched on an inadequate ostrich, with a scared wife clinging to the neck of a giraffe. The shy ploughman rode solemnly alone in the red-plush sumptuousness of a car. The blaze of brightness scooped out of the pressing dark gave the whole scene a curiously unreal effect, so that, watching the mechanical rise and fall of the flying circle, Lanty's mind, reacting from the strain of the three days' audit, grew gradually quiescent and dazed. Dandy spoke to him, but he did not hear her. Close at hand in the crowd, Brack had turned to face him, but he did not see him. The lights dimmed suddenly, became lanterns swinging and dipping in a night as dark as hell. The blare of the trumpets was the shattering roar of a big wind as it tore the air to tatters, and the wailing of the reeds grew into the shrieks of women and the thin crying of lambs. He was conscious of intense, paralysing fear, of a frantic necessity to shout, choked on his lips by the pressure of the gale. And through it all he felt that he was listening, straining his ears to madness against the tumult of an inferno let loose, just as, at Ninekyrkes, he had seen an old woman strain and reach through the tense stillness of coming thunder. The deadly helplessness of nightmare weighed him down as he writhed against the horror, certain that, if he could speak *now*, hear *now*, the unspeakable danger would pass. Through the torture a hand came up on to his, a hand that he had never touched before to recognise, but which held and drew him up and out of the abyss. He thought vaguely that it must be Hamer's—the clasp had the same comfort—but when he had struggled blindly back to the present, he found it was not Hamer's, but his daughter's. He saw Brack then, his eyes as they rested on him unnaturally brilliant, the pupils unnaturally large, before he dropped his still swaying gaze to Dandy's face.

'What was it?' he asked. 'I heard—water!' And as he said it he caught a little click in a man's throat, as of satisfaction and justification, but when he looked again Brack was gone. Dandy drew him out of the crowd.

'You looked as if you had gone blind!' she said. 'I was frightened, and you trembled as if you were frightened, too. And you called first to your own father and then to mine, just as though you were drowning and wanted help. I expect you're tired out, and ought to rest. Let me take you home in the car. You can send over for your horse to-morrow.'

But he refused. He wanted the quiet ride home in the night for thought.

'Jogging along in the air will do me good—thanks all the same! I *am* tired—you're right, there—but I'm as strong as an ox and can stand anything. I don't usually behave like this, even after a rent-audit! I'm dreadfully sorry if I upset you. I expect the glare of the lights hypnotised me on top of the landlord's punch! You won't trust yourself to me again, if I'm going to see visions in your company.'

She gave him her hand a second time through the window, and he looked down at it in his own. 'It *is* like Hamer's!' he said curiously, marking the resemblance in miniature, small, but square and strong. She withdrew it with a shade of embarrassment.

'Yes, I know, but what made you think of it, now? I'm proud of it—dear old Dad! You'll start at once, won't you?—and do keep your wits about you on that lonely road!'

At the top of the hill he pulled up for a last look down into the little blaze of life below him, throwing its brilliance over the pile of the church and the looming canopies of the trees. The lights still circled madly, the music still crashed, but they had no power over him now. What was it that had used them to the forcing of that terrible moment? Vague words of Brack's about clairvoyance drifted back into his mind. He had laughed with Bluecaster over a mental picture of Brack evoking spirits. Was he responsible for that tortured nightmare? Perhaps he had really been trying to tell him something; or was it just hypnotic reaction from that theory of his, obsessing him to madness? For himself, he could do nothing now. Even if he had believed it, he could not doom the Lugg on the strength of a prophecy—after a rent-dinner, too! And he did not believe it. His faith stayed where it was.

He quickened his horse along the silent highway, the healing of the night gathering him into quiet; and, as he rode, there went with him the pressure of the hand that was so like Hamer's, cool and firm and blessedly kind.

CHAPTER XV

THE BEGINNING OF THE END

It was a very dreamlike day on which Lup left Nine-kyrkes, turning his back upon the marsh and all that had filled his life hitherto. He made no round of good-byes, no flurry of preparation, but when the time came, he went, just as he would go at the end of his day on a further journey yet. He would 'bide still and die light,' as taught the unhurrying philosophy of Wiggie's song.

Not even for Francey had he a farewell; yet she had her moment with him, all unknown. Lifting her blind in the first showing of dawn, she saw him standing on the sea-wall, looking over the bay. He was still in his rough clothes, and the dull shade of the worn stuff was one with the colourless growth of the breaking day. He stood perfectly still, his hands dropped at his sides, his head a little bent, more like a symbol than a breathing human. On either side of him a shadowy wraith of a sheepdog lay crouched with pricked ears, as if watching for an invisible flock to come shoulder-ing out of the dim space beneath. They had scarcely left him a moment during the last few days, clinging like burrs, and all the last night they had whimpered and wept, until in desperation he rose and called them out. Francey knelt at the window with her black hair looped on either side of her pale face, and saw the day come up to the feet of her parting love.

He was going, and by a finger she could have held him, but something kept her back that did not seem part of her at all. If she had but known it, the tragedy that was coming was in her hands to force or to with-hold; but she did not know. The question was still purely personal, still hung on the one point, whether or not her real happiness lay in the primitive figure on the bank. There were tears in her eyes as she thought of the coming dawns when she might look to find him there and all in vain, but she was prepared to shed them. He would leave desolation behind him, but it would pass. She knew that she was able to let him go, and while she realised that she would not keep him.

Yet she longed for a last look, however far, and from her post under the lifted sash she tried to will that he should turn and send his climbing glance over the house to her window, as he had done so many times before, but her fixed gaze did not reach him. Brack would have answered it, she knew— Brack, sensitive, impressionable, ultra-self-conscious; but Lup looked straight before him with his tranquil eyes, and all the hysterical telepathy in the world might have shrieked in his ear and found him deaf. And just for that, just because he did not look, nor heed, nor answer, Francey felt wounded and full of longing; for it is always the man that turns his back that pulls at a woman's heart.

There was a clink of milk-pails on the stone floor beneath, followed by steps on the stairs; and then the door opened, and her mother stood at her shoulder.

'You'll get your death at yon window! For the land's sake don't be staring at nowt, like poor Martha at Ninekyrkes! She fair gives me the creeps. It's about time to be stirring, I've been down a bit, and t' master's out an' about. Yon's Lup, I reckon. What's he at? Feeling a bit down in the mouth, likely, but he'll get over it. Westmorland folk be gey ill to shift, but they do rarely when they get going. Lup'll be a sight better for a change. Canada'll happen make a man of him—same as Brack!'

Francey said nothing, watching the pale day grow round the figure on the wall. The mother kept her light tone, but her unslept eyes were red.

'It isn't as if he hadn't a bit of brass. Wolf's not the sort to send him off with his thumb in his mouth, for all his jye looks! He's doing well by the lad, and Lup'll be fit to do his best back again. What, I shouldn't wonder if he's home in a two-three year, as like Brack as one pea to another! It's a sad pity Brack didn't hold on till Ninekyrkes was empty. It would have been pleasant-like, having him next door.'

'Brack at Ninekyrkes!' Francey fired contemptuously. 'Why, mother, he knows nothing of farming! You should hear the tales going about him. You should see his fences and his thistles! Mr. Lancaster will be having a word with him, if he doesn't mend. He knows less about crops than I do, and I can handle a rake with him, any day!'

'Why, there's nowt to that! Brack's got a snack o' yon culture you reckon so much on. He can handle that puffin' billy o' his, anyhow, an' carry a smart coat an' finger the banjo. Yon was a rare good tune he give us, t' other night at Sunflatts, with his face blacked an' all! Lup'll never shape for owt o' *that* sort, I doubt.'

On the bank Lup turned sharply without lingering or hesitation, and dropped down into the road, the dogs springing on the instant, as if part of him. Looking straight before him, he made off towards Ninekyrkes, and they saw his fine, dark profile as he stooped to hasp a gate. Then he was gone, and the waste was empty as before. And in that moment Mrs. Dockeray forgot her daughter and forwent her methods, pressing her working face to the cold glass. Francey heard her say: 'Good lad, Lup! God bless you; good lad!' and when she stood up beside her, she saw the quick tears running down the kind cheek.

'He'll come back!' she found herself saying, vaguely wondering how the post of comforter had come to be reversed, and the elder woman nodded, passing her hand over her eyes, her subtle diplomacy broken at last to plain words.

'Ay, he'll come back, I reckon, but he'll happen

come too late! Folks change—there's no getting past
it; we've got to face it out! I've always thought a
deal of Lup. He's the real thing, all through. Eh!
an' there's poor Martha losing her lad! It doesn't
bide thinking on. I doubt it'll just about finish her;
there's lile or nowt to her as it is. It's her happiness
as'll drive off atween the shafts o' the cart. Ay, my
lass, and it's your happiness as'll take the road along
wi' him an' all! What's the use o' schoolin' an' such-
like if it sets you snirpin' at the right stuff? I've had
a good man myself, mannerly and decent, but I've
had to be the grey mare, as I reckon you know.
Michael's that soft an' easy led. He leans on me, does
Michael, and I'd not have it different, nay, nor him
neither; but there's something better than that for a
woman, and you'd have had it from Lup. He'd have
been master; he's strong enough for both an' more,
and you'd have been glad of it, every year. I'm not
blaming you. It's me that's to blame, being over
fond an' wanting the best for you could be got. You
were such a bonny barn an' that smart, I'd have
scraped the roads to get you learned an' done by like
a lady! Ay—*fond*—I was that! But what was to tell
your happiness lay just over yon fence, an' me blinding
your eyes to it? I've done you a terrible big wrong. I
can see that now, right enough. You'll sorrow for it
all your life, if you send him off. You've just to say
the word, and he'll bide. Say it, my lass! You'll be
rare an' glad when it's done.'

The door opened wider very gently, and Michael
looked in.

'That you, missis? You're wanted. Francey badly,
this morning?'

Mrs. Dockeray wiped her eyes hastily and bustled
towards him.

'Nay, nowt o' t' sort! You get along downstairs,
an' the lass'll follow. You might have given a body
a shout, instead of bursting in as if t' house was afire!'

At the door she turned.

'You've just to say the word!' she urged.

But Francey did not say it.

.　　　.　　　.　　　.　　　.

Denny had begged the honour of driving him to the station, and turned up with the ramper about nine, a small 'Jack' at one lamp-bracket, and the 'Stars and Stripes' at the other. Lup stayed stolidly on the step until he removed them. The dogs sniffed and whined at the bags as they were lifted into the trap. In the dull light everything took on a deadened effect, utterly dismal and forlorn, from the melancholy house on the edge of the dreary flat to the two worn figures with their set faces and shut hands. At the gate the cowman waited for a last word. Through the window the 'girl' peered at the little scene. The dogs leaped at Lup, whimpering and beseeching, refusing to be stilled.

Denny's efforts to lighten the atmosphere did not go far. His flags had not drawn even a smile; his new tale about Brack died on his lips. In the silent trouble before him even his frothing joy in life sank and drowned.

Lup took a step towards the cart as though meaning to leave without farewell, and then stopped. As if driven by whips, he strode back to his mother and kissed her; to his father he gave his hand. None of the three spoke. Their eyes did not meet. The tradition of silence, of fatalistic stoicism, gripped them all alike in that last moment.

At the gate he dropped a word and a shake to the man as he wished him luck, and out in the road turned —once—to look behind, set against the skyline in the high-wheeled trap. But only the 'girl' at the casement waved; the couple in the porch made no sign. Only their weak, old eyes, strong in inward vision, followed him tirelessly on the long miles.

Passing Ladyford, master, mistress and hands were

out to speed him. A horseshoe took the place of the discarded 'Jack.' Mrs. Dockeray was weeping again —into a large muffler meant for his wearing on board. Something of value passed in Michael's grip, but there was no word either of or from Francey, and this time he did not turn on the road. He did not dare. It might be that he would see her, after all, come too late.

He slid a hand over the back of the seat, and a tongue came up and licked it. Behind the tongue was a brown dog-body hidden between the bags. The miles flew by in the misty morning. The drifting hails of friendly tongues came mistily to his dulled brain. Even Denny seemed very far off. Only the ache in his heart was real, and the warm tongue reaching comfort to his hand.

In Sunflatts they met Lancaster, and drew up for a last word, and long after they had disappeared the agent stood staring up the street. The changes were beginning. Lup was gone. What came next?

He was to take the express at Oxenholme, and as they pulled into the station, Brack's car snorted up behind, setting the ramper on end, and scaring the brown dog between the bags. They had already met him, miles away, taking an opposite direction altogether, yet here he was at their heels. He seemed uneasy, too, fixing them when they were not looking, and walking away when they turned. If he had been meeting anybody, he would have said so, surely, and he took no ticket himself, only loitered on the platform, tugging at his moustache and staring. However, when the train thundered in, and Denny was busy holding to the ramper with one hand and the howling brown dog with the other, he seemed to make up his mind.

'Just pulling out, I reckon?' he observed at the carriage-door, his casual tone rather more casual than usual. 'Well, I hope you'll find my luck meeting you

on the other side. Tell them I sent you along, with
my love, as one of the best! And—and—we'll see to
your folks for you, those of us left behind.'

Lup nodded something that could scarcely, even
with the best intentions, have been termed gratitude.
The other lighted a cigarette nervously. The luggage
was in, the guard looking round for the last time.
Suddenly Brack jumped to the footboard.

'When do you sail?'

'Thirtieth March.'

'Liverpool till then?'

'Ay. Take time! We're moving.'

'What address?'

'Nay, what it's no—get out, man! We're off!'

'*The address?*'

'Five, Derby Rd.'

Angry hands tore Brack from the express, and more
or less hurled him off the station and into his car, but
for once he was too distracted to resent interference
with his personal dignity. He did not hear Denny's
polite inquiry after the pigs. He even drove away
with his hat on the exact middle of his head, and a
dead cigarette hanging limply from his mouth.

.   .   .   .   .

The sale was over. The Whinnerahs had seen their
possessions catalogued and scattered, saving only a
remnant for the furnishing of the little Pride. Wolf had
gone the round of the house, handling each piece for
the last time as if it had been a pet beast, but his
wife had made no sign, refusing to quiver at the blow
of the hammer. When the end came, it was she,
lately so shrinking and afraid, who led the man out
into the waste.

The closing door echoed its drear Amen through
the deserted building. The empty house followed them
with its desolate, hollow eyes—the bent man clinging
to the frail woman in her old-fashioned mantle and
neat bonnet, the dispirited dogs slinking at their heels.

He would have turned again for a last wander through the shippons had she not held him with her thin fingers. To the left, as they walked, the heaving grey of the sea reached out into the still grey of the sky. The Lugg itself looked grey, and ruggedly old. Below it the tide was running strongly, lipping far up the Let and filling the estuaries. It seemed a forty years' travel in the wilderness, this sad progress out of life, but at last, a few hundred yards beyond where the road ceased and became a track, their new home waited their slow approach.

Mrs. Dockeray and Francey were there to welcome them, and had brought a cheerful homeliness into the isolated cottage, setting a kettle singing in the kitchen, and a bowl of Ladyford snowdrops on the wooden table. The old couple's chairs were in their usual places at the hearth. Wolf's patchwork cushion was ready to his shoulders, and the last week's *Gazette* put to his hand. On the wall, Mrs. Whinnerah's proud 'Peter' hung in all his glory of burnished copper, and a set of cherished willow-pattern stood at attention in the little pot-rail. A thick cloth hearthrug promised comfort to the dogs. On the miniature oak-floored landing the Ninekyrkes 'grandfather,' an ancient Whinnerah name on its brass face, swung a deep, almost human note down the shallow stairs.

The mantelpiece held a tobacco-jar and a tin or two, and, cheek by jowl with a Sheffield candlestick, was a photograph of Lup, looking very black and white and square and fierce and awkward and dull. In the waiting moments before they caught the slow footsteps, Francey looked long at this travesty of the original, and knew that, just as the cold negative had ignored his living, breathing humanity, so her own cold, critical sense had robbed him of sympathy and glamour. They should have no eyes to see, she thought bitterly, who have not also wide, tolerant hearts to feel, brewing their own transmuting elixir of love. Yet she had thought to taste it, once, had stooped her head to it to drink, before Wolf, at that fatal supper, had coarsened it on her lips.

She heard her mother in the passage, sweeping in the outcasts on a breeze of cheer that made even the dogs lift depressed ears, but she herself stayed rather nervously on the hearth, stirring the brisk fire into a mighty 'low,' and filling the pot as soon as the wayfarers were snug in their seats. Over the cups a little consolation crept up and took hold, and now and then there was actually weak laughter in the lonely little house. The afternoon died, and presently, when Wolf began to nod in his chair, when the dogs had finished exploring and settled on the rug with great, sleepy sighs of satisfaction, the comforters took their leave.

There were other visitors, though, even then; Michael, looking in for a short chat, and Denny flying over with a few pounds of apples and a present of twist; even their late cowman, 'just to see if they were settling-like'; but when the last figure had passed the window and melted into the dusk, the vast loneliness came down upon the Pride, swallowing it as before.

The soothing sounds within—Wolf's quiet breathing, the soft snoring of the dogs, the crackle of the fire, the patient speech of the clock—seemed to intensify the mighty silence without. There was no voice from shippon or dairy to give a sense of warm nearness and surrounding companionship. Facing the still-glimmering window, the wakeful woman gathered no feeling of protection from the well-built walls; seemed, rather, to be out unsheltered in the green emptiness, with the chill night settling heavily down. She could still mark the Lugg, dark against the paler sky, but the tide beyond it had been gone more than an hour; she knew it, though she could not see it. She folded her hands and laid her head against the woollen antimacassar, looking back over the years. The time for looking forward was past. Gradually, the pain of exile drew away. Here, in the very shadow of her great dread, it ceased to hold her, leaving her lapped in peace. There came to her, too, the consciousness of power, of victory almost, in the mere fact of having lived, which gives to old age, however humble, its own peculiar dignity. '*My* life!'—says every soul—'that sum of happenings which is mine and mine alone, that wonderful and dreadful pilgrimage that I have made with Time. Whatever the record, I have lived, finished the course, bound myself to Eternity by the tendrils of experience and growth.'

Her eyes closed slowly as the Lugg faded from view. The fire sank a little; the dogs turned and sighed; the shadows crept in. On the flickering hearth the old man and the old woman slept, dreamless.

CHAPTER XVI

SPURS TO GLORY

SLOWLY, very slowly, the faintly-shifting kaleidoscope of the months adjusted Dandy to her new conditions. The first sense of stagnation, following on the hurry of Halsted, was replaced gradually by a feeling of steady movement and expansion. The days were alive but never feverish. She came to see that rampant activity does not always mean progression, that the stimulant of rush may finally produce stupefaction, and flying feet carry one over all the great truths of life. The country's gift was hers—time to grow.

But the gift came gauntleted, she found. It had its Judgment Book, its Black List, its Penal Code. There were long evenings with nobody at hand to deliver her from herself, long, hopeless days with a heart like a spurless steed, and long, terrible nights when the ghosts of the place woke her to clamour in cold hate at her presence. For Watters would not always own

her. It had its brutal hours, when the very garden
was sinister and the eyes of the house had no soul, and
terror waited at every turn of the stair. She came to
know, too, the penalty of identifying her mood with
that of the weather—the cruel relentlessness of storm,
the utter soullessness of glaring heat, the cynicism of
an edged wind, the inquisition-beat of hail.

Yet for these what exquisite consolation! Exhilara-
tion of frost, peace of still days swung on a soft, low
wind, inspiration of light and shade and mist and
evening sun. She learned, too, to look on the rain as
a dominant personality ruling great issues. At Halsted, after scorching days of tennis, a healing drizzle
soft as down, blotting out the day and whispering
through the night, brought no comment except 'Filthy
weather! Shut it out!'—but here they said of it:
'It's doing rarely—coming down nicely—doing
grand!' thinking in the dark of tarns filling in the
lonely hills, and listening to the drinking earth with
a sense of personal benefit, and almost of personal
achievement. And when the big winds came, so that
the lights quivered and the beds shook and the carpets
flapped like bunting, you did not say, as at Halsted:
'Just the night for "Everybody's Doing it"—what?
Somebody order the closed car!' but you wondered
under which hedge the sheep had gathered, and
whether the tide was over the road at Sandfoot, and
if, by some miracle of endurance, the frail old ash
would live till morning.

Moreover, the country sense of clannish common-
ness in so much took her by degrees, giving her whole
new world into her hand.

'I believe I'm beginning to understand,' she said to
Hamer, one day when the mood of analysis was upon
her. 'I know now why old James was so angry when
we cut down that sycamore, just after we came. Why,
I could hate the whole District Council for pulling
down the ferny old wall at Abbey Corner, just because

you and I ran round it into the Chairman! Everything seems to get up close to you in the country and make a personal matter of itself without being asked. Haven't you noticed how people say, "Oh, the harvest is all in, with *us!*" or, "*We* did splendidly in roots!" even if they own nothing but an ivy-strangled cottage with a lean-to hen-pen and a border of nasturtiums? It grows on you, somehow. Everybody does it. Why, only last week, when those horrid cousins of mother's motored through and did nothing but grumble about the Westmorland butter, I found myself saying: "It can't have been local. *Ours* has been winning all over the place!" just as if I'd been raising prize pats on my own account, instead of Harriet and Mrs. Wilson!'

'It's great!' Hamer answered irrelevantly but comprehensively, as he had answered, months before. He had a fat book or two in his arm.

'Doing anything this evening, Dandy Anne? I'm going over to Wild Duck with these, and I thought of bringing Knewstubb back with me.'

'*Need* we have him to dinner again to-night?' Dandy sighed. 'No. The V.A.D. was yesterday, and the S.P. something-or-other's to-morrow. I'm sure I know every hair on that wretched Lapwing, by now! And two of the maids have threatened to give notice if he goes on calling them "Skirts." Harriet says it's his generic term for all women-servants, just as he calls all the men "Whiskers," but it isn't very polite. I wish you'd give him a hint, Daddy dear.'

Hamer looked troubled.

'Of course I don't want to pester you with him, little girl, but I can't help worrying and wanting to lever him out of his rut. A man with my luck ought to be handing it round if he can. Knewstubb isn't bad all through. He's only—careless. He's begun to take an interest in one or two things going, lately.

And, anyway, my whisky's better than the "White Lion's".'

'How you are scooping in the shekels up aloft, Daddy dear! If you're not careful, you'll break the bank. Why, yes, Stubbs is quite a different creature already, and you've started others stretching a hand to him, too. They made him a platform ornament at the last Conservative meeting, and several good souls are trying to push him into positions of trust. It won't be your fault if you don't waft him into heaven among you!'

Hamer looked more troubled than ever.

'You're not sneering at me, are you, Dandy Anne?'

'Oh, DARLING!' Dandy took the fat books from him and put herself in their place. 'Now may the Bald-Head Bears come out of Crag Yeat Wood and gobble me up! As if I didn't just worship you and your trams, and mean to ride into glory at the tail of one of them! Ask the Stubbs, by all means, and I will get him to teach me the Farmers' Shuffle for the fifteenth time, while you have your after-dinner nap. And you might ask the Forgotten Parson and the Lonely Lady with the Policeman's Rattle. Let's have a real Tram-Party while we're about it. There's the Grammar-School Master, too, who blew himself up, last week. I met him, this morning, wandering about in bandages and a splint. He hasn't a spare hand, so you'll have to feed him. Shall I tell mother dinner for seven? And then let me walk over to Wild Duck with you, and help to carry the books. I want to see Harriet about "Elijah".'

They found the lady farmer round by the shippons, on the point of climbing into the float between the shining milkcans. It was growing dusk as they went up the gravelled path, and already a light showed in the pretty farm-house. Snowdrops were thick in the garden, and a band of yellow crocus edged the foot of the whitewashed porch. Over the dividing wall they could hear Harriet directing the lighting of the sparkling lamps.

'Just taking the milk to the Workhouse,' she informed them, as they appeared through the little gate. 'Martindale is laid up with rheumatics, and there's some complaint I want to settle in person. Stubbs is indoors, if you've brought that dull-looking inkhorn stuff for him. You might keep him stodging at it till I get back. I shan't be long, so don't clear out before I've had a chin with you. Right, horse—get along off!'

She spun out of the yard with the flashing cans, flourishing her whip as she rounded the turn, and swaying easily to the swing of the trap. Hamer looked after her admiringly.

'I like a woman with a straight back!' he observed. 'It means a lot more than you'd think. It's a pleasure to watch that girl move. She's real grit bent on getting there all the time!'

'Ay, she's a devil to meet, but an angel to follow!' Stubbs commented, at his elbow. 'She's got my figure'—the check swelled proudly—'but I'm hanged if she's got my face! Deuced plain, *I* call her. Don't know where she picked it up. And the very dickens for language, though I'm d——d if I know where she gets *that*, either! Come along in, won't you, and have a glass'—— He checked himself hastily—'snow somewhere about, I'll swear!'

Through the deep-seated porch into the narrow passage, where a staring stag's head threatened their own from the pink-washed wall, they came into the snug parlour, and soon Hamer and Stubbs were happy with a fat book between them under the lamp on the round table. The fire chuckled merrily, and the lustre ornaments on the mantelpiece caught the dancing light and flashed it on to the brass candlesticks and a gilt beer-barrel of a clock. Above the clock was a black paper silhouette of Harriet's grandfather, *the* John Knewstubb, Prop of the County. It was a man's room, from the business-like bureau to the prints and the books—county, agricultural, sporting and veterinary—the leather leggings flung at the side of the hearth, and the silver-bound carriage-whip in the corner. Yet it was here that Harriet spent most of her scanty indoor hours, and the room was as much hers as her father's. There was no sign of feminine occupation, not a single softening touch, but for all that it was cosy and cheerful with the homeliness that clings imperishably to the farm-house, the fundamental, abiding home of all. It had the real farm-house smell, too—Dandy was beginning to recognise it, and was proud of the fact—the smell that registered it as the Holy of Holies of many a past generation.

A kitten was flung, white-pawed and drowsy, on the red window-seat, and, drawing it to her knee, she looked through the narrow panes into the gathering shadows. Hamer glanced up from the printed page and across to her dreaming face, and a look of whimsical distress came into his own. He had lost his girl, he knew that; had known it ever since the night she had danced with the fairies through a Gate of Vision.

The minutes slid by, bringing no roll of returning wheels, but presently, across the men's talk and the song of the furry sleepiness in her lap, Dandy caught the sound of voices on the path—Helwise's first, penetrating as escaping steam, and then Lancaster's, deep and abrupt, followed by the framing of their figures in the arc flung on the night. Helwise plunged in at the porch, still babbling, but Lanty stayed a moment, arrested, and through the little, old casement he and Hamer's daughter sent glance to meet glance. So had he seen her in the car, he remembered, her charming, wistful head aureoled in light. That picture had remained; this, too, held him. There was to be a third also, kept for an hour as yet mercifully hid from both.

Meanwhile Helwise had streamed into the passage and through the parlour door, and had addressed at least half a paragraph to Harriet before she discovered that she wasn't in the room. Stubbs said 'H—ll of a bore!' under his breath, and 'Milk. Back in a jiff!' above it, and retired into the fat book without more ado. He couldn't stand Helwise at any price. It was Hamer who got up, put her into the rocker and lifted her feet to the fender, loosened her furs and plunged a poker into the red coals. The big man loved waiting on the piece of deceptively-appealing inconsequence, and of course Helwise loved it, too, so they were both happy. Dandy moved her eyes from the window with a start, and stood up politely to offer her a cushion.

Stubbs looked relieved when he saw Lancaster, and drew him down to the table, pointedly turning his back upon his female relative, but she soon wore him into silence. She was upset, it appeared, about the forthcoming oratorio in Bluecaster. The church was small, and it seemed that there would be a squash for the Choral Society. Forms would have to be added to the choir stalls. The Vicar had written Miss Lancaster, as Secretary of the Society, to know whether Elijah and Co. might be accommodated on chairs on the chancel steps, and, if so, whether the chairs should be plain or upholstered. Miss Lancaster was of opinion that the chairs in question ought to be the Vicar's best saddle-bags, and had answered to that effect—a suggestion indignantly vetoed by the Vicar's wife. The Vicar had replied that, according to *his* humble judgment, large and bulgy saddle-bags were in keeping neither with the appointments of a church nor with the original *entourage* of Elijah and his troupe. Helwise had responded with quotations: 'The Lord loveth a cheerful giver,' and 'Whatever, Lord, we lend to Thee, repaid a thousandfold will be,' envisaging the terrible prospect of countless saddle-bags prancing cumbrously up the Vicarage drive. This

Biblical trespassing had been taken in bad part by the other side, and Elijah bade fair to fall between two stools. Lanty having refused to show any interest whatever in the matter, Helwise had flown to Harriet, who, it seemed, was at the Workhouse. Stubbs audibly wished them both at Hong-Kong, and Elijah along with them.

Hamer came soothingly to the rescue. He happened to have some old chairs that were exactly the thing. In fact, he rather believed that they had been church-wood, to begin with. He would be delighted to lend them, and also to send them, if they would be of service. He even borrowed notepaper from the disgusted Stubbs, and sat down to write to the Vicar at Helwise's dictation. Lanty, in the window, stroking White-Paws on Dandy's lap, growled a remonstrance, which she checked. 'Oh, please let him!' she begged under her breath; and, remembering that Wiggie would occupy one of the chairs, he said no more. Stubbs rattled off a string of all the most swear-sounding rotifera he could think of.

To the tune of a spanking trot Harriet dashed into the yard, and strode in, a fine colour in her sallow cheeks, and every fighting bristle raised for war. Hospitality dragged from her a brief recognition of the later arrivals as they rose to greet her, but she paid it no further dues. Stubbs brightened. Evidently there had been a row.

'Worm!' said Harriet, slapping down her hard gauntlets under Helwise's nose. 'Caterpillar! Blood-less, backboneless caterpillar! To dare to talk to *me* about milk—ME! Knewstubb of Wild Duck! Centi-pede — white-livered, backstair crawler — Earwig! CROCODILE!'

The Shaws paled—this was a new and dreadful Harriet—but Stubbs merely hallooed: 'Sick 'em, lass! Good dog—hie on to him!' snapping his fingers with keen enjoyment, and even Helwise seemed unconcerned. As for Lanty, he laughed with evident understanding.

'Thorne, I suppose, is it? I've seen him slinking into the Workhouse once or twice lately as I passed. Afraid he thinks no great shakes of me as his fellow Guardian. It isn't often I get time to look in. I fancy he gives them a pretty thin time there, poking about and finding fault.'

'Yes. Ollivant Thorne. "Creeping Jesus" they call him in the village, with his slimy voice and his shifty eyes! What are you all on your hind legs for, by the way? I've a lot to say, so you may as well ease up to it. That's better! It was like this: Lambert sent me a private note to say that Thorne didn't think the milk up to standard, so I went round myself to see about it, and there if you please was the Creeping Jesus, waiting ready to sniff at the milkcan as soon as it stopped at the door. Of course I asked him where the devil he had learned anything about milk with his death's head always stuck in a ledger, and he said he was there to see that the poor were not being fleeced by a flummoxing farmer. I replied that the milk was the best in the county, as anybody but a long-eared sarsaparilla raised on barley-water and lemon wouldn't need telling, and he said that language wasn't allowed in the Sacred Precincts of the Pure Pauper, and that he should parley with the Board, and have the contract taken from me. I told him he could sue me for jumping it on the spot, and tried to come away and the milk with me, but Lambert nearly wept, so of course I turned soft and let him have it. He said awful things about Thorne when the Creeping Jesus had bunked, but, of course, that's unofficial, so you must keep it dark. The creature's had his knife into me ever since I chucked him out for trying some stuff on Stubbs that he called a perfect substitute for whisky. Stubbs was ill for days afterwards—weren't you, Stubbs?—and I had to stick upstairs nursing him and let the farm slide.'

'Thorne?' Hamer pondered. 'I know the man. Excise—insurance—law—what is he? Something parchmenty, anyhow. Had two hours of him, one day, and never guessed what he was after until the last five minutes, when he tried to get some work out of me. Wouldn't trust him as far as I could throw him. County odd-jobber, isn't he, as well?'

Lanty nodded.

'Rural District Council. Attends like his prayers. I share the honour with him. We've been returned unopposed at least twice, and there's nobody coming up against us this time either that I know of. Election in March. Afraid I don't lay myself out much to oblige. The estate carries me, and Thorne has a select band of slummites that he beats up for the occasion.'

'Estate be hanged!' Harriet jeered. 'Lanty's shoving his head in the sand, Mr. Shaw. He doesn't need to canvass, because the district, in its rational moments, happens to know a useful man when it sees one. Thorne always works like a black if he thinks there's a chance of a fight. You'll find him slumming for months beforehand—the carping old milk-sniffer! I've half a mind to stand against him myself.'

The words meant nothing, spoken in a last leaping spasm of annoyance, but after a pause Hamer said 'Why not?' very quietly; and after a second pause—of astonishment this time—Stubbs suddenly said 'Why not?' too. Indeed, he got solemnly to his feet and repeated it, extending a check arm.

'Why not? In the family. Always in the family! Rur'l D'trict C'cillor myself, once upon a time'— so he had been, in forgotten ages—'father Rur'l D'trict C'cillor, too. Chairman, in fact. Chairman myself but for accident. Other important business—you all know! Father great man, very highly respected. Chairman. In the family. Always in the family!'

Harriet said—'Oh, cheese it, Stubbs!' looking embarrassed, but the colour had risen again in her cheeks, and she pulled the gauntlets back and fidgeted with them.

'We all remember John Knowstubb,' Lancaster paid tribute. 'His work for the county will stand for many a long year.' He looked laughingly at Harriet. 'Come on! I'm sure his grand-daughter will find plenty of backers.'

'Bunkum!' Harriet frowned uncomfortably. He was not serious, she knew, but her colour mounted higher. 'You're talking through your hats. Of course I can't do it!'—and again came the query, placidly from Hamer, importantly from Stubbs.

'But isn't she too—young?' Dandy put in, gazing with awe at the proposed candidate. 'Of course, I know they do have ladies sometimes, but not—not like Harriet.' Excitement conquered doubt. 'Oh, Harriet, do, and we'll all help! Dad and I will canvass for you, and Miss Lancaster and Wiggie—Wiggie will love it, and nobody ever refuses him anything'—she pulled up suddenly, biting her lip. 'We shall all be so proud of you, if you get in!'

'Lancelot won't let me canvass,' Helwise lamented. 'Such a good opportunity for collecting subscriptions, too! He says they're side-issues, whatever that may mean. But I'm sure they'd put you in, Harriet, even without me. You know you always get the egg-accounts within a shilling or two.'

And Stubbs said: 'In the family. Always in the family. Rur'l D'trict C'cillor!' with a final wave that abolished one of the lustres, and the diversion gave the visitors their chance to move. Harriet refused the Shaws' invitation both for herself and her father.

'I'm going to write to the Creeping Jesus, and it'll take me all evening. I've remembered lots of things I could have said and didn't, and I'll want Stubbs by me to put in the adjectives. He'll be as happy as a king with that and the microbes. We'll come some other night, if you'll have us. You'd better take a light, hadn't you? It'll be as black as a hearse in the lane.'

She lighted a lantern, and walked with them to the gate. Behind her straight, boyish figure the well-kept house spoke of comfort, honesty and respect. She snapped the latch after them with a firm hand.

'Good-night.   And   good   luck!'   Lanty   called laughingly. 'I shan't mind standing down to John Knewstubb's successor!'

Harriet grunted with annoyance.

'Stow all that piffle! You're as safe as houses, and you know it. It's Thorne I'd be out to rattle; I'd make no difference to *you*. And in any case I'm not doing it. You'll only set Stubbs agitating. I wish you'd chuck it!'

But as she went slowly back up the path, the stray-flung idea settled and took root. It was absurd, of course, and she was much too young, too insignificant, and—only a woman; but after all she was doing a man's job in a man's place, and doing it well. She had earned respect in her own line—there was no doubt about that—and she'd as good a head-piece as most of the old buffers on the Board, thank the powers! It would be a fine old crow over the Creeping Jesus if she bagged his post. Might be a help in business as well, now she came to think of it. She was bred to it, too, as Stubbs had said. A certain knowledge of Poor Law and county management comes the way of most country people, but Harriet, brought up by her grandfather, had breathed it in with her native air. She could still cite many a point of importance which he had made familiar, repeat stories of difficulties triumphantly solved. She loved it, too, all the machinery and the ceremony and the cracking of nuts with Nasmyth hammers. Association and instinct alike made the dull things dear and vivid.

There are few stronger claims in certain families than this obligation of service, passing from one generation to another. On the backs of its often inadequate but willing gentry the agricultural county moves forward, exorbitant with them because it has bred them, exacting more of them with each succeeding year, and only they know what it gives them in return. Titles—silver—illuminated addresses—a squad of police to walk before their coffin—a portrait to hang behind their empty chair—these make their testimony; but the real guerdon is surely immeasurably different and beyond.

Later, in her own room, the deeper reason—the woman's reason—spoke for itself. Dandy had said: 'We shall all be proud of you.' 'All?' Would *he* care if she went in to fight and came out victorious, honour her because honour had come her way? The suggestion had amused him; he had not taken it seriously, but it had roused him to new interest in her, nevertheless. She had thrilled at his homage to her grandfather; *that* had been serious and genuine, without question, and the reflection, if pale, had yet been hers. The possible venture would surely bring her a little nearer! She would share some measure of his work, lay her hand to it beside his, join in the common endeavour. Thorne and the milk insult were forgotten. The woman's reason, the woman's hope, urged her forward. Lighting a candle, she slipped silently down to the sitting-room, and drew out one of her grandfather's books.

CHAPTER XVII

THE GREEN GATES OF VISION—IV. DARK— THE LONELY PLOUGH

In the road, Dandy came to halt, dismayed.

'It's too late, now, for the rest of the Tram-Party, and there's all that food hurrying to meet them! Miss Lancaster, please come and help to eat it.'

'The boy, too,' Hamer added. He often called Lancaster 'the boy,' with a quaint, protective accent. 'We'll catch it from Mother if you don't lend a hand, giving her all that trouble for nothing. Don't you hark to Dandy Anne—the Tram-Party's only her nonsense. She wanted to give one or two down-in-the-mouth folk a bit of a feed, but they'll have to have their particular wire-in another night. You'll come, won't you now? We'll send you back in the car.'

Lancaster hesitated, his business-conscience pricking, but his aunt's declaration that she could not remember whether she had ordered tinned sardines, or tongue, or both, or neither, for their evening meal, did not tend to waken his homing instinct, and he found himself following up the Lane, swinging the lantern over Dandy's path. It was black, as Harriet had prophesied. In the shifting light the hedges looked huge and dense, climbing to where their sombre tops scarred the fainter dark of the starless heaven, and every curve and turn loomed a barrier impenetrable as the Sleeping Beauty's Forest. The dream-traps yawned emptily, with witless mouths and vacant eyes.

'Will Harriet really stand, do you think?' Dandy asked, keeping with difficulty in the middle of the narrow road, so subtly were track and hedge blended by the Northern night. 'It was only a joke, wasn't it?'

'Well, it started as a joke, of course, but I shouldn't

wonder if it didn't end there. It would be an innova-
tion, just here, but there must always be pioneers, and
the lot may have fallen to Harriet. She's young, but
she's a better man than Thorne, not only in position,
but in business and brain. I shouldn't be surprised if
she does have a shot at it. You see, her grandfather's
name still carries weight, and in this county half of us
run our reputations on those of our forebears.'

'That's true enough!' Dandy laughed. 'Why, only
the other day, when we were going over Bluecaster, I
heard you say to the housekeeper: "Tell me who her
mother was, and I'll know what she is!" It all comes
back to the same thing.'

'There's a lot of reason in it, though, don't you
think? You'll hear the very man who breeds prize-
dogs and specialises in orchids insist that all human
beings are equal. He'll sniff at a cross-bred mongrel
and sneer at a dandelion, but he'll tell you straight
that he himself is as good as the bluest blood and the
finest stock, though he may be sprung from a collier's
cot or twenty nameless mixed strains. 'Tisn't common
sense, to my thinking! There is no good or evil done,
fine thoughts put into shape or base ones grown secretly,
but blossoms again somehow in later lives. We've got
to fight our own way, but there's both help and bind-
ing from those gone before.'

'But you—surely you stand alone?'

They were well on towards Watters by now, and
the rhythmic dance of the light had broken over one
of the gaps, catching a sudden reflection from clean
steel. They stopped to look.

It was only a plough, flung on its side in the hedge,
waiting the morrow and renewal of toil. The bright
share told that it had been in use that day, and Lanty
knew that, near it in the dark, the long, clean furrows
curved up over the hill. It seemed a small, inadequate
tool for its great work; simple, too, as are all enduring
things; yet it had the whole of history behind it.

'Yes, I suppose I do,' he said at last. 'We all stand alone, if it comes to that. We drive our furrow single-handed, out of the dark into the dark, though we've got to reckon with the soil that others have left, just as others must reckon with our leavings after us. But it's our job while we're on to it, all the same. It's our job, while the light lasts, to make the best of it we can. It's always one man's hand on the lonely plough.'

For a long moment they stood silent, ringed round by the night, in closer communion than they had ever found themselves. Strange talk still and new was this, but she did not shrink from it, now; and he, opening his heart, did not find it shuttered by an alien hand. Together they looked through the dim Gate, so near that, when he stooped his head to the lantern, he felt her hair against his face.

Calls for help came out of the vast beyond, and they took guiltily to pursuit, to find Helwise and Hamer marooned up a blind alley in the swamping sea of the dark, and, as they set them right again, a new elf-candle appeared from the opposite direction, having Wiggie somewhere in its vicinity. He was just back from an engagement in town, and in the glowing hall at Watters looked shockingly thin and ill, though excellently clothed and brushed, making Lancaster conscious of muddy boots and the general wear and tear of a busy day. He began to have his favourite complaint of feeling old, and when Dandy, after a miracle-change into something softly-pink, danced in to dinner on the singer's arm, the lightly-welded link of the Lane snapped as lightly, leaving her farther than before.

Wiggie had brought her from town an infinite variety of excitements, new books, new music, even new fashions, described after his own manner. There was also an umbrella-thing meant especially for country use—so they had told him in London; indeed, they had been quite feverish about it. You could sit on it when you went shooting or fishing or mushrooming or marketing on Saturday, and it had buttoned pockets for carrying anything from grouse to reels of cotton, and collapsible spokes that could be adjusted to cover any part of a hat, and a purse and a pocket-handkerchief and a plate with the owner's name. He had practised with it in the train, but he had been dreadfully stupid and allowed it to take steck in the door, so that, when the train stopped, none of the ordinary umbrella-people inside could get out, and a very cross inspector on the platform couldn't get in. However, the collapsible spokes had collapsed before they were carried on to Carlisle, and he was quite sure that Dandy would manage them in a few lessons. Dandy was quite certain of it, and could scarcely live through the enormous Tram-Dinner in her anxiety to try. It was a first-class Highways-and-Hedges Dinner; and now that Wiggie had turned up, they were only one or two short, after all.

He was immensely thrilled about Harriet, and full of hope that the 'joke' would prove serious. He hadn't another engagement for—oh, next door to never!—except of course, 'Elijah' in Bluecaster—and would love to run round and help if they would let him stay so long. His joyousness set Dandy shining like a clear light on gems, bringing home to Lancaster how different she was with himself. Probably he seemed old and staid to her, certainly dull and one-sided. Wigmore's was her natural atmosphere. Wiggie could ring every pretty change on her as easily as he rippled the vocal octave, but the elder man had no key to her moods. The sympathy in the Lane had been shallow and fleeting. Not here—not *here* was the making of his 'silly home'!

He said little during the evening, and, in the car, showed scant enthusiasm for his aunt's surprise-

packet from town—a large pot pug, with a chocolate-
box interior and an almanac on his chest. Wiggie
loved people's little weaknesses, and saw no reason
for refusing to pander to them. He did it charmingly
enough, too, but, after all, it wasn't Wiggie who had
to live with the pot dogs.

Helwise was in ecstasies over the luxurious car, and
more than once nearly wrecked them all by switching
on the electric light just as the unhappy chauffeur
rounded a bend. She thought Lancelot might see his
way to giving up his horse and buying a motor.
Bluecaster would help. Look what he had done about
the bath!

Lanty answered unkindly that if ever he did own
a car it would certainly not be at Bluecaster's expense,
and that he preferred the old gee to all the petrol-
puffers in creation; and then felt ashamed when she
sighed and was hurt. No doubt he did sound cross
and discourteous after Wiggie's chocolate-box consideration, just as in all probability he had seemed
countrified and slow beside the singer's wit and
finish. That was the worst of these pandering sym-
pathisers! They showed you up as a very bad second,
though you might really be carrying a big load quite
respectably. Still, he need not have snubbed Helwise
so brutally. It was partly Bluecaster's own fault that
she looked upon him less as an employer than as a
free emporium and family asset. He could see him
buying her the car without a murmur. He had to
admit, too, that the padded elegance of the limousine
fitted her to a nicety, just as the luxury of Watters
seemed her natural setting. There was no doubt you
couldn't expect the best of people out of their
special environment—certainly not weak creatures
like Helwise, formed for others to pity and sustain.

Nevertheless, his philosophy did little to soothe
him on arrival at their own cheerless dwelling. The
fires were all out, of course, and they were met by a

wandering odour of kippered herring not to be located anywhere, certainly not in the burnt slices of chilly ham congealed on the dining-room table. He found a telephone-message from the House ingeniously concealed in the barometer, and could have sworn that there was a fresh scratch on the maltreated wall. He waited while Helwise introduced the new pug to the old collection, and then requested a candle for his empty stick. His nightly tour discovered bolts unshot, gases burning and taps half-turned, not to speak of a general back-premises condition sufficient to set a fastidious taste hunger-striking for weeks. And so upstairs with the rocking candle to his cold bedroom, and had barely shut his door before Helwise called him to unhook her gown. There was only carbolic soap to wash with, and the kitchen fire had long ago left the cylinder in the lurch. Probably the flue wanted cleaning, anyhow. He thought of the bathroom at Watters, with its hot rails and shining taps, and hated himself for even remembering them. They reminded him, however, that there offered to be a sharp frost in the early hours, and he betook himself to an icy attic to see that a certain pipe was properly wrapped. Finally, to a lumpy bed with wandering sheets. Sleep brought oblivion, but no magic. He did not dream, as Dandy, of swung lanterns in a lover's lane.

·   ·   ·   ·   ·

But before that dream-flower blossomed, she asked Hamer whether he really meant to back Harriet's attempt. She was curled on the hearth at his knee, with her mother nodding asleep at one side, and Wiggie's overbright eyes on the other. Hamer took his cigar from his mouth, and pressed her head against him before replying.

'I'll let it lie till morning,' he said thoughtfully, 'and then, if it doesn't seem too much of a forlorn hope, I'll run over and set her going. She won't need overmuch

persuasion! I'm new, of course, but I can do a bit of
talking and getting folks interested. *She's* well enough
known, and there's a good many that think a lot of
her judgment. They'll laugh, at first, but I shouldn't
wonder if she went through, and I don't mind laying
that they'll find her pretty useful. She's not the
ordinary woman. She looks at things like a man, and
she's get-up-and-git enough to run a train. She wants
more outlet, too, and Fate owes her more than a bit
for that halma-board of a father, especially as all the
elections in the kingdom will never get her the one
big thing——'

He stopped abruptly. Wiggie was looking at him.

'Tramming again, old dear?' Dandy put up her
hand to meet his. 'It's rather a dangerous experi-
ment, playing Providence in your wholesale fashion.
And what do *you* know about Harriet's "one big
thing"?'

'I was only talking. Probably I'm right out of it,
but one just wonders. Hadn't you and Mother better
be getting off to bed?'

But when they had taken his advice, and Wigmore
had closed the door behind them, Hamer got up
slowly and knocked his ash into the fire, a sorrowful
expression on his handsome face.

'Some have Paradise and some Elections,' he said,
not looking at Wiggie, collapsed now like a tired child
in his chair. 'And the others—what have the others
got, Cyril, my boy?'

'Dead candles and a tune in the throat!' Wiggie
answered, with closed eyes, and began to croon—

> 'Ma chandelle est morte,
> Je n'ai plus de feu '

Good Hamer sighed.

CHAPTER XVIII

HAMER'S SECOND TRAM

As it happened, Harriet's attempt seized the skirts of Happy Chance exactly at the right moment. Election fever had been rampant during the last six weeks, setting everybody canvassing his neighbour with delirious zeal. First, a county by-election had been rushed through in a glorious fourteen days of crowded life, taking the eye of the whole country by the fact that it was fought upon a pioneer question of national importance. Then the County Council reorganisation came on, loosing all the grinders at each other's throats; and when that had passed, leaving the different divisions to settle down for the next three years, the District and Parish Councils followed. All sorts of unaccountable hatreds and differences were abroad, as well as still stranger enthusiasms for individuals who had not counted a snap of the fingers before. It was amazing how blood bubbled and boiled for or against some harmless person whose existence had hitherto mattered about once in a blue moon. Both men and women made each election a question of personal insult or exaltation, and said so as often and as loudly as possible; while the grinders ran from pillar to post, setting everybody by the ears and talking loudest of all.

Into this whirlpool was flung the announcement of Harriet's candidature as Rural District Councillor for Bluecaster. The district was still seething, but the strain was beginning to tell, and its enthusiasm showed signs of needing a fillip. Harriet gave it this fillip. The older generation was scandalised, the younger amused or contemptuous; while the earnest ladies who sit on Boarding-out and School Committees pronounced it publicly to be horrid presumption, and privately wished that they had thought of doing it themselves. In her own neighbourhood, however, when the first shock was over, she soon began to find supporters. Thorne was disliked by most outside his own peculiar, gullible clan. The story of the milk-fracas soon got round, bringing the farmers solidly to Harriet's defence. Wild Duck milk needed no bush, and though Thorne's slummites had a pleasant habit of shrieking 'Milk O!' after his opponent, they did not succeed in bringing the blush of shame to the Knew-stubb cheek of innocence. Ratepayers of standing signed her nomination, and all went merry as a marriage-bell. And in his thin, deceitful-looking, wedge-shaped boots, Ollivant Thorne shook.

Harriet did not do very much canvassing on her own account. She hadn't the right grinding touch, which is either very bluff and 'Come-along-be-a-good-dog!'-ish, or silkily insidious and appealing. Her request for a vote was apt to sound more like a County Court judgment, so she prudently left the work to her backers. Wiggie said little, but then Wiggie's very presence smoothed the wrinkles out of the atmosphere and demoralised resistance; and Dandy sat behind, ready to hand out fresh suggestions when Hamer came to a halt. As for Stubbs, he had but one argument, the inevitable 'In the family. Always in the family!' but it carried weight; and it seemed as if, in reminding others of the family honour, he was reminded of his own, for he certainly pulled himself together during this fateful time. But still it was Hamer who was the real canvassing success. These local elections are carried largely on the women, and Hamer went down with the women all the way. He turned up each evening at Wild Duck with his reports, triumphant over the certainties, miserable about the failures, and worried to death over the doubtfuls.

Wiggie often came with him, and on the first occasion was so delighted with Harriet's dwelling that he couldn't be made to attend to business. Wild Duck captured him from the start. While Hamer waved a pencil over the lists, he wandered round the room, worshipping the silhouette and the carriage-whip and the beer-barrel, and was positively childish about the clover-leaf into which Grandfather Knewstubb had squeezed the Lord's Prayer. He sank happily into the comfortable rocker pulled close to the glowing bars, cuddling the kitten in his arm, and watched the colours floating in the lustres until Harriet's voice in the background—'Oh, *he's* no good! Let him slack' —brought him to his feet as if a live coal had sprung at him. She looked a trifle ashamed at his earnest apology, and, after a minute or two, muttered a word of excuse and went to fetch him a glass of new milk from the dairy; and when, on the following day, she found him at the gate with a message, she actually condescended to show him round the buildings. He looked regretfully behind him as he turned back into the road.

'I've always known there was a place like this somewhere, he said, 'ever since I was top angel in St. Somebody-Something's choir, but I hardly believed I should ever really find it. It's so beautifully restful, it almost makes me glad to be tired. I love Watters, and it's very patient with me, but after all it only kind of shakes hands, whereas Wild Duck opens its arms and takes you on its knee. You won't sell it, I suppose? You should have what you wanted for it. You're a very honest person, I know. I wouldn't haggle a farthing.'

'It's Bluecaster property,' Harriet explained, 'though I mean to buy it in the long run, if I can get his lordship to let me have it, and if Lanty doesn't want too thieving a price. When my grandfather died, we had to turn out of the old place, and I took Wild Duck on the money he left me, though everybody said I'd have had enough in a year. But I haven't; and I wouldn't go back, not if I was paid! I'm sticking to the farm all right, so I'm afraid you'll have to look elsewhere as long as I'm over sod.'

Wiggie went a little further, looking sadder than ever.

'I'm sorry,' he said. 'I mean—I'm sorry we can't both have it.' And as he vanished under the hedge, the wistful voice finished its speech—

'I believe I could get well here. I'm sorry.'

A surprising touch of concern startled Harriet as she heard him, prompting her to call him back to the rocker and the kitten; but she shook it off with impatient disgust. He suffered from nerves—anybody could see that. He lived too much in stuffy rooms and microbe-ridden railway-carriages, and ate all the poisonous messes they give you in towns. It was doubtful, indeed, whether he got enough to eat at all. His clothes looked prosperous, but he was as thin as a match; you could hardly see him sideways. These artist-people had to make a show, so probably he economised in food. No doubt he smoked excessively to make up for it—that was why he coughed and always looked tired. He was thoroughly under condition altogether, out of training and in a bad way generally. What he wanted was a stiff walk and a run with the bassets and ten miles or so on a push-bike, new milk, good butcher's meat, and one pipe a week—poor, weedy rotter! Harriet drew up her own splendidly-working collection of organisms, and went within to swing dumb-bells.

And all the way home the voice repeated—as if it simply couldn't get away from it: 'I believe I could get well there. I *do* believe I could! I'm very sorry.'

Bluecaster affairs were keeping Lanty very busy just at this time, sending him to London more than once, and otherwise pinning him to his office, so that the electorate saw little of him and his particular friends less. His clerk, a young person of enthusiasms, with a vivid admiration for everything Blue—and Lancastrian—scamped his meal-hours in order to put in a little electioneering on his own, but he generally returned convinced that he had risked his digestion for nothing. The men he interviewed assured him that as long as a Lancaster was putting up he could be certain of their word. Happen they'd vote for Miss Harriet as well—Mr. Shaw (him over at Watters) seemed to think they ought to be having her on, and they weren't saying but she'd her head set straight enough on her shoulders for a lass, and they'd all thought a deal of the old man, and pity there weren't a few more like him—but Mr. Lancaster anyhow could be sure of their cross when the time came— ay, that he could! But he never got as far as the women, and indeed he never worried about them at all. The women always voted for Lanty, because he was young and unmarried. The clerk had a penchant for the study of human nature, and rather fancied he knew all about women—at least, politically. Perhaps he did; but straws may blow different ways in the same wind.

The poll opened on a Monday at twelve, but long before that hour the Watters cars—the limousine, driven by the chauffeur, and Dandy's little Delage cheeping like a scurrying chick behind Hamer in the touring Austin—were running through the ring of villages. They made quite an effective little procession, carrying Stubbs' old racing colours flying from the screens, and wonderful placards devised by Hamer: 'Wild Duck Wins!' 'Vote for the Old Stock!' 'Help for Harriet!' etc. The candidate, rolling down the hill in the float five minutes after noon, with no more ostentation than lay in shining harness in front of her and a well-trimmed Stubbs at her side, frowned a little at the flaunting gaiety before the booth; but objection was impossible in face of Hamer's joyful excitement as he hurried to her with outstretched hand. Thorne's thin, furtive countenance could be seen peering round the doorpost for the children he had stationed at the gate with milkcans labelled 'Watered Wild Duck.' He was puzzled to know why the war-cry arranged for Harriet's arrival had missed fire, but the reason was not far to seek. On the front seat of the limousine sat Grumphy, very black and fat and swathed in ribbon, with a collar of snowdrops round his neck and a red rose nodding over his ear, smiling eternally at the wondering childish faces below.

Inside the booth the polling-clerk greeted the lady farmer with polite amusement tinged with admiration, and the early voters, brought in by the Watters contingent, shook her warmly by the hand. Even Thorne offered her the same pledge of goodwill, and she returned it brusquely.

'I doubt you'll be too much for me, Miss Harriet!' he remarked, with his thin smile. 'You're so popular, and those friends of yours have been working terribly hard. *I've* no cars to fetch folks along to vote for me, so I must just depend on a little kindly feeling and any service I may have done the district in all these years. That may carry me a bit of the way, but I fear it won't go far against motors and ribbons!'

'Thorne's funking you—that's a sure thing!' Hamer observed outside. 'He's thinking he's out of the game from the start. Lancaster's certain to go through—everybody says that—so the Creeping Jesus has a very thin chance, I'm afraid. Now, Kavanagh, off you get to Stone Riggs for those almshouse folk—four of 'em, mind now! Dandy Anne, the Sunflatts district's yours; you know how we mapped it out. I'll run over to Halfrebeck for that old chap I couldn't get a promise from. It might help a bit, Harriet, if you came along, too. It's only about a mile.'

Wiggie, who was wearing her colours in his buttonhole, gave her his seat beside the driver, and hopped

in behind; and, as they slid over the hill, found himself observing the candidate from a fresh mental
standpoint. There was something new about Harriet
to-day that wasn't to be accounted for by the dark-
grey tailor-made and trim *suède* hat. The impression
of strength, almost of rough power, already familiar,
was now fused with a more courteous dignity and a
nervous self-possession very different from her usual
sledge-hammer assurance. Memory had leaped upon
her from under a snapped lock, showing her similar
crises in her grandfather's career. Just so had he said
this, done the other, looked and thought—one of the
fine men a county never quite forgets. It was pretty
fair cheek, perhaps, to think she was fit to follow him.
It would be a rotten turn-out if she made a mess of
it. For all our vaunted superiority, what trembling
children we are, in the first moment of feeling for our
fathers' shoes!

Lanty had arrived by the time they came back, with
the wobbler triumphantly installed in the tonneau,
and shortly afterwards Bluecaster motored down.
Voters were coming in quickly now, and a cheerful
crowd was collecting round the booth, Helwise's voice
being easily distinguishable above the rest, as she
informed his lordship that he must certainly call and
see the perfectly sweet 'porcelain on legs,' and there
was also just one other little matter of a washhouse
boiler. She had worked him up to offering her an
entire kitchen range when the Watters limousine
groaned round the corner, with four inside, a few
more in front, and Grumphy fatly ensconced within
the luggage-rail; and under cover of its entry he
escaped.

The day wore on, but still the untiring cars ran in
and out, and smiling ladies were dug from dark
corners in strange garments that seldom saw the sun.
After six o'clock the rush quickened again until clos-
ing-time at eight. and then, under the fallen curtain

of night, began the weary wait during the count. The crowd that had ebbed and flowed all day now drifted back, and where the motor-lamps flung their rays, familiar faces stood out whitely. The door of the booth had shut with a final click as the last strokes from the church clock died, and the mean face of the Creeping Jesus had peered out for the last time. The black figures hung patiently round the railings, while the slow half-hours spoke over their heads. In the grouped cars the weary canvassers turned anxious eyes to the one bright window of the dark building. Grumphy alone slumbered soundly, with a fat head laid on the knee of the yawning chauffeur. It was very chill and dismal, and the lights ringing the square seemed lost in separate hollows of gloom. Dandy was sitting in the Austin with Helwise and Wiggie, exchanging conversation with the doctor and his wife, who had given them tea; and the passage of the fateful minutes filled her with vague depression. Close to the Austin's lamps her father was standing with Bluecaster and Lanty's clerk, Stubbs leaning against the door, and it struck her that they all looked worried. The clerk was talking rapidly in a low voice, hammering in his statements fist on palm, while Bluecaster nodded assent from time to time. The shrieking children playing on the outskirts of the crowd quietened suddenly, and the clerk's words came up sharply over the car.

'It doesn't do to take a thing for granted with the women! There's never any getting at what they understand and what they don't. You can explain till you're black in the face, and then have to start at the beginning and say it all over again. Why, at the Parish Council Elections, I've known them stick their mark against every man-jack on the card, though the whole boiling had been at them telling them they could only vote for nine! They do other daft things, too—put the cross half-way between a couple of names, or plump for the very man they don't want,

thinking it'll out him, and then swear afterwards
that you told 'em to do it! I don't know what sort
you breed in Lancashire, Mr. Shaw, but some of our
lot up here want a lot of looking after. A deal of them
don't bother much about politics in between election-
times, and I'm not saying they're any the worse for
that; but it makes it a bit stiff working with them
when it comes to the vote. You've got to be dead sure
that they know what you want of them, and then you
have to go back and see that they haven't got it upside
down in the meantime! I may be wrong, sir, and
nobody's wishing it harder than myself, but I'm very
much afraid that you've gone and done it, this time,
without meaning to. It'll be a bad day for Bluecaster,
if you have!'

Dandy looked questioningly at Wiggie as their
acquaintances melted into the dark.

'Is there anything wrong? They seem put out,
over there.'

He shook his head.

'I haven't an idea. I saw Harriet about half an
hour before the poll closed—all three of them have
scarcely stirred out of the place since six o'clock—and
I thought she looked tired and rather white, but it has
been a big ordeal for her, and she's—well—different
to-day, anyhow. It just entered my head to wonder
whether things were going right. Thorne was somewhere in the background, looking rather pleased with
himself. They said Harriet's votes were coming in
like smoke, this afternoon, but of course the luck may
have turned since then.'

'Oh, I do hope she won't be out!' Helwise lamented.
'It will send Stubbs simply running to the White Lion,
and her grandfather will be so disappointed up in
Heaven, or wherever it is Rural District Councillors
go when they're finished with. Lanty was saying only
yesterday that Lancaster and Knewstubb had represented Bluecaster for many a long year, so it would be

quite like old times to have the two names going to
the Board together. I'm sure he will be disappointed
if he has to be coupled with Thorne again. Lanty
always gets in, of course. You see, he's so frightfully
well known. He always gets in.'

Inside the room the last vote fluttered down, the
last figure cut the air, and, at long last, Harriet, white
to the lips, looked up and across at Lancaster. He
smiled as he met her eyes, a smile of franker, kinder
comradeship than he had ever given her, putting out
his hand to her as she passed, and she felt the hot
tears fill and burn her throat. Thorne smiled also,
his own thin, furtive smile. The polling-clerk looked
with some curiosity at all three, as, paper in hand, he
turned to the door.

Outside, there was a sharp murmur as the square of
light broke the dark mass of the house, framing the
figure in whose hands lay the will of the people.
Dandy saw the keen face of the Bluecaster clerk
thrust forward like that of a leashed hound, and afterwards her father's, braced as if for shock; and then the
far-away voice from the door came thinly over the
heads of the silent crowd—

Harriet Knewstubb   104
Ollivant Thorne   99
Lancelot Lancaster   95

Through the roar that followed she heard Helwise
burst suddenly into tears, and saw the clerk spin round
on Hamer with a fierce nod and exclamation, his face
flushed violently as if he had been struck. She turned
blindly to the comforting of Helwise, surprised to find
her hands trembling and her own eyes full of tears.
Wigmore slid from the car, and joined the little band
of men as Lancaster came up. He met them with a
cheerful shrug, and they stood in silence while
Harriet, head of the poll, spoke her thanks to her
supporters. It was strange to hear her steady, strong
English, devoid of slang adornments—old inhabitants

thought of Grand Old John as they listened—stranger
still to hear her voice quiver as she added her regret
at Mr. Lancaster's defeat. More than one of her
friends wondered secretly if they were meeting the
real Harriet for the first time. Only Stubbs, shining
with happiness, muttered: 'In the family. Always in
the family!' with an uplifting pride worth all the
temperance sermons in the world.

When the cheer had died, Thorne said his few,
plausible, little sentences. His cheer was isolated to
a deliberate section, but he seemed quite satisfied with
it. He had expressed his pleasure that the lady was
to be his partner on the Board, and now he turned to
her, offering a furtive paw with something like real
admiration in his shifty eyes.

'It's to be you and me, after all, Miss Harriet!' he
said kindly. 'I'm not sorry I interfered in that milk
business, if it's ended in bringing you to this!'

And John Knewstubb's grand-daughter, whose fine
diction had so recently filled delighted ears, remarked:
'Go to the devil, you Creeping Jesus!' and strode off
into the crowd.

Hamer Shaw laid a hand on Lancaster's shoulder.
'See here, my boy!' he began, looking old and
troubled in the sharp light. 'Your lad here says it's
my fault they've outed you. He says I was so taken
up asking the women to vote for Harriet I forgot to
remind 'em to vote for you, too. He asked at least
ten as they came out, and they all said they'd plumped
for Harriet and that I'd told 'em to! Of course, I
didn't do anything of the sort, but it's true enough I
never thought of bothering them about *you*. Everybody said you were safe, that the usual crowd always
voted for you. Anything else never entered my head.
Your lad says I was so busy running Harriet I made
them think they could only vote for one candidate.
He says those ten female plumpers could have put
you at the head of the poll. If that's so, I deserve to

be shot—drowned—anything—as the most interfering old ass in England!'

Lancaster laughed as cheerfully as he knew how. Hamer he might deceive, but there were too many natives round him who knew exactly what he must be feeling.

'Oh, Garnett's talking through his hat!' he said lightly. 'They put me out because they were tired of me and wanted a change; it had nothing to do with you. Let's get home. It's been a long day. Harriet came out fine, didn't she? Nothing like the old stuff! Really, my dear Mr. Shaw, there's no need to worry.'

'But the female plumpers!' the clerk put in eagerly, still writhing and bitter.

'Oh, stop it, Garnett!' Lanty frowned, then softened. The boy's partisanship was sweet, after all. 'I'm sorry, Jimmy. It's hard lines on you, after the way you slaved for me in your off-time, but it can't be helped. As for the women, half of them have forgotten what they did by the time they get outside the door.'

The young man opened his lips again, but shut them at once with an effort. Only, as he turned and groped for a bicycle leaning somewhere against a tree, Dandy heard him reviling the female plumpers with bitter if bated breath, ending with his original statement: 'It never does to take things for granted with a woman!'

She also heard Stubbs inquiring for Harriet, and when it appeared that that undutiful daughter had driven off without him, the stranded parent was stuffed into the Austin. Bluecaster had taken charge of the still-sobbing Helwise, murmuring incoherent consolation in the shape of boilers, and persuaded Lanty to come with him as well, leaving Armer, whose groans could be heard all over the square, to follow with the trap. But first the ex-councillor went back for a final word with the ex-canvasser.

'It's really all right!' he said, feeling as sorry for Hamer as for himself. 'I've far too much on my hands, anyhow, and this will ease me a bit. Don't you think any more of Garnett's nonsense. These young 'uns are always too clever by half. He's wrong, I tell you—dead wrong!'

But he knew, and Hamer, looking down at him, knew that the 'young 'un' had been perfectly right.

At Watters, the poor man tried to eat his wife's carefully-thought-out supper and could not; and Dandy played an intricate game with a chicken-wing that was always on its way to her mouth and never got there, while Wiggie ate nothing either in his efforts to keep Mrs. Shaw from observing the others. They drifted to a warm hearth and were presently comforted a little, but Hamer was still very low when he took his girl in his arms for her good-night kiss.

'This is the Last Tram, little one!' he said sadly. 'I've made a fine mess of it, and I'll never forgive myself. There'll be no more tramming for Hamer Shaw!'

.   .   .   .   .   .

Soon after eleven o'clock, Harriet, standing at her window in the dark, caught the shuffling of feet in the road, and directly afterwards a lusty cheer startled the sleeping peace of Wild Duck. She knew at once what it meant. So, in her grandfather's time, had his supporters come to seal his victory. She remembered to this day the thrill of pride with which, as a child, she had listened to the demonstration, creeping from her bed to peep at the massed enthusiasts without. Lighting the lamp, she called to Stubbs and threw up the window, to meet a second cheer as she came into sight. Standing there, with her father's hand on her shoulder, she thanked them briefly and told them to get off home, with just the same rough humour that Grand Old John had used with such effect; and after a final tribute they withdrew. She went to bed with the warmth and the pride of it glowing at her heart.

.   .   .   .

But in the night she woke and saw the thing that she had done in all its naked, irrevocable folly, saw how her stratagem had twisted in her hand, to the undoing of the man she loved. Power and adulation were sweet, but real love will have first place even in a Knewstubb heart. She had meant to-day to draw them together—deep down she knew that she had had no other hope but that—and instead it had set them leagues asunder, probably for ever. She had put herself in the very place where he could not love her—his own place. She had cut her throat with her own so subtle weapon, the clever lady of Wild Duck Hall. She hid her face in her hands and wept.

CHAPTER XIX

UNDER THE JUNIPER TREE

HAMER's chairs in the chancel looked very select and correct. There were four of them on the stone steps, their fine austerity fittingly framed by the rough arch. The Vicar gazed at them lovingly, and from them over the fast-filling building. Carriages and cars were lining up busily at the lych-gate, dropping an audience drawn from every side of the district. Things looked promising for the Missions over the Seas; even for the K.O.s.

The Bluecaster Choral Society, numbering over sixty, was packed tightly into the choir-stalls, with a surplus of men on forms. Late comers were greeted with despairing shakes of the head, and stood about in the aisle, looking lost, but in a minute or two they had always miraculously disappeared, stowed away somewhere in the serried ranks. The chancel had been partially decorated in honour of the occasion,

and through the fronds of palm and fern could be
traced exotic blooms of mystifying shape and colour,
appearing presently as ladies' hats. There was a good
deal of whispered conversation in progress—the sort
that misses your neighbour's ear but can be heard
well across the aisle—and a fluttering of leaves like
a fretted wind up an autumn glade. Hymn-books
and direction-papers were being handed about, and
anxious-looking tenors stood up and signalled to
worried-looking basses. The male portion of a choir
is always economical of concentration. No matter
how its part in the programme has been explained,
it will generally wait to wonder about things until the
stick is well up on the opening beat.

A twin fluttering was going on in the congregational
forest, and feathers and fur bent towards each other
in the throes of lowered comment. So Nancy Leyburne *was* going to be the soprano—the Widow—after
all! A little pointed, surely—curious, anyhow—so
soon after her broken engagement! And really it was
a shocking pity that Graham-Langwathby insisted
upon considering himself a tenor, when it was perfectly plain to anybody—anybody *musical*—that he
was simply a pushed-up baritone. They might have
been sure he would be the Obadiah. You met him at
every old thing—like other people's clothes.

'The Angel—oh, my dear, *do* remember you're in
church!—the Angel, "Fidge" Morseby! Let me see
—was it *last* night I saw her on the luggage-carrier of
Captain Gaythorne's motor-cycle? And at the Gay-
thornes' theatricals—well, perhaps I *had* better wait
till we get home!'

'Who's the Elijah?—something Wigmore—C. or
G.? Oh, I believe he's a friend of the new Watters
people. I seem to have heard of him—the only one
of their old set that they weren't able to choke off.
Colossal cheek to tackle a big thing like "Elijah," but
perhaps he thinks it doesn't matter here. It's really

very distressing how little outsiders realise our
extremely high standard of culture!'

Hamer and his wife were in a convenient position
for admiring both their own chairs and their daughter's head through the palms. Helwise was at the
extreme end of a stall under the reading-desk, just
where her wandering soprano would sail straight into
Wiggie's sensitive ear. There was a pretty colour in
her delicate cheeks. She had just been having words
with the Vicar about the necessity of providing his
best silk drawing-room cushions for the unyielding
oak seats of Hamer's property. Harriet was in the
altos. If you are not quite sure whether you possess
a voice or not, they always shove you into the altos,
or else into that last refuge of the destitute—the
second trebles.

Bluecaster was talking to Lanty in the porch when
a long grey car, covered with mud, slid up to the gate,
setting down a young man, thin and eager-looking,
and an older one, broad-shouldered and dark, with
sad eyes. They were evidently strangers, from the way
they looked about them, and in the porch the thin
man appealed for information.

'I understand there is to be a performance of the
"Elijah," this afternoon. Shall we find seats, do you
think? We've come some distance to hear a friend
sing.'

Bluecaster took them in tow and persuaded the
verger to put them in the Vicar's pew in front, the
Vicar's wife being securely jammed in the chancel
sardine-box. The strangers looked tired, as if they
had come far, and they talked to each other in little,
snapped-off, troubled sentences. Once, the hatchet-
faced man rose as if set on an errand, but the big man
dragged him down again. His voice was low, but
singularly penetrating, on account of its curious
inflections.

'It's no good. You can't make a fuss, with this

crowd. He would never forgive us. Sit still, man,
and trust to Heaven. You'll have the congregation
thinking we're the bailiffs!'

In the vestry, the Bluecaster schoolmaster, an
excitable little man with a beat like an aeroplane
propeller, was giving the last instructions to his
soloists. The Obadiah was making quite sure of his
moustache in the clerical looking-glass, while the
Angel, in the very latest of earthly fashions, followed
Wiggie round the room, declaiming: 'Elijah! Get thee
hence, Elijah!' with playful fervour. The Widow
looked out of the window, rather sad and pale, and to
her Wiggie drifted by degrees. She was young and
evidently very nervous, and because she had blue eyes
rather like Dandy's, he wanted to speak to her; so he
opened his neat, leather-bound copy, asking how she
meant to take a certain phrase.

As he closed it again, she caught the name on the
cover, and gave a little cry, putting out her hand.

'It *was!* I knew it was! I heard you——'

Wiggie grabbed the hand and squeezed it, he was
so anxious to stop her. The conductor looked round
hurriedly.

'Thought you were going to cry or have hysterics,
Miss Leyburne! Don't be nervous. You'll feel as
right as rain the minute you hear the first note of your
beautiful voice. (I think everything is ready, now, so
we can go in.) Look at Mr. Wigmore there, as easy
as you like!'

Elijah smiled politely. His hands were icy, and his
heart was beating in great, wavering bumps, but that
had nothing to do with the conductor.

'He's wrong, isn't he?' the Widow whispered—she
had touched his hand—and he nodded.

'It's my belief you don't do anything great if you're
not frightened beforehand. A self-possessed per-
former may get at an audience's admiration, but it
takes the inside-frightened person to get at their

hearts. It's like going into battle—the trembling
Tommy hits hardest when he starts.'

Seated at last under the reading-desk palm, with
the Angel beside him, the sea of faces so near seemed
to rise and engulf him, turning him faint. His heart
still hammered its wavering stroke, like a bad work-
man. It was a blessing Gardner could not hear it—
Gardner in London; though it was almost a wonder,
it thumped so loudly.

And then he saw Gardner, with his hatchet-face
over the pew-front as if he meant to leap it—Gardner
and the other dear old watchdog!—and the sickening
nervousness changed to a freakish joy, a mischievous
delight. Edgar looked upset; he had forgotten poor
old Edgar. There were the children, too—but it didn't
do to think of them. Edgar would understand. He
would have done the same himself. He sent a brilliant
smile to the men in the front pew, a smile so gaily
defiant that Lancaster, far behind, wondered. The
organist played the first of the four big chords, but he
was too busy smiling to heed, until the Angel nudged
him, alarmed. But, once up, he forgot the watchdogs,
forgot the palm tickling his ear, forgot even the children of whom he would not think. He was Elijah,
flinging out his mighty message to a cowering people.

During his long wait following, he did not look at
the audience again. They did not matter any more.
The big thing that was happening was not on their
side of the building. Most of the time he sat with his
eyes on the well-known notes, but when he turned
ever so little to the right, he could see Dandy singing
with every inch of her, her rapt gaze fixed on the
whirling beat. How the Dandy Shaw of Halsted
would have scoffed, not unkindly, but with sincere
amusement, at such rustic enthusiasm! He saw an
admiring young joiner offer her a paper bag when the
close air caught her throat during Obadiah's pushed-
up solo, and watched her abstract the offering without

a qualm. Absurd details like these were little wind-arrows, pointing the trackless way along which she was drifting, further and further from him.

All the delinquencies and hiatuses of the plucky little chorus smote his trained ear in a succession of torturing shocks. He knew when the Infant Basses asked for bread exactly half a bar too late, and heard Helwise cast her burden upon the Lord at a moment when she had no business to be singing at all. Through all the shades of alto he could detect a queer grumbling like that of a home-sick cow, and traced it correctly to Harriet. Yet you could not have told from his face that the Second Tenor Angel had dashed his foot against several stones in the way of accidentals, though the conductor moaned and wept, and knocked a mauve hat eastwards in one of his volplaning move-ments. The professional knew so much better than anybody else just what was the real standard of the big work, and the long rehearsal on the night before had set him marvelling at the perseverance which had brought it into presentable form. He had been told the miles the choir came through wild weather, opening his eyes at the record of attendance; and when he had grasped their deeds achieved, in face of the average of knowledge among them, he saw each member a Hercules striving to seventy times seven, and the little aeroplaning schoolmaster a hero storming Valhalla.

The Widow trembled to her feet, and Wiggie guessed that there were real tears behind the first words of pleading for the sick child. He got up presently, long before his time, and stood beside her to give her courage; and when he broke at last into the thrice-repeated, conquering prayer, with eyes fixed on a far window, unheeding the woman's inter-jected lament, it seemed to the girl, bitterly conscious of her personal trouble, that it was her own spirit, her own future, that he gave back alive again into her hands.

But, curiously enough, it was not the praying but the fighting Elijah that Wiggie loved best. The pale, diffident young man saw himself as the fierce, tanned herald of woe, and made others see him as such, too. It was glorious to curse kings, run before chariots and slay false prophets by the hundred! He felt the inspired words hot on his lips, the racing blood in his veins, the warm dust spurned by his swift feet. In the great 'hammer' solo he worked to such a pitch of intensity, beating out the last iron strokes of the *più lento* so strongly that the audience almost winced beneath his power, and the hatchet-faced man shook like a whippet on leash, uttering sharp little sounds remarkably like oaths. But after that—after the Reproach to Ahab—Elijah sank back into Wigmore, quivering under the virulent words of the venomous Queen as if they had been live blades. The Queen was a strenuous member of the Society, with a bludgeon air that reminded him of Harriet, and he shrank before her condemnation as he had shrunk many a time under Harriet's scorn. The tired protest under the juniper tree, in face of the fresh task—'Oh, Lord, I have laboured in vain! Yea, I have spent my strength, have spent my strength for naught. O that I now might die!' brought the tears chasing down Hamer's cheeks, but it was Wiggie, not Elijah, who brought them there, though he did not know it. It was Wiggie's own cry from a desolate heart and an almost finished body, looking into a future void of the one hope that had kept him alive for long—the terrible cry of the human, seeing the strength of the flesh break, taking the strength of the soul with it. He was in the wilderness, and no God could set his feet for Horeb.

But the pitiful personal note was felt, if not recognised, bringing the Angel to 'O Rest in the Lord' with a style very different from her famous 'Sing me to Sleep' imitation, and aweing the basses to an unwonted mellowness of mumbling in the tender balm of 'He that shall Endure to the End.' And at the close of it, the quiet figure on Hamer's chair lifted his eyes and smiled the same whimsical smile at the strangers in the front pew. The man with the sad eyes smiled also. The leashed whippet sank back and was still.

It was over at last, the last brave spurt of confidence and hope, the swirl of the final choruses, followed by the stillness of a prayer; and then the organ burst out again, the doors flew open, the sardine-box unpacked itself and stretched. A hum of wonder was running through the congregation. *Who* was the collapsed young man with the perfect voice at least six sizes too big for him? Quite extraordinarily good, and with a great look of—something like 'Quagga'—the man who was commanded to Windsor last month—but of course they all knew that he was nothing more exciting than the Shaws' last, unthrottled-off pal.

Wiggie saw the watchdogs spring up and leave the pew, to be checked at their first step by the Vicar's wife, strongly suspicious that they had been sitting on her best Prayer-book; and as the stream from the chancel joined the human sea below, he seized the opportunity to escape from the adoring conductor, and steer his swimming head towards the vestry door. Here the Vicar had his word, but at last he was out on the step and in the air; and there he found Harriet.

'Saw you bolt for the vestry,' she began, 'so I came round outside, as I wanted to speak to you. I say, you *did* do us all proud! Hefty sort of song, that hammer-yell—what? You must be stronger than you look, to put all that weft into it. By the way, there's a couple of outsiders waiting at the lych-gate, asking for you. I suppose they didn't see you bunk for the short cut. Look here! Will you play hockey for me to-morrow?'

He gazed at her with the patient surprise of one, half-crossed to the other world, surveying the caper-ings of those still firmly anchored to this. At that

I

moment he could not have run from one tombstone
to the next, and a hockey ball, bounding down the
path, would have taken to itself a dozen nebulous
brethren under his reeling sight. Except in the case
of her own employees, who were rigidly well looked
after, Harriet, with her superb health, rarely troubled
about other people's, unless they were yellow with
jaundice or pink with scarlet fever. And she had
already decided what was the right treatment for
Wiggie.

'I haven't played for years,' he hedged, 'so I should
be worse than useless. And I'm afraid I've—a—a very
bad headache!' he added apologetically.

'No wonder! The atmosphere in there was enough
to lift the roof clean off its hinges. But your head will
have gone by to-morrow, won't it? As for being out
of training, it doesn't matter; at least, it *does* matter,
but it can't be helped. You can always get in the way
and let the ball hit you. Every little helps. It's
Dandy's fault. She was one of the team, and now
she and her folks are scuttling off to that Motor and
Aero Show to-morrow. Don't say you're going with
them, because you can't. They'll let you stop on by
yourself, won't they? You might help me out of a
hole—especially as it's Dandy's hole. We're up
against a classy team, so I don't want to be short. I
ought to have a girl, of course, but I don't suppose
Witham will mind our playing a man extra, as it's
only you.'

Wiggie pondered, expecting every minute to see
the watchdogs round the corner, and felt again that
frivolous longing for a last snap of the fingers in the
relentless face of Fate. He had been a keen player in
his early twenties, before the Moloch of music clasped
him in its searing arms. There had even been inter-
national visions, at one time. It would be rather fun
to feel the ugly old stick again, jumping and ready
under his hand, to put out a foot in the path of the

whizzing ball and nurse it neatly up the hugged touch-line. Of course, he couldn't possibly last more than five minutes, and Harriet would be extremely angry if he went and died suddenly in front of a clean clearing shot, but he wanted that five minutes very badly. Moreover, for some curious reason, he had never been able to disobey Harriet's mandates. He did things for Dandy because it was as natural as eating and sleeping, not in the least because he felt he had to; but he was always conscious that Harriet was pushing him, and he seldom tried to resist, for, deep down somewhere in his drifting soul, was a queer sense of comfort in being pushed.

'Togs?' he asked weakly, and Harriet's face brightened.

'Oh, Lanty will rig you out! He's got all the necessary kit stowed away somewhere, if Helwise hasn't shifted it to the nearest rummage-sale. I'll tell him you'll send over for it in the morning, if you don't see him yourself. I say—it's jolly decent of you! Hope you don't really mind missing the old 'buses! It makes all the difference to *me*; and the fresh air will do you no end of good—you take my word for it!—that, and a bit of hopping about. D'you suppose those friends of yours are still kicking their heels? Perhaps they're wanting to cocker you about the hammer-yell. Oughtn't you to be scouting round?'

'They're not friends,' Wiggie answered absently—he was trying to remember that neat little twist of the stick point that had been such a favourite of his—'they're police. At least, I mean——' He stammered, catching her surprised eye. 'I say, my head is really rather bad! I think I'll take the path across the fields, and miss everybody. You might shunt the—the friends for me, captain, and whisper a word in Hamer's ear!'

'Right O!' She swerved off with a nod as he opened the little gate and fled across the green to the stile in the opposite wall. There he heard her hail him a second time, just as he was stepping into safety.

'You know where the ground is, I suppose? The big meadow just below Wild Duck. Don't forget. Bully-off at 2.30, *sharp!*'

He stood a moment with a foot on the hollowed stone. The feel of the farm came back to him, and the rocker, and the furry cat. He was glad the ground was just there—wherever it was. If he might not live at Wild Duck, he might at least, when the match was over, go and die in it.

He kept close to the hedge until he was safely out of the danger-zone, like a hare lying low in its form for the wind to bring news of the pack. He began to feel a little better in the cool and the quiet, and the same mischievous excitement crept upon him that had roused at the sight of Gardner's face. He would have a good run for his money, wherever it ended, but he must be careful, or the watchdogs would nab him before he was ready. For all he knew, they might be at Watters when he got there, which would be more than awkward. He must keep out of their way until he had stood long enough in front of a hockey ball to please Harriet, even if he had to tell lies to do it. He wondered whether lies counted when you were finishing with everything, and breaking all the foolish little threads of life, or whether a special concession was made by the Angel of the Judgment, just as, in some fatal illnesses, you may eat anything that you fancy because nothing can possibly harm you ever any more. He laughed a little. It was all quite amusing, and he wondered why he had felt so dismal under the juniper tree. But of course he hadn't remembered then just how that neat little point-twist snatched the ball from under an opponent's nose. He pulled a stick out of the hedge, and began to practise with it, and when he found the old turn still oiled after all these years, he laughed again, and a farm-lad heard him over the fence, and confided to his dog that there was somebody on the loose 'as mun sewerly be a bit wrang in t' garrets!'

At Watters there was no sign of the long grey car, but he reconnoitred carefully before committing himself to the prisoning of four walls. Dandy was a little bit hurt because he had elected to walk home alone, escaping all laudation. She was very excited about the performance, and perfectly convinced that it must have been faultless in every detail, seeing that she herself hadn't sung a single wrong note from beginning to end. But her momentary chagrin vanished at sight of the star's drawn face, and she pushed him into a chair and brought him tea, comforting him with pleasant little words of praise. He received her attentions without protest because he was still thinking about that point-twist, and practised it mentally with the teaspoon.

'You'll have to take a long rest, Cyril, my boy!' Hamer said kindly. 'You must have to raise a deal of steam to keep that rock-breaking business going up to time. It made me feel sore inside, just watching you breathe! It can't be good for you, to my way of thinking. You'll please just keep quiet for a bit, or we'll have you going to pieces altogether.'

'Oh, I'll soon be having a lot of quiet!' Wiggie answered cheerfully, twiddling the spoon. (He wondered whether they would think him silly if he asked to have a hockey-stick buried with him. Working out a new point-twist would put him on nicely until the Judgment.) 'You know, I haven't any more engagements for a long time.' (He hoped they wouldn't collar him at once for the Heavenly Choir. He would like to sit and listen for a bit, and hear somebody else getting up steam, for a change.) 'I'm glad I had "Elijah" as the final bust-up.'

'Why, you talk as though you never meant to sing again!' Dandy exclaimed curiously. 'You *do* look tired, Wiggie dear! I feel anxious about you. Don't you think you'd better stop here quietly, to-morrow, and just lounge about and do nothing, instead of coming up to the Show? I'm sure you're not fit for a hard day, and we'd be back at night, you know, so you wouldn't be alone for long.'

This suggestion was loudly encored by both parents, and Mrs. Shaw offered to stay down with him, but Hamer wouldn't hear of it.

'No, no, mother! We know what you and Cyril are, when you get together. He'd be carrying jam-pots for you, or reading your crochet-patterns and singing you little snooze-tunes when he ought to be resting. He'll be best alone, brutal as it sounds.'

'It will be horrid, leaving you behind!' Dandy added regretfully, and Wiggie felt a little spasm of happy warmth, and then a little twinge of shame because he was going to deceive these kind souls so completely. He grasped the teaspoon a little tighter, and tried not to care. It would be no use trying to make them understand how impossible it was to disobey Harriet.

'I forgot to tell you I heard two men asking for you,' Dandy went on. 'They were sitting in the front pew—perhaps you noticed them? They wanted to know the way to Watters, and just as I was thinking of telling them you belonged to us, Harriet came up and said you'd gone to the station to meet the 4.45. I was so taken aback that I missed my opportunity, and let them escape, and when I tried to get at Harriet, to ask her what she meant, she just nodded and disappeared. I'm afraid she's dreadfully vexed about the hockey match. I hope she'll get somebody all right. *Did* you go to the station, Wiggie, or was I dreaming? I suppose you don't know who the men are? They'll probably come on here, I should think, if they didn't find you.'

'Probably!' Wiggie agreed. 'Oh yes, I think I know

them all right. They want to worry me about something, and I don't think I could stand being bullied to-night. They're terribly difficult people to get rid of, any time. Don't you think we might tell them to call again?'

'In the morning,' she suggested, 'just for a few minutes before you begin your nice, quiet day? How would that do? We're starting before nine, you know, so I'm afraid we shan't be here to protect you, but we'll leave Blenkinship's Marget in charge. She's very brave with all the one-foot-on-the-mat people, and she'll simply stand on her head for a chance of nursing somebody, so I do hope you'll lie on the sofa and let her bring you beaten-up eggs and things.'

'And treacle-posset? I love treacle-posset!' Wiggie murmured happily; then got up quickly, dropping the teaspoon. He had heard a car turn in at the gate. 'May I go and see her about it now?'

But instead of seeing Marget, he slid silently through the old gun-room into the stable-yard, and shinned up the Jacob's Ladder in the loose box to the loft above, and sat on a rusty old turnip-chopper and shivered in the dark until there had been time to rout the enemy's attack. It was Dandy who caught Blenkinship's Marget in the hall, and whispered instructions that set that warlike damsel yearning for battle. She was a little surprised to find two quite pleasant, if rather tired and troubled gentlemen on the doorstep, but her orders were definite. Yes, Mr. Wigmore had been in, and gone out again, leaving word for them to call and see him at eleven o'clock in the morning. Well, could they see the master, Mr. Shaw, or say, Mrs. Shaw, if there was one? They couldn't. The master was up to his ears in letters for the post, and as to whether there was a mistress or not, that was none of *their* business! How *was* Mr. Wigmore? Alive and kicking, if they cared to know, and fit to stick up for himself against anybody, any day. No,

they couldn't come in and wait. They'd lost two
silver candlesticks off the hall-table, that way, already
—but they might leave cards if they had such things—
considered doubtful. However, the cards were forthcoming, and the disappointed callers drew back on
their tracks. Watters had received them odiously
altogether. They had found difficulty in turning into
the drive, to begin with, and, when once safely through,
had nearly run into a wheelbarrow that some idiot
had left in the middle of it. Then they had been
allowed to shiver unregarded on the step, and afterwards treated with contumely. The gate that had
refused to open when they entered, swung heavily on
their tail-lamp as they drove out. Decidedly, this
wasn't their day.

Blenkinship's Marget, studying the cards with
interest, found Wiggie at her shoulder, and handed
them over, though under protest. 'They said as they
were for t' master,' she explained, but Wiggie only
smiled and began to talk about treacle-posset. It
was just as well that Hamer shouldn't see those cards.

Everybody was very kind to him, that evening, and
thought he should not only have a nice, quiet day
following, but a nice, quiet night straight away, so
he was packed off to bed soon after dinner was over.
As he crossed the hall to the foot of the stairs—very
slowly, for he was afraid of the night—Dandy came
out of the smoke-room to meet him. She looked
singularly radiant, he thought, from the depths of his
own chill fear. Beyond, he could hear Hamer at the
telephone.

'You're going up? That's right!' she said with a
relieved air. (People always think things are going
to straighten themselves out when they have persuaded you to do something unpleasant.) She gave
him her hand with a kindly pressure. 'Are you sure
you have everything you want? Isn't there *really*
something more we can give you or do for you?

You've had such a fearfully hard day, and you're so tired! And, look here, you must promise—promise faithfully, or I won't let you go—that if you feel bad in the morning you'll let us know, first thing. I'd never forgive myself if we went off for a day's pleasure, leaving you to be ill all alone.' She wrinkled her brow, looking at him very earnestly. 'I sometimes wonder, Wiggie, whether you tell us all the truth. You never do talk much about yourself, do you? We know who you *are*, of course, and we've been friends for years, but you never tell us your troubles, and though you always say there's nothing the matter with you that matters, I don't think I quite believe it. You look so'—she laughed rather shakily, and put a comforting hand on his arm—'so dreadfully "gone before!" Don't you know how precious you are to us all, Wiggie dear? Let us have a chance of taking care of you if you really need it, won't you?'

With his own hands tightly clasped on the banister, he stood looking down into her eyes, and at her hair, tossed into a mesh of gold by the little watchman's lamp at the foot of the stair, at the pleading mouth and the pearls at her throat, at the whole, terrible, beautiful want in his life that she represented, and an impulse came over him to tell her the truth, and see the mouth quiver, and the tears so near the surface brim over for his sorry plight. He had always taken care of *her*, thought for *her*, lived for *her*, but perhaps she had had help for him, too, all the time. If he broke now, completely and in utter thankfulness, would he find himself, if only for a little, within the comfort of her arms?

The telephone rang off, and instantly, as if snatched by a cord, Dandy dropped her hand and turned, her lips opened to an unspoken question as Hamer came into the hall with a pleased expression on his face. He nodded to her as he advanced.

'Not gone yet, Cyril? Come, now, be a good lad,
and get tucked up! The missis is still set on stopping
behind, but I tell her she'll only fuss you. I've got
Lancaster persuaded to come, Dandy Anne! He
hung fire for some time, talked about work and
umpiring a hockey match, but I made him promise
to cry off and join us. I'm talking of to-morrow,
Cyril. I had an idea at dinner. As you're a bit under
the wind, I've asked Lancaster to come along in your
place.'

Wiggie moved a few steps up the stair.

'Glad you thought of it! And awfully glad he'll go!
He doesn't give himself a day off very often. Hope
you'll have a first-class time, all the lot of you!' He
glanced at Dandy, thrilling with a happy excitement
she could not repress. (No, he had no right there.)
'Sleep well, Dandy Anne, and don't worry your dear
head. I'll be as fit as ever, after my nice, quiet day.'

Inside his silent lavender room with the rosy curtains, he found a well-groomed spink sitting on the
rail of his bed. It cocked its head on one side when
he closed the door behind him, and they surveyed
each other with interest. Harriet had said that birds
in your room meant disaster, and Harriet was always
right. He had thought, for a moment—one crowned,
delirious moment on the stair—that Harriet would
not find him at her hockey match, after all, but Fate
did not mean him to fail her. Lancaster was going to
the Show. Lancaster would have his place in the car.
Very well! Let Lancaster have his Show and his
seat, and his share of Life Everlasting. *He* would have
his five little minutes of the point-twist.

He laughed aloud as he had done in the fields,
scaring the bird from its perch, and after a minute or
two he caught it deftly in his thin fingers. How frail
it felt! he thought, as he opened the window and
tossed it lightly into the night. Would the Almighty
find him just so, he wondered—a piteous, frightened

heart beating the walls of its fragile tenement—when His Fingers closed softly round him for the last, light fling into the Dark?

CHAPTER XX

WIGGIE'S FIVE MINUTES

IT was still scarcely day when he heard the house rouse to action, and dragged his miserable body out of bed for a look at the weather. He had not slept much—most of the night he had been toying with an imaginary hockey-stick in a dull stupor—but every time he had waked to acute consciousness he had been certain that the rain was dripping heavily down the pane. He would have been bitterly disappointed if Harriet's hockey match had been frustrated, and that little ecstasy of five minutes had slipped his reach. But he might have remembered that Harriet always got everything she wanted—almost everything; little things like weather and Rural District Councillorships, anyhow. And certainly it was not raining now, though the brightening earth had a watery look which would be dried presently from its clean, green face, sparkling through its veil of soft, grey air, and clothed around with the dark zone of wood. It was going to be just the right sort of day for hockey, with the ground springy and true, and the air soft but strong, and all the little spring-voices calling to you as you line up, light and free. He wondered what sort of a stick Lanty would be able to find him, and hoped it wouldn't be a Bulger. You wanted something lighter and whippier to bring that point-twist off properly. But of course it *would* be a Bulger. It was just the right sort of steady whacker for a respectable person like a land agent, playing back. He was absolutely certain Lancaster had played back. He always seemed to be behind things, somehow, on guard and keeping watch.

Then he heard Hamer's voice in the passage, and realised suddenly that he was very cold, and the bed a terribly long way off. However, he got back there all right, and was busily reminding himself about the nice, quiet day, and trying not to think of the Bulger, when Hamer knocked and entered. How was he? Oh, topping, thanks! Just a bit tired, though. Hoped they'd excuse him for not showing to see them off. Would get up after a bit and have a nice, quiet breakfast. It was awfully decent of them to think they would miss him, but he was sure the Show atmosphere would have bowled him over at once. He hoped Hamer would buy that motor lawn-roller they were advertising. It would save the gardeners a lot of work, and he might lend it to Harriet, perhaps, for the hock—well, why on earth shouldn't he say 'hockey-ground'? The motor-roller kept his host off the guest's health for the next five minutes, and by that time the car was at the door.

He had handled Hamer rather artistically, he thought, sinking back with somewhat weary satisfaction, and then came Dandy's fingers drumming lightly on the panel.

Was he better? *Sure* he was better? If he didn't say it more convincingly than that, nothing on earth would induce her to leave him. She wasn't half-certain she wanted to go, as it was! But it was going to be a lovely day, and she loved the long run, and of course she loved the aeroplanes and the lovely, big cars.

. 'In fact, God's in His Heaven, and no doubt about it, my lovely dear!' Wiggie observed sadly to his sorry self, and, because the panel was between them, put into his hearty wish for her day's happiness all the melody of the beautiful things he would never say to her now as long as she lived. And then there came the pulsing roar of the car beneath his window, throttled down after to a steady purr, and the big wheels gripped the drive and slurred off and out into the distance. He lay in bed, listening to the sudden silence of the house, and feeling in every nerve the desolation of being left behind.

After an argument—carried on, it seemed, independently of his own brain—between a body which flatly refused to arise, and something brandishing threats with faces like Harriet's—he found the body dressed and at breakfast, by some curious conjuring, and feeling a little braver and bigger by virtue of a large bath, strong coffee and the bright morning. Blenkinship's Marget waited on him with ardent devotion, and he began hastily to lay his evil plans, seeing sofa-cushions and beaten-up eggs quite plainly in her yearning eye. With a royal air he ordered the limousine and the under-chauffeur for ten minutes to eleven.

Blenkinship's Marget stared, as well she might, for although she knew that everything at Watters was entirely at Mr. Wigmore's service, down to the last salt-spoon, he had never so much as ordered a wheel-barrow before. Wiggie read the newspaper upside down, and tried not to look as though he knew she was staring.

'I thought you'd to keep quiet, sir, to-day, if you'll excuse my mentioning it,' she ventured at last, 'and you're looking that poorly, it fair makes my heart ache! There's them two gents., too, as was to call at eleven. You'll just miss them.'

'No, Marget, I shall not!' he replied firmly. 'I shall meet them on the road, and so you will be saved answering the bell. And we shall both be saved having to throw them out of the house, because they will never be inside it. You can't say it isn't keeping quiet to sit perfectly still on a padded seat while things called spiggots and stub-axles and tappets and gudgeon-pins pull you along. And I'm looking poorly this morning because you didn't bring me that treacle-posset you promised, yesterday. You can't expect me to be very hearty and blooming after screaming with hunger all night.'

Marget looked conscience-stricken, and then brightened. The treacle-posset might atone in some measure for the lack of egg-and-sofa treatment.

'You shall have it this evening, sir, honest and faithful! I thought it was only your bit of joke. Then you'll see the gents., sir?'

'Oh, I'll certainly *see* them!' Wiggie promised cheerfully. 'And look here, Marget, if they come worrying again to the house, and make out that they haven't met me, just pretend you're all dead or something, will you, and keep on keeping out of the way? I've to have a nice, quiet day, you know—master's orders.'

And see them he did, meet them he did, quite five minutes before their time, just as the limousine had cleared Watters and settled down into the straight. But it is quite easy to see and yet not be seen in a closed car with a deep back seat, and at the wheel an enthusiastic under-chauffeur, blessed with the Heaven-sent chance of 'letting her rip.' Wiggie was over at Crabtree asking for garments by the time the 'two gents' had finished knocking and peering at an apparently deserted house. As they were leaving, in intense irritation and disgust, they met a gardener's boy, who told them that the whole family had gone to the Show. Which Show? 'Why, t' gert 'un i' Manchester, o' coorse!' Mr. Wigmore too? Yes, certainly Mr. Wigmore, too. The gardener's boy was always at least twenty-four hours behind the clock, so his knowledge of Wiggie's indisposition was not due for some time yet.

The wily quarry found Helwise in the attic, hunting for the shirt and shorts that she had assured Lanty were safe in the green ottoman on the front landing. She had believed her own statement quite honestly, and, as Lancaster was in a hurry, he believed he

believed it, too, which he would not have done in a
calmer moment, but no amount of belief had conjured
the garments into the ottoman. Wiggie joined in the
search with zest, and though it was not Wiggie's attic,
it was certainly Wiggie who suggested twenty hiding-
places and discovered the treasure in the twenty-first.
And after Lanty's hockey-stick had been run to earth
in the jam-cupboard, it was nearly lunch-time, so at
Miss Lancaster's request the borrower stayed to join
her at the scrapings of something potted. She was
driving over to the match, in any case, so he sent the
car home and changed in Lanty's room. He fell
asleep by the dining-room fire while he was waiting
for Helwise to decide whether she looked more
sporting in her own golf jersey or Lanty's aquascutem,
and dreamed he was the sparking-plug in a very large
motor-roller at the Show, over which Dandy's face
was bent in earnest struggle after comprehension.
Hamer had bought the motor-roller, and wished to
see it roll something, if only a little Manchester mud,
so it was trotted out and set to work, and then everything went to smithereens in a hundred and forty
different directions, and he could hear Dandy's voice,
far and very far off, remarking: 'Something wrong
with the sparking-plug! I knew it last night on the
stairs!'

He woke gasping and clutching at things, and if
Helwise (in Lanty's 'scutem) had been anybody but
Helwise, she would have rung all the bells and ordered
doctors and hot bottles and brandy, but instead she
asked him to button her gloves, and thought him
tiresomely stupid and fumbling as she tried to see
exactly how sporting she looked in the sideboard
mirror.

He felt better again, however, as they jogged along
to the ground, and began to experience joyful thrills
as strenuous figures with bare knees and flapping
overcoats push-biked past them, armed with sticks.

He drew his own from under the rug so that the push-bikers could see it. It was a Bulger, as he had anticipated, slightly elegantised by wear and tear, but a Bulger, for all that. Still, it might possibly bring off the twist all right, if he hurried it a bit.

The field under the farm was already dotted by the red shirts of the opposing team, and a sprinkling of spectators edged the neat touch-lines. The white-topped Bluecastrians were grouped beside the little pigeon-house of a pavilion (where at least two people who liked each other might have found room to shelter) listening to Harriet's barked directions. When the trap drove up, she looked at a very strong watch on her wrist so emphatically that Helwise tried to leap the wheel, and tore Lanty's 'scutem on the lamp-bracket.

The home team stared curiously at Wiggie as he came in, carrying a few mufflers and a camp-stool belonging to Helwise, for half of them had heard him sing the day before, and the half that hadn't, wished it had, while both halves had just been told by Harriet that of course he wouldn't be the slightest use in the game, so that they must all back him as much as they could. Certainly, he did not give an impression of superfluous strength; indeed, when he had taken off his coat, he looked as fragile and hopeless an athlete as you could possibly expect to see, so much so that the brawny captain-back of the opposing side came up and implored Harriet to 'put it somewhere where I can't hit it!'

Wiggie didn't hear him, but he wouldn't have cared, if he had. The soft, bright air was wine in his blood. The press of the spring turf lent him a buoyancy not his own. The strength of union, of interdependence and support, put fire into his slack muscles. He stole the ball from the red shirts when it shot out suddenly from the circle, and was trying to persuade the Bulger that he had always belonged to it, when Harriet stalked up. She looked very trim and hard and clean and extremely well put together. You could picture her lasting through half-a-dozen matches without losing so much as a hairpin.

'Where do you want to play?' she demanded. 'You'd better go and stand about somewhere at the back, hadn't you? I'm putting all the strength into the attack—it's the only thing to do with this team. Johnson' (the brawny captain) 'loses his head if you keep on nagging at him. Suppose you take the right, and mark that little black-headed curate on their left outer? You'll be worth your salt if you only keep *him* occupied. He's a terror! Cut him over the shins if he won't behave. There's plenty of weft in that stick of yours.'

Wiggie twiddled the Bulger discontentedly, showing the 'L. Lancaster' cut clearly on the blade. A tinge of colour came into Harriet's face.

'It's too heavy!' he murmured mournfully. 'You see, when you get going up the field, it's always just a second behind your wrist——' He tried to execute a double twist that didn't come off. Harriet looked scornful.

'You don't need to "get going" when you're back. All you've got to do is to let out, but I suppose you won't be able to clear far. And if the thing tires you' —she looked down casually at her own lighter, handier weapon—'I don't mind changing. An ounce or so makes no odds to *me!*'

'Oh, but I shouldn't dream—I didn't mean——!' Wiggie protested, and then stopped. 'If you're sure you don't mind, I dare say I should get on ever so much better.'

Harriet did not mind. You could see how little she minded, running her firm fingers along the rubber where Lancaster's hands had so often gripped. Wiggie tried the double twist with ecstatic success.

'This'll do me all right.' Harriet tucked the stick

under her arm with a kind of savage shame. 'By the
way, of course you know Lanty let me in, too? I've
the rottenest lot of friends anywhere—barring you, of
course! *You've* been a sport. Very well, then, you get
along back and do what you can if anything comes
your way. Johnson won't have to worry about you,
then. He seems nervous of breaking you. Don't get
crocked up or anything—it wastes time so rottenly;
and let Saunders have as much of the game as he
wants, otherwise he'll sulk. For goodness' sake remember that the goal-posts are none too steady, so
don't get shoving against them. And keep an eye on
the curate!'

Wiggie walked sadly to the back. He had never
played back, and he had no wish to begin now. How
was he to get his glorious five minutes if he stood
about and did nothing? He would just dodder and
shiver and wither away into thin air, and there was
nothing dramatic about *that*. And the point-twist
simply wouldn't get a show. Delicate art of that kind
wasn't needed at back. You hit out slashingly, and
then stood with your feet crossed and bowed to the
crowd, until the idiot in front whom you had fed so
prettily allowed another idiot to grab the ball and
send it back again. He wouldn't clear far, having
parted with Lanty's sledge. Harriet's possession was
nearly sure to sting if he began putting anything into
it, and in any case Saunders was to have the limelight.

Saunders, fair-haired and finely built, greeted him
without enthusiasm. He had just been telling the
goalkeeper that he would have all the work to do,
just as if that wasn't exactly what he wanted. Five
minutes before, he had told her that, owing to the
rotten scheme of attack, he never hoped to see a ball
all afternoon, but he expected her to have forgotten
that. The goalkeeper said it was a shame to both
remarks, and prayed that, if a ball ever did arrive, he
wouldn't knock her down inside the goal-posts and

sit on her, as he had a trick of doing. She was a bright-faced young person in pads, who nodded genially to Wiggie as he came up shyly. She wanted to tell him that she had heard him sing, and though of course she liked this sort of thing much better, she could do with a tune, now and then. Wiggie thanked her sweetly for doing with it, and told Wiggie how much he admired her in her perilous position. At least Harriet had not put him *there*, to combine the philosophy of a fisherman with the stoicism of an Aunt Sally.

Saunders suddenly felt rather jealous, and came and joined them. He was pleased to be patronising and instructive, if somewhat contra-law-and-order.

'The great thing is to keep in your *place*!' he said kindly. 'Never mind if you think the ball is six yards nearer your side than mine; it probably isn't. You leave it to me. *I'll* see to it all right. But if you come barging in just as I get there, we shan't hit anything but each other, and the ball will be pushed through; whereas, if you keep out of the way, I can give our forwards a chance. You spend your time looking after the left outer. He's always offside—know what that is, of course?—and fouls every other minute, but it's no earthly use appealing. Knewstubb is much too busy looking after his legs to remember he's a whistle in his mouth, and in any case no referee pays any attention to appeals about Davids—they're too fed up on 'em. So don't waste your breath yelling over his operations, but sneak the ball from him any way you can get at it, and if he starts shoving, just shove him back!'

Wiggie cheered a little. The glorious five minutes were evidently not to be his, but something offered. To go down to death in a locked struggle with the curate was not exactly an heroic finish, but it was better than shivering into nothingness. He went to his post with more hope.

The teams lined up under the faint but kindly sun, between the clean white lines and the clean flags at the corners. There was a graceful, curly-headed youth bullying-off for Bluecaster, with Harriet at centre half a good deal closer behind the ball than was safe for her excellent front teeth. On her left she had a strong Army Major, backing a wild and ineffectual left outer with masses of hair on the point of descent, and a clever left inner, the kindest and most unselfish player in the team. At her other hand was a long-legged person of the male persuasion, excitably pretending to support the best right outer in the county, a young girl with a tightly tied mane and the cheerful trot of a Shetland pony. As her inner she had a meek little man who lived only to get rid of the ball to somebody else, after the manner of cowards who funk the sixpence in 'Up Jenkins!' Stubbs was in the middle of the field, with a nervous eye revolving round him. Raymond, the opposing centre-forward, had a trick of lifting the ball about the level of your knee-cap. If it came his way, he should skip. He blew the whistle, and skipped.

Harriet's offensive policy answered very well at first. The home team knew the tiny drop in the gradient that carried a sudden rush irresistibly into the net, and made the most of it. For some time a furious warfare raged round the visitors' circle, and then the Shetland pony got a pretty shot home, passed her politely by the unambitious inner. After that, though Bluecaster still kept in the foreign half, they were held away from the ring, and Wiggie watched the curate edging slowly up, waiting for the hungry backs to rush into the fray, leaving him offside and well ahead for his centre-half's clearing drive. He was a black-headed, blue-eyed, boyish little thing, as strong as a horse, with an impudent, twinkling smile and no sporting conscience whatever. Wiggie, drooping wearily on the exact square foot of earth appointed him by Saunders, tried to intimidate him with a glance, and failed.

The drive came, a long, low, steady shot with half the field before it, aimed clean and true at the red shirt on the line, and Wiggie's white shirt stepped out to meet it. But even as he stopped it neatly with his stick, earning a cheer from the spectators, a plunging, leaping Saunders fell upon him out of the far distance and squashed him to the earth, hacking wildly as he tumbled after him; and while they were busy disentangling themselves, the ball was passed to the waiting curate, who banged it in at the net, regardless of the shrieked appeals of the deserted goalkeeper. Stubbs had met Saunders in his kangaroo career and was badly injured in the ribs, which rendered him incapable of listening to claims of any kind. He gave the goal with a mule-like obstinacy. He knew Harriet would make it hot for him afterwards, but he didn't care. He would give that galloping Saunders something to remember him by—dashed if he wouldn't!

And all the way back to their posts, Saunders pointed out to his colleague that that was what came of not playing the game, and hoped he'd profit by it.

'You see, my dear fellow,' he said earnestly, 'everything went wrong just because you didn't follow our arrangement. If you'd stayed and minded the curate, as I think you *said* you would, I should have got the ball away nicely, and you wouldn't have been there to hamper me when I arrived. Yes, I know it *looked* as if it was coming straight to you, and as if it was in your half of the ground and not mine, but it doesn't do to be led away by these things. I admit I was a second late, because I ran over that idiot Knewstubb, who was watching you instead of attending to me. And, by the way, it really isn't safe on a ground like this to stop a long shot with your stick. All very well on South-Country cricket-pitches, but no use on rough stuff like ours, up here. Very pretty and swanky, of course, if it comes off, and goes down A 1 with the crowd, but it's too big a risk to be really sporting. Use your feet, man—use your feet!—and do give me a free hand. A really first-class player has no chance, my dear fellow, if he isn't allowed to have his head.'

Wiggie didn't answer because Saunders had flattened all the breath out of him, and the next minute Harriet came up and pitched into both of them. He felt a hearty, uprising hatred of several people, but especially of the curate, twinkling cheerfully where he now stood decorously with his front line.

The little imp grew shameless, after that, and Wiggie had his hands full with him. He had all the engaging tricks of the trade—turning on the ball, putting his foot on it, pushing with his shoulder or his little black head, and using more or less any part of his stick that came first; perpetrating each offence with the same maddening, childlike gaiety and delight. The gentle Wiggie could gladly have strangled him. They fought away in a far corner—Stubbs turning a blind eye, and Saunders behind, shouting a lordly—'Here, sir, here!' —the little, scratching, jabbing, twisting, poking game that kills quicker than the wildest spurting, until the singer was sick and stupid, with a swimming brain and a clamour in his ears. Bits of the 'Elijah' joined forces with Saunders and added their quota to the muddle in his poor head. 'What have I to do with thee, O man of God?' 'Here, sir, here!' 'They have laid a net for my feet.' (The curate had his wicked little stick hooked firmly round Wiggie's leg.) 'Yet doth the Lord see it not.' 'Behind you, sir! Back to your left. . . . LEFT, I said, you ass!' 'Mark how the scorner derideth. . . . It is enough. . . . See mine affliction!' 'Shoot! Shoot!' 'There is no breath left in me.'

By the end of the first half he was trembling, gasping

and half-blind, and he had had no five minutes.
Harriet came up and looked at him anxiously.

'Bit done, aren't you,' she said. He was working
for her at the present moment, so must be cared for,
just as he had had to have glasses of new milk during
the election. 'Afraid you've had a thin time with
Davids. I can't think why the clubs don't combine
and refuse to play against him. He's quite a decent
little chap, though, off the field. Doesn't take the
thing seriously enough—that's what's wrong. I
thought that stick of mine wouldn't be any good to
you—you want something beefy for Davids. Perhaps
you'd like to have Lanty's back again? Saunders
brought you down a nasty whack; must have hurt you
somewhere. He's a clumsy ass. Only last week he
got his stick fast in a girl's hair, and pulled some of it
out by the roots. Look here, hadn't you better knock
off altogether? We'll get along somehow. Saunders
hasn't begun to stretch himself yet, and I can do a
bit more, too. I'm resigned to lose, anyhow. Stubbs
will just simply give the whole blooming game away
if Saunders hits him again. I wish Lanty had been
here! There'll be no saving us in any case if Teddy
Dunn' (the centre-forward) 'loses his wool after half-
time, as he always does. His nerves aren't guaranteed
to wear the whole seventy minutes. Well, ease up for
a while, won't you? Hang about on the touch-line
if you don't care to go up to the house, and if you feel
like chipping in again later, well, chip!'

She brought him his coat, and snatched the camp-
stool from a bleating Helwise, and a kind, little, kid-
gloved lady, who had been calling somewhere, produced some smelling-salts from a russia-leather bag.
He sat on the camp-stool with his head in his hands,
bitterly ashamed but helpless, and wishing with all
his heart that Saunders had finished him off completely. He had not meant any of it to be in the least
like this. He had hugged a vision of fleeting, soaring

ecstasy, and—with God be the rest!—but it seemed that things didn't happen like that. This was shrieking farce and despicable exhibition—no saving grace about it anywhere. But he would not go up to the house, though his face burned every time anybody looked at him. He was an object of utter derision, and, worse—pity, but he would not go up to the house, though his whole soul turned to it with longing. He must stop until the last chance of glory was past; so he clung to his stick, refusing to give it up, and sniffed bravely at the smelling-salts, hoping and praying that he might feel able to 'chip in again later.'

The second half opened with instant trouble for Bluecaster, for the visiting team, having now the better of the gradient, ran through like greased lightning before Saunders had finished impressing upon his goalkeeper that she was perfectly equal to doing both Wigmore's work and his own without her stepping out of the net. Harriet said nothing—just looked at him—and he was a good deal more careful after that. Wiggie found himself admiring her as he sat on his camp-stool, noticing her steady control of the team, absence of fuss, and the neat strength of her play. She spoke out when necessary, but she did not nag, and she took reversal with stoic calm. She had not even opened her lips to Stubbs when he had failed her so disgracefully. There was something rather fine about her, even if she did push you; and again he felt the queer sense of comfort in being pushed.

The curate came and condoled with him, standing the while in his usual illegal and colossally impertinent position, and Wiggie found him quite a decent sort, after all, if somewhat weak in customary sporting ethics. Nevertheless, he had a philosophy of his own which he expounded with charming insouciance.

'What's the fun of sticking to rules?' he asked brightly. 'Any old donkey can stick to rules, but it

takes brain to be always just on the wrong side of the
law without getting collared. Besides, it's frightfully
interesting seeing how the other man gets his hair up
when you foul him all round the place. *You* took it
first-class, like a regular turn-the-other-cheek Sunday-
school teacher. You were jolly nippy, too—took me
all my time to keep ahead of you! Awfully sorry if
I worried you too much; you do look rottenly off
colour. Wish you'd buck up, though, and come on
again. I can't get any fun out of Hoofy Saunders—
he doesn't enter into the spirit of the thing like you.
Hoofy just gets his hair blazing and lams into you and
yells for help, and there's no seeing past his feet when
once the ball's on the other side.'

Play kept pretty well to the middle of the ground
for some time after this, the Witham attack being
warded off by Harriet and a somewhat humbled
Saunders. Then the Most Kind and Unselfish
Member of the Team put in a kind and unselfish
goal, so gently that the goalkeeper did not even see
it; but there the luck ended. Fresh disaster fell upon
Bluecaster. Teddy Dunn 'lost his wool.'

Teddy was a pretty player, supple and light, very
quick on the ball, and very easy with his stick, but
the excitement of the game invariably set his usually
pleasant temper bubbling hot. In common with the
whole team, he had been thoroughly ruffled by
Stubbs' cruel behaviour in presenting Witham
with a patently unearned goal, and when, fifteen
minutes before time, the opposing centre-half caught
him napping over a simple shot at the nets, incidentally waking him with a drive across the shins, he
shook off Harriet's yoke and let himself go altogether.

Ceasing to take any notice of the game, he concentrated his attention upon following up the centre-half
in order to pay him back in his own coin, and various
unauthorised persons dug the ball from under their
feet as the murderous debt was cleared. General

disorganisation ensued, ending in a passionate on-
slaught on the Bluecaster goal, setting Wiggie
quivering to help. When he could bear it no longer,
he dragged off his coat and took himself back to his
place. Nobody noticed him in the hurly-burly, until
the ball clove a miraculous path out of the crowded
circle, leaving a fiery sting running clean up to his
shoulder, and the first thrill of exultation that the
game had brought him yet. But as the centre-forward
was still adding interest to payment, the ball soon
came back again, and the frantic scramble resumed.
Wiggie slammed and rammed, saved and better
saved, listening as in a dream to Saunders' mechanical
'With you, sir! Here, sir, here!' and to Stubbs'
announcement—somewhere on the lip of hell—that
there wanted only five minutes to time. He had a
vision of the curate standing practically inside the
nets, imperturbably ignoring the goalkeeper's ex-
postulations, and then, as if dropped from heaven,
his own chance rushed upon him. The ball was
suddenly in the crook of his stick, cuddling there as
though it loved it. He caught a glimpse of a Shetland
mane away on the rim of the circle, and slipped
through to it between a horde of clashing weapons.
Saunders, drunk with agitation, tried to drive the ball
back again, catching him on the foot with his heavy
swing, but he hopped free, and was out in open
country. Then was seen the shocking spectacle of a
centre-forward far behind, doggedly leaning on his
stick, while a staid full-back carried the game home.
The Shetland pony swung into line with a jolly little
chuckle, and a second later the M.K. and U.P. came
up on Wiggie's left. The three passed up the field as
the wind-shadows pass above clover. Harriet was
not far after them; he could hear her call to the other
halves to follow up, and was conscious of complete
independence of all the halves in the United Kingdom.
Now he felt the lift of the elastic earth, the free, flying

joy that he had craved all afternoon. *Now* his choice of stick was justified, the ball running steadily before the sharp, little strokes. Wiggie might be fragile, but he was the right shape. His sally had the grace of a flying Mercury, and the Shetland pony, keeping easily level, chuckled a second time. She nodded across to the M.K. and U.P., and he sent back his own M.K. smile of content. This was the real stuff, the smile and the nod said alike. What on earth had this treasure been doing at the back?

He knew that he had no business where he was, the newly-imported rotter who ought to have been minding his nets, the miserable failure who so lately had sat on a camp-stool and sniffed at smelling-salts. He felt certain that Saunders sulked behind in utter scandalisation, but he did not care. Still inside the Bluecaster goal, the curate gaped in open-mouthed astonishment, but he had forgotten the curate. He had his five minutes. The gods had heard his prayer, and not allowed him to pass away shamed.

'He that shall endure to the end. . . . Arise, Elijah, for thou hast a long journey before thee. . . . Forty days and forty nights shalt thou go.' Not every part of him seemed to be working at once, but some of him would get there. His feet were still moving, and his wrist, but his eyes—'Night falleth round me, O Lord!' Saunders would say he hadn't kept his place—Hoofy Saunders—but Harriet would be pleased, anyhow, and that was the chief thing. Here were the backs, Johnson and Co.—'Go, return upon thy way! Then did Elijah the prophet break forth like a fire'—*that* got him all right, and it was quite simple! If he fell down suddenly, would his feet still go on running, running? They seemed to know all about it, more than he did, but he would get away from here soon and lie down in Harriet's parlour. 'Though thousands languish and fall beside thee'—nasty E♯ that for the tenors in the fifty-seventh bar! There was a rocking-chair, too, and a kitten, and somebody with a black face. 'Through darkness riseth light, light for the upright'—awful jar for Saunders, his getting away like this! Ah, but what came after? 'Shall the dead arise, the dead arise and praise thee? Lord, our Creator, how excellent thy name is! My flesh also shall rest in hope.'

The Witham left-back came out steadily and with discretion, and Wiggie's twist carried the ball round him as easily as a dancer spins a pirouette, leaving him staring. The right sprang to meet the attack, and he passed out to the Pony, who passed back just as the racing left crossed them a second time. The Witham halves were coming up, thudding and panting, but the three were not to be caught. The right-back sprang again, shouting to his partner, and Wiggie passed to the Most Kind, who dribbled cleverly to the line as if meaning to shoot, and then, with a lightning turn, centred back to the stranger. Wiggie took the ball daintily on his stick, Saunders or no Saunders, meeting the final rush of the recovered left with the same bewildering trick, and, as the goal-keeper danced and slashed, aimed delicately past her into the net. The whistle blew.

But as the teams came up, both sides ready with praise (always excepting Saunders, limping vain-gloriously), Wiggie walked straight off the ground without looking at anybody, not discourteously, but as if very pressing business were hurrying him away. Indeed, from the moment he took the ball in the Bluecaster circle until he had scored his goal, crossed the field and disappeared, he never really stopped at all. It didn't do to stop. He must go on walking . . . walking . . . 'Lord, our Creator' . . . not rushing, but just walking, or he would never get to the other end. The curate tore after him, waving a coat, but he did not look back. If he turned his head, he would never reach the farm, because he couldn't see it any longer. He could only go on walking towards the place where

it had been a minute ago. There was a stile somewhere in the field; his feet would find it all right. He
had really wonderful feet; it was only all the rest of
him that was wrong—his heart and his lungs and his
head and his blind eyes. Well, it was something to
have feet, anyhow. Gravel path, surely? Feet again!
And then steps and a flagged floor. It was time he got
there, because even his feet would have to stop soon.
Yes, he was there . . . he could feel the fire, though he
could not see it . . . there would be the kitten and the
rocker. . . . 'Lord, our Creator . . . Lord, our——'

Harriet explained that Mr. Wigmore was knocked
up, probably wanted to rest. No, she had not known
he was *that* sort of player. He had given her to understand he knew nothing about the game. Anyhow, he
had won the match for them, snatched it out of the
fire at the last moment; not but what they had won
it by rights already! If they would kindly make their
way to the house, they would find tea in the usual
place.

She shepherded them up to the back of the farm, and
through the kitchen into the house-place, where tea
was set on the long table, but in her heart she was
troubled. Wiggie had not joined them. Perhaps he
was not in the house at all. Perhaps he had gone for
quiet to the parlour. She had her hand on the door
when a long, grey car drew up at the gate, and the
men she had seen at the church hurried up the path.
The tale of the gardener's boy at Watters had not
satisfied them, and after a dismal lunch at the 'Four
Feathers' they had started out on a fresh hunt.
Rumours had met them at last of a match and a
stranger playing for Bluecaster—'a lile chap what
sings a bit'—and in spite of incredulity had come on
the wanderer's trail to Wild Duck. The hatchet-faced
man pushed past Harriet into the house.

'Is he here?' he flashed. He looked ready to drop.
Harriet put her hand back to the parlour door and

hesitated. She understood him at once, and for some reason she felt frightened, frightened as she had never been in her life.

'I—don't know!' she stammered, holding the knob tight; then made an effort to pull herself together. 'If you mean Mr. Wigmore, I am just looking for him. He may be resting in here, away from the crowd. He seemed very tired after the match.'

The hatchet-faced man echoed '*Match!*' in a tone that was half bitter irony and half a snarling curse. The big man behind laughed a sad and perfectly hopeless laugh. One of them took the knob out of Harriet's hand and pushed the door. On the hearth by the steel fender Wiggie was fallen, the comforting glow of the fire playing over his white shirt and his closed eyes. The rocker stood empty above his quiet head. The kitten curled, purring, in the curve of his helpless arm.

But he was not dead. Sitting alone in her own room, Harriet willed it with all the force of her personality. He *should* not be dead! The men had said he was, and he had looked it, lying there without a breath, but she would not have it so. After they had carried him up to Stubbs' room and shut the door on her, she had gone across to her own and willed him violently back to existence. He had been her player, her loyal man; he was her guest. He could not die under her roof. In some inexplicable fashion he seemed to belong to her, this stranger from another life and another world.

Downstairs, the teams made merry, wondering a little what had happened to their hostess. Somebody had seen a car come up; perhaps she was wanted on business. That Wigmore chap had disappeared, too. Pity! They would have liked a word with him. Somebody said he was stopping at Watters, so probably he had cleared off at once. He had certainly

looked thoroughly played out. Stubbs, explaining to
a bursting Saunders exactly how and where he would
not be hit by him again, was unaware of any tragedy
passing overhead. Only the little curate, emerging
last from a flying bath, with his round face glowing
above the neatest of clericals, paused on the landing
upstairs, brought to halt by a sure instinct of trouble.
As he did so, the door sprang open in his face, and a
desperate man strode out on top of him. He recoiled
when he saw the parsonic figure, as if it had struck
him.

'What's brought *you* along?' he demanded roughly.
'He's not dead, yet—not going to be dead, I tell you!
You can take yourself and your psalm-singing off
again!'

Davids said: 'Hockey—bath—just passing—can I
help?' with cogent simplicity, and the other relaxed.
He thrust a paper into the curate's hand.

'Fetch the nearest doctor, will you, and ask him to
bring anything he can? Car at the door. There's a
chemist somewhere in this county, I suppose? If
not, send the chauffeur to Lancaster—Manchester—
anywhere. Fire along, and never mind limits. We
pay. But for God's sake, hurry!'

He shut the door as abruptly as he had opened it,
and the little curate slid downstairs as if dropped
from the banisters. They called him in to tea as he
passed, but he did not stop to reply. Hungry but
valiant, he tore down the path, sending before him
the name of the profession that sets every wheel racing
and every hoof at the beat. The chauffeur had his
engine started before the passenger was in the car,
and leaped back to his seat. They became a very
sudden blur in the distance. Whatever his philosophy,
the curate certainly had the knack of being always on
the spot.

Tea finished in the house-place, and Johnson,
shouting down a perfect roar of argument and con-

tradition, was busy illustrating with Harriet's china just how Wigmore had got his goal, when a cool medical voice broke across the hubbub.

'Will somebody kindly tell me who owns this house?'

Stubbs took his head out of a teacup, and came forward and said that he did, which was not in the least true, but sounded well.

'Then perhaps you will forgive me for asking that it may be kept as quiet as possible? Mr. Wigmore is upstairs, dangerously ill. I doubt if he will live through the night.'

He disappeared before anybody's breath had come back, and the stricken teams hunted hats and coats in a graveyard silence, stealing forth as if from a meeting in the Catacombs. Queer that Stubbs shouldn't have known!—but then Stubbs never did know anything for two minutes together. Made a chap feel such a bounder, yelling and roaring with a sick man overhead! Certainly, Harriet had vanished clean off the earth; they might have guessed something was up, from that. It had been a queer match altogether; one they wouldn't be likely to forget in a month of Sundays. The push-bikes crept down into the road, and silently faded away, and a death-like, terrible peace descended upon the farm.

The car came back, bringing a local doctor and a nurse, who disappeared upstairs without asking for anybody. The curate had been explicit. He himself stayed outside with the chauffeur, munching a penny bun. Harriet came down into the parlour, and was joined by Stubbs, whose voluble demands for explanation she strangled savagely into silence. Nobody took any notice of either of them. They might not have existed.

The shadows were well down in the little room when the hatchet-faced man was heard in the garden, directing the chauffeur to take the curate to the station, and then the door opened, and the strangers came in. Harriet asked 'How is he?' and Stubbs looked around and behind him, not recognising the voice.

The hatchet-faced man opened the fingers of an expressive hand, and shut them again.

'A long way on!' he answered, and wondered at himself. He had never heard the expression until a minute before, when the nurse had used it on the stairs. 'But we shall bring him back,' he added—'perhaps. We won't waste time discussing that. I have to apologise for taking possession of your house in this extraordinary manner. We cannot thank you enough for allowing us to do so. I should be glad to explain.'

Harriet said 'Sit down, won't you?' in the same voice that had set Stubbs peering into corners. She found a match and lighted the centre lamp. The big man said nothing.

'My name is Gardner. I am a Londoner—Wigmore's medical adviser, and incidentally his oldest friend. Before he left town, last month, I told him—though he didn't need telling—that his voice was killing him. I warned him that any out-of-the-way effort would probably finish him; that in any case he would not last another year unless he took instant precautions. He had just had a big concert in London, and I knew—what I knew. He promised me to throw up all his engagements and come down here for absolute rest, and I let him go because I believed he would keep his word. On Monday night I discovered by the merest chance that he was to sing here on Tuesday, and I left London before six in the morning —*we* left London—but we were too late to stop him. He would neither have listened to us then, nor forgiven us ever after. God! but I thought he would die before the thing was through! *That* was mad and bad enough, but on top of it he goes and plays in a

hockey match, after leading us a dance round half the
county to prevent us finding out. What's at the back
of it all I can't possibly imagine! Perhaps *you* can.
Who is the insensate fool that led him to fling away
his last little gasp of life?'

Stubbs stirred uneasily. He thought Dr. Gardner
should be told that such language was unfitting the
company of both a past and present Rur'l D'trict
C'cillor. The big man by the window still said
nothing, and nobody introduced him. His eyes
travelled from one face to another with pathetic,
questioning intensity.

And, at last, '*I* am the insensate fool!' said Harriet,
in the voice of Eve after the Fall. '*I* bullied him to
sing. *I* pestered him to play. I told him that all he
wanted was fresh air and hopping about. He tried to
say no, but I said yes, and he always did what I told
him. I made him.'

The doctor drew in his breath as if physically hurt.
He struck his hands together with a little movement
of passionate regret.

'Then you will probably have the satisfaction of
knowing that you have killed the finest singer in
England.'

She winced sharply, but surprise came uppermost.

'I don't understand! We knew he was a singer, of
course, but not of any importance. His name is never
in the papers.'

'He sings under his mother's name—the famous
Quetta. You've heard of *her*, I suppose, even at this
Back o' Beyond? You must have heard of him, too.
He's the great Quetta, now—makes pots of money and
is wanted everywhere. His agent in town was tearing
his hair to come along with us. He can close his
account now. Quetta's done! I suppose you *might*
not know, though. He liked to be incog. here, and
his friends respected his wish for quiet. Well, *you've*
quietened him all right! He should have stopped

singing, years ago, but he had a reason for going on, a good reason——' He caught the big man's eyes fixed earnestly on his lips, and checked himself with a vexed start. The other stood up slowly and looked at Harriet. (It was strange how both seemed to forget Stubbs.) His voice was low, with a curious intonation.

'I am that reason,' he said quietly. 'I am Cyril's half-brother, and once—it seems a very long time ago now—I was a singer, too. I had my own share of our mother's gift, and I was getting on well. I might have been a great Quetta also. Then I had an accident which left me totally deaf. I had no other trade in my hands, and I had both wife and children. Cyril was just coming out, and he took every engagement that came his way to bring us in a living. It was in those first hard years of fight that he broke his health. He kept us all then, and he keeps us all now. I do not know why he never told. Perhaps he was afraid that Mr. Shaw—his friend—would give him money. I do what I can for him—I learned the lip language, and I am now his secretary—but I do not earn half we cost him. And I have never heard him sing. I would give everything I have or ever hope to have, just to hear Cyril sing.'

.   .   .   .   .   .

Stubbs was sent down to the White Lion to telephone to Watters, and a middle-aged damsel at the other end clasped a treacle-posset to her bosom and wept. Long into the dawn Harriet sat by a burnt-out lamp in the little parlour. The walking-mail went by in the smallest hours, the creak of wheels alone coming up to her like a ghostly, undriven hearse of the dead. And when the first cock crew, just as if it were Harriet's imperative voice calling him, the great Cyril Quetta, who was, after all, only Wiggie, struggled back to life, and observed that he was a sparking-plug.

K 2

CHAPTER XXI

THE TROUBLE COMING

THE twenty-ninth of March. Lancaster had been at the Pride. Now he was walking along the north road, where he had stood with Francey Dockeray, months ago. They had had a good winter, just enough hard weather and little wind, and the spring was wonderfully early. The whole countryside breathed an atmosphere more like that of late Easter than wild March. But March had had no lion in it, this year. It had come in like a lamb, and continued to frolic softly onwards, crowned with garlands, like a sacrifice frisking to the altar.

He walked slowly, loving the kind air and the delicate light lying over the land, and his soul was at peace. His visit to the Pride had left him happier than he had expected. For long, the necessity of it had haunted him, and he had shrunk, without admitting it, from what he possibly might find. But there had been nothing to disturb or alarm. Wolf looked very old, but in better spirits than when he had last seen him, for old age has its own medicine of the mind. He spent most of his time at the last Ninekyrkes fence, looking over the fields. The new tenants were not into the house yet, but they were at work on the land, and he found a queer, half-bitter interest in watching others till his soil. Mrs. Whinnerah was a great deal thinner, seemed to have no more substance than a blown straw, but she was much softer in manner than Lanty had ever known her. Her eyes, grown large as she grew small, had the exalted, aloof, almost happy expression of the martyr-fanatic, but they rested more kindly upon him than of yore.

The little Pride was a model of neatness and comfort. He found himself envying them its cosy quiet, until, looking up, he saw the Lugg towering in at the window. For a moment he had the impression that his own satisfaction, the woman's calm and the man's quiet were all alike due to one terrible fascination, the charm that holds a fated creature still before a beast that springs. It was gone directly, and, as he walked with Wolf on the new land, they talked again of his father's planning. He saw it broken up, portioned out, houses built, fences set, a new estate growing under the shelter of the Lugg. When there was a little colony there, the loneliness would vanish, and those that had never known it would laugh at the old tale of a dead fear.

Bluecaster was still at home, waiting. He seemed bored and rather restless, but he would not leave. When Lancaster suggested a Swiss trip, or at least some sort of a party in the big house, he could generally produce some halting excuse; but one day, when hard pressed, he said simply: 'It's March!' and looked at the barometer. Lanty wanted to laugh, but forbore. There were days when it did not do to laugh at Bluecaster. He could make you feel that you were laughing, not only at him, but at nine other Baron Bluecasters behind him.

Well, March was passing, wearing a dainty face showing neither fear nor frown. This was Friday, and Sunday would be mid-Lent Sunday. The worst of the year was over, thank goodness, and with luck there should be a second good season in front. He was almost sure there would be another good season.

He asked after Lup. He would sail to-morrow, it seemed. They had had a letter, saying a last good-bye after the most circumscribed method of good-byes. Lanty had the letter to read, and wondered how long it had taken him to frame the clipped sentences. At the bottom of the page, far below the abrupt signature, three words were scribbled. as if jerked into being by some ghost-hand gripping his elbow. Almost indecipherable, they evolved themselves on inspection into 'Wait of me,' and no more. Completely out of touch with the letter both in spirit and position, they gave the impression that the writer might have sealed the cover without ever knowing they were there.

Mrs. Whinnerah saw the agent's eyes on the message, and smiled faintly.

'There's that as waits for nobody,' she said enigmatically, and turned her face to the window. And again the thought came to him, as it had come months before, that she saw what no other eye could envisage.

The old couple walked with him to the fence, and there he bade them farewell.

'I'll be back again before long,' he said cheerily, shaking each by the hand. 'I'll be looking you up again soon'—and knew not what truth he spoke. So they parted, with mutual kindly smile and thought and word; and as they turned from each other at last, a magpie fluttered out of the fence and stood between them, lonely and alone on the alone and lonely road.

Young Rowly came out from Ladyford at his hail, and his sister behind him. Mother and father were away for the day, it seemed. Francey met him with her usual pleasant manner. Lup's departure had left her apparently untouched, he thought. Perhaps, after all, it had been best for him to go.

'Have you seen Bracken Holliday, lately?' she asked, as he put a foot into the boat, a subtle change coming over her tone.

Some undercurrent of sympathy made Lanty start, realising that the man had been in his mind also.

'Why, no!' he answered, steadying himself in the boat, and looking at her instead of crossing to the stern. 'What's his Loftiness been doing with himself? Getting engaged, or making ready to stand for the county? I hear he was a great man at election-time.'

Young Rowly looked up from his seat with a ripple of mirth running over his clear, young face.

'Nothing o' *that* sort! He's got religion. He's taken to going to church!'

'Not just Sundays, to show off the fit of his coat,' Francey explained. 'He's done that, all along. Rowly means Lent Services—weekday Services. Brack's there, every time!'

'But what's taken him? Some girl gone back on him? Or has he lost another pig or something?'

She looked down at the sand. There were words on her lips, plainly enough, but she did not utter them. Rowly, however, supplied the deficiency with the same happy haste.

'If you want to know, sir, he's praying for *you!*'

'For me? What in creation——! For *me?*'

'Yes, sir—for you. He says there's something awful coming along, and you're responsible for it. Says if he can only get the Almighty to listen to reason, He'll happen let you off and give you another chance. So he goes to church every day, motor-machine, better-mer clothes an' all!'

Lanty scrambled over, and sat down with a bump and a laugh. It was difficult to take any theory seriously that included a vision of Brack, pale-grey suit, Trilby and S.-F., waving wild arms in supplication before the Lord.

'Seems to me Brack must have collected a germ or two on the other side of the pond! He's a queer specimen. Well, I'm grateful for anybody's prayers. Who knows? Brack's may do me a good turn yet!'

Over the sand, he went to Pippin Hall for his horse. Uncle Willie was in the yard, and walked with him for some distance along the dyked road. He remembered afterwards how many people seemed to have stopped and held him, as if loth to let him go, on that last journey round the banks.

'I suppose you'll be over at this feed to-morrow

night, you and your lads?' he inquired—'Mr. Shaw's hotpot supper at the "Duke." '

'Ay, we'll happen show up. T' element's quiet enough at present.' He cast a keen look over the sky, and then the deep-set eyes twinkled, dropping to Lanty's face. 'They seem a likely sort, the new folk over to Watters. They do say as you're looking round there, Mr. Lancaster. Time you got wed an' all!'

Lanty laughed as he mounted.

'Oh, they've had me fixed up more often than I could count, but it's never come off yet! I'm over-throng for that kind of thing, with the Government setting me a different sort of sum every other week. The estate's my wife. I'll never have any other.'

But, as he rode away, he knew that the real reason had been left unspoken. True, the estate had the whole of his heart at present, but it had not yet claimed all his dreams. The Lady that had walked between his box-borders was not forgotten, though still yet to be found. The shadows would have to lengthen further before he ceased to hope.

He would have no half-gods, this blunt, absorbed business-man of the land. Thorough as he was in every detail of his work, he carried the same demand for perfection even to his private, human joy. It had always been said of the Lancasters that they would have the best—the best stuff, the best workmen, the best methods, no matter at what cost. And the last Lancaster of all added that, in little things like love and marriage, he would also have the best—or go wanting them.

He had had a very pleasant day in Manchester. Hamer had treated him royally, and Dandy's joyous enthusiasm had shed brilliance over the expedition. For once she had shown for him the rare sparkle that she always kept for Wiggie. He had felt free and gay and almost as young as she as they wandered round the Show, tasting the charm of fellowship and mutual interest, but even then it had failed as it had always failed before. He had told her that she must persuade Hamer to take her to the Royal, and she had mocked: 'Cows and turnips!' passing on to show rapturous interest in the latest type of plane. He could not know that, five hours before, on the Preston Road, she had decided that Hamer should certainly take this very same party to the Royal. He only felt like a turnip, and wished that his boots were more like those of the nearest showman, and wondered if he could possibly tolerate an overcoat with a waist to it. And when they had turned their backs on the city lights, she had wriggled from under the rug to look behind her over the hood, and had sighed: 'Dear Manchester!' It had always been for her a city of wonder and delight, paved and padded by the genie-hands of Hamer's gold, but there hung no gleam of hard cash over it to-night, only the will-o'-the-wisp lantern of new love. But Lanty remembered the thermos flasks and electric hair-curlers, and believed that she turned sadly from the rich man's city, where such comforts were as common as dog-roses in Westmorland. *He* would never have an electric thingumbob in *his* house, he reflected savagely and childishly. They had a thermos flask already, in spite of him, given to Helwise by Hamer, last Christmas, and she had found it a glorious boon on the servant's day out, when she happened to want a day out, too. Lanty had had many a cooped-up cup of tea out of it, longing the while with a foolish bitterness for a singing kettle and a fresh brew. The Lady would never give him tea out of a thermos—he was certain of that.

The shock of Wiggie's illness had laid the final lever to the reopening gulf. During the following anxious weeks, Dandy's one thought had been for her old friend, so that the new seemed completely put aside; and the latter, hearing her self-reproach and seeing her genuine trouble and anxiety, was more than ever convinced that, in spite of their day together, she belonged to the Wiggies of the world, and could never be rightly his. With a very little incense she might be a half-god—his rebelling soul confessed that!—but he did not mean to burn it. He would swing no single censer, nor strew a single flower.

As he climbed out of the marsh on to the main road, he met Brack in the Flanders. A church-bell was ringing somewhere on the hill-side, and on the empty seat at Brack's left lay a Prayer-book. When he saw the well-known figure, he pulled up with a jerk that ground fierce complaint from his tyres. Lanty looked at the Prayer-book in mild surprise, and then at its owner. The angry colour flew into Brack's face, but he did not put out a hand to the strange object. Let the d——d agent look if he liked!

When the colour faded, Lanty saw that he was thinner, less superior, less exaggerated, less—well, less Brack. The superciliousness that had marked him at the rent-audit was gone, the splendid self-possession changed to mere nervous defiance. His eyes were restless, frightened. He looked as though, at any moment, he might bolt like a startled deer.

Lanty stared at him curiously, with more contempt in the curiosity than he knew. It was impossible to take Brack seriously; the man must have dropped a screw or two, somewhere 'across the dub.' The Prayer-book alone, sitting blandly on the seat of the car, stamped the situation.

Stung by his expression, Brack pulled himself together with an effort, drawing out his cigarette-case with shaking hands.

'Been looking out for you!' he began, coughing to steady his voice. 'Just come from calling at Watters!'

'Indeed?' The agent raised his eyebrows. Was Brack aspiring to that particular orbit? The younger man flushed angrily once more.

'Westmorland Holliday blood need touch its hat to no manufacturer's cash, Mr. Lancaster!'

'Granted!' Lanty said heartily—'though it lifts it to honest success!'

His manner changed, however. The little outburst pleased him, coming as it did not from vanity, but from heritage, showing the man to be really one of the old stock. He dropped into the coaxing tone he kept for the long-time tenants. 'Come, Brack! What's worrying you? Not the same old tale, man, surely? You're looking as nervous as a cat, and more fit to be in hospital than driving a car.'

But Brack ignored the question, struggling with his obstinate cigarette, and cursing under his breath (despite the Prayer-book) as the wind took the flame.

'I went to Watters,' he continued, speaking very carefully, 'to see about this hotpot supper. I went to tell Mr. Shaw I reckoned he'd better put it off.'

'Put it off?' Lanty's eyebrows went up again. 'What on earth for? Measles or something broken out at the "Duke"? He must have thought you had a pretty fair cheek! What did he say?'

'Say?' Brack raised himself in the car, shaking suddenly with distorting rage. 'He heard me right out without bucking in once—all I've told you from the start, and a bit more—and then he said what the whole durned crowd of them say, every bright boy among 'em, but what I reckon they'll soon be shutting their mouths on for ever and ever, Amen—he said, "I'll ask Mr. Lancaster!" That's the ticket—always has been. "I'll ask Mr. Lancaster. What a Lancaster says, goes!"'

His hand fell accidentally on the Prayer-book, and he quietened. The bell had ceased ringing up on the hill. Lanty regarded him gravely.

'I know what you believe, Brack—it didn't take long to guess who sent that chapter out of the Bible—but you can hardly expect us to believe it, too, just on your word. You'll admit it's a queer story. And what's it got to do with the hotpot?'

Brack fiddled with the wheel, suddenly embarrassed and distressed, his personal animosity fading before the pressure of his inexplicable fear. His tale had run fluently enough to Hamer, a listener from without. Before the agent's steady contempt it fell to pieces.

'Dead woolly things!' he muttered, incoherent and unintelligible, and other words completely lost. And then again: 'Wet little woolly things! Dead!'

Lanty might be forgiven for thinking that his sudden religious mania had been backed by the 'Duke's' ale. He touched up his horse, but Brack put out a hand.

'I've just been slinging a word over the wire!' he said queerly.

'Really?' Lancaster was wearying to get away. 'To the Clerk of the Weather, I presume?'

'No! Will you listen, if I tell you?' He leaned forward eagerly, and then got his hands back to their place as the sound of wheels warned him from the near corner. Denny tore round it, and pretended to have a heart-attack when he saw Brack.

'Danged if it bain't the Judgment hissel! Runnin' about in a motor an' all!' He put his hands together, and turned his eyes to heaven. 'Give us a bit of a prayer, Parson Brack, do!'

Livid, Brack snatched at the Prayer-book with quivering fingers, and stood up.

'Guess you shall have it right now!' he cried, and raised his hat. The book fell open instantly at the Forms of Prayer to be used at Sea. By the fierce rush of his words they guessed that he knew the page by heart.

'O most glorious and merciful Lord God. . . . Look down, we beseech thee, and hear us, calling out of the depths of misery, and out of the jaws of this death, which is ready to swallow us up! Save, Lord, or else we perish. The living, the living shall praise thee. . . .'

His voice steadied as he read, the greatness of the need taking hold not only of the speaker, but of the two men hearkening. Mechanically, Lanty put his hand to his cap, and Denny awkwardly followed suit. The last words came out quietly into calm.

'Stir up thy strength, O Lord, and come and help us; for thou givest not always the battle to the strong, but canst save by many or by few. . . . Hear us thy poor servants begging mercy, and imploring thy help.'

And Lanty, with his face turned to the sea, answered 'Amen!'

Denny passed him as he rode on, saluting him with a lifted whip. His pleasant, uncaring face was troubled and wondering. He met the agent's eyes with a question in his own.

Lancaster broke into a trot in the fair evening, and, behind him, over the sea, there came up a cloud no bigger than a man's hand.

CHAPTER XXII

COMING

ROBERT WHINNERAH looked in at the door of the little bedroom, and saw Lup standing by the window, knitting his dark brows over a sheet of flimsy. The yellow envelope lay on his bed.

'What's amiss, lad?' He had seen him take the telegram in, and wondered; and presently he had followed him up. He was a tall, gaunt, white-bearded man, with a look of Wolf about the eyes.

'Nay, I can't make top nor bottom on it!' Lup puzzled. 'If there's owt amiss, it's the sort as doesn't bide shouting down a wire. It just says "Come at once!" with never a why nor wherefore to its tail. "Come at once!" Ay, yon's all there is to it.'

'From Wolf? From your dad?'

'Not it! It's from Bracken Holliday. You'll mind the Hollidays o' Pippin Hall, I reckon? Well, old Willie's Brack's uncle. He took him in an orphan and tried to put him in the way o' things, but Brack was all for something fresh, and made off to Canada afore he was sixteen. He raised money there an' all—he's smart in his way, is Brack—and then come home to farm at Thweng. He's in fine fettle, nowadays, and as throng as a dog wi' two tails, aping quality and driving his own motor-car, but he's no friend o' mine. That's why I'm capt to reckon up the meaning o' this here.'

'Happen it's a joke.' With Lup's arrival, Robert had fallen speedily to the use of the old words.

'Nay, I thought of that, but I don't hold by it. Brack thinks overmuch of himself for such-like daft lakin'. Besides—I'd a notion he'd his own reasons for wishing me out o' the road.'

'Best wire your folk, asking if there's owt wrong.'

Lup shook his head, folding the paper back into its cover.

'I reckon nowt o' wire-talk an' trumpet-talk an' such-like! Seein's believin', when all's said an' done. I'll gang myself. There's a train somewheres about midnight, isn't there?'

Robert stared.

'You're forgetting you sail to-morrow, lad, at noon!'

Lup reached for his overcoat.

'Happen—if I'm not sailing across t' Wythe in-stead!'

'Ay, but your passage booked—your gear aboard!'

'Let em bide!' said Lup tranquilly, and went out to the station.

. . . . . .

He was in Witham before seven o'clock. It was a dreary morning, and offered to be a wild day. Passing Hest Bank, he could both hear and feel a

big wind whistling in from the sea, and it was raining
heavily.

In Witham it was raining, too, and the wind ran
in fierce gusts up the narrow streets and down the
innumerable entries. Overhead was a sky like a
sodden blanket. He had his big coat, however, and
after some breakfast at the 'Green Dragon,' he went
into the streets as they began to fill for market, seeking
news and a friendly lift out. One after another of his
acquaintances met him, open-mouthed and incredu-
lous, but from none could he glean that there was
anything wrong with his folk. This man had seen
them quite recently; that had had news of them but
yesterday, and so on. All was well on the marsh—
Pippin Hall and the rest. Ninekyrkes still empty, of
course. 'What of Ladyford?'

This brought sly jibes from the growing ring of
farmers round the late deserter. 'So *yon's* what fetched
tha back i' sic a ter'ble scufter like, eh, lad? Nay,
now, there's no use lookin' as slape as an eel-tail! We
ken all about it. Oh ay, Ladyford's snug enough.
Here's Michael to speak for hissel!'

Dumbfounded, Dockeray stared as at a ghost, but
when he had gathered his wits, had nothing different
to say from the rest. He urged the young man to make
some attempt to catch his boat, but could not move him.

'Ower late, now,' Lup said, running his eye over
the wet street for Brack in vain. He had kept his own
counsel about the telegram, scarcely knowing why.
'I've missed it, right enough.' And as in Liverpool,
so he said in Witham: 'Seein's believin'!'

There was no sign of Brack all morning, but
presently he ran into Denny, who fell upon him in
delight, and cared not a rush what reason had brought
him back as long as he *was* back. To the dogged
inquiry he returned the common denial, but his
usually open glance shifted a little when Lup asked
for Brack.

'Nay, he's not in town this morning. Leastways, there's nobody clapped eyes on him yet. He's a bit rocky in the upper storey, nowadays, is Brack. Going clean off his nut, I reckon!'

They had dinner together at the 'Dragon,' and afterwards he suggested that Lup should drive back with him and spend the night at Lockholme. Dockeray was for taking him to Ladyford, but Denny clung jealously to his prize, and though Lup's heart turned to the latter farm, his courage shrank unmistakably. He would go with Denny. If all was right at the Pride, there was no haste till morning.

'There's yon do of Mr. Shaw's, to-night, at the "Duke," ' Denny went on, heartened out of his vague doubts by the 'Dragon's' ale. 'What d' you say to going down? I'll lay Mr. Shaw'll be glad to see you, and there's Brack's invite going begging, anyhow. I hear he's not for turning up. You can slip over to the Pride first thing while morning. The old folk'll be feared to death if you come knocking at the door to-night. If you can hang about a bit longer, I'll be through with my job, an' then we'll get out.'

After some hesitation, Lup agreed. He had had no sleep, and was bewildered almost to helplessness by the sharp turn of events and the puzzle of the situation. He had a feeling that he ought to go with Michael, but he did not know why. If he went now, he could get over to the Pride before dark without running any risk of alarming the old people, but if there was nothing wrong, what would they think of his sudden return, cropping up in this aimless manner, having thrown away Ninekyrkes on the one hand, and like enough his passage-money on the other? Wolf would call him a fool. He began to feel a fool, too—to wonder what could possibly have taken him. Drink heartens some and depresses others. Lup wondered and worried. Francey would have something to say, as well; unsaid, even, he would see it in her eyes. In any case, she would be certain to think that he had come crawling back to her because he could not keep away, and at that his Westmorland pride took fire. The powerful instinct that had drawn him blindly but surely so far, checked in the last ten miles before the possibility of a woman's scorn. No! He would not go with Michael.

Yet, when Dockeray drove out, he watched the retreating trap with something like a very agony of desire to follow. He wanted to tear down the crowded street and leap up behind; he could scarcely hold himself back. But the Westmorland farmer does not tear, especially after dinner on a market-day, so he stood where he was, and let the trap drop out of sight.

Waiting for Denny, he wandered aimlessly here and there, stopping now and then for a chat under some shelter, or to stare, with little interest, at a shop-window. There was a hat he thought would look a regular knock-out on Francey. It was of extensive diameter, with two wild wings beating the air far behind. The marsh wind would have taken it mightily to heaven, but he did not think of that. He thought, though, of the gulls he had seen driving inland in the dawn, as the night-train hugged the edge of the wind-swept bay.

The confectioner next door had a window of cakes with knobs running round them like castle-ramparts —Simnel cakes they called them. Then it must be Simnel Sunday—Mothering Sunday—to-morrow! A slip of paper pasted on the wet pane informed him that it was. The old custom was gone, leaving, as in the case of so many customs, merely something in the way of eating as its memorial. He remembered hearing the parson preach about it, last year; how the farm lads used to go home to their mothers, taking flowers with them. Francey had been in the choir, and they had driven home together. If he slept at Lockholme to-night, it would be Mothering Sunday by the time he reached the Pride. Seemed appropriate, somehow. Perhaps, after all, he had been right not to go with Michael—so he tried to comfort the puzzle out of his heart. In any case, he might take the old folk a remembrance of some kind, even though it might not be over and above well-received, in view of the lost passage-money. Shag for the old dad—that would do *him* all right!—but his mother was a harder problem. He had often heard her say she had all she wanted and a bit over. After a while, he sneaked ashamedly into the florist's and bought some violets, large, dewy and sweet. The girl watched with amusement as he sank them gingerly into a capacious pocket. He would put them in water at Lockholme if he could possibly escape Denny's inquiring eye.

The boisterous wind that had roared through the town all morning was still as high as ever when they drove out in the late afternoon, calming no whit even at the dead ebb of the tide, and it was raining with the same steady violence. Crouching low against it, Lup was glad that he had not to meet it on the Northern marsh. He wondered if Michael had got his horse to face the driving storm, or whether he had had to trudge at its head—a weary-enough job even for a young man. He had done well to stay with Denny. Yet at the first turn leading to the marsh, he threw off the rug and put out a foot to the step.

'I doubt I'd best be making tracks for home, Thomas! It'll be a bit of a drag across the moss, but better now than when tide gets turned. We're in for a wild night, by the look of it, an' there'll be no getting to the Pride after dark. It'll be dark soon, an' all.'

Denny expostulated.

'Losh save us, man, you'll never win out to the Pride to-night! Light'll be gone afore you're at Ladyford, and Mrs. Dockeray 'll never let you cross door a second time.' He had set his heart on taking

Lup down to the supper, and, in spite of the rain, was still aglow with 'Dragon' confidence. 'What's got you, Lup? You're as queer as Dick's hatband! You've never Brack's bee in your bonnet, surely?'

'How's the tide?' Lup asked unmoved.

'Sometime after midnight. Nowt to speak of. There's nobody looking for trouble on the marsh, barrin' Brack, as I said. Holliday o' Pippin has yon prize beasts o' hisn down on the low land, an' there's sheep in plenty out an' all. Tide's low, I tell you, and it's only been blowing since morn. We've seen many a worse day, you an' me. Come on with you, lad! I tell you what it is'—he brought out the joke that had been going round all day—'it's yon lass o' Dockeray's you're after. We all know what skifted you to Canada, but I reckon you found you couldn't quit, after all!'

And again Lup put his purpose by, yielding his last chance for fear of a woman's eyes.

The turn was passed, and Denny's stepper, eager for home, rocked over the bridge and along by the towering wall of Doestone, which, with the swaying, dripping trees facing, formed a darkening avenue in the quickening night. Then up the hill and sharp to the right, sliding down towards the west. Once on the low land, with nothing betwixt them and the sea, the whole panorama of sky and sand lay blended before them in one buffeted veil of grey, torn by the sheets of rain. Only Denny's voice kept the horse to the wind, and now and again they had to draw into a curve of the hedge for breath.

'We'll fair catch it, coming back from the "Duke"!' Denny observed, in one of these pauses. 'But it'll likely blow itself out by daylight, an' tide's nowt, as I said.'

They called at Thweng as they passed, at Lup's request, but Brack was not indoors. His doddering old housekeeper, more than anxious to be shut of

them and back to the warm kitchen, told them he
was out somewhere on the land. Had he left a message
for one Lup Whinnerah? Nay, what, he'd left a
parshel o' messages for more than one body, and
the visitor could take his choice! Yan body was to
gang, an' another body was to bide, an' there was
summat about a motor-car an' summat else about
wool, wi' a bit o' the Bible thrown in like, for luck.
T' master'd talk t' hind leg off a dog, any day, an' if
they could mak' owt of any on it, they were welcome.

The draught round the door was growing unbearable, so she promptly banged it, and they withdrew,
pondering. Brack and his housekeeper seemed much
of a piece, and neither of them more than elevenpence
in the shilling. The conviction grew upon Lup that
the telegram, if not a joke, had at least been the out-
come of a mad obsession, and saw himself the laughing-
stock of the district. Whether he told or not, the out-
ward circumstances would never be forgotten—how
Lup Whinnerah turned tail on Canada at the last
minute, and ran home as hard as he could lick. Well,
Ladyford at least should have the laugh last. To-
night, Denny must see him through. He stumbled
thankfully into the warmth of Lockholme, and fell
asleep before the fire. Denny, trying to rouse him
later, heard him muttering as he slept. 'Wait of me!'
he was saying. 'Mother! Wait!'

.   .   .   .   .

After infinite trouble, Hamer got Lanty on the
telephone towards one o'clock on that Saturday
morning. The agent was deep in deeds in some
Witham lawyer's office, and excessively annoyed at
being snatched from them. Hamer, at the other end,
sounded anxious and started badly.

Did Lancaster know it was raining?

Lancaster was safely under cover and furiously
occupied, and did not care a toss what it was doing
outside. Why should Mr. Shaw care—if he did care?

It seemed he did. He recounted Brack's conversation of the day before—at least, as much of it as Lanty
would deign to receive—and found himself cut off
before the end of it. After five minutes' patient
waiting, the agent's voice came back to him, slightly
breathless.

'I say, I beg your pardon! Saw a chap out of the
window that I mightn't catch again for a month of
Sundays, so I just sprinted. I'm always pressed on
Saturday, so you must overlook it. By the way, it's
raining more than a bit, as you say, and I'd no
umbrella. But I give you my word it's not the Day
of Judgment or anything of that sort! You don't
know our weather, yet; we've had such a fine year.
As for Brack, didn't he strike you as being a little off
his chump? I'm rather anxious about him. . . . Why,
no! Hotpot it for all you're worth! They'll turn up,
you'll see. There's nobody minding rain in this
district except Brack. Right! Thanks very much.
I'll come over by the Lane. How is Wigmore this
morning? . . . That's good. By the way, Harriet
turned in to the Board to-day for the first time. Great
doings, I hear! Put the Chairman right on a matter
of some cubic feet, and trotted out a point of law that
cleared up that supply difficulty like magic, and left
them all gaping. All the old hands are saying it's
like old times and John Knewstubb over again.
Harriet will shake them up before she's through!'

Hamer, still worried, observed that there was a
wind, and Lancaster groaned.

'My dear sir, it can't always be summer! We'd do
badly if we didn't get a wind now and then. It's to
be expected, you know. Time o' year. March.'

March! The fatefully-returning word smote on his
ear like a blast. He hung up the receiver and stood,
thinking.

CHAPTER XXIII

COME—THE GREEN GATES OF VISION—V. THE OUTER DARK

IT was dark when Brack got in, pitch-dark and blowing the very roof off the world. He found his housekeeper slumbering peacefully in the kitchen, with a bottle of gin peeping coyly from under the table. He shook her into some measure of wakefulness, but coherence was beyond her. Ay, Lup Whinnerah had called, sure enough, and kept her yammering in a draught fit to blow the flesh off her old bones. 'Message? What-like message? Nay, now, master, ye said nowt o' t' sort! T' lad didn't bide long or say much neyther, barrin' he'd happen look in later. Ay, he'd a manbody o' sorts wi' him, but I don't mind who. It was ower black.'

She had let out a screech at first sight of the dripping figure with haggard cheeks and staring eyes, and even after he had thrown off his coat and emerged as the elegant, somewhat ineffectual master she knew, her fear of him scarcely lessened. He told her to make him some tea, shooting out sharp questions as she dragged to and fro, and swearing helplessly at the maddening vagueness of her replies. When the tea came, he drank it black and strong, and ate nothing, sitting at the table with his wet hands locked, the flying firelight on his white, strained face and drooped shoulders. At every fresh blow of the gale he started, and more than once he went to the door to peer into the dark, looking for Lup's form on the step, and returning breathless from the fight with the entering storm. As the hours wore on, he could not sit still even for a few minutes together, but was forced to pace the flags, straining and listening, his restless eyes on the banging windows and the shaking rugs, coughing as the wind in the chimney drove great clouds of smoke into the room. The housekeeper had fallen asleep again, taking no heed of his mutterings as he passed continually behind her.

The stock was safe, anyhow, up in those far pens. Were they doing anything at Pippin?—Pippin, on the very edge of the sand, hobnobbing with every tide that ran in? Probably they were all gallivanting off to the 'Duke,' eating and drinking with that Lancaster-worshipping fool from Watters. Was Lup there, too, blind and deaf to the call of the storm? And, if not, where was he? That was the torturing, unanswerable problem. He'd never have come to Thweng, though, if he hadn't thought something was up—why, he would never have left Liverpool at all! What had that old hag *really* told him? She might easily have given him the message, after all, and forgotten all about it. If he had gone straight to the Pride, Brack would certainly never set eyes on him to-night. If, on the other hand, it was true that he meant to call again, he might be here any minute. Should he wait, or should he go himself? God! What was that? A fresh, tearing roar from the gale drove him to a scream that brought the old woman leaping out of her happy, drunken sleep. He was struggling back into his coat, trying to control himself. It had only been the wind, after all.

'I'm off out again!' he threw at her, tying a scarf over his mouth to keep the force of the air from choking him. 'Come and bar the door after me, and if you don't stop awake with your eye on that fire, you'll sure be cinders in hell by to-morrow morning! Do you take me? And if Lup's round again, tell him I've gone to the Pride!'

It took all their united strength to force the door back when once it was open, and after the bolts were shot, the old creature sank on the floor, shaking with long, sobbing breaths. She could not hear what

direction the master took, nor catch the note of the
car as it turned out presently through the yard. She
could only hear the song of the wind as it swept up
from under the door in a maniac scream, playing over
her crouching form like the gust of a thresher's flail.

.   .   .   .   .   .

Within the cheer of Ladyford, the storm seemed of
less account, and there was no tide yet, washing at
its foot, to add the sinister dread of live water close at
hand in the dark and a flying gale. They had known
many a night as wild, though none worked to such
a pitch in so short a time; yet the women looked
anxiously at the clock, and wished Michael safe back
from the 'Duke.' He had turned out again reluctantly
—nothing but an urgent business-matter to be put to
Lancaster would have dragged him to Sandwath—
and would have a bad time, coming back. It was
nearly midnight now. He should be home before long
behind a horse who knew his road like a homing
pigeon; yet in the warmth and jollity of the 'Duke'
the wildness without might pass unfelt. Mrs. Dockeray
fidgeted, sighed, set the kettle boiling, stole a look at
her daughter and sighed again.

Michael had told them of Lup's return, and, between the three of them, thrash it out as they might,
they could make nothing of it. He seemed anxious
about his folks, but that hadn't prevented him
stopping the night at Lockholme instead of coming
on to the far marsh. He'd no call to be anxious,
either, unless some busybody had been writing him
lies. Happen he'd taken boggle at the big ship and
the far-off country, but that wasn't like Lup, who had
always found the hardest thing in life to be turning
back or changing his mind. Happen he was home-
sick, or just taking steck and no more: happen, and
happen to it. The riddle would not read, any way
round.

Left alone, for young Rowly was in bed with a

foot sprained on the shore the night before, the two
women dropped the subject like a split egg, and
wondered in silence, the mother glad and relieved,
the girl resentful, though longing. She knew now how
the dead ache of parting had weighed her down, but
she had no welcome for the knowledge. She did not
want him back to begin the struggle again, yet
hungered for the sight of his face. Thinking he could
not leave her, she despised his weakness, yet fretted
because, having returned, he had nevertheless stayed
at the last mile.

He would not come in as he had come with Michael
so often, wet but cheery out of the night, filling the
house with a sense of safety, and stealing the fear from
the storm. Yet it might have been, if she had not
willed it otherwise. She might have sat in another
house, too, listening and longing for her man, and
have had Lup come back to her and her alone. But
that also she rejected. She had put the dream from
her for always, but to-night it came every hour,
passionately and insistently real, though never in
all her life was it to come true on the Northern
marsh.

Going to the window, as the two of them had gone
by turn for the last hour, she saw blinding lights climb
up the dark to the porch. They were too strong and
too low set for the lights of the trap, as she thought
after the first instant, and even as she called to her
mother, Brack burst in at the door. He looked
distraught enough in truth as he stood with his
shoulder to the panel, the rain shining on his tossed,
uncovered hair, his brilliant, frantic eyes scouring the
kitchen as he asked for Lup.

Mrs. Dockeray exchanged a puzzled glance with
her daughter.

'Lup? Ay, Michael said he was back, setting all
Witham gaping, but he's never got the length of
Ladyford. He's to bide with Denny, isn't he, after

the supper at the "Duke"? We're not looking for
him to-night. Whatever's set you seeking him here?'

'I thought he'd sure come right out.' Brack turned
as if to go. 'No, I've never put eyes on him myself.
I just reckoned I'd look in, on the chance.'

'Have you heard what's brought him?' she asked
curiously, and he shook his head impatiently. There
was scant time for talk, and less use. She pressed him
to a warm drink before leaving, but he refused; then
turned again, blurting out quick speech.

'Guess I'll trot on to the Pride! It'll be bad going,
but I reckon I can get the car most there, even to-
night. She'll come back smart enough, anyway! I
promised Lup I'd keep an eye on his folks, and I've
heard say the old woman used to funk the tide something cruel. Guess she'll be scared out of her skin,
to-night! If I can get them to move, will you take
them in?'

She stared again. This was not like Brack—this
unnecessary consideration and struggle for others.
She was amazed, too, at his agitation, the terror-
stricken eyes that would not meet her own, and the
ghostly echo of lightness over hollow fear.

'Why, Whinnerahs need never go wanting as long
as there's Dockera's, that's certain! But they'll be
to bed a while since, lad. You'll never stir them.
They'll not feel the wind over yon like us here. The
Lugg'll break it a good bit. You're never really
feared o' the Lugg, as they make out? What, it stood
yon storm as tore up the front at Bytham, an' t'other
as broke Cunswick Pier, ay, an' many more! It'll
stand to-night an' all.

'You'll never get Martha off the spot!' she added,
laughing.

'I must! I must!' Brack beat his clenched hand on
the door. 'Guess you might come along and help.'

'What? Me?' She laughed again, but with less
heartiness. Brack was so strange, so daft. 'Nay, I'd

have all the breath out of me afore we'd reached the first gate! Stop here, lad, and make yourself easy.'

Francey stepped forward suddenly. Mad or no, Brack had made her afraid.

'I'll go!' she said. 'We'd be happier with them here at Ladyford. Anyhow, we can see if they're all right and not anxious.'

Brack gave her no time to retract, but thrust her roughly into a wrap close at hand, paying no whit of attention to motherly protests, and had her out in the yard before she had drawn the streaming ends of her scarf around her head. Scrambling over her to his seat, he bade her crouch on the floor for protection, for the rain made the screen worse than useless, and, moreover, he was afraid for it against the gale. In the whirling dark he dared not reverse out, so set the car head on to the gateway, trusting to luck to turn her in the open road. With the wind behind her, she took the slight gradient free like a greyhound, and he threw in the clutch at the bottom just in time to save her mounting the sea-wall. Then, with infinite trouble and labour on the narrow track, he wrenched her head round into the storm, the gale fighting him all the time. Brack had done many a pretty piece of driving for the impressing of his friends, but to-night both vanity and pose were as far from him as the black gulf of heaven above. Straining and gasping, he pulled round on his road with a sob of relief, not even conscious of the crouching girl at his feet.

Then began the struggle out to the Pride, the engine biting its way yard by yard through the opposing force, often almost stopping, as an extra weight of air drove upon it, but always gallantly picking up again. Brack had learned to see through slashing rain, like most drivers, but this torrent of wind and water made as though it would hurl him off the face of the earth. With numb hands he kept the car on the road by some sense that seemed outside himself altogether.

Francey, with her head buried on her knees, feeling the striving engine growing hot and hotter beneath her, and Brack's feet moving beside her, wondered what tremendous motive could have brought them both to this shared nightmare. She remembered the former occasion when he had asked her to drive with him, and she had refused, little dreaming of this that lay before. In the comparative tranquillity of Lady-ford it had seemed easy to talk of going over to the Pride. On a reasonable day it was no more than fifteen minutes' walk. To-night, behind a powerful engine, it seemed as far away as Whitehaven.

She had little hope of persuading the Whinnerahs, and, indeed, dreaded for them the shock of this sudden midnight descent, but at least they would know that they were not unthought of at their lonely post. Did Brack really think that the Lugg might go to-night? She remembered all the tests it had passed, trium-phantly as Wythebarrow itself. She thought of the gale that had overthrown the Whitehaven express in the dead of a black night on the viaduct crossing the sands. The fury and passion of that tempest had left the Lugg untouched, as had many another. Why should Brack fume and fret and struggle to reach the lonely house on the farthest marsh? And—still more —why should she have joined forces with him? Her heart gave her the answer. She went to carry the news of Lup's return. Whatever they might say, however puzzle and condemn, how glad they would be over the main fact, the three of them together, father, mother, and lover!

The road ceased suddenly, and they were on the grass-grown trail leading to the Pride, the wheels squelching and sticking on the sodden land; and at once, by the lessened force of the wind, they knew the Lugg to be risen at their left hand. They were still swept and buffeted, but not with the pitiless malignancy of the open, and the run along the difficult waste was accomplished in less time than that on the metal. So thick was the darkness, however, that they did not raise the Pride until practically at its door, and saw a warm-eyed window peer unblinking into the immeasurable solitude. Through the unshuttered pane they could see Wolf and his wife at either side of the hearth, staring into the red cavern of magic and memory that was built between them. The light of it fondled the old faces and shot along the walls, turning steel to silver and copper to gold, drawing the deep blues out of the china, and chasing itself in molten streams along oak and stone. Only the fire and the dogs stirred in that absolute, happy peace of reaching back. The latter were plainly uneasy, lifting themselves out of sleep with pricked ears; and at intervals the older dog laid a wistful muzzle on his master's knee and cried softly. Then Wolf would set a hand on its head without look or word, and it would sink back to the hearth, yet keeping its questioning eyes on his dreaming face. It was a curious picture to be seen in the heart of a waste that should by rights have been covered with rolling billows, and to the watchers it had the effect of a tiny gem on the mourning folds of a widow's robe, of a lost star in an illimitably shrouded heaven.

Brack's knock broke the peace like a hammer, and through the wind they heard the dogs bark, springing, bristling, on guard. Wolf came presently to the door.

He let them in at once when he knew them, for talk without was impossible, but they found more bewilderment than welcome awaiting them.

What, for the land's sake, had brought them out on such a night at such an hour, scaring folks out of their senses? Brack, exhausted with his fight, was almost speechless, but Francey broke into the kitchen with her woman's wit alive and ready.

They'd been worrying about them at Ladyford, she explained quickly. They felt lonely, somehow, with

Ninekyrkes at hand empty, and their old friends such a way off. It was the first wild night for many and many a winter that they had spent so far apart. Brack had been calling with his car, so she'd taken it into her head to come along with him to have a look at them. Father was down at Sandwath, at Mr. Shaw's supper, or he'd have been over himself. And there was news, too, clamouring to be out.

Kneeling between the dogs and spreading her cold fingers to the flame, she told them of Lup's return, startling the whole neighbourhood by its apparent lack of reason. Brack fidgeted in the background, chafing to get at their chief cause for coming, but she checked him with a look. There was only one way of working to that.

Wolf dropped back into his chair, clinging to his stick, interrogation, wrath and wonder stamped out in turn by unwilling and sharply-suffocated joy, but the old woman said nothing, smiling and staring on into the fire. She did not even look surprised, Francey thought. Had *she* summoned him back at the last moment? How strange and reasonless it all was! And what would be the end?

Catching Brack's agonised glance of entreaty, she went on hurriedly, laying her hand on the mother's knee.

Lup was at the hotpot with Denny, but there was more than a chance Michael would bring him back to Ladyford. He'd never get out to the Pride to-night on foot, and he'd be wearying to see them. Wouldn't they venture the short run in Brack's car, in the hope that he might turn up? Her mother was looking for them, and with the wind at their back they'd not be more than five minutes on the way. Like as not, they would find Lup waiting on the doorstep. They must wrap up warm, and with the dickey seat they could manage somehow. She could sit on the step.

She got no further than that, for Wolf growled her

into silence with the utmost fierce contempt, having
battered down his first delight. He was like to gang
scuttering off to meet yon wastrel as had ought to be
well loosed out o' dock by now—ay, wasn't he! He'd
see him strung afore he stirred a foot on such a night
to reach Ladyford or any spot in the kingdom! The
news could well have kept while morning. They might
have spared themselves their trouble, and the sooner
they were away and back at home the better for all
concerned. Mrs. Whinnerah stared and smiled.

Brack broke in, then, bursting into a torrent of
entreaty and command.

'I'll not leave you! I'll not stir without you! You're
sitting here snug and asleep, putting your trust in
your one-eyed Lancasters, and you'll drown in your
trust like rats in a trapped hole! But it's up to me to
see you don't. I'll hike you out, with or without your
will. I'll get a move on you in spite of you!'

He seized the old man by the shoulder, but Wolf
shook him off, striking at him furiously with his heavy
stick. Then he turned to the woman, stammering,
hysterical, almost weeping, his voice rising in desperate appeal.

'*You* know what's coming! I guess I needn't tell
you! You know what the tide's bringing, 'way out on
the dark sand! *You* hear it, same as I do, what it's
seeking, what it sure means to have. It's all in for the
Lugg to-night, and yet you'll set your life and his to
foot the account, just to make good on a Lancaster's
word, a Lancaster's honour going plumb to hell for
ever and ever and ever——'

He stuttered into silence before the smiling dread-
fulness of her eyes on his working face, and, when he
stopped, she turned them again with complete and
horrible definiteness to the fire. Wolf staggered to his
feet, the dogs close at his knee, half-crouched to
spring. Across Brack's hand where he had struck him
the blood showed in a vivid streak.

'You'll say nowt agen the Lancasters under *this* roof, Bracken Holliday! We all ken the trouble you've made on the marsh, and the tales you've set agog about the Lugg and the old master; an' I tell you now, if it's with the last breath God Almighty puts into my mouth, that they're every one on 'em lies! The Lugg'll last many a long year after us as saw it built, an' many a year after such as you an' all, just as the Lancasters' honour will stand, an' their word an' their righteous judgment, long after the likes o' you is mouldered away an' forgot!'

He tottered across to his wife and held out his hand for hers.

'Wilta bide wimma, Martha?' he asked in a dropped voice, and she looked up at him, resting her grey head against his sleeve.

'Ay, lad, I will that!' she answered in the same tone of rarest intimacy, and he remembered in a lightning-flash how she had spoken those very words, in just that way, to his rough courting of long ago.

Cursing and sobbing, Brack tore out into the night, calling to Francey to follow, and after a last look of pity and pain she obeyed, the tears rolling down her cheeks. In that moment all her theories and doubts and surface convictions went by the board. Before her eyes she saw made manifest the one thing that holds human life safe and unafraid against all the unknown terrors of the dark, and knew that to end it thus with Lup, her hand in his, her cheek against his arm, was to have for ever all of the very best that God could offer.

The car went back as rooks go home on a slanting gale. More than once Brack felt her slide up and off the bank, on the other side of which lay the waiting sands. And, as they fled, with the tempest-roar in their ears, above it and behind them they heard the voice of the coming tide.

.   .   .   .   .

Over the telephone, Hamer had offered to motor
Lancaster to the 'Duke,' and the latter had accepted,
adding that he would walk to Watters by the short
cut. Driving home from Witham, his mind had been
so deep in ruts of law that he scarcely noticed the
increasing violence of the sinking day, but when he
left the house again about seven o'clock he was
appalled by its gathered strength. He wished now
that he had asked Hamer to send the car round, but
the Lane would soon take him, and he would be
sheltered under the tall hedges. Knowing the road
so well, he carried no light, and consequently stumbled
into Dandy in the pelting dark, feeling her way home
in a state of abject misery. To his astonished questioning she made answer in a voice very close on tears,
and she was more than a little cross. She had had a
trying experience, and even her beautiful temper had
snapped under the strain.

'I've been losing myself!' she explained, conscious
of sopping boots, clinging skirts, rat-tail hair and ting-
ling fingers, from which she had long since cast away
ruined gloves. He could not see her here, but he
would certainly see her in the hall at Watters, and
though, out of all heaven and earth and any other
stray universe, he was the one and only person she
wanted, she naturally used him as the whipping-boy
of her pent-up wrath and distress.

'I've come from Wild Duck. Harriet had gone to
Witham—perhaps you saw her—so I went over to
have lunch with Wiggie, and as I knew the car would
be out again to-night, I said I'd walk back. It's not
so far, and I meant to be home long before dark.
However, Harriet was late in coming in, and I didn't
like to leave Cyril alone with Stubbs (the nurse was
resting, and Stubbs talks him to death), so tea was
over before I got away. It was still light, then, but very
wet and blowing hard, so Harriet told Stubbs to see
me home, and we started off, but we hadn't got

far before he announced that he wanted to call at
Rakestraw. He'd got it into his head that it would do
Wiggie good to go out in a bath-chair, with himself
to push, and he knew they had a bath-chair at Rakestraw, which he meant to borrow. I asked him if he
couldn't go some other time, but he said no. No time
like the present was his motto. It had been his father's
motto. In fact, it was in the family. Always in the
family. I said that Wiggie might not care about a
bath-chair, but that, if he did, father would hire him
the latest pattern from Manchester, but he wouldn't
hear of that; and when finally I suggested that he
should go chair-hunting by himself and let me go
home, he wouldn't hear of that, either. He said that,
coming from a town, I must naturally know all about
bath-chair charges, and he would want me to tell him
what to pay if he couldn't get it borrowed. If I
wouldn't help, he'd have to call for advice at the
"White Lion," so for Harriet's sake I went. The
Rakestraw people dug the chair out of the barn, and
said they'd be delighted to lend it, and Stubbs was so
overjoyed that he started practising on it at once, with
Newby's daughter as passenger. He'd evidently
forgotten all about me, so when I was thoroughly
tired and chilled to the bone I slipped out, hoping he'd
go on practising until I was safely away. Unfortunately, I took the wrong turning and had to ask the
road, as I didn't dare to go back. A boy told me to
keep on up the ginnell, and I'd strike a gate opening
on to the main road, so I rushed on without taking
much notice where I was going, until I'd lost the farm
and everything else as well. It was getting dark, by
then, and every bush looked exactly like every other
bush, and I suppose I went on walking round them,
as I never found the gate at all. I ginnelled and
ginnelled and ginnelled *and* ginnelled, but nothing
ever ended anywhere. I found all sorts of glades and
walls and little woods and streams I'd never seen or

dreamed of before, and that I'm perfectly sure are not there at all in the daytime, but there was no way out. I felt just as if I were bewitched, and all the bushes seemed like little stunted men jeering and leering; and when it got quite dark I was properly lost altogether. I was just getting ready to die and deciding what I meant to say about Stubbs at the Judgment, when young Newby ginnelled up and found me. He'd thought he'd seen me wandering about, earlier, and was anxious in case I was really lost, so hunted me up. He wanted to bring me home, but I knew he'd to get down to the "Duke" by eight o'clock, so I wouldn't let him. He'd only just gone when you caught me up. They'll be out of their minds about me at Watters, and I shall probably die there if not in the ginnell; but even if I don't, I mean to file that Judgment Bill against Stubbs!'

It was certainly quieter in the Lane, so that Lanty was able to catch most of her troubled story, and though he sympathised warmly, and reviled Stubbs heartily, he could not help laughing, too, and when he laughed she felt hurt, and wetter than ever.

'I'm frightened of your horrid country!' she said miserably. 'I'm sure there was something queer about it to-night, anyhow. I felt as if it were playing cat and mouse with me, and watching me run round and round and yet never out of reach. *Don't* laugh! *It* laughed at me, too—I could hear it—and the wind set all the bushes catching and clawing at me as I passed. Young Newby says it's going to be the worst storm for years, and that he's very glad he's farming inland—not on the bay. He says that, after midnight, if it keeps on, the marsh will be holding to its hair!'

A chill not of the striving elements came over Lancaster. For the first time he thought of Brack since Hamer's call on the wire. Where was he to-night? He had prophesied this storm, and prayed over it. Was his madness really about to be justified?

He would know by the time he got down to the 'Duke.' If Brack was there he needn't worry, though of course he wasn't doing anything so absurd. But if he wasn't there? Bluecaster too; not a sign of him all day. Well, to-morrow he would laugh at all this! In the meantime, he heard Dandy speaking again. He had made no answer to her last words, but had merely gone on splashing beside her without offering to help her, probably with his head full of some stupid farm person she had never heard of. She thought him more unkind with every minute that passed.

'It will be dreadful at Watters to-night if the wind keeps up!' she went on presently. 'I shall lie awake all the time, and shiver and shake. Watters just purrs in a wind! You'd think it liked to feel its joints cracking and its slates flying and the big trees threatening it on all sides. It isn't frightened an atom, but I am. I never remember being frightened at Halsted. I wish we were back there. I used to think I was getting to love the country, but now I'm almost sure I hate it!'

In her vehemence she stumbled into the side, and when he had picked her out again they could see, grown accustomed to the dark, the straining blackness of a giant tree beyond the still, black break in the hedge.

They could hear it groaning, too, above the storm, and, in the sense of fearful battle and pain, felt it as the impotent writhing of a soul in hell. In this his Lane, where the magic set his fancy at full play, Lancaster wondered what the soul really felt, the impotent, lost soul! As Dandy had said, there were strange things abroad to-night.

'I doubt the old shippon at Pippin will never stand,' he said absently, thinking all the time of the soul, and scarcely for an instant of the shippon, and started when she uttered a sharp little sound of misery and contempt.

'I'm sorry, but may we go on? No doubt it is very

important, but I'm afraid I'm too wet and tired to care!'

He begged her pardon instantly, and then, because behind the shippon had been all his anxious thought for the men of the marsh, 'You don't understand,' he added quickly. They were the opening words of much that he wanted to tell her, seeking comfort from her and strength; but she could not know that, and she did not wait to learn.

'No, I do not understand!' she said passionately. 'I am an outsider, and you always take care to make me feel it. Very well. I will remain outside. And I do not wish to understand.'

They trudged on in silence, and after she had again walked into the hedge he offered her his arm in a detached voice that might have come from the nearest stump. She took it without answer. On her wet cheek the wind could tell no difference between salt tears and the rain.

. . . . .

In spite of the weather and the busy season, the men turned up fairly well at the 'Duke,' making light of their wet drive. Some of the elders were absent— Holliday of Pippin, for one; but his sons were there, and Dockeray's arrival from the far marsh was greeted with applause. He drew Lancaster into conversation at once, and, almost immediately after, attention sprang to Denny, leading in Lup with the swagger and importance of a hen with a single chick. The latter met the general curiosity with the defensive imperturbability he had shown all day; only, when Lanty came to him, wondering, he asked for Brack. He saw the agent start, and the eyes of the two men met in a dumb perplexity, almost as those of trapped creatures walked stubbornly to the same snare. But neither Lancaster nor anybody else knew anything of Brack, save his late church-going mania, though they had plenty to say about *that*. As they sat down at the long table, his name was shuttle-cocked from mouth to jesting mouth.

It was just about the time that Brack burst in at Ladyford that Bluecaster came into the 'Duke' and opened the supper-room door. The warm air was full of light and comfort, smoke, fellowship and song. The 'Duke' stood well protected by the surrounding buildings, so that the storm was not only shut out, but forgotten. His lordship came to the head of the table and shook hands with Hamer. At the far end, Lancaster stood up.

Bluecaster looked round the assembly with his shy, appeasing smile. His face was rather pale, but his voice was even quieter than usual.

'Are there many sheep out on the mosses, to-night?'

After the first stare of wonder, anxiety rolled like a wave from one face to another, each looking into each and back again to his lordship, and then the answers broke round the table: 'Twenty in t' lower meader—fourteen on t' middle moss—nay, I've all mine penned—seventeen—ten—why, what's the stir? Storm's nowt, is it?'

Holliday's lads got up and looked at the door, remembering the precious stock on the lowest land of all. Other men followed their example. Only Lup sat on, with his eyes fixed on Lanty.

'The tide is for one o'clock,' said Bluecaster. 'The wind may bring it earlier. It will be a big tide.'

He said no more, but the room emptied as if by magic, the men jerking their good-nights over their shoulders as they went out.

'You will forgive me?' the intruder said to the host. Outside, he motioned Lancaster into his car. 'Pippin!' he ordered, and——'if we can get there,' he added, under his breath. The agent looked at him.

'Is it coming?' he asked.

'It is here,' said Bluecaster.

.   .   .   .   .   .

As Brack caught the dread sound that had risen so often through his tortured dreams, he uttered a cry of such agony that Francey shrank beside him. Thrusting her out at the gate of Ladyford, he leaped after her to the ground and stood straining into the dark over the sea. Then suddenly he began to run in the direction from which they had come, gasping and beating against the air in a fresh effort to get back to the Pride. But before he had gone a hundred yards, he saw ahead of him, towering over the Let, a white mountain of water as if the whole of the tidal wave had swerved and mounted its barrier. On a screamed prayer he turned and raced for his life with the monster behind him, and, as he reached the gate, a galloping horse and rocking trap burst past him into the yard, a flood also at its heels. The water poured after them up the slope, and above the shriek of the wind they heard the roar of the full tide as it swung on and past to the top of the bay.

In the kitchen, the frightened women and the roused hands were busy moving food and valuables as the sea came in at the door, until presently it was standing two feet deep on the flags. Michael and Lup (for they had driven together) came in at the back after they had stabled the horse, and a short consultation was held in the larder, raised by stone steps above the level of the kitchen. Brack had sunk into a kind of stupor in a corner.

'The banks are giving on all sides!' Michael said, as the household crowded round him. 'We were near caught time an' again as we came along. The water kept bursting through behind us before we were barely clear. The marsh road's gone—ay, an' the main road an' all, I doubt! There's a gap like the mouth o' hell just below there where we galloped in. The Let's going all round the marsh, but the Lugg's not gone yet!' He looked at Lup, rigid and silent, and went on slowly. 'I feel somehow we'd know right off if the Lugg went.'

Young Whinnerah nodded. He had not looked at Francey since he came in, nor attempted to question Brack. The time for wonder was past.

'I must get out, some way,' he said. 'I must learn if they are safe. Happen it'd be possible back o' t' house, over the land. Which of you's game to come along?'

They were all game—no question about that—and the women made no protest. Storm and tide were no new things to the folk of the marsh, and in this case friends of tried worth were in peril out in the night. Brack dragged himself up, and joined the rest as they furnished themselves with sticks and splashed across the yard to the drier land. He had done his share already, but that did not keep him. His car was sunk in a swirling torrent, but he never thought of it. Through the web of conceit which had sealed his heart to his kin, there had sounded at last the call of the clan.

They formed a human chain and groped, with the big sticks scouting before them, in imminent danger all the time, and more than once utterly bewildered and all but lost. Wading often to their waists, trapped by deep holes, by wire fencing wrenched into sunk snares for their stumbling feet, blinded, dripping, breathless and stunned, buffeted by the wild gusts and clouds of spray beating in through the mighty breaks in the bank, they yet held on until there seemed to stretch before them a limitless expanse, and knew that the floodgates at Ninekyrkes must have smashed. For long enough they tried to get round, but in vain, and at last, in the same perilous fashion, they struggled back to the house. All over the marsh men were doing the same, risking their lives for news of each other's safety, or in attempts to rescue stock, counting it all as just so much in a bad day's work.

In the big bedroom upstairs, the women had lighted a fire and set food, and called the weary band to it. Michael, the old man, heartened himself to hearten the rest.

'The Lugg's standing,' he said more than once. 'I tell you we'd know right off if the Lugg went! It'll hold it's own as it's always done. It'll win through this lot an' all.'

And Brack held his peace.

.   .   .   .

'For Loyalty is still the same
Whether it win or lose the game,
    True as the dial to the sun
    Although it be not shined upon.'

At the Pride the fire sank a little, and the dogs grew more restless with every five minutes that passed. The clock on the stairs struck half-past one, and Wolf stood up stiffly.

'Time we were abed,' he said.

She looked up at him for a minute without moving. She would have preferred to stay where she was, gleaning a little false assurance of security from the red coals, but, after all, what difference could it make? She raked out the fire after her usual custom, and Wolf turned the lamp to a dying flicker and lighted the bedroom candle. The whittering flame caught their son's eyes looking down under drawn brows from the mantel, and they stared at him together in silence. At that very moment Lup was fighting to get to them in vain, and all the way his heart was saying the same words: 'Wait of me, Mother! Wait—*wait!*'

There was no change in the wildness of the night; only upstairs it seemed more apparent. The frightened dogs scratched and howled at the bedroom door until it opened, when they fled under the bed and lay shivering and whining in mortal fear. The old clock beat steadily on the stairs. A shrieking gust tore at the window as the old couple knelt at the bedside for their evening prayer, but they were not afraid. In the kitchen, love had wrapped them round with a golden moment from the past, but here a higher angel spread protecting wings.

The roar of the night increased suddenly in volume, and after it there came the special voice that had called the whole trembling marsh to listen—the voice of the sea. And, as if listening also, in the middle of its steady swing, without whirr or warning, like the last, soft, never-repeated breath of the gently-dead, the clock stopped.

.   .   .   .   .

His lordship's car never got to Pippin.

About one o'clock, old Willie woke as if a finger had touched him, and struck a light. He had barely flung on his clothes before the tide had leaped the bank and swung round the farm like the turning flow riding a stranded yacht. By the time he had roused his wife and daughter, the water was in the house, half a dozen feet on the ground floor and climbing the stairs. The elder woman crouched on the bed and wept for her best parlour furniture, bumping below like rocked boats anchored aside; but Holliday thought of his prize beasts drowning in their pens; of his ewes choking in the fields, and—lastly—of his lads racing home against the sea. Would they trick the tide? And more —if saved themselves—would there be any home at all for them by morning?

He guessed what had happened. The river Wythe, semi-ringing the farm, had been in flood all day, and, meeting the driven tide, had flung terrific pressure on the whole of the marsh banks. Here and there they had quickly burst, letting the tide through, and Pippin had been taken in its first stride. From the top of the stairs he watched the water, wondering how long it would continue to rise, and listening to his wife's lamentations over the parlour carpet. He let her alone, though he knew all the provisions in the house were gone, and that they were cut off from help on all hands. What he did not know was that in the bank outside was a gap a quarter of a mile wide, but if he had known he could have done nothing. He could only watch the water creeping up.

His daughter came out to join him, and leaned a second light over the sliding, heaving enemy below. When it had passed by six inches the Great Tide-Mark on the stairs, recording the big storm of his childhood, he remembered suddenly how he had denied his nephew in the flooded room below. Brack had said this would come, and they had none of them believed or cared.

Now the water was three stairs from the top. Stooping, he could touch it. Each stair was a foot wide, and the black water over the black oak seemed to hold the depth of the bottomless pit. When it reached the third step it stayed as if uncertain, listening, waiting for some ghostly order from without. The light gleamed along the yard of shining baluster rising from the well, lending a silvery whiteness to Holliday's bent head, and the shimmer of gold to his daughter's drooping plaits. With strained, almost inhuman faces they leaned above their doom, waiting, as the water waited, for a fate that hung in the balance. And at last, after incredible years, something happened. Holliday let out a hoarse cry that rang through the house, and father and child, staring into each other's eyes, read the same flashed message of sickening horror and passionate relief. The tide had dropped a foot in sixty seconds.

They fell on their knees, shuddering, and Holliday spoke.

'T' Lugg's brast!' he said. 'Whinnerahs is done. T' Lugg's brast!'

CHAPTER XXIV

MOTHERING SUNDAY

DAWN saw a boat-load of haggard faces under the walls of the Pride. There was water as far as eye could see, and the grim light filtered through six great gaps in the bank. The Let had given in all directions, and from Watch How the whole Wythe valley showed like one vast lagoon.

Lup stood up in the stern to hail, and found his voice a dead thing in his throat. All night long it had been calling, but it was dumb now. In his pocket his icy fingers crushed the forgotten violets meant for his mother.

Lancaster, at an oar, looked up at his terrible face, and shivered. Somebody called, and they rowed closer. Across the sill of an upper room the wind had blown the silvery strand of a woman's hair. They hailed once more, and drew towards it; but when they saw the watermark, they were silent.

So, on Mothering Sunday, Lup Whinnerah came home again.

CHAPTER XXV

ONE MAN'S WORK

IT was a strange and fearful world that lifted its mangled face to the growing day. The wind was still blowing, but with less violence, and the rain drifted in a kind of desultory fretfulness between the weary greys of earth and sky. From all the districts round, folk had come to see what the storm had made of the marsh, and the wreck of Lancaster's Lugg had sped on wire and rail through the country. On all hands men were at work saving what they could of the remnant of stock; here, a sheep crawled on a fence within a few inches of the reaching water; there, cattle still deep in it long after noon had struck. Pippin Hall was completely surrounded, but friends had crossed the swollen river with food, and from an upper window Holliday asked shakingly for news of the Pride. Pippin had lost almost everything it could lose—ewes, new lambs, calves, poultry, stacks, turnips, mangolds, carts—and had half a ruined house to top the account. Only, by some miracle, the prize beasts had been saved. Standing up to their necks, half a mile from dry land, they could be approached only by boat, and the difficult and dangerous rescue extended far into the afternoon. Poor Denny had lost a valuable horse as well as half his flock. Nearly every farm had suffered with its sheep, and the 'dead, woolly things' of Brack's prophecy covered the marsh.

On the sea-roads the water rose level with the hedges all day, and, when it left, the scars of the land crept shudderingly into sight. Great holes five and six feet deep where had been metalled surface, uprooted fences and railings twisted like cord; and everywhere dead things, rabbits, hares, poultry—and always sheep. The peaceful, cared-for country lay broken and horribly disfigured, as if by the riving hands of a maddened giant.

And over it all—grey; the grey of desolation, of cowering shame, of finished defeat and despair.

Lancaster stood in the wet kitchen at Ladyford, and stared at his wrecked world. He looked utterly changed, years older, stunned and almost wondering, like a man struck from empty skies. His face and hands were blue with cold, and his wet clothes clung to him soddenly. Before him he could see the Lugg heaving out of the clearing sands, and the Pride still girthed in flood—guard and trap, betrayer and betrayed. In the room above him he could hear footsteps, hushed and slow. The Pride had given up its dead that Ladyford might take them in.

Lup was dropped at the table with his head on his arms, and opposite him Francey stood stiffly, white as the new scrubbing-stone on the hastily fettled hearth. When Lancaster turned from the window with a definite movement, Whinnerah lifted his face and looked from him to the girl. So, to the slow music of the hushed steps, they stared at each other, the three who had sent the proud old couple to their doom.

'They went on my word!' Lancaster said at last, in a curious voice. 'I wonder if they forgave me before they died?'

'They went because of *me!*' Francey put in passionately. 'They could have stopped at Ninekyrkes, but I drove them out. They went because of *me.*'

And though he was right, she was right, too. Far away, far back had been sown the seed of this trouble, when an upright, loving pair had put their savings to the bettering of their only girl.

But Lup denied them both with a sharp gesture full of the dignity of possession.

'They were my folk—not yours. If I'd stopped, they'd be here to-day. They were my folk, and I drowned them!'

And he also was right.

Yet Lancaster, listening, knew that from the leader and not the led is toll exacted, on the head and not the hand is judgment passed. This debt was his, this judgment his. The two had been but tools in the carving of his fate.

He saw Lup sink back, and Francey fall to her knees beside him, and he went out and shut the door. They would mend their broken lives together, but he was alone.

.   °   .   .   .   .

Michael ferried him to a point from which he could reach an untouched road by means of climbing fences and skirting meadows. The day was fading into quiet and dusk with the death-exhaustion more terrible than the height of wrack and pain. The trouble that was passing was physical, rending the body and stupefying the mind. The trouble that followed was the still, corroding trouble of the soul.

Behind him the Lugg, broken monument and draggled standard. Behind, the Pride, tomb of more than human flesh. Before him, Pippin, with the water still at its door, and the stretch of ruin around. With the marks of the long hours upon them, agent and tenant parted on the soaking grass.

'Don't fret yourself overmuch, sir!' Michael said earnestly. 'It had to happen. It was nobody's blame. It had to come.'

And all across the marsh he met men who said the same, men spent with giant exertions, who had lost heavily, and saved even their lives only by sheer good luck.

'It had to be, sir! It's bad, but it might have been worse. If the Lugg hadn't given, the whole of the top marsh would ha' went, and that would have settled a deal more folk than just two. There wasn't room for a tide such as yon. Why, it was like to have taken the whole Wythe valley! It wasn't anybody's blame. Who would have looked for such a flood, and that sharp like? The Lugg had been a smart bit of framing, and had done its best. There were volcanoes and such-like abroad, ready to brast up any minute, but that didn't stop folk building nigh 'em. With luck, the Lugg might have stood another fifty year. It was nobody's blame.

And not one of the well-meant words lifted the load an atom, or carried a shade of comfort home. It had been his choice, and he had chosen wrong; his team, and he had pulled the wrong rein. This thing had happened in his time, this record would be written against his name. The cheering words went with the wind. And as he turned for the last time to look behind, seeing always the faces of the newly dead, there came over him a hard rage against the man who had tied his hands with his plans and his pride. He cursed his father as he stood on the wrecked shore, and in that loss of faith fathomed the darkest depths of all.

His circumambulatory journey took him past Thweng, and, done though he was, a sharp impulse turned him to its door. Within, he found Brack and Denny, and, seated at the kitchen table, Bluecaster.

For more than a dozen hours he had forgotten Bluecaster completely. They had lost each other in the dark, and had gone to help, one at one farm, the other at another. He had thought of the whole matter as his own, and wondered at himself now even while he clung to the thought, for here was the real master. Yet, had Bluecaster ever been master? Again, as at Ladyford, he recognised that always the leader paid.

'You *knew?*' Denny was saying, half-fearful, but resentful and distressed. 'Nay, you're just getting at us! You *couldn't* know.'

'I *did* know!' Brack answered wearily. 'Guess I might as well tell the table, though, for all the understanding I'd get. I played myself out trying to make you see square, but there was no getting past that bleat of yours about the Lancasters. Well, I reckon you've got your head in your hands, this time! Keep to your bleating and see what you'll get, next. Seems to me folks that don't bleat aren't wanted any on Bluecaster—folks with their eyes skinned ahead. For I knew—that's sure!' He paused suddenly. 'And his lordship knew!' he added.

'No,' said Bluecaster.

Brack swung round with a piercing look and opened his lips, but Bluecaster kept his eyes steady with an effort. Lanty stepped into the room.

'I thought you'd have been gone long since, my lord! They'll be getting anxious at the House. Can you drive us home, Thomas?'

Denny turned with quick gladness on his poor, troubled face.

'Ay, that I can, sir, though I've lost the best horse in my stable!' He reached out and laid a hand on Lanty's arm. 'There's folks, sir—none so far off, neither—as say the Lugg ought never to have been built, folks as think 'twas pride as put it there and pride as kept it there. But there's other folks as say the Lancasters may build a score o' Luggs an' drown the lot of us; an' the fust on 'em's Thomas Cuthbert Dennison o' Lockholme!'

He hurried out, leaving Brack staring curiously after him.

'What's the cinch you've got on 'em all?' he asked, at last. 'What's the receipt for making blind, boot-licking fools of thinking men, setting them kissing your feet and your kid gloves? How have you fixed these kow-towing cranks on the marsh?'

Lancaster came forward to the table.

'There's only one tie, Brack, between man and man that will stand a week, and that's just simple faith. You think we're out of date up here because some of us still trust each other, still hold a man's word as his bond, unbacked by a Government stamp. You think that folks should trust themselves and nobody else, should keep looking out all the time for other folks getting ready to do them. Now, *I* tell you, who have seen my own faith go down to-day—*I* tell you, it is better to keep trust and be betrayed—ay! better even to betray trust in keeping trust, than never to have trust at all. What you knew, you knew of yourself; it could not help us. We at the helm had to take our chance, and failed. Do not doubt that always, and in every way, we shall pay.'

A flush came into Brack's haggard cheeks. He gave a short laugh of pure nervous excitement. He straightened himself. His elegance came back to him. You looked instinctively for the Trilby and the

S.-F., though both had been swept out to sea. He stepped in front of Lanty, clicking his heels together, and flinging up a hand in salute.

'Mr. Lancaster, you're great!' he exclaimed, at his most colonial. 'You're the real goods, all the way. You've got me, any time you like. I'll take a top line, please, in that drowning-list of yours, along with friend Thomas Dennison!'

He gave the same nervous laugh and went out. But, as he went, he cast one last keen and curious glance at the young man at the table.

.   .   .   .   .

'Sit down, won't you?' Bluecaster said. 'Dennison will be some little time yet. You look thoroughly done up.'

Lanty took the chair opposite. They were both tired out, but there were things yet to be said, things that might never be possible, perhaps, on any other day but this.

'I spoke for us both, my lord. If I took too much on myself——'

Bluecaster lifted a hand.

'You have always had to take everything. It isn't the first time. I have never helped you. Do you think I don't know it?'

'That's not true!' Lanty answered warmly. 'How could I achieve anything without your consent? In the end, everything comes to you, and you've never hindered. There's no better landlord in the kingdom.'

'It's easy to be kind without lifting a finger; easy to agree to a judgment you know to be right; but there's a final responsibility that is mine and mine only, and that I've never faced. In this matter of the Lugg, for instance——'

There came to Lanty a memory of the meeting at which, with a single look, Bluecaster had passed the fate of the bank into his hands.

'Of course you couldn't know!' he exclaimed

incredulously. 'That's only Brack's raving. But'—
he stopped suddenly, stared, stammering and half-
rising—'you don't mean that you agreed with him,
thought the Lugg ought to go—did not trust it, all
the time?'

Bluecaster bowed his head without reply.

'You thrust the problem on me, convinced in your
own mind of the one right course—bade me answer
for us both, unjust as it was, biassed as you knew I
must be, certain that my answer would not be yours?
I took it that you had no opinion, could not and would
not choose. For that reason only I stepped into your
place. Have I failed so far in my duty that you dared
not set your will against mine?' Doubt assailed him,
the fearful doubt besetting the strong of the uncon-
vincedness of the consenting weak. 'My lord—was it
that?'

'No, it was not that,' said Bluecaster.

'It must have been! I thought you wanted help—
but it was that.'

'It was *not* that!' Bluecaster spoke very firmly.
'Sit down again, man, and listen to me. We're
neither of us fit to see very clearly to-night, but I
want to get this said. You've never bullied me—
don't worry your head about that. You've been the
stronger man, that's all, and you're suffering for it.
It's always unfair on the servant to be the stronger
man. But sometimes'—he smiled his pleasant smile—
'sometimes, Lancaster, old man, the master is jolly
glad of it!

'I'd always thought the Lugg might be a menace to
the top marsh. The neck of the bay is so narrow—it
used to look to me as if the Lugg was choking it. And,
like Brack, I've seen storms—one does see things,
knocking about as I do,' he added half-apologetically,
the idle, rich traveller to the home-keeping worker.
'And the reclaimed land always made me creep a bit.
It looked so—well—*snatched!* I've a fear of the sea,

although I've been out on it so much in all sorts of
cockle-shells. It always has something in hand. You
may trick it, but it generally gets its own back in the
end. And though I know all the marsh has been
fought out of it, yard by yard, it seemed to me to have
a queer kind of grudge about the land behind the
Lugg. I'd have been glad to see it go, and that's the
truth! But then—your father had built it, and I'd
been brought up on the things your father did. They
used to call him the Big Man of the North. *He* said
the Lugg would stand, and it did, long after he wasn't
there to see that it was doing as it was told. Then
you came—as good a man as your father—*yes !*—and
said the same thing, and I kept quiet. All the marsh
knew my opinion wasn't worth the flick of a whip
against yours. If I'd touched the bank, they'd have
taken it that I meant to slight you, and I would have
cut off my head rather than do that. See?'

He smote the table suddenly with his clenched fist.

'God! What a liar and a coward I am! That's all
lies—you know it, don't you, Lancaster?—no—not
lies, perhaps, but side-issues. The truth is, I was
afraid, as I've always been afraid when it came to a
big shove. I shirked having to speak out, having to
decide, so I put it on to you. I knew *you* wouldn't be
afraid, that you would take the straight path as you
saw it. I knew you'd shoulder things for me, as you'd
always done. You must have despised me often; and
yet I don't think that, somehow. But I'd despise
myself more than I do if I didn't feel that they've
given me overweight to carry—the powers up above
that fix our place for us down below. I wasn't meant
to handle men. It isn't my job. I shouldn't have
been slung up like St. Simon what's-his-name on his
pillar. I was cut out a quiet, retiring, harmless
individual with a taste for sailing and rather a good
eye at tennis, and I'm expected to be a symbol, a
father-confessor, general caretaker, referee and prop

of the State! I haven't been any of all that except in spurts. You've had to be it for me; but in the end it all comes back to me. It's slated down to my account. The responsibility's mine. It isn't that I don't love the place and the people, and the feel of it all belonging to me, but those of us who stop to think what it means are paying for it all the time, even chuckle-headed idiots like myself. Do they never realise—these men who are always going for the landlords—that power and place have to be paid for, and in bitter coin? It all looks so easy from the outside; but it's loading a horse a ton too much, setting a seasick chap to furl the tops'l, when it comes to poor beggars like me!

'But you're clear in this,' he added presently. 'The final responsibility's mine, as I said. It's I who will have to face the music for those lost lives when the bill comes in.'

Lancaster shook his head without lifting it from his hand where he had leaned it, listening.

'I took the responsibility from you. I need not have done it. I could have refused it. But I didn't refuse. This is *my* work.'

And, as at Ladyford, so here, he saw clearly that in every crisis one particular soul holds the scale. Bluecaster was right, as Lup and Francey had been right, but there was a more stringent law beyond. The words that had haunted him all day came back to him now with redoubled force. 'It is always one man's work—always and everywhere.'

CHAPTER XXVI

HIS SILLY HOME

HE dropped from the trap at his own gate, and walked up the drive. There had been no sound of his coming, so the door was not open, and the lack of welcome hurt him somehow, as if the house meant deliberately to shut him out. He did not come to it as to a place of healing, but at least it was his own hole to creep into when wounded. The blank door seemed to deny him even that.

It was very dark in the high-walled garden, but a ray from a side-window caught the Church Army summer-house across the lawn, and sprang a text into being. 'Feed my sheep,' said the text, in reference to scrambled teas dispensed by Helwise under the Reckitt's roof, but it brought many other things to his mind to-night. He stood still and looked at it, thinking of the helpless stock the sea had taken. Brack's dead, woolly things would cry to him for many a long day to come. He thought, too, of the marsh-folk, broken and spent to-day because of his father's building and his own seal upon it, of the two at Lady-ford sleeping their last sleep; and out of the dark from over the west there seemed to come to him an exceeding bitter cry: 'Where is the flock that was given thee, thy beautiful flock?'

As he turned again to the house, the door was flung open, and Helwise peered into the night.

'Is that you, Armer? Whatever are you doing so late? I thought you had gone home long ago. But as you *are* here, you may as well bring a pound of bacon when you come in the morning, or there'll be none for breakfast. Sliced. One pound. And remember I will *not* have those brown boots blacked!'

Lanty stepped inside.

'It isn't Armer,' he said.

Helwise jumped and stared. It was certainly not Armer, but in that first instant it seemed to her as if it was not Lanty, either. Her voice was almost hushed.

'Why, Lancelot! When I saw you on the step, I thought for a moment it was your father!'

'Thank God it is not!' he answered, and moved towards his office. Across the hall, where the drawing-room door stood slightly ajar, he could see that there

was a warm fire in the loathly grate, though the grate
itself he could not see, nor the pot-dogs on the mantelpiece. There was no light in the room but the light
of the fire. On a low stool Dandy was sitting, staring
into the red glow as it poured out and wrapped her
round, setting a thousand torches to the brightness
of her hair, and racing with golden feet over her
slender grace. She looked curiously lonely, he thought,
since there was somebody else in the room, whose voice
he placed without hesitation. If the somebody else
hadn't been there, he might, perhaps, have entered,
drawn by the first real glimpse of heart's joy the house
had held for years. At least he might have stood on
the threshold and looked within, before his personal
tragedy dragged him back into the desert; but instead
he turned to Helwise, still staring at him with that
half-look of fear.

'Can I have something to eat? I don't seem to have
had anything all day—I don't remember.'

At the sound of his voice Dandy sprang up, looking
nervously towards the hall, and Harriet came out of
the dusk and stood beside her. Helwise threw the
door wide.

'Don't go into the office, Lancelot! There's no fire,
and the gas has been escaping. What a dreadful
storm, wasn't it? I felt certain every minute that the
house would be blown down. I don't know why I
didn't have a heart-attack! Dandy and Harriet came
over for news, so I made them promise to stay until
you got back. I really *couldn't* be left alone, and it's
Our Agnes's night out.'

The two girls came forward into the hall.

'It was very good of you,' Lanty said mechanically,
looking at them with tired eyes. Behind them he
could see the grate, now, and the pot dogs. Helwise
chattered on.

'I'm sure I don't know if you can have anything to
eat! I expected you'd get some food at one of the

farms. You always say you like it best there. We've had supper some time since, and it's the girl's night out, as I said. There isn't any meat in the house, I know, and there won't be any bacon for breakfast, as you weren't Armer, after all, but I dare say you can have some tea, if you care about it. I put some into the thermos at five o'clock, thinking you might turn up, so you can't say I don't remember your comfort sometimes! I'll go and get it.'

'Hot whisky do you a jolly sight more good!' Harriet shot out bluntly, without looking at him. She looked instead at the sign-manual of her bicycle on the wall. Dandy, in an apologetic tone, murmured 'Soup!'

Lanty smiled faintly. What a mixture life was—bathos dancing on the edge of the Pit! Now he came to think of it, he did not want anything to eat. He had asked for it as one asks for some small alleviation in an unbearable trial. He would not have the thermos, anyhow.

'It doesn't matter. I don't really care anything about it.' The smile was slightly satirical, this time. 'I'd forgotten it was Our Agnes's night out!'

Helwise looked upset, and as if she might be getting ready for another heart-attack.

'I dare say there's a tin of something somewhere, but I shouldn't know what to do with it, if there was. You'd much better let me get the therm.—*not* in the office, Lancelot! I meant to have had it all tidied up before you got back, but Dandy brought another crochet pattern and that was how I didn't turn off the gas. What I mean is that I've been hunting through your old papers for accounts of the Lugg when it was first built. I thought it would be so interesting to have them pasted in a book now that the thing's gone altogether, and then there'll be all the fresh paragraphs about it, this week. I felt sure you would like to see them, but there were so many years back to look through, and the stickphast stuck such lots of

other things beside the right ones. Oh, and do you
know, Lancelot, there was a photograph of your
father taken on the top of the Lugg, with his foot on
the last spadeful, and on the right—no, left!—that
poor old Whinnerah person who was drowned?
Underneath they'd put: "Conqueror of the Sea!"
Don't you think that it would be nice to have the
photograph reproduced in this week's paper, while
everybody is so interested? People forget so soon.
There might be a companion one of you, too, don't
you think, looking at one of the breaks?'

'With my foot on a coffin?' Lanty's voice, risen a
little, had in it something strange and wild. He stood
gazing at her with a fixed expression on his face,
striving to measure the exact immensity of the gulf
between them, seeing her thousand selfish follies climb
out of it like mocking gnomes. He had done all he
could for her, not all she wanted, perhaps, but everything within his power, and at his greatest need she
gave him nothing—no, much worse than nothing—
in return. In this his hour of bitterness she would drag
his dead into light, holding it up to public calumny
with a pot of stickphast. He closed the office door
between them, and heard her burst into terrified tears
on the other side.

'It was his father!' she sobbed and gasped, as the
girls attempted to soothe her. 'It's no use telling me
it was Lancelot, because he never looked at me like
that in his life. They say the dead come back sometimes, and stare at you through the children's eyes,
and I'm sure it's true! He never liked me—the other.
He always said I was silly, and I was frightened of
him. I believe Lancelot is drowned, and this is his
father come back in his place! No, it's no use talking
to me about eggs and bread-and-butter! If he's a
ghost, how can he eat? I won't stay down here—no,
I daren't! He might come out again, and I should
never get over it!'

She tore herself out of their hands, and stumbled, panting and weeping, up the stairs, and immediately they heard the bolt of her door shoot home. They were left in the hall, looking at each other, awkward and uncomfortable.

'This is rot!' Harriet observed presently. 'Helwise must have gone clean off it. We can't let the man starve. We'd better see if we can't dig up something. That soup notion of yours was first-class.'

'We might try,' Dandy agreed, 'but I'm afraid I know next to nothing about cooking.'

'Well, *I* know everything!' Harriet answered calmly. 'I can make soup that will fetch you galloping from the top of the house. You good-looking people haven't bagged quite *all* the tricks in this unjust world!'

They went exploring into the dark larder, and both the rich man's daughter and the mistress of the spotless farm-house exclaimed at the patent evidences of neglect.

'No bread!' Harriet commented, leaning over the big pot with a guttering dip. 'Wish I'd left that last tough old crust at supper. Weren't there some biscuits in that sixpence-ha'penny glass thing in the dining-room? Just think on about them, will you? Half a blanc-mange and a few pine-apple chunks— *that's* no use to a hungry man! It's all he'll get for breakfast, though, by the look of things. I wonder if it's any good going down into the cellar? Helwise said there was no meat, didn't she? Eggs? No, I'm afraid not! There *must* be some milk, though—I wonder where? Might be in the boot-cupboard, on *this* system. Come on! We've got to unearth that soup somehow!'

They found the full tin stowed thoughtfully among a stack of empty ones, and, in the dirty kitchen, Harriet began her labours by the light of a gas-jet that burnt one-sidedly with a shrieking flame. Fortunately for present conditions, though not for the master's pocket, the fire had been left piled up high; but this piece of criminal wastefulness was the only happy accident that befell them.

'What beats *me*,' Harriet remarked, sniffing disgustedly at pans, and flinging half-washed spoons into a slimy tin in a stopped-up sink, 'is why Lanty hasn't been poisoned before now, or at any rate sold up and carted to the Workhouse. It's too bad of old Helwise, it really is! After all, he keeps her, and he works jolly hard. She might have done him a bit better than this. Do you mind cleaning a few of these things while I open the soup?'

So while Harriet boiled, Dandy scrubbed, and produced, by some conjuror's wand, a bowl and silver spoon, a small tray and a passably clean traycloth, also the biscuits. When the soup was added, steaming and strong, they looked at each other with conscious pride, on the heels of which came a sudden sense of guilt and confusion. After all, it was open to question that a couple of outsiders should be cooking food for a man in his own kitchen without his permission or even his knowledge.

'How are you going back?' Harriet asked, covering in the range, and slipping a plate over the lidless bowl. 'I meant to have cleared out long before this. I hope Stubbs hasn't been worrying Cyril.'

The name came out naturally enough, but Dandy started a little. The use of it by Harriet seemed to put her old friend Wiggie in a new light.

'Father is coming for me,' she replied. 'He had to go to Manchester to-day, but he said he'd run over as soon as he got back. He wanted to see Mr. Lancaster. You'll wait and come with us, won't you? He should be here any time now, and I can't stop alone, with my hostess locked away upstairs.'

'Right you are!' Harriet lifted the tray with reverent care. 'Put out that one-eyed gas, will you, and light the candle? There's a cockroach crawling up you—don't know if you're keen on 'em! You'd better go on in front and yell out if there are any booby-traps. I nearly broke my shin over a clothes-horse, and we can't afford to lose the soup.'

But in the hall she stopped, even as her hand was raised to knock, for Dandy, with flushed cheeks, had stepped back into the firelight from the drawing-room, bringing to the other's mind how Lanty had paused—from her corner she had seen him—paused, weary as he was, to look at the same picture. There had been in his face something of which he had not known, but which even Harriet, unobservant and callous, had not failed to read. It was as if, in that instant, he had seen at last the 'silly home' of his desire.

She drew back, holding out the tray.

'*You* take it in, will you? I'm not fit to be seen, after grubbing about in that region of the lost.'

Dandy started, and shook her head violently.

'Nonsense! It's *your* cooking. Go in and collect your own credit. If it comes to that, *I'm* not fit to be seen, either!'

'Don't fish!' Harriet snarled. 'Buck up, I tell you! The stuff's freezing. I'm not going in, anyway, so if you won't take it I may as well sling it through the window.'

'But——' Dandy advanced with reluctance. 'I don't like to! It's your place. You know him so much better than I.'

'That's just it. He doesn't want the folks he knows. They know too much. I'd probably be giving him my opinion before he asked it. You walk in as if you were used to it, and he'll probably think you're only Our Agnes.'

Dandy took the tray slowly, still doubtful.

'Git!' said Harriet, and knocked. Without waiting for an answer, she opened the door and pushed the girl in, closing it again instantly. Not content with that, she went out into the porch, and shut the inner

door behind her. She would not even be within reach
of their voices. The damp cold swept in from the west
as she stood in the dark, biting her lip. The standard
of action is mercifully adjusted to each of us, and perhaps Harriet's funny, homely, big-little sacrifice
formed a fine enough leaf in the laurels of love.

She had been there barely a couple of minutes before
the Watters limousine turned in and drew up at the
step. She went forward, expecting to see Hamer, but
instead, out of it came Wiggie. He came carefully,
with the chauffeur's hand under his arm, a wavering
shadow uncertain of its feet, but yet he came, smiling
a ghost of his old smile at Harriet's amazement and
concern. The chauffeur planted him safely within
reach of her assistance, and returned to his car.

'Hamer's a little way behind,' the new-comer
explained breathlessly. 'We met a certain Mr. Dennison going home from Bluecaster, and Hamer wanted
to ask him things, so I came on.'

'But what on earth are you doing here at all?'
Harriet demanded angrily. 'What were Stubbs and
that cap-and-apron nurse thinking of? Go back at
once, or you'll die!'

Wiggie looked guilty, trying to lean against a
flower-stand afflicted with a chronic wobble, and she
put her hand beneath his elbow.

'Oh, I needn't die yet, need I, please? Hamer
came round on his way here, and I—he seemed
lonely. Dennison said Lancaster was back.'

Harriet nodded, opening the glass door, and sup-
porting him inside.

'You'd better come out of the cold, as you *are* here.
Yes. About an hour since. Looking about twenty
years older, and half-cracked. Sent Helwise upstairs
in screaming hysterics. He's in there.' She jerked her
head towards the office. 'Dandy's with him.'

Wiggie gave one long, quiet glance at the closed
door. No sound of voices came to the two equally

silent outside, the absence of speech within that shut room conveying an intimate isolation that no exchange of words could have held. In that look it seemed almost as if he were saying good-bye. Then he turned to Harriet, smiling as on the step.

'I did not come for Dandy,' he said gently. 'I came for you.'

Harriet blushed violently. She looked angered almost to tears.

'You've no need to lie to *me*, Cyril! I should have thought you ought to know that, by now.'

'But it is true!' he said simply. And it *was* true. The look had been merely the seal set on a renunciation made weeks ago on the Watters stairs. 'It's been such a dreadfully long day without you! Dear old Stubbs has been hunting germs, and the nurse told me all the diseases I'd just missed having, and all the diseases I might have yet, if I'd hurry up. Can't we slip away now, and send the car back for the others? Hamer won't mind.'

'But don't you want to see Lanty?'

'Perhaps I'd better not worry him to-night. I'll be ready for him when he wants me, poor old man! Please take me home.' His voice was very weak, and she felt him heavy on her arm. 'You might, you know. You're not the only lonely pebble on the beach!'

Harriet blushed again, but without anger, this time. Wiggie had known, all along, and the thought had never hurt her or made her ashamed. And no matter where his own love was placed, he yet had an urgent need of herself. She remembered how he had turned to Wild Duck as his refuge. It was queerly pleasant to be needed. She would take him home.

They got him back to the car with some difficulty, and, once inside, he lay against the cushions so still that she was afraid, until she found that he had simply fallen into exhausted sleep. He had spent all his little store of strength in coming to her in the dark hour when she had deliberately shut herself out of Heaven. It was strange that he should always be digging her out of deep places. It seemed almost like fate.

The Rur'l D'trict C'cillor drew the rug more closely round him with an oddly motherly touch.

.   .   .   .   .   .

There was indeed a vile smell of gas in the office, and an unlighted fire, astonishingly badly-laid, showed yesterday's cinders still unraked. A perfect sea of newspapers heaved along the floor, and across them Lanty's boots had trodden a path to his desk at the far end, where his private documents had been swept aside to make room for more *Gazettes*. A large island of stickphast sat smugly upon the fine leather. The shelves had been ruthlessly rifled. Cupboard doors stood open. The newspapers themselves, evidently long folded away with neat precision, had been crushed and crumpled, slashed or torn across. For a second, Dandy forgot her nervousness in sheer amazed horror.

Lanty was standing by the desk, with one of the myriad sheets in his hand, looking down at it with a still intentness and absorption. When he heard the door he lifted his head without turning, clutching the paper close as if afraid that somebody might see it over his shoulder.

'Who is it?' he asked, still with the air of being on guard, and Dandy of the Tray, in a faint and rather frightened voice, wishing herself safely back at Watters, answered: 'Our Agnes!' The silver spoon clinked against the bowl.

Lanty had been well-trained by weekly nightmare meals to the stern remembrance of the 'girl's night out,' but in the present stress of circumstance his weary brain had again let slip the important fact. The voice might easily have belonged to Our Agnes, who boasted an organ varying between the colourless twitter of a new-fledged sparrow and the discordance of the tom-tom. It certainly carried no faintest reminder of Dandy. Moreover, in his passionate concentration upon the paper, yielding to it entire heart and soul and quickened, yearning memory, Dandy was as if she had never been.

He did not turn, because he was afraid to let even a vacant mirror like Our Agnes reflect his face; and also for another reason. The fragrance of Harriet's galloping soup reached him quickly across the room, waking him to the violent realisation that he had not tasted food for many hours. If he saw it, he might be driven to a fierce snatching which would send Our Agnes to join Helwise in her orgy of hysterics upstairs; so he stood fast, clasping the paper like a child in peril.

'Will you put it down—whatever it is?' The tray touched the table. 'Thanks! And, while you're here, do you mind lighting the fire? I couldn't find any matches.'

He sat down in the desk-chair, struggling with his consuming hunger, and cursing himself for having kept her a moment longer than was necessary. She would take hours to light the fire—she always did—and he would have to sit in torture until she had finished. But he was very cold, chill with hunger as well as damp, and the mere consciousness of a woman's presence had roused the weary man's instinctive claim for help. Perhaps she would not find the matches, either, and while she went for others he could retreat in dignity with the food. But she did find them. He heard them rattle as she drew them out from behind the clock. Why on earth hadn't he thought of looking there himself? It wasn't like Our Agnes to be so quickwitted. Now he would have to sit through an eternity of craving while she fumbled with the wet sticks. He fixed his eyes furtively on the paper, and was back again sharply in his former atmosphere of longing and regret.

Dandy, on her knees, fighting the unwilling sticks, fought also the strangling tears and pitiful laughter in her own heart. Harriet's jest was become fact; he had indeed taken her for Our Agnes! Her voice had sounded strange even in her own ears—she admitted that; but, if she had ever had a real place in his life, ever stirred, if only for an instant, his difficult heart, ever been to him even a fraction of more worth than the slattern in his kitchen, would he not have known that there was somebody quite other in the room? She looked at his tired back and roughened hair with a great rush of pity and pain and longing to help, but it did not reach him. His wet wristbands and soaked boots blurred before her misty eyes, but he did not guess or care. Love was round him, kissing his hand, begging at his knee, pressing his aching head to rest, but he could not feel it. She might have drawn his attention with a word, a touch, but she left the one unspoken, the other unperformed. There are rights belonging to unself-conscious friendship that shrinking, fastidious love will never claim.

How could he *not* know? Ah, but he *ought* to have known! If he had cared ever so little, he would have guessed at her presence; cared much—sprung to meet it; and, last of all, if he had loved her, he would have looked for her to come to him somehow from the very ends of the earth.

But he had done none of these things. There was no answer to her prayer. If he never guessed, never turned, she would know that she meant nothing to him at all.

The soup was getting cold. She fretted, battling with the fire. Harriet would be annoyed if their labour was wasted, and he seemed too deep in his reading to remember that she had brought him food. Nervously she pushed the basin up the table within reach of his hand, and went back to her task. When she looked round again, it was empty, and he had buried himself afresh in his paper. After the thrill of joy that she had at least given him some shred of comfort came the renewed certainty that he was quite unconscious of the giver. It was more than plain that she was outside his thoughts altogether.

The fire was crackling merrily now, and with a last strained hope that he might yet know her, she began to gather the papers into a corner, but before she had set the last on the pile, she saw him stir as if distressed and irritated through his absorption by her quiet movements. She stopped instantly, then, and moved to the door, yet slowly, and looking towards him, and all the way her heart was begging, begging for a sign. She knew that all these months her little taper of hope had burnt bravely, bending at times to the wind of disappointment, but always brightening and glowing. Now it was dying. By the time she reached the door it would be dead. Yet she would not call, nor speak aloud the words that the soul only could utter and its twin-soul only should hear. Even a commonplace he might possibly resent in this his trouble. He had said she did not understand. He might certainly say it now, if, in her ignorance of the real conditions, she tried to comfort him. She could only speak to him dumbly from her heart, and he did not hear. His home, his resting-place, were at hand, and he held his face from them. The little torch flickered low. The handle turned, and turned again. Outside the door Dandy stood, hugging her dead candle.

. . . . .

Hamer came in like an anxious bear in his large coat, and found her there.

'All alone?' he asked, stooping to kiss her. 'Where's the boy?'

'In the office. Miss Lancaster is upstairs. She seems rather upset.'

'That so? Poor little woman! I'll go up and have a look at her. She wants stroking a bit, I reckon.

Can you wait any longer, little girl, or are you aching to get home? I'd like just to have a word with the boy, if he'll see me.'

'Yes—do. I don't mind how long I wait.'

'I'll get Miss Lancaster down to keep you company.' He stopped, his foot on the first stair, lowering his voice. 'Does the boy look bad, Dandy Anne?'

She nodded.

'I doubt he'll take it terribly hard—worse than anybody else would have done. He didn't say anything to you, I suppose?'

'No. Nothing.' (And, verily—nothing!)

'You look a bit white, dearie. Getting tired, are you?' He came back to her. 'Didn't *you* say a word to him, Dandy Anne? Didn't you try to comfort the poor lad?'

She smiled bravely.

'I took him some soup, Daddy! Harriet made it, and I "dished up." I don't think he wanted to talk. He's very tired.'

Hamer said no more, looking down at her anxiously, trying to read her face. Sorrow was for bringing folks together, said Hamer's simple philosophy, but it seemed to have failed here. He couldn't think of any trouble in which his first longing would not be to feel Dandy's arms round his neck. Things were wrong somewhere for his little girl. Had he brought her to Watters only to seek diligently for pain?

'Please hurry a little bit, Daddy dear!'

He gave her a last glance, turning reluctantly, with words evidently trembling on his lips, then marched off up the stair. Above, she could hear him pounding at Helwise's door, and presently he had her out on the landing.

'It was his father!' Helwise chattered still.

'Nonsense, my dear! You're a bit overstrung, that's what it is! You want somebody to pet you and tuck you up on the sofa with a hot bottle—that's it, isn't it? Now you put your hand through my arm and we'll trot along down to the fire. Why, you're just shivering, poor dear! I've got a plan to propose to you, if you'll take it on. What do you say to sending Lancaster for a trip after he's got things in working order again—say Egypt or the Canaries—and you shut up house and come over to Watters? If we get a fairish spring we might try a motor-tour after Easter— how'd you like that? Cathedral cities, perhaps, or something of that sort. You keep Dandy company for a bit while I look in at the boy, and see if she can't persuade you to think it over!'

So Helwise, purring with excitement, was stayed with cushions and comforted with cathedrals in front of the drawing-room fire, and Dandy, very heart-sick and resentful at her selfish neglect, yet remembered that she was something of Lanty's, and was patient and sweet with her therefore, mapping out a tour on the hearthrug, with the whole of her being reaching across the hall.

Hamer knocked once, and went straight in to the lonely figure without a moment's hesitation, setting big, raising hands on its shoulders. The Hamers of the world may do these things with impunity, for in their rare, angelic sincerity they carry an Open Sesame through the locked gates of the furthest shrinking sorrow. And though a dreaded somebody was looking over his shoulder at last, Lanty let his paper lie, and neither moved nor minded. Hamer's eye passed over it as he drew up a chair and sat down close.

'I had to go to Manchester. Only just home, or I'd have been down—*there*—with you. I was some-where on the marsh, as it was, until after three. Had anything to eat?'

'Yes, thanks.' Lanty's voice sounded as if pulled by a string. 'I'm afraid I frightened Helwise a little, but the girl brought me some soup. She lighted the fire, too. She's not usually so useful.'

Hamer stared a minute, but said nothing. What game had Dandy been playing? Had Lanty really mistaken her for the 'girl'?

'Miss Lancaster's all right now, anyhow. She and Dandy Anne are having a cosy chat in the drawing-room, snug as snug. She's very easy thrown out of gear. Dandy's cosseting her a bit.'

'It's very kind of Miss Shaw.' Hamer glanced at him shrewdly, but found the answer purely mechanical. No; this wasn't Dandy's hour, he decided with a sigh.

'I heard the—bad news—before I left. Lancaster, I can't forgive myself for having that show of mine, last night!'

'It made very little difference.'

'A deal, surely! There'd have been many more sheep saved, if the men had been on the spot.'

'I doubt it. You forget that they didn't think the storm anything out of the common.'

'Except Brack. It was queer how he knew, wasn't it? I'm blessed if I can make it out! He certainly did his best to warn us.'

'Perhaps. But Brack's was hardly a business pro-position.'

His tone was cold, and Hamer felt suddenly silenced. He raised his eyes to the portrait above them, vivid with energy and pride, remembering Helwise's hysterical conviction, and the likeness between father and son, always marked, struck him strangely to-night. Reversion to type is always the first strong instinct to emerge under great stress. There had been something much deeper than she knew behind Miss Lancaster's chattered fears.

'Well, I'll fix no more hotpots till I get the weather ruled to order!' Hamer sighed. 'I suppose the Lugg's broken its back out and out? I saw a paper in Man-chester. Those poor old souls at the Pride! I met Dennison, just now. He said Whinnerah was set on going there. You'd no choice but to let him have it, had you?'

Lanty thought a moment. There *had* been choice, perhaps, at the very beginning. He hardly knew; so swift had the hour of forced decision come upon him.

'They made it the test of my belief in the Lugg,' he said. 'If the storm were to-morrow instead of yesterday, I would still let the cottage to-night!'

'Then you think you were right about the bank? You don't blame it—you still think it justified?' Hamer stammered, taken aback.

For the first time Lanty turned and looked him straight in the eyes.

'Shaw, I've *got* to think it! If I didn't, I should shoot myself. I've *got* to believe, in spite of everything, that the thing had a right to its existence. I'm not of the class that judge their fathers. I was brought up to see mine as the standing emblem of right thinking and right doing, and though out on the marsh I lost my bearings awhile and forgot it, I found my faith again here. This was his house, his office, his desk. There's his face above it. Even now the place seems almost more his than mine, and, sitting here, I see what he saw, feel what he felt.' He laid his hand on the paper. 'This is the full account of the building of the Lugg—how it was opposed and condemned, and finally sanctioned, fully sanctioned by expert authority—yes, and praised and copied! My father *had* the right to take the risk, both for himself and for posterity. That's the faith I lost—and regained. The success was his. The rest—the failure—is mine.'

Hamer shook his head.

'The world won't agree with you, my boy! It will say you had no chance, that you were bound to stand by your father's work. It will place the fault with the man before you.'

'It will be wrong! It isn't that I don't believe in

inheritance, in reaping and sowing from one generation to another. I've seen the dragon's teeth come up
too often for that. We're bound both before and
behind—I admit it all the way. Thinking of a race,
from father to son, I always see—what is it?—"the
lean, locked ranks go roaring down to die." We've
a hand in more fates than one. But, in spite of that,
I hold that a strong man wins out on his own—wins
out, or goes to the wall. There's no other self-respect-
ing creed. This thing fell to me. Judgment is due on
me. I wouldn't have it otherwise. Each of us in his
little day represents all the rest, and in his own person
stands by what he reaps. I say, I wouldn't have it
otherwise!' And he said to the father as he had said
to the daughter in an hour of sympathy forgot: 'It's
our job while we're on to it. It's our job, while the
light lasts, to make the best of it we can. It's always
one man's hand on the lonely plough.'

After the long silence, Hamer rose.

'I must be getting back to my little girl. Promise
me you'll be off to bed soon, and not stop the night
here, fretting and thinking. And for Heaven's sake
get out of those sopping clothes! No—don't come with
me. Dandy'll understand. Cyril came over for a word
with you—did you know?—but he thought he'd better
not bother you to-night. And Mother sent her love.
Save us! I'd have caught it if I'd forgotten that!
You'll look us up, sometime?'

'When I've made my world over again.'

'Lancaster'—the words came hesitatingly, almost
as if the speaker wondered at himself and them—
'there's one thing I envy you, anyway! I'm just a
plain business-man who's never run up against much
except money that everybody else doesn't taste equal,
but you and your father between you have had something bigger and grander than comes to most folk,
something that sets you near alongside the gods. They
say old Whinnerah stuck it out because of you both,

though Brack went to fetch him. For how many of us others, I wonder, would a man die to prove our pledged word?'

Before he went upstairs, Lanty opened the door and called to Helwise, still purring over her prospects. She rose startled, and came fearfully. He was standing by the table, and upon it the *Gazette* lay wide. The whole world might see it now.

'I hope you haven't waited up for me,' he said quite gently. 'I just wanted to tell you that I should like those cuttings in a book, after all. I should be grateful if you would finish them for me.'

The tears rushed back to her eyes.

'I didn't mean to vex you. I didn't mean to be prying and unkind! I thought all the fine things they said about the Lugg might comfort you a little—help you——'

'They have helped me.'

'Of course I know you'll blame yourself because those two old people got themselves drowned, and the sheep and the mangolds and everything like that, but everybody thought it was very wonderful when it was built, and admired your father and said he had such a good leg! He was ever so proud of that photograph when it came out.'

'I am proud of it, too,' Lanty said, leaning over the paper. He looked long from his father's face to that of Wolf behind. It was hard to think that both were dead—men of a personality that never really dies, but lives on in its effects. Taking a pen, he added a letter to the inscription below, and left the paper lying.

'CONQUERORS OF THE SEA'

CHAPTER XXVII

THE GREEN GATES OF VISION—VI. SWEET-HEART TIME

In the late October afternoon Lancaster rode through the Lane fast, for he was behind time with his promise. Therefore, he looked ahead of him to each flying curve, letting the Gates of Vision pass without notice, nor culling one magic thrill from the garden of enchantment. Yet he checked suddenly where the Lane ran off at right angles like a darting trout, half lest his pressed horse should take the hedge, half in joyful recognition. Out on the drifting distance—of the land, yet of the sky also—his Ghost Mountain smote his eye with its strange twin-qualities of edged clarity and floating opaqueness, like the Shoulder of God made manifest, yet not clothed upon with flesh. What help had it for him, after all these desolate months?

He could spare it only a moment's greeting, but for some reason his heart was lighter as he rode on. Amid the wreck of much the Ghost Mountain had foundered too, forgotten. Its vivid, unexpected return set a faint hope beating that somehow, through some outside power, other lost things might come to resurrection also.

The spell of the 'back-end' had its will again, and in spite of him caught him in its wound gossamer of remembrance. Though he looked between his horse's ears, he knew well enough that round him on every hand were soft distances, melting, blending and changing from blue to purple and purple to grey, with filmy pillars of smoke raised like the standards of home against the stark, stripped woods. He could not keep his cheek from the mild fingers of the gentle air, nor from his lungs the smell of the fresh, damp

earth, going rain- and dew-washed to its winter sleep.
And under the horse's hoofs the dry leaves rustled and
the wet leaves crushed into a still, soft carpet of
stamped crimson and bruised gold. Far in the amber
sky a black little bird was singing, swung on a twig
like a poised finger, and over Dick Crag he could hear
the baffling music of tired hounds on the last spurt of
the afternoon. Little by little he was taken and held
by the old wonder and the familiar glory, so that the
last terrible months dropped away, and his heavily
self-raised prison unlocked. Through the cruel
summer he had come mechanically and doggedly,
with all his joy in his work gone like a blown petal,
together with the quivering sympathy that had made
him the perfect instrument of atmosphere and environment. For this is the last punishment of souls ordinarily
attuned to Nature, when bent to the yoke of pain or
sin. They cry to her, and she does not answer; she
calls to them, and they do not heed; for though the
eyes look abroad on the same beauty, the ears gather
the same music, the spirit and meaning are fled,
leaving only soulless mirages and jangled wires. But
to-night Lancaster came back again to his kingdom.

The look of sudden age, stamped on that far death-
dawn, still clung to some extent; the stern lines of his
face were hammered and set; he was thinner, and his
hair had whitened a little. But for compensation he
had a new self-reliance, a new quietude born of the
absence of nervous struggle. His was now the unfearful poise of one who has fallen and risen again before
the hammer of the gods.

The inquest, the long, dreary spell of wild weather,
intensifying the merciless handling of the marsh—the
dismal rent-audit, the interminable hours of cal-
culating and planning, of patient hearing of complaint, of ordering and overseeing repairs—all these
were behind him now. The new tenant was settled
at Ninekyrkes, and the Dockerays had taken both

him and his to their robbed hearts. For Francey was
in Canada with Lup, and though the old folk were
for ever planning a future that held Rowly with a
wife at Ladyford, and Lup back at the twin-farm—
Dockera's and Whinnerahs as of yore—they knew
well enough that for the wanderers there could be no
place ever again on the Northern marsh.

Slowly the wreck of things was pulled back into
symmetry and order—houses carpeted and papered,
Dutch barns rebuilt, fences set up again, the mutilated
roads laid and rolled. The Let, too, had had all its
yawning mouths filled and strengthened, and the
dykes and cuts were deepened and increased. So the
patched marsh grew trim again, and by the time the
haycutter sang on the hill, the land below had gathered
itself out of the horrors of destruction into a growing
likeness of its old beauty. Only the Lugg and the
Pride were left untouched, derelicts at the will of
wind and tide.

The story had roused a storm of interest throughout
the country, coming as it did at a slack time for news,
and carrying with it the precious breath of long
romance. Lanty refused all dealings with reporters
and kept his eyes from the papers, yet knew well
enough that both his father's career and his own,
their private life, and probably his personal future,
were all common property in a highly decorated
fashion. Into a seething world of clashing interests
and warring classes the tale of the Northern property,
where the flower of ancestry still sprang purely as
well from yeoman and peasant stock as from patrician,
where law was less than loyalty, long service a matter
of course, friendship and understanding things born
of inbred knowledge—dropped like a mediaeval,
blazoned shield into the arena of modern warfare.
Men picked it up wonderingly, fitting it clumsily to
an unaccustomed arm, only to discard it with a laugh.

'No agreements? *That's* a lie, anyhow! You've

got to have everything down in writing, nowadays, or else it's just simply putting your neck in a halter. Landlord's personal charm—tenants' appreciation— sounds like the days of Magna Charta, doesn't it?— tenure by knight service, socage, villeinage, and all the rest of it! I must say these journalists know how to pile on the colour. Amity between agent and farmers—well, I just *don't* think! Why, it's an under-stood thing that they're always at each other's throats! Scion of Hugh Lupus of the Conquest gives his life for an old trust—feudalism dug up by the spadeful, and plastered on with a trowel! *Lies!*"

Yet the true picture was there all the time, defying the brush of maudlin sentiment, as a masterpiece glimmers through a daub.

The rights of the case spun between blame and praise like a feather between two mouths. Both Lancasters were strong men of a rare type that should be stuffed and labelled. They were also murderers, and should both have been drowned; truth-lovers, peace-rulers, regarding their charge as sacred; specious liars and hypocrites, afflicted with a grossly inordinate ambition.

But, as a matter of fact, there was plenty of sym-pathy for the son, the supposed victim of forced loyalty to a weak employer and an arrogant parent, the creature of destiny, bound to take the course he did, a helpless, doomed sheep, like all the other martyrs of the marsh. There were certain well-meaning souls who pursued Lanty with such com-forting extracts, but even these smug blunderers did not do it twice. Only Lup and Francey, over the sea, and Hamer, sadly silent, knew what he really felt about it all; and not they fully. There are debts a man pays in himself alone.

He had resisted all attempts to get him away— Hamer's pleasant plan for the Canaries had had a short existence and a sudden and violent death—but

Helwise had not been defrauded of her tour. For a
month she had spun luxuriously from place to place,
petted and considered, chattering incessantly and
happy as a singing kettle. And after that they had
kept her at Watters for long enough; while Blenkinship's Marget, lent to Lanty during his aunt's absence,
scrubbed and organised like an inspired fury, ruthlessly forcing the twittering Agnes through the mill
of discipline and method, and feeding the silent
master as he had hitherto been fed only in dreams.
The transfer had been brought about by Dandy,
cognisant, through bitter experience, of his need. But
now Helwise was coming home, and King Muddle
would have his own again.

Wigmore, slowly returning to a semblance of health,
had spent the summer recruiting at Bournemouth
and yachting with Bluecaster, and was now at Watters,
while over at Wild Duck Harriet entertained the
whole Quetta family (whose real name was something quite different) with reckless generosity. Lanty
had seen her with them at the various Shows, preach-
ing Westmorland agriculture into puzzled foreign ears.
He had also seen Stubbs, no longer requiring to be
soothed with rotifers, hung about with Quetta-lings
like a family elephant.

But of Dandy he had seen nothing—nothing, that is,
but, at intervals, a smiling, daintily-gracious trans-
parency hovering on the borders of his clouded
existence. Blotted out in a night of storm, she, who
had come so near to meaning everything in his life,
had ceased to mean anything at all. But to-night the
old transfiguration was upon the once-loved fields,
and everything was human and dear again, even as
the friendly earth. At eventide there was light.

To a groom crossing the drive at Watters he handed
over his horse, and went up through the gate at the
top of the garden to the fields above. The house
behind him lay silent and apparently deserted, but

in Hamer's meadow there was a busy little community, receiving that particular instruction in butter-making which comes under the County Council heading of 'Higher Education.'

The Travelling Dairy Van from Asprigg was planted on the breast of the hill looking over the tiny, half-hidden village below, the long curve of the North Road, and the upward sweep of the park. In the big tent stretching from the side of the van a dozen churns were at work on the wet boards of the temporary floor, and in the frame of lifted curtains on the far side the white gowns of pupils and instructress showed vividly against the green of the hill beyond. There was quite a little crowd on the surrounding benches, for this was examination day, and relatives and friends were present to support the last supreme effort. On the raised platform of the van, Mr. and Mrs. Shaw, together with Helwise and a county lady or two, backgrounded by a couple of husbands, an odd parson and Grumphy, surveyed the final throes of competition. The examiner, moving about among the workers, was very busy being taught his business by Harriet, mightily full of contempt for all Dairy Schools and officials thereto attached. In the last little gleam of sun outside Wiggie was walking slowly with his brother, while a gentle, foreign-looking woman struggled with a trio of joyous ruffians rolling down the hill. Stubbs had a fourth in the Rakestraw bath-chair, and was wheeling it patiently if awkwardly over the steep slope. The fourth was a sad little boy of eight, with black eyes swallowing up a pathetic face, conducting the bath-chair progression with the solemnity of high ceremonial. He smiled once, though, when a rapturous thrush, enamoured of the growing sunset, flung it a little flutter of song from a near hedge; and Lanty suddenly saw Wiggie in the smile.

From the middle of the tent, where the scales

awaited the butter, the caretaker ruled teacher and taught alike, by virtue of ancient standing, peculiar wit, and a deficiency in hearing which made mutual wordy warfare impossible. To this autocrat Lanty handed his onlooker's threepence, stopping to exchange a word with the examiner before joining Hamer on the platform. Harriet, however, was still saying her say.

'Of course I know you think you're doing no end of good, but it's all rot! None of that butter will be *really* fit to eat—you know it as well as I do. You wash and work all the goodness out of it, for one thing. Yet, in a minute, you and all the rest of the crowd will get up and say what first-class stuff it is, just because it looks pretty squatting on that table, with a silly pattern sprawling over it. You've admitted yourself that I sent you in the best cream of all the farmers round. Very well! I can send you in a sample of the best butter to match. But I didn't learn how to make it in a rotten tent from a mass of theories walking about with a notebook. I learned it from hard experience and Stubbs's swears when he had to eat the result. Butter-making on the stage, *I* call it!' Harriet finished, glaring round at the trim, white figures. 'Might be a Gaiety chorus getting ready to sing "We are the Churniest Churners!" or, "Never forget your Plug!" Let 'em go home and learn the real thing from their mothers!'

Wiggie looked in over the heads of the pleased crowd.

'Harriet, I'd be awfully obliged if you could persuade Geronimo to come out of the duck-pond! And I rather believe that Stubbs has emptied the Little Great Quetta out of the bath-chair.'

Harriet flew, nearly annihilating the examiner. Wiggie met Lanty's eyes with the smile that he had already seen on another pair of lips.

'Oh, nothing dangerous! Come out and talk, will

you, when business is over? Isn't this jolly? I don't care *what* Harriet says. I should like to eat *all* that butter myself!'

He moved away, followed by looks of passionate gratitude from the disheartened competitors, and Lanty mounted the platform.

'Seen Dandy Anne?' Hamer asked him in a loud whisper, when he had shaken hands all round, and found a chair. Grumphy crawled from under the table, and snored against his knee. Hamer laughed with suppressed jollity.

'She's making butter!' he announced in a joyful undertone. 'Insisted on having a shot at seeing what she could make out. Taken all the ten lessons as serious as seven Sundays all in a lump! Our Dandy Anne! Funny, isn't it?—though you needn't say I said so. I hope she'll pull through all right. Mother here'll be sadly vexed if she comes out with a duck-egg!'

He pointed surreptitiously, and, looking along the lines of farmers' daughters, running his eye from faces he knew personally to others whose parentage was easily placed, Lanty found Dandy at last no more than two churns away.

She looked extraordinarily serious, as Hamer had said, and not only serious but anxious; not only anxious but even—just a little—dishevelled. Her butter had been a long time in coming, and though she had it on the worker by now, it would be a race to finish it. She had seen Lanty when his head first topped the hill, and after that she had done everything wrong, forgotten her plug, made a thorough hash of lifting out the butter and had then over-salted it, so that the marks against her were totting up like a washing-bill, to the distress of the examiner, who admired her exceedingly. That poor four pounds was worked and overworked until it didn't know itself, and was received for weighing with grunted contempt. With flushed cheeks and escaping hair, Dandy took it back to finish, and tried to console herself with a perfectly-executed pattern. Lanty watched her with interest, and decided that he liked her—just a little—dishevelled.

And then at last came a stir of relief from the patient audience, and the white figures retreated to a form, looking excited and hot. The examiner prefaced his report with a short lecture upon butter in general, keeping a nervous eye on Harriet the while. She was on the point of argument more than once, but Wiggie, close at hand, always seemed to know when the explosion was due, and conjured up a Quetta-ling to distract her.

The examiner was very pleased to be there, that day, and very pleased with results, and everything that had gone wrong had, of course, been pure accident, or a passing spasm of forgetfulness, or sheer evil fate. Because everybody had meant excellently, and that, of course, was the main thing, as where there was a will there was a way, and the person who made a mistake to-day would most certainly correct it to-morrow, etc. etc. Still, mistakes, that day, were in such negligible quantity that they were really not worth mentioning. Indeed, he was happy to say that he had been able to place the whole of the competitors in the first-class, with one exception only. Here he looked with such agonised care at least six feet over Dandy's head that everybody else instantly looked six feet lower. This, of course, did not imply that the aforesaid competitor was hopelessly behind the rest; it only meant that her work was not quite up to the standard. Indeed, any one who had watched this particular competitor could see with half an eye that she knew perfectly well how to make butter, only she had been unfortunate. Everybody knew that butter could turn nasty, if it liked, and it had treated her badly. She had had other misfortunes, too—little troubles connected with the plug, etc.—but it was really hardly worth while to dwell upon them. He was most decidedly pleased to be there! And this time he looked six feet down and straight at Dandy, so adoringly that all the audience who had really nice feelings instantly looked six feet up.

Then one of the pretty county ladies rose and said how pleased she was to be there, and how pleased everybody else was pleased, and how more than pleased everybody would be when they read about it in the papers, while the competitors wished she would hurry up and put them out of their misery, and thought how infinitely more desirable it was to stand on a platform and look charming and sweet and say all the right things in exactly the right way, with an adoring husband somewhere behind, than to make the best butter in the Three Kingdoms.

After that, the certificates were given out, and the noble first-class came up blushing and bowing to receive the spoils of war. Finally, Dandy, for her duck-egg.

It seemed to her that the tent was ten miles long and packed like a Military Tournament. She saw the examiner's eyes bulging with pity, and wondered absently why they didn't fall out. She heard her father's big whisper: 'Now then, Mother, don't you fret! Don't fret, Mother!' and knew that he was patting his wife's hand. She heard the caretaker's grunt. And at the foot of the steps she felt exactly as if hot needles were dancing red-slippered all over her, simply because there was one very ordinary person sitting on the platform, engaged in staring at his boots.

But as she curtsied to the pretty lady and the duck-egg, wishing herself at Halsted for the last time in her life, Harriet came suddenly to her rescue.

'Good lad, Dandy!' she bawled, clapping like a small thunderstorm, and the general embarrassment

broke in a burst of amusement and applause. Everybody laughed; competitors, audience, the miserable
examiner—thrilling with gratitude towards his late
tormentor—and Dandy herself. Grumphy waddled
forward to the extreme edge, and reached out a long,
loving tongue.

'I am sure we all appreciate Miss Shaw's sporting
effort!' the pretty lady said prettily, and there was
more applause. Dandy looked up bravely and met
Lanty's eyes, turned on her at last as if they really
saw her.

'It was very bad butter!' she said candidly, putting
out a hand to the rolling tongue, and raising a fresh
laugh by her cheerful honesty. Lancaster leaned
forward, smiling.

'May I buy it for that thin dog of mine?' he asked;
and instantly the Lane was about them both instead
of the crowded tent, and a vision of rippling wind
on the turning corn. They had been alien, then; he
had almost frankly disliked her; but that was long
ago, and in this moment they were all the nearer for
it. She had said that she was looking for herself, even
as Grumphy, galumphing through new wheat; and
in looking for herself she had found somebody—ah,
how much dearer! And *he* had said that the whip was
the only teacher. Well, she had come through many
a scourging of longing and revolt, unbearable pain,
self-hatred and contempt, and had learned many
things; but in this hour of absurd humiliation she
knew that the one great thing she had learned she
had at last taught him also. She turned and went
blindly through the still cheering crowd to her seat.
But it was twenty miles back, because she went from
him.

As they streamed out of the tent, Bluecaster came
over a hedge on a splashed hunter, and the Quetta-
lings, who had a passion for all locomotion that did
not include plain walking upon their own legs,

swarmed up him. Harriet stalked after them, and lifted the Little Great Quetta down again, because he was precious. The big, black eyes filled with tears, but he did not rebel. He knew that he was precious, and it had very serious drawbacks.

Lanty ran into Denny, standing in tongue-tied admiration before a Miss Braithwaite. So had he stood all afternoon, from the first whirl of the swinging churn to the proud moment when she had laid before the examiner the four best pounds of the day. He started when Lanty tapped him on the shoulder.

'Your wife will have plenty of sale for her butter, Thomas!' he told him slyly.

Denny reddened hotly, and found his tongue with a rush.

'Ay! an' yours'll likely be her first customer!' he retorted briskly, with meaning, and chuckled as he saw his embarrassment reflected. He had caught the episode of the duck-egg. Lanty went away hurriedly.

Wiggie joined him on the slope, with Edgar and his Southern wife, and they went down together to Watters, to find Dandy and the examiner putting the last touches to the waiting meal, while Helwise rooked the instructress for a bazaar. Harriet and Stubbs followed with the rolling ruffians, and then Bluecaster. Bluecaster had taken the Little Great Quetta to see the horse stabled, because you may sometimes look on at interesting things, even if you *are* precious. And lastly, Mr. and Mrs. Shaw, with their other butter-supporting guests, who were still as pleased about everything as ever. They did not stay long, though, having some distance to drive; and then the Quetta-lings were able to let themselves go with Italian shrieks and wild, operatic gestures. Only the Little Great Quetta sat silent and could not eat for quivering excitement, because a real, live, large horse had munched out of his thin, little hand; until Bluecaster, with a furtive air of removing his neighbour's landmark, took him on his knee and fed him himself.

Lanty looked round the big, joyous, crowded room, and in spite of the buzz of talk and the soaring, staccato shrieks, felt again the peace that had met him, months ago, on his first entrance. He was happy, too. It came to him with a shock, since he had been so sure that he could never be happy again. Hamer made him happy, moving about gloriously contented with the swarm under his roof; and Mrs. Shaw, presiding with conjuring cleverness over her teapot. Dandy had given hers to Helwise, who loved the effect of her white fingers on the silver handle, and took care to do nothing more active than to incline the spout gently towards each cup. Dandy did not make him feel happy, though. She made him feel breathless, and as if he would like to climb on the table and shriek with the Quetta-lings. It was safer not to look at her.

Wiggie, however, murmuring at his side, busily bridging a big gap with his summer experiences, filled him, as usual, with little chuckles of content. Lanty noticed that he never forgot to turn his face so that his brother might read his words. Presently he went a step further back still.

'Did I ever tell you that all the players in that hockey match turned up again, one after another, to say how sorry they were I was ill? I thought it so awfully decent of them! It helped a lot, I can tell you. Saunders *did* say that, if only I had stayed in my place, he could have done all the work and perhaps saved me something, but that's—well—just Saunders, isn't it?—and he brought me a book on the actinic force of light, to cheer me up a bit when I was getting better. Do *you* know anything about the actinic force of light? Neither did I till I met Saunders, but I do now. I learned it up to talk to him. The little curate said that he had saved my life, and that I owed him

a penny bun. Harriet was very angry—you've no
idea! She said there was plenty of food in the
kitchen, and that he had done nothing but sit still
while a motor-car took him somewhere, and that
anybody, even an idiot or a parson, could have done
that. The curate said the point was that he was the
body on the spot. It was his motto. In the family,
he said, like dear old Stubbs. I like him. He lent me
a novel by—perhaps I had better not say it out loud.
The others were all awfully kind, too. I liked them.
I remarked to Harriet one day that they seemed to
be really keen on music, up here, and she just snorted.
She said: "You don't imagine, do you, that they care
a straw about your being a singer, any more than I
do? They're simply stuck on you because you stole
that goal!" Edgar wasn't a bit pleased—were you,
old man?—and Gardner said awful things, but I
think I liked it.'

'He is the Great Quetta!' Edgar put in, with a note
of indignation in his deep, curious voice.

Wiggie laughed.

'Do you know that they say I may—perhaps—be
able to sing again in a year's time? I've still a half-
crown or two in the toe of a stocking, and Edgar's
got a post somewhere where they waggle their fingers
instead of their tongues, so the babies won't starve
yet awhile. We'll keep the pot boiling, somehow, but
I do not think I shall ever be the Great Quetta again.'

Edgar uttered an exclamation of angry pain, and
his brother smiled at him affectionately. Blenkinship's Marget came up and handed him a medicine-
glass, and he finished the tail of the smile on her.

'What does it matter? Anyhow, I can always
teach; and the Little Great Quetta will keep us all
out of the Workhouse when we're old! You must
hear him sing, Lancaster. He has the true singer's
throat, and cords like the harp of all the winds.
Perfect ear, of course. Even the Quetta-lings, shrieking

themselves hoarse over there, have *that*. He will
be the Greatest Quetta some day, please God, and
make up to Edgar for his poor old ears, and to me
for all the poor other things that have gone wrong in
my inside—won't he, old man?'

'He looks very sensitive,' Lanty observed, watching
the child.

'The instrument has to be tuned,' Wiggie answered
rather sadly. 'It is out of wrung strings that both
God and man make their sweetest music.'

'Still jabbering about your stupid singing!' Harriet
scoffed, thrusting a plate of scones into his face. 'Try
these. They're buttered with Wild Duck. I told the
examiner it was the stuff from the Van, and he
cleared out like a shot, and hasn't been seen since.
By the way, the L.G. knows what you call your
Quetta-Song perfectly now. He was singing it all
morning.'

'It's a song I used to sing,' Wiggie explained for
Lanty's benefit, 'a song about lambkins and resting-
places and things. We call it the Quetta-Song because
the Quettas never have a resting-place. They are
always on the move.'

'I know a song like that,' Lanty said slowly, out of
far depths when Harriet had turned away, and
nobody but Wiggie could hear. '*I* call it my Home-
Song. I heard it years ago at the Westmorland
Festival.'

'You heard *me*,' Wiggie said simply. 'I remember
singing it there. It is known as the Quetta-Song in
the profession, so the others do not sing it. It was
when I first came out and was plump and pretty, with
my voice not quite full grown, so of course you wouldn't
remember me. But I thank you ever so much for
remembering the song.'

'I always remembered it, but I lost faith in it,' Lanty
said. 'I could find no home to match the song.'

'But you will find it soon!' Wiggie answered with a

quick look, and saw where the other's eyes turned.
'I have found mine,' he added. He stood up as Harriet
came back. 'Harriet—when may I come home again?'

'Home?' Harriet stared.

'Home to Wild Duck—for good!'

They gazed at each other over the plate of scones,
and then, still clasping it, the Rur'l D'trict C'cillor
fled from the room. The Great Quetta (who was only
Wiggie) followed.

'Seen Brack lately?' Hamer inquired in a low tone,
dropping into the vacant chair. Lanty nodded.

'Yes, I've come across him a good deal. He often
looks in to see me, too. But he's leaving—did you
know?—giving up Thweng in the spring, and going
out to Canada again, to join Lup. They say he wants
to take Braithwaite's youngest girl with him. He's
money, you know, so he can afford to play about
between the Continents. I'll be sorry to lose him—
yes, it's come to that, though I'd never have believed
it! There's nothing he won't do for me, nowadays.
Oh, he's the old Brack again, of course!—all the
stage-effects piled on as thick as ever—but the old
Brack with a difference. He still goes to church, by
the way.'

'New life for everybody,' Hamer mused. 'There's
not much doubt where Cyril will end, is there? You'll
be putting out your hand, too, my boy!'

Lanty looked at him with a question in his eyes.

'Put it out soon!' said Hamer.

Bluecaster left, shortly afterwards, and the agent
walked part of the way with him.

'You'll come back?' Hamer begged, concerned.
'You'll stop to dinner, you and your aunt? I've
scarcely had the tail of a word with you, with all those
folks to see to. Come back!'

And all the rest of the party gathered on the steps
and called after him as he went down the drive—
kindly Shaws and gentle Quettas, Helwise, smilingly

satisfied and perfectly at home, and Stubbs, untroubled by the least alluring vision of any White Lion, all under the long, creepered house in the opal evening. 'Come back! Be sure you come back!'

The two men turned into the Lane, walking by the tired horse, and after their short business chat was finished they went on some way together in silence. Bluecaster was going abroad again soon to his usual winter round, but to-night he went back alone to his big, lonely house. Lanty was glad that, behind himself, the friendly, happy party awaited him at Watters.

Bluecaster's would always be a lonely life, he thought, unconsciously prophetic. Such a temperament as his would send him weaponless into every battle, and receive him back more sure than ever of the forces arrayed against him, yet pathetically ready to the bitter end. And each defeat would leave him more silent and more shy. Yes—and more lovable, he said to himself, holding his stirrup for him while he mounted, and watching for the last courteous salute that he knew would be sent him from the turn. Bluecaster might be little more than a symbol of great ideals beyond his perfect grasp, but even as such he met a passionate need in the stronger man behind him, since every brave Viking-soul sails forth the happier for the figurehead and the spilt wine.

There was coming into the sky the steely clearness of still autumn, and a faint breath of frost was promised by the yellow bar yet lingering on the horizon and the starkening edge of the woods. It was darker and stiller in the Lane, and when Dandy grew out of the mist creeping up from the earth beneath, she came with the hush and mystery of vapour-borne elves. Not only was she not outside any more, but she had looked right into the fairies' haunts and bent her ear to their rippling talk. Across the almost fiercely-pure sky the birds went home.

Close at hand, she had still her mystery, but now it

was human and breathing, with kind, shy eyes and delicate colour coming to and fro.

'Wiggie sent me!' she said rather breathlessly. 'He told me to stop you at the last gap as you came back. He said you had lost something, and would find it there if you looked. Do you know what he meant? He wouldn't explain—just packed me off with the message. I don't know what to make of him—he's like a schoolboy to-night! It's glorious to see him getting well, isn't it? You wouldn't believe how pleased Watters was to have him back! Two roses bloomed in the night under his window, and at dawn there were half a dozen birds waiting on the sill.'

'I believe he's a wizard!' Lanty smiled. 'Look at Harriet! He has her at the end of a string.'

'Harriet has fallen in love with him! I believe it happened the night he came to Crabtree—the dreadful night after the storm when I brought you the soup —I mean, when Our Agnes—Wiggie—Harriet——' She floundered, agonised and helpless.

He stopped, looking at her with a frown.

'When *you* brought me the soup?'

'Yes. No!' She was almost in tears at the unmeant revelation. 'It was Harriet! *She* made it, and there were cockroaches—a tin of something—I washed the pan.'

He held doggedly to his question.

'When *you* brought me the soup?'

'I carried it in—that was all—and you didn't know. You thought it was the servant! But I only found the tray-cloth. It was Harriet——'

'Bother Harriet!' he said cruelly, and put his hands on her shoulders, trying to see her face. 'It was *you* who fed me, *you* who lighted the fire and tidied up those horrible papers, and were good to me all round? And I didn't know!'

'No, you didn't know!' She let her pride slip through soft fingers and looked up at him, all the pain of that gone hour in her sobbing voice. 'But you ought to have known—oh, you ought, you *ought!* I wanted to be good to you more than anything in the world, and you wouldn't let me. I asked you—I begged in my heart—how was it you did not hear? I did not dare to speak aloud. You had said I did not understand—do you remember?—and I was afraid. So when I found you did not hear, I went away, and you let me go. You let me go!'

'I was out on a far road, sweetheart, and I had lost you in the dark. I doubt I haven't got back to you, even yet!'

'Come soon!' she whispered, in his arms.

Behind them, a crystal voice broke into singing, and, turning, they looked together through the last Green Gate of Vision. On the hill-side a little child was standing with his face turned to the bar of sunset, as if he sang to listening souls behind that dying door of gold. Far out of sight, the Quettas stood arm in arm, risking their Little Great Quetta in the autumn mist. There was nothing framed by the Gate of Vision but the sleeping land and the singing child.

He sang the Wander-Song of the Quettas, that was Lancaster's Song of Home.

> 'What can lambkins do
> All the keen night through?
> Nestle by their woolly mother
> The careful ewe.
>
> What can nestlings do
> In the nightly dew?
> Sleep beneath their mother's wing
> Till day breaks anew.
>
> If in field or tree
> There might only be
> Such a warm soft sleeping-place
> Found for me!'

With the last note he stayed, looking up at the door

of Heaven closing before him. Almost he might have seen the long years of wandering and struggle, searing glory and usuried fame, before he came to his last, soft sleeping-place on the Arm of God.

'And *my* place?' Lanty whispered. 'It is cold in the dark.'

'It is warm in my heart,' she said.

CHAPTER XXVIII

HAIL AND FAREWELL!

ON the marsh there was the breath of mown hay that comes when the grass is ready, before ever the scythe is swung or the cutter yoked. On the eve of his wedding, Lancaster walked the ribbon of road alone.

To-morrow Helwise would be gone, joyfully transplanted to Watters for life, and in her place his dear love, with all his joy in her hands. He closed a reverent palm on the leaping thought, and turned to send his tribute out across the sea.

The Let had come through the winter months unharmed, but the unbuttressed Lugg looked pitifully rent, with its six doors set open for any flood to charge unchallenged. Year after year it would shrink and crumble, beaten and torn, until the memory of its fame would be but a tale mumbled in old men's mouths. And not a hand had been laid on the Pride since the Whinnerahs had gone out with the dawn. Tide after tide swam cold into its wrecked rooms, and took its flotsam of broken sticks. In the little fire-lit home the waves swallowed the empty hearth and fretted the mouldering walls. Where the kettle had sung and the tired dogs breathed in a happy sleep, the bitter water plashed and moaned.

Yet the sea had not won. Wolf was its victor, though it had dragged him down and strangled him out of life. For many waters cannot quench love, neither can the floods drown it.

On this the eve of blessed beginnings, Lancaster gave himself wholly to his faithful dead.

> '*Who hath remembered me? who hath forgotten?*
> Thou hast forgotten, O summer swallow,
> But the world shall end when I forget!'

PRINTED IN GREAT BRITAIN AT THE UNIVERSITY PRESS, OXFORD
BY JOHN JOHNSON, PRINTER TO THE UNIVERSITY

A LIST OF THE
WORLD'S
CLASSICS

Oxford University Press

THE WORLD'S CLASSICS

A SERIES in constant progress, already containing over four hundred volumes, and offering in a size adapted for the pocket, and at a low price, the most famous works in the English language, with more than a few translations. Many of the volumes contain introductions by the best modern writers.

POCKET SIZE, $6 \times 3\frac{3}{4}$ inches (as this list). Large type, on thin opaque paper. Obtainable either in superfine art cloth or sultan-red leather.

A NUMBER of the volumes are issued also in brown antique leather, embossed design, gilt top. These are specially recommended for presentation.

THE volumes are obtainable only through the booksellers.

IN THE FOLLOWING LIST the books are classified as below:

Anthologies	*Letters*
Autobiography	*Literary Criticism*
Biography	*Philosophy and Science*
Classics—Greek and Roman	*Poetry*
Drama	*Politics, Political Theory,*
Essays and Belles Lettres	*and Political Economy*
Fiction (Short Stories are	*Religion*
grouped separately)	*Short Stories*
History	*Travel and Topography*

AN INDEX OF AUTHORS is given at the end of the list.

LATEST ADDITIONS

¶ *Biography*

TREVELYAN (SIR G. O.). Life of Macaulay. 2 vols. With a prefatory note by *G. M. Trevelyan* (401, 402).

¶ *Poetry*

DANTE'S DIVINE COMEDY. Italian text and English translation, by *Melville B. Anderson*, on facing pages, with notes. 3 vols. (392-4).
English translation only, with notes, in one volume (395).

GOETHE. Faust, Parts I and II. Translated by *Bayard Taylor*, introduced by *Marshall Montgomery*, annotated by *Douglas Yates* (380).

¶ *Essays, &c.*

AMERICAN CRITICISM. Representative Literary Essays. Chosen by *Norman Foerster* (354).

CHESTERFIELD. LETTERS. Selected, with an Introduction, by *Phyllis M. Jones* (347).

STERNE (LAURENCE). A Sentimental Journey. With Introduction by *Virginia Woolf* (333).

¶ *Fiction*

AUSTEN (JANE). Northanger Abbey. Introduction by *Michael Sadleir* (355). Persuasion. Introduction by *Forrest Reid* (356). Sense and Sensibility. Introduction by *Lord David Cecil* (389).

AUSTRIAN SHORT STORIES. Selected and translated by *Marie Busch* (337).

CRIME AND DETECTION. Second Series (351).

DISRAELI. Coningsby. With Intro. by *André Maurois* (381).

FIELDING. Jonathan Wild (382).

GISSING. Veranilda (349). Will Warburton (348).

HARRIS (JOEL CHANDLER). Uncle Remus (361).

HOLME (CONSTANCE). The Lonely Plough (390). The Old Road from Spain (400).

SHORT STORIES OF THE SOUTH SEAS. Selected by *E. C. Parnwell* (332).

SPANISH SHORT STORIES. Sixteenth Century. In contemporary translations, revised, with an Introduction, by *J. B. Trend* (326).

STORIES OF AFRICA. Chosen by *E. C. Parnwell* (359).

TOLSTOY. Childhood, Boyhood, and Youth. Translated, with an Introduction, by *Aylmer Maude* (352).

TROLLOPE (ANTHONY). The American Senator (391). The Eustace Diamonds (357). Last Chronicles of Barset. 2 vols. (398, 399). Tales of all Countries (397).

¶ *Politics*

SPEECHES AND DOCUMENTS ON THE BRITISH DOMINIONS (1918-1931). Introduction and Notes by *A. Berriedale Keith* (403).

COMPLETE LIST OF THE SERIES

¶ *Anthologies*

A BOOK OF NARRATIVE VERSE. Compiled by *V. H. Collins.* Introduction by *Edmund Blunden* (350).

AMERICAN CRITICISM. Representative Literary Essays. Chosen by *Norman Foerster* (354).

ENGLISH ESSAYS, chosen and arranged by *W. Peacock* (32).

ENGLISH ESSAYS, 1600–1900, chosen by *S. V. Makower* and *B. H. Blackwell* (172).

ENGLISH ESSAYS, MODERN, from 'MARK RUTHERFORD' to J. MIDDLETON MURRY. Selected by *H. S. Milford* (280).

ENGLISH LETTERS (Fifteenth to Nineteenth Centuries) (192).

ENGLISH PROSE from MANDEVILLE to RUSKIN, chosen and arranged by *W. Peacock* (45).

ENGLISH PROSE, chosen and arranged by *W. Peacock* in 5 volumes: I, WYCLIFFE to CLARENDON; II, MILTON to GRAY; III, WALPOLE to LAMB; IV, LANDOR to HOLMES; V, MRS. GASKELL to HENRY JAMES (219–23).

ENGLISH PROSE, Narrative, Descriptive, Dramatic (MALORY to STEVENSON), compiled by *H. A. Treble* (204).

ENGLISH SONGS AND BALLADS, compiled by *T. W. H. Crosland.* New edition, with the text revised, and additional poems (13).

ENGLISH SHORT STORIES (Nineteenth and Twentieth Centuries), from SIR WALTER SCOTT to KATHERINE MANSFIELD, selected by *Hugh Walker* and *H. S. Milford*, with an Introduction (in Series I) by *Hugh Walker*. Three Series (193, 228, 315).

ENGLISH VERSE. Edited by *W. Peacock.* Vol. I, Early Lyrics to SHAKESPEARE (308). Vol. II, CAMPION to the Ballads (309). Vol. III, DRYDEN to WORDSWORTH (310). Vol. IV, SCOTT to ELIZABETH BROWNING (311). Vol. V, LONGFELLOW to RUPERT BROOKE (312).

LETTERS WRITTEN IN WAR-TIME (Fifteenth to Nineteenth Centuries), selected and arranged by *H. Wragg* (202).

A MISCELLANY OF TRACTS AND PAMPHLETS. Sixteenth to Nineteenth Centuries. Edited by *A. C. Ward* (304).

PALGRAVE'S GOLDEN TREASURY, with 190 pages of additional poems by *FitzGerald, Tennyson*, the *Brownings, Arnold*, &c. (133).

¶ *Autobiography*

AKSAKOFF (SERGHEI). Trans. by *J. D. Duff.* A Russian Gentleman (241). Years of Childhood (242). A Russian Schoolboy (261).

CELLINI (BENVENUTO) (300).

DE QUINCEY (THOMAS). Confessions of an Opium-Eater (23).

FRANKLIN (BENJAMIN). The Autobiography, edited from his original manuscript by *John Bigelow* (250).

GIBBON (EDWARD). Autobiography. Intro. *J. B. Bury* (139).

HAYDON (BENJAMIN ROBERT). The Autobiography. Introduction and Epilogue by *Edmund Blunden* (314).

HOLCROFT (THOMAS). Memoirs, continued by *W. Hazlitt* (302).

HUNT (LEIGH). Autobiography. Intro. *Edmund Blunden* (329).

MILL (JOHN STUART). Autobiography. Introduction by *Harold J. Laski* (262).

MORITZ (C. P.). **Anton Reiser.** Introduction by *P. E. Matheson* (299).

TOLSTOY. **A Confession, and What I believe.** Translated by *Louise* and *Aylmer Maude* (229).

TRELAWNY (E. J.). **Adventures of a Younger Son.** Introduction by *Ethel Colburn Mayne* (289).

TROLLOPE (ANTHONY). Autobiography. Introduction by *Michael Sadleir* (239).

¶ *Biography*

CARLYLE. **The Life of John Sterling.** Introduction by *W. Hale White* ('*Mark Rutherford*') (144).

DOBSON (AUSTIN). **Four Frenchwomen: Charlotte Corday, Madame Roland, Princess de Lamballe, Madame de Genlis** (248).

EMERSON. **Representative Men.** (With *English Traits*) (30).

FRANCIS OF ASSISI (ST.). **The Little Flowers; and The Life of Brother Giles.** Translated into English verse by *James Rhoades* (265).

GASKELL (MRS.). **The Life of Charlotte Brontë** (214).

HOUGHTON (LORD). **Life of Keats** (364).

JOHNSON (SAMUEL). **Lives of the Poets.** 2 vols. Introduction by *Arthur Waugh* (83, 84).

MAUDE (AYLMER). **Life of Tolstoy.** 2 vols. (383, 384).

SCOTT (SIR WALTER). **Lives of the Novelists.** Introduction by *Austin Dobson* (94).

SMITH (J. T.). **Nollekens and his Times.** With Introduction by *Walter Sichel* (322).

TREVELYAN (SIR G. O.). **Life of Macaulay.** 2 vols. With a prefatory note by *G. M. Trevelyan* (401, 402).

WALTON (IZAAK). **Lives of Donne, Wotton, Hooker, Herbert, Sanderson.** Introduction by *George Saintsbury* (303).

¶ *The ' Classics ', Greek and Roman*

AESCHYLUS. **The Seven Plays.** Translated into English Verse by *Lewis Campbell* (117).

ARISTOPHANES. **The Acharnians, Knights, Birds, and Frogs.** Translated by *J. Hookham Frere.* Intro. *W. W. Merry* (134).

HOMER. Translated by *Pope.* Iliad (18). Odyssey (36).

SOPHOCLES. **The Seven Plays.** Translated into English Verse by *Lewis Campbell* (116).

VIRGIL. **The Aeneid, Georgics, and Eclogues.** Translated by *John Dryden* (37).

—— **The Aeneid, Georgics, and Eclogues.** Translated by *James Rhoades* (227).

¶ Drama

BROWNING (ROBERT). Poems and Plays, 1833–42 (58).
[*Contents*: Pauline, Paracelsus, Strafford, Sordello, Pippa
Passes, King Victor, and King Charles.]

CONGREVE (WILLIAM). Complete Works. 2 vols. Introduction by
Bonamy Dobrée. Vol. I, The Comedies. Vol. II, The Mourning Bride, with Letters, Poems, and Miscellanies (276, 277).

EIGHTEENTH CENTURY COMEDY. Edited, with an Introduction,
by *W. D. Taylor*. The five comedies are FARQUHAR'S Beaux'
Stratagem, STEELE'S Conscious Lovers, GAY'S Beggar's Opera,
FIELDING'S Tom Thumb, GOLDSMITH'S She Stoops to Conquer
(292).

EIGHTEENTH CENTURY, LESSER COMEDIES OF THE. Edited by
Allardyce Nicoll. The five comedies are ARTHUR MURPHY'S The
Way to keep him, GEORGE COLMAN'S The Jealous Wife, MRS.
INCHBALD'S Everyone has his fault, THOMAS MORTON'S Speed
the Plough, and FREDERICK REYNOLDS'S The Dramatist (321).

MARLOWE'S Dr. Faustus (with GOETHE'S Faust, Part I, trans.
J. Anster). Introduction by *Sir A. W. Ward* (135).

RESTORATION TRAGEDIES. Five Plays, with an Introduction by
Bonamy Dobrée (313). The five tragedies are DRYDEN'S All for
Love, OTWAY'S Venice Preserved, SOUTHERNE'S Oronooko,
ROWE'S Fair Penitent, and ADDISON'S Cato.

SHAKESPEARE. Plays and Poems. Preface by *A. C. Swinburne*.
Introductions by *Edward Dowden*. 9 vols. Comedies. 3 vols.
(100, 101, 102). Histories and Poems. 3 vols. (103, 104, 105).
Tragedies. 3 vols. (106, 107, 108).

SHAKESPEARE, Six Plays by Contemporaries of. DEKKER, The
Shoemaker's Holiday; WEBSTER, The White Devil; BEAU-
MONT and FLETCHER, The Knight of the Burning Pestle, and
Philaster; WEBSTER, The Duchess of Malfi; MASSINGER, A
New Way to pay Old Debts. Edited by *C. B. Wheeler* (199).

SHERIDAN. Plays. Introduction by *Joseph Knight* (79).

TOLSTOY. The Plays. Complete edition, including the posthu-
mous plays. Translated by *Louise* and *Aylmer Maude* (243).

¶ Essays and Belles Lettres

BACON. The Essays, Civil and Moral (24).

BROWN (DR. JOHN). Horae Subsecivae (Rab and His Friends,
&c.). Introduction by *Austin Dobson* (118).

CARLYLE. On Heroes and Hero-Worship (62). Past and Present.
Introduction by *G. K. Chesterton* (153). Sartor Resartus (19).

DOBSON (AUSTIN). At Prior Park, &c. (259). Eighteenth-Century
Vignettes. Three Series (245–7). Four Frenchwomen (248).
Old Kensington Palace, &c. (258). A Paladin of Philanthropy, &c.
(256). Rosalba's Journal, &c. (260). Side-walk Studies (257).

EMERSON. English Traits, and Representative Men (30). Essays, Two Series (6). Nature, and Miscellanies (236).

ENGLISH CRITICAL ESSAYS. Selected and edited by *Edmund D. Jones*. 2 volumes. I, Sixteenth to Eighteenth Centuries. II, Nineteenth Century (240, 206).

ENGLISH ESSAYS, chosen and arranged by *W. Peacock* (32).
—— (A BOOK OF), 1600–1900. Chosen by *S. V. Makower* and *B. H. Blackwell* (172).
—— MODERN, from 'MARK RUTHERFORD' to J. MIDDLETON MURRY. Selected by *H. S. Milford* (280).

ENGLISH PROSE. MANDEVILLE TO RUSKIN. Chosen by *W. Peacock* (45). Also a selection in 5 volumes by the same editor; WYCLIFFE TO CLARENDON (219); MILTON TO GRAY (220); WALPOLE TO LAMB (221); LANDOR TO HOLMES (222); MRS. GASKELL TO HENRY JAMES (223).

ENGLISH PROSE. Narrative, Descriptive, and Dramatic (MALORY TO STEVENSON). Compiled by *H. A. Treble* (204).

FROUDE (J. A.). Short Studies on Great Subjects. Series I (269).

HAZLITT (WILLIAM). Characters of Shakespeare's Plays. Introduction by *Sir Arthur Quiller-Couch* (205). The English Comic Writers. Introduction by *R. B. Johnson* (124). Sketches and Essays. Essays on Men and Manners (15). Table-Talk (5). The Spirit of the Age (57). Winterslow (25).

HOLMES (OLIVER WENDELL). The Autocrat of the Breakfast-Table (61). The Poet at the Breakfast-Table. Introduction by *Sir W. R. Nicoll* (95). The Professor at the Breakfast-Table. Introduction by *Sir W. R. Nicoll* (89).

HORNE (R. H.). A New Spirit of the Age. Introduction by *W. Jerrold* (127).

HUNT (LEIGH). Essays and Sketches. Introduction by *R. B. Johnson* (115). The Town. Introduction and Notes by *Austin Dobson* (132).

IRVING (WASHINGTON). The Sketch Book of Geoffrey Crayon, Gent. Introduction by *T. Balston* (173).

LAMB. Essays of Elia, and The Last Essays of Elia (2).

LANDOR. Imaginary Conversations. Selected, with Introduction, by *Prof. E. de Sélincourt* (196).

LEOPARDI. Essays (365).

MILTON. Selected Prose. Intro. *Malcolm W. Wallace* (293).

MONTAIGNE'S ESSAYS. Florio's translation. 3 volumes (65, 70, 77).

REYNOLDS (SIR JOSHUA). The Discourses, and the Letters to 'The Idler'. Introduction by *Austin Dobson* (149).

RUSKIN. (*Ruskin House Editions, by arrangement with Messrs. Allen & Unwin, Ltd.*) 'A Joy for Ever,' and The Two Paths. Illustrated (147). Sesame and Lilies, and Ethics of the Dust (145). Time and Tide, and The Crown of Wild Olive (146). Unto this Last, and Munera Pulveris (148).

RUTHERFORD (MARK). Pages from a Journal (358).

SMITH (ALEXANDER). Dreamthorp, &c. (200).

SMOLLETT. Travels through France and Italy (90).
STERNE (LAURENCE). A Sentimental Journey. Introduction by *Virginia Woolf* (333).
STEVENSON (R.L.). Virginibus Puerisque, & Across the Plains (296).
THACKERAY. The Book of Snobs, &c. (50).
THOREAU. Walden. Introduction by *Theodore Watts-Dunton* (68).
TOLSTOY. Translated by *L. & A. Maude*. Essays and Letters (46). 'What is Art?' and Essays on Art (331).
TRACTS AND PAMPHLETS, from JOHN KNOX to H. G. WELLS (304).
WHITE (GILBERT). The Natural History of Selborne (22).
WHITMAN. Specimen Days in America (371).

¶ *Fiction* (For SHORT STORIES see separate heading)

AINSWORTH (W. HARRISON). The Tower of London (162).
AUSTEN (JANE). Emma. Introduction by *E. V. Lucas* (129). Pride and Prejudice. Introduction by *R. W. Chapman* (335). Mansfield Park. Introduction by *M. Lascelles* (345). Northanger Abbey. Introduction by *Michael Sadleir* (355). Persuasion. Introduction by *Forrest Reid* (356). Sense and Sensibility. Introduction by *Lord David Cecil* (389).
BETHAM-EDWARDS (M.). The Lord of the Harvest (194).
BLACKMORE (R.D.). Lorna Doone. Intro. *Sir Herbert Warren* (171).
BORROW (GEORGE). Lavengro (66). The Romany Rye (73).
BRONTË (ANNE). Agnes Grey (141). Tenant of Wildfell Hall (67).
BRONTË (CHARLOTTE). Jane Eyre (1). Shirley (14). Villette (47). The Professor, and the Poems of CHARLOTTE, EMILY, and ANNE BRONTË. Introduction by *Theodore Watts-Dunton* (78).
BRONTË (EMILY). Wuthering Heights (10).
BUNYAN. The Pilgrim's Progress (12). Mr. Badman (338).
CERVANTES. Don Quixote. 2 volumes. Translation by *Charles Jervas*. Intro. and notes by *J. Fitzmaurice-Kelly* (130, 131).
COBBOLD (REV. RICHARD). Margaret Catchpole (119).
COLLINS (WILKIE). The Moonstone. Introduction by *T. S. Eliot* (316). The Woman in White (226).
COOPER (J. FENIMORE). The Last of the Mohicans (163).
DEFOE. Captain Singleton (82). Robinson Crusoe. Part I (17).
DICKENS. Barnaby Rudge (286). Christmas Books (307). Edwin Drood (263). Great Expectations. 6 Illustrations by *Warwick Goble* (128). Hard Times (264). Old Curiosity Shop (270). Oliver Twist. 24 Illustrations by *George Cruikshank* (8). Pickwick Papers. With 43 Illustrations by *Seymour* and '*Phiz*'. 2 volumes (120, 121). Tale of Two Cities (38).
DISRAELI (BENJAMIN). Coningsby. With an Introduction by *André Maurois* (381). Sybil (291).
ELIOT (GEORGE). Adam Bede (63). Felix Holt the Radical. Introduction by *Viola Meynell* (179). The Mill on the Floss (31). Romola. Introduction by *Viola Meynell* (178). Scenes of Clerical Life (155). Silas Marner, &c. (80).
FIELDING. Jonathan Wild (382). Joseph Andrews (334).

GALT (JOHN). The Entail. Introduction by *John Ayscough* (177).
GASKELL (MRS.). Cousin Phillis, and Other Tales, &c. (168).
Cranford, The Cage at Cranford, and The Moorland Cottage
(110). Lizzie Leigh, The Grey Woman, and Other Tales, &c.
(175). Mary Barton (86). North and South (154). Right at
Last, and Other Tales, &c. (203). Round the Sofa (190).
Ruth (88). Sylvia's Lovers (156). Wives and Daughters (157).
GISSING. Veranilda (349). Will Warburton (348).
GOLDSMITH. The Vicar of Wakefield (4).
HARRIS (JOEL CHANDLER). Uncle Remus (361).
HAWTHORNE. House of the Seven Gables (273). The Scarlet
Letter (26). Tales (319).
HOLME (CONSTANCE). The Lonely Plough (390). The Old Road
from Spain (400).
KINGSLEY (HENRY). Geoffry Hamlyn (271). Ravenshoe (267).
LE FANU (J. S.). Uncle Silas. Intro. *Montague R. James* (306).
LESAGE. Gil Blas. Ed. *J. Fitzmaurice-Kelly*. 2 volumes (151, 152).
LYTTON. The Coming Race, &c. (327). Harold (165).
MARRYAT. Mr. Midshipman Easy (160).
MEINHOLD. The Amber Witch. Intro. by *J. W. Mackail* (325).
MELVILLE (HERMAN). Moby Dick (225). Typee (274). Omoo
(275). White Jacket (253).
MORIER (J. J.). Hajji Baba (238). Hajji Baba in England (285).
MORITZ (C. P.). Anton Reiser. Intro. *P. E. Matheson* (299).
PEACOCK (T. L.). Headlong Hall; and Nightmare Abbey (339).
Misfortunes of Elphin; and Crotchet Castle (244).
SCOTT. Ivanhoe (29).
SMOLLETT. Roderick Random (353). Humphry Clinker (290).
STERNE. Sentimental Journey (333). Tristram Shandy (40).
STEVENSON (R. L.). Treasure Island (295). Kidnapped; and
Catriona (297).
SWIFT. Gulliver's Travels (20).
TAYLOR (MEADOWS). Confessions of a Thug (207).
THACKERAY. Henry Esmond (28).
TOLSTOY. Translated by *Louise* and *Aylmer Maude*. Anna
Karenina. 2 volumes (210, 211). Childhood, Boyhood, and
Youth (352). The Cossacks, &c. (208). The Kreutzer Sonata,
&c.(266). Resurrection (209). Twenty-three Tales (72). War
and Peace. 3 volumes (233-5).
TRELAWNY (E. J.). Adventures of a Younger Son (289).
TROLLOPE. American Senator (391). Ayala's Angel (342). Bar-
chester Towers (268). The Belton Estate (251). The Claverings
(252). Cousin Henry (343). Doctor Thorne (298). Dr. Wortle's
School (317). The Eustace Diamonds (357). Framley Parsonage
(305). The Kellys and the O'Kellys (341). Last Chronicles of
Barset. 2 vols. (398, 399). Miss Mackenzie (278). Rachel Ray
(279). Sir Harry Hotspur (336). Tales of all Countries (397).
The Three Clerks (140). The Warden (217). The Vicar of
Bullhampton (272).
WATTS-DUNTON (THEODORE). Aylwin (52).

¶ History

BARROW (SIR JOHN). The Mutiny of the *Bounty* (195).
BUCKLE. The History of Civilization. 3 volumes (41, 48, 53).
CARLYLE. The French Revolution. Introduction by *C. R. L. Fletcher*. 2 volumes (125, 126).
FROUDE (J. A.). Short Studies on Great Subjects. Series I (269).
GIBBON. Decline and Fall of the Roman Empire. With Maps. 7 volumes (35, 44, 51, 55, 64, 69, 74).
IRVING (WASHINGTON). Conquest of Granada (150).
MACAULAY. History of England. 5 vols. (366–70).
MOTLEY. Rise of the Dutch Republic. 3 volumes (96, 97, 98).
PRESCOTT (W. H.). The Conquest of Mexico. 2 vols. (197, 198).

¶ Letters

BURKE. Letters. Selected, with Introduction, by *H. J. Laski* (237).
CHESTERFIELD. Letters. Selected, with an Introduction, by *Phyllis M. Jones* (347).
CONGREVE. Letters, in Volume II. See under *Drama* (277).
COWPER. Letters. Selected, with Intro., by *E. V. Lucas* (138).
DUFFERIN (LORD). Letters from High Latitudes. Illustrated (158).
ENGLISH LETTERS. Fifteenth to Nineteenth Centuries (192).
GRAY (THOMAS). Letters. Selected by *John Beresford* (283).
JOHNSON (SAMUEL). Letters. Selected, with Introduction, by *R. W. Chapman* (282).
LETTERS WRITTEN IN WAR-TIME. Fifteenth to Nineteenth Centuries. Selected and arranged by *H. Wragg* (202).
SOUTHEY. Selected Letters (169).
TOLSTOY. Essays and Letters. Trans. by *L.* and *A. Maude* (46).
WHITE (GILBERT). The Natural History of Selborne (22).

¶ Literary Criticism

AMERICAN CRITICISM. Representative Literary Essays. Chosen by *Norman Foerster* (354).
COLERIDGE (S. T.) Lectures on Shakespeare (363).
ENGLISH CRITICAL ESSAYS. Selected and edited by *Edmund D. Jones*. 2 volumes. I, Sixteenth to Eighteenth Centuries. II, Nineteenth Century (240, 206).
HAZLITT (WILLIAM). Characters of Shakespeare's Plays. Introduction by *Sir A. T. Quiller-Couch* (205). Lectures on the English Comic Writers. Introduction by *R. Brimley Johnson* (124). Lectures on the English Poets (255). The Spirit of the Age. (Essays on his contemporaries) (57).
HORNE (R. H.). A New Spirit of the Age (127).
JOHNSON (SAMUEL). Lives of the Poets. 2 volumes (83, 84).
SAINTE-BEUVE. Causeries du Lundi. (In English.) 8 vols. (372–9).
SHAKESPEAREAN CRITICISM. (HEMINGE and CONDELL to CARLYLE.) Selected and Introduced by *D. Nichol Smith* (212).

¶ *Philosophy and Science*

(For POLITICAL THEORY and RELIGION see separate headings)

AURELIUS (MARCUS). Thoughts. Translated by *John Jackson* (60).

BACON. The Advancement of Learning, and the New Atlantis. Introduction by *Professor Case* (93). Essays (24).

CARLYLE. Sartor Resartus (19).

DARWIN. The Origin of Species. With a new preface by *Major Leonard Darwin* (11). Voyage of a Naturalist (360).

HUME (DAVID). Essays (33).

REYNOLDS (SIR JOSHUA). Discourses, &c. Intro. *A. Dobson* (149).

TOLSTOY. What then must we do ? (281).

WHITE (GILBERT). The Natural History of Selborne (22).

¶ *Poetry*

(For AESCHYLUS and ARISTOPHANES see ' Classics ' on p. 5)

ARNOLD (MATTHEW). Poems, 1849–67 (85).

BARHAM (RICHARD). The Ingoldsby Legends (9).

BLAKE (WILLIAM). Selected Poems (324).

BRONTË SISTERS, THE. The Professor, by CHARLOTTE BRONTË, and Poems by CHARLOTTE, EMILY, and ANNE BRONTË (78).

BROWNING (ELIZABETH BARRETT). Poems. A Selection (176).

BROWNING (ROBERT). Poems and Plays, 1833–42 (58). Poems, 1842–64 (137).

BURNS (ROBERT). Poems (34). Complete and in large type.

BYRON. Poems. A Selection (180).

CHAUCER, The Works of. 3 volumes. Vol. I (42); Vol. II (56); Vol. III, containing the whole of the Canterbury Tales (76).

COLERIDGE. Poems. Introduction by *Sir A. T. Quiller-Couch* (99).

CONGREVE (WILLIAM). Complete works in 2 volumes. Introductions by *Bonamy Dobrée*. I, The Comedies. II, The Mourning Bride, Poems, Miscellanies and Letters (276, 277).

DANTE. Italian text and English verse-translation by *Melville B. Anderson*, on facing pages, with notes. 3 vols. (392–4). Translation only, with notes, in one volume (395).

DOBSON (AUSTIN). Selected Poems (249).

ENGLISH SONGS AND BALLADS. Compiled by *T. W. H. Crosland*. New edition, with revised text and additional poems, 1927 (13).

ENGLISH VERSE. Vols. I–V: Early Lyrics to SHAKESPEARE ; CAMPION to the Ballads ; DRYDEN to WORDSWORTH ; SCOTT to E. B. BROWNING ; LONGFELLOW to RUPERT BROOKE. Edited by *William Peacock* (308–312).

FRANCIS OF ASSISI (ST.). The Little Flowers of St. Francis. Translated into English Verse by *James Rhoades* (265).

GOETHE. Faust, Parts I and II. Translated by *Bayard Taylor*. Introduction by *Marshall Montgomery* (380).

GOLDEN TREASURY, THE. With additional Poems (133).

GOLDSMITH. Poems. Introduction by *Austin Dobson* (123).

HERBERT (GEORGE). Poems. Introduction by *Arthur Waugh* (109).

HERRICK (ROBERT). Poems (16).
HOMER. Translated by *Pope*. Iliad (18). Odyssey (36).
HOOD. Poems. Introduction by *Walter Jerrold* (87).
KEATS. Poems (7).
KEBLE. The Christian Year (181).
LONGFELLOW. Evangeline, The Golden Legend, &c. (39). Hiawatha, Miles Standish, Tales of a Wayside Inn, &c. (174).
MACAULAY. Lays of Ancient Rome ; Ivry ; The Armada (27).
MARLOWE. Dr. Faustus (with GOETHE's Faust, Part I, trans. *J. Anster*). Introduction by *Sir A. W. Ward* (135).
MILTON. The English Poems (182).
MORRIS (WILLIAM). The Defence of Guenevere, Life and Death of Jason, and other Poems (183).
NARRATIVE VERSE, A BOOK OF. Compiled by *V. H. Collins*. With an Introduction by *Edmund Blunden* (350).
NEKRASSOV. Trans. by *Juliet Soskice*. Who can be happy and free in Russia ? A Poem (213). Poems (340).
PALGRAVE. The Golden Treasury. With additional Poems (133).
ROSSETTI (CHRISTINA). Goblin Market, &c. (184).
—— (DANTE GABRIEL). Poems and Translations, 1850–70 (185).
SCOTT (SIR WALTER). Selected Poems (186).
SHAKESPEARE. Plays and Poems. Preface by *A. C. Swinburne*. Introductions by *Edward Dowden*. 9 volumes. Comedies. 3 volumes (100, 101, 102). Histories and Poems. 3 volumes (103, 104, 105). Tragedies. 3 volumes (106, 107, 108).
SHELLEY. Poems. A Selection (187).
SOPHOCLES. The Seven Plays. Translated into English Verse by *Lewis Campbell* (116).
TENNYSON. Selected Poems. Intro. *Sir Herbert Warren* (3).
VIRGIL. The Aeneid, Georgics, and Eclogues. Translated by *Dryden* (37). Translated by *James Rhoades* (227).
WELLS (CHARLES). Joseph and his Brethren. A Dramatic Poem. Intro. *A. C. Swinburne*, and Note by *T. Watts-Dunton* (143).
WHITMAN. A Selection. Introduction by *E. de Sélincourt* (218).
WHITTIER. Poems : A Selection (188).
WORDSWORTH. Poems. A Selection (189).

¶ Politics, Political Economy, Political Theory

BAGEHOT (WALTER). The English Constitution. With an Introduction by the *Earl of Balfour* (330).
BUCKLE. The History of Civilization. 3 volumes (41, 48, 53).
BURKE (EDMUND). Letters. Selected, with an Introduction, by *Harold J. Laski* (237). Works. 6 volumes. Vol. I : A Vindication of Natural Society ; The Sublime and Beautiful, &c. (71). II : The Present Discontents ; and Speeches and Letters on America (81). III : Speeches on India, &c. (111). IV : Writings on France, 1790–1 (112). V : Writings on Ireland, &c. (113). VI : A Letter to a Noble Lord ; and Letters on a Regicide Peace (114).

ENGLISH SPEECHES, from BURKE to GLADSTONE. Selected and edited by *E. R. Jones* (191).

MACHIAVELLI. The Prince. Translated by *Luigi Ricci* (43).

MAINE (SIR HENRY). Ancient Law (362).

MILL (JOHN STUART). On Liberty, Representative Government, and the Subjection of Women (170).

MILTON (JOHN). Selected Prose. Intro. *Malcolm W. Wallace* (293).

RUSKIN. 'A Joy for Ever', and The Two Paths. Illustrated (147). Time and Tide, and The Crown of Wild Olive (146). Unto this Last, and Munera Pulveris (148).

SMITH (ADAM). The Wealth of Nations. 2 volumes (54, 59).

SPEECHES AND DOCUMENTS ON BRITISH COLONIAL POLICY (1763–1917). Ed. *A. B. Keith.* 2 volumes (215, 216).

SPEECHES AND DOCUMENTS ON THE BRITISH DOMINIONS (1918–31). Ed. *A. B. Keith* (403).

SPEECHES AND DOCUMENTS ON INDIAN POLICY (1756–1921). Edited, with Introduction, by *A. B. Keith* (231, 232).

SPEECHES ON BRITISH FOREIGN POLICY (1738–1914) (201).

TRACTS AND PAMPHLETS, A Miscellany of. Sixteenth to Nineteenth Centuries. Edited by *A. C. Ward* (304).

TOLSTOY. What then must we do? Translated, with an Introduction, by *Aylmer Maude* (281).

¶ Religion

THE OLD TESTAMENT. Revised Version. 4 vols. (385–8).

APOCRYPHA, THE, in the Revised Version (294).

THE FOUR GOSPELS, AND THE ACTS OF THE APOSTLES. Authorized Version (344).

THE NEW TESTAMENT. Revised Version (346).

À KEMPIS (THOMAS). Of the Imitation of Christ (49).

AURELIUS (MARCUS). Translated by *John Jackson* (60).

BUNYAN. The Pilgrim's Progress (12). Mr. Badman (338).

KORAN, THE. Translated by *E. H. Palmer.* Introduction by *Reynold A. Nicholson* (328).

TOLSTOY. A Confession, and What I believe. Translated by *Aylmer Maude* (229).

¶ Short Stories

AFRICA, STORIES OF. Chosen by *E. C. Parnwell* (359).

AUSTRIAN SHORT STORIES. Selected and translated by *Marie Busch* (337).

CRIME AND DETECTION. Two Series (301, 351). Stories by H. C. BAILEY, ERNEST BRAMAH, G. K. CHESTERTON, SIR A. CONAN DOYLE, R. AUSTIN FREEMAN, W. W. JACOBS, EDEN PHILPOTTS, 'SAPPER', DOROTHY SAYERS, and others.

CZECH TALES, SELECTED. Translated, with a Preface, by *Marie Busch* and *Otto Pick* (288).

DICKENS. Christmas Books (307).

ENGLISH SHORT STORIES. First Series. Nineteenth Century: SIR WALTER SCOTT to HUBERT CRACKANTHORPE. Selected by *H. S. Milford.* Introduction by *Prof. Hugh Walker* (193).

ENGLISH SHORT STORIES. Second Series. Nineteenth and Twentieth Centuries: MARY LAMB to GERALD WARRE CORNISH. Selected by *H. S. Milford* (228).
—— Third Series. Nineteenth and Twentieth Centuries: HAWTHORNE to KATHERINE MANSFIELD. Selected by *H. S. Milford* (315).
GASKELL (Mrs.). Introductions by *Clement Shorter*. Cousin Phillis, and Other Tales (168). Lizzie Leigh, The Grey Woman, and other Tales, &c. (175). Right at Last, and other Tales, &c. (203). Round the Sofa (190).
GHOSTS AND MARVELS and MORE GHOSTS AND MARVELS. Two Selections of Uncanny Tales made by *V. H. Collins*. Introduction by *Montague R. James* in Series I (284, 323).
HARTE (BRET). Short Stories (318).
HAWTHORNE (NATHANIEL). Tales (319).
IRVING (WASHINGTON). Tales (320).
PERSIAN (FROM THE). The Three Dervishes, and Other Stories. Translated from MSS. in the Bodleian by *Reuben Levy* (254).
POE (EDGAR ALLAN). Tales of Mystery and Imagination (21).
POLISH TALES by MODERN AUTHORS. Translated by *Else C. M. Benecke* and *Marie Busch* (230).
RUSSIAN SHORT STORIES. Chosen and translated by *A. E. Chamot* (287).
SHORT STORIES OF THE SOUTH SEAS. Selected by *E. C. Parnwell* (332).
SPANISH SHORT STORIES. Sixteenth Century. In contemporary translations, revised, with an Introduction, by *J. B. Trend* (326).
TOLSTOY. Twenty-three Tales. Translated by *Louise* and *Aylmer Maude* (72).
TROLLOPE. Tales of all Countries (397).

¶ Travel and Topography

BORROW (GEORGE). The Bible in Spain (75). Wild Wales (224). Lavengro (66). Romany Rye (73).
DARWIN. Voyage of a Naturalist (360).
DUFFERIN (LORD). Letters from High Latitudes, being some account of a voyage in 1856 in the schooner-yacht *Foam* to Iceland, Jan Mayen and Spitzbergen. Introduction by *R. W. Macan* (158).
FIELDING (HENRY). Journal of a Voyage to Lisbon, &c. Introduction and Notes by *Austin Dobson*, with an Illustration (142).
HUNT (LEIGH). The Town. Introduction and Notes by *Austin Dobson* (132).
MELVILLE (HERMAN). Typee (294). Omoo (275).
MORIER (J. J.). Hajji Baba of Ispahan. Introduction by *C. W. Stewart*, and a Map (238).
SMOLLETT (TOBIAS). Travels through France and Italy in 1765. Introduction (lxii pages) by *Thomas Seccombe* (90).
STERNE (LAURENCE). A Sentimental Journey. With Introduction by *Virginia Woolf* (333).

INDEX OF AUTHORS, ETC.

Further Volumes are in preparation.

Jan. 1932.